THE CARRY OUT

Published by Seacoast Press, an imprint of MindStir Media, LLC
1931 Woodbury Ave. #182 | Portsmouth, New Hampshire 03801 | USA
1.800.767.0531 | www.seacoastpress.com

Printed in the United States of America
ISBN-13: 978-1-7367342-0-9

THE CARRY OUT

KALI GADOMSKI

SEACOAST

PRESS

For my parents, husband, and daughter;
thank you for always believing in me.
I love you.

CHAPTER ONE

"Just stay down. I won't hit again."

Max wasn't sure the boy could hear him over the roar of the crowd, despite being one inch from his ear. When the cowbell sounded, Max had immediately pinned the boy against the back wall of the stall, the only one without spectators leaning over to listen. He had the boy pinned with his forearm across his throat, and although he wasn't applying any pressure, Max flexed his arm to protrude his veins, giving the illusion that he was. The initial slam had startled the boy, and he looked at Max as if genuinely offended.

The abandoned barn smelled of coagulated blood, the hay and wooden floor beneath their feet stained a painful shade of pink. An old spotlight shone in on them, and as usual, Max could not make out the faces of the spectators surrounding the other three sides of the stall. Unfortunately, he didn't need to; he knew all too well what the picture looked like. He could hear them bellowing like incomprehensible barbarians. Men leaning over the wooden half-walls against the chain-linked fence, waving wads of cash over their heads and sloshing beer on one another. It was obvious the boy was new from the way his eyes squinted to take in the scene, more confusion than terror.

"What are you waiting for?" Max stifled an eye roll at his older brother's voice. He sure had a lot of advice for someone that never fought himself. But then again, he was invested; Max's winnings funded his stoner lifestyle.

Max tried to focus on the boy, who was now squirming in an attempt to get away in a spastic manner atypical of a fighter. Truth be told, the boy didn't seem like a fighter, just someone in the wrong place at the wrong time.

Max knew how that felt. He slammed the boy again, kicking the base of the wall with his heel to make it sound harder.

"Man, I'm serious," Max hissed in the boy's ear. "Just stay down, I—"

"MAX!" The voice roared over the rest of the crowd, dripping with a hatred that made Max tense up. "TAKE HIM OUT!"

"—I won't hit again," Max finished as he pushed away and squared off against the boy. They held eye contact as Max wound up and right hooked him across the face. The boy didn't even put his hands up as the crack of skin on skin echoed through the stall, and he crumpled to the floor on impact. Max aimed between his eye and temple, more disorienting than damaging, in an attempt to keep him down. The crowd jeered around them, and the boy gasped, looking at Max with a pained understanding before collapsing again onto the floor.

Max turned on his heel and strutted out of the stall, his calculated cockiness distracting the crowd from the length of the fight. The longer the fight, the longer scumbags had to bet on them, and this fight had been one-tenth of the usual length. But if there was one thing Max learned from his time in this hellhole, it was how to work the crowd, especially in the name of self-preservation. "One and done," he grandstanded, and the crowd ate it up, pouring beer over his head and exchanging bets with one another.

"Too much hesitation." His brother fell into step beside him. "You gotta go in quicker for the first hit. Give them a taste of what's coming." Max wiped the beer dripping from his forehead and continued to draw the crowd away from the stall with the boy. A rough hand grabbed Max by the elbow and yanked him around, his shoulder dangerously close to dislocating.

"What the hell was that?" The alcohol on his father's breath panted across Max's face as he spoke. "Cut the theatrics. We got three more tonight." He shoved Max toward the next stall where another opponent stood waiting. They fought before, and Max was not concerned, but the shove from his father made him bristle. Self-preservation was impossible when it came to him.

Asshole.

The word described all of the disgusting men surrounding him, but in Max's eyes, his father easily stood out as the worst.

As he entered the stall, Max stole a glance back in the direction of the boy. He knew all the fighters on the circuit and had never seen him before. The boy hadn't seemed scared or even weak. He was an intriguing mixture of defiant and accepting, as if he too had been through enough to understand how the cruelties of life liked to hide behind the façade of normalcy.

Max wondered if he had that look too. How long had his father been bringing him here on the weekends to make a quick buck? Long enough for it to be Max's normal; his painful, screwed up normal. His eyes combed the crowd, the bumbling degenerates coming to bet on him again obstructing his view. Max was able to make out two henchmen dragging the boy's limp body outside before the spotlight blinded him, and the cowbell rang again.

Damn.

. . .

Harold the Fireman careened into the sixth story window, startling Tate out of his chair and onto the carpeted floor. His father pretended not to notice as Tate scrambled back into his seat to watch the parade. The young firemen on the street below fought to regain control of their giant balloon, managing to get Harold the Fireman back on course as they continued down the street.

Tate and his father watched the Macy's Thanksgiving Day Parade every year, but thanks to his new job, this was the first year they got to watch it from an office in the Twin Towers. Granted, it wasn't his father's office, which was many floors above, but it beat perching on shop windowsills trying to see over the bustling crowd. Tate had sealed the deal to their new vantage point, his six-year-old crooked smile more than enough to charm his father's boss into lending them his office for the day.

"Tate, look!" Tate followed his father's finger to the black-topped, purple-bottomed uniforms coming into view. He could feel the beating of the drumline thump against his heart as the marching band approached. The sun reflected off the trombone slides racing back and forth to the rhythm, glistening an impossible shade of gold. Tate leaped from his chair and pressed himself against the window, music belting from their instruments as they marched behind their leader.

The drum major!

Tate bounced with excitement as the band stopped beneath them, marching in place as the drum major hurled his baton into the air. It was about the same size as Tate, and it rotated as if in slow motion. Tate and his father kept their eyes glued to it until it landed back in the drum major's hand in an effortless catch.

As long as Tate could remember, he wanted to be a drum major like his father was. The leader of the band, confident and skilled at the helm of the ship. Tate stole a sideways glance at his father, who watched as the drum major continued on, band in tow. Both of them strained to watch the band until it completely disappeared from view.

"It's such a work of art," his father said, pulling Tate against his side. "Marching."

"I'm going to be a drum major one day," Tate declared. His father smiled and patted his back.

"And you'll be the best drum major there ever was."

Tate thought about that for a moment. "Even better than you?"

His father paused, lost in thought. He liked to remember his days as a drum major, and a smile played at his stubble as his eyes watched something Tate couldn't see. "Definitely." He returned Tate's smile with a crooked grin of his own.

"Daddy." Tate spun himself in circles in the boss's chair. "Did you ever march in this parade?"

"No." His father glanced out the window as a giant ice cream cone floated by. "But I wanted to."

Tate stomped his feet on the carpet to stop himself, stumbling as he stood in a fight to regain his balance. "Someday, I will!"

The golden crucifix dangling from his father's neck bumped Tate in the nose as his father leaned over to kiss his forehead. It glinted in the sun, not unlike the trombones, the reflection of light dancing around Tate's face like a kaleidoscope. "I hope so," his father murmured into his hair.

A grin spread across Tate's face as another drumline sounded on the horizon, and they pressed themselves against the window once more. All those years of floats and balloons and attractions, yet the only thing that excited them were the high school marching bands. Even though it was always the two of them against the world, thick as thieves, Tate never felt closer to his father than when they watched the marching bands play on Thanksgiving.

. . .

When Tate regained consciousness, he was sprawled face down in a grassy clearing outside the barn. He had no idea how long he had been out, but the throbbing around his left eye indicated it had been a little while. Long enough for him to remember his father.

His foster father had left the minute Tate hit the floor. He could have stayed like the other fathers betting on their sons, but he hadn't come for the money. His sole purpose for coming tonight was to teach Tate a lesson, and that he did.

Tate could hear the fights continuing inside, the cracking of bone piercing the night air like stormy waves against the side of a boat. Two men stumbled past him from the woodline behind the barn, zipping their pants as they balanced beer bottles in the crooks of their elbows. Tate assumed they were on their way back from taking a piss.

Charming.

"Hey, look at this kid," the shorter one said, gesturing in every direction but Tate's, despite his best effort. His skin was the greyish red of a man who was simultaneously stimulating himself with alcohol and slowly drinking himself to death. The taller man turned around, the sores on his face and arms proving he was plagued by more than one bad habit. "I didn't know they used fire in the fights now."

The taller one took a step closer, leaning over to examine the scarring on the left side of Tate's cheek beneath the swollen eye. His breath smelled like rotting trash, and he couldn't keep his balance, stepping on Tate's arm with his boot as he stumbled. "Uh," he grunted in agreement. "Got burned up good." The man leaned over and brushed Tate's hair out of his eye with yellow fingernails. Tate wanted to recoil but thought it best to assess the situation first. "I wonder if his face is purty enough on the other side to spend some time with us."

He glanced at the shorter man, already unzipping his pants when the swift kick of Tate's shoe connected with his crotch. The man stumbled backward into his friend in a slur of curse words.

Tate scrambled up and took off toward what looked like the only opening in the clearing before the man could catch his breath. "Screw you!" the shorter man yelled as he struggled to keep himself and his friend upright.

"No wonder someone burned him." Tate heard the man he kicked growl before they toppled into the grass in a fit of inebriated rage.

Tate didn't look back until he reached the deserted dirt road on which they had driven in. Rusty old pickup trucks lined the clearing's left side, the barn flaking dark bits of red paint onto the ground on the right side. Men and boys trekked across the clearing from the barn to the woodline for what Tate now understood was not to piss, and shuddered at the thought of what he just escaped.

Heavy tree cover hid the barn as Tate trudged down the road, trying to catch his breath. His adrenaline was pumping, and he could feel his swollen eye pulsing with every heartbeat. The horrific sounds were swallowed by the immensity of the forest that filled the growing gap between himself and the barn.

Couldn't have picked a better spot for a shithole like this.

He followed the road until it met another road he somewhat recognized. Tate looked back at the path leading into the woods. It looked like one of the abandoned snowmobile trails scattered throughout the otherwise urban grouping of towns, nothing about it raising the slightest suspicion of the violence going on a few miles in.

Tate walked on, matching his steps to the pulsing beat of his eye until he reached the foster home. From the outside, it looked like any other house in the neighborhood: a rundown Cape Cod for a working-class family of four. But on the inside, there were two bedrooms packed with fourteen kids, who kept enough government money coming in to keep their foster parents happily unemployed.

Tate was sent here years ago when his father died, and he'd been butting heads with his foster father ever since. Although their basic needs were minimally accounted for, there was no love in that home. They were all just pawns in a government game, and Tate had always wanted more than they were willing to give him. He wanted to be somebody, and he wanted somebody to believe he could.

Tate stared at the house for a long time, his fists clenching and unclenching as he tried to figure out his next move. His foster father would be waiting to berate him when he got in. They had gotten in an argument earlier that day, his foster father baiting Tate by mocking his dreams of becoming a drum major. He told Tate he was too useless, too weak, to ever make his dead father proud.

And Tate tackled him.

Aggression wasn't Tate's go-to, but his foster father had pushed all the right buttons, and stupidly, Tate had fallen for it. His foster father had been waiting for an excuse to extinguish what was left of Tate's hope for years now, and the barn tonight almost did it.

Tate didn't want to do it anymore.

At twelve years old, he was the oldest of the bunch, and he felt his hope for a better life slipping further away the longer he stayed. Right then and there, the moonlight illuminating the left side of his beat-up face, Tate decided he'd had enough. He dreamt of leaving from the moment he arrived years ago, but he never thought the decision would be so easy. He was a realistic person with a realistic view on life, but he had never quite been able to quiet his soul, and it wanted more.

Without a doubt in his mind, Tate crept to the shed aside the yard and pulled his father's guitar from its hiding place underneath. It was one of his most prized possessions, and Tate had scampered away to hide it the day he arrived here. The other was the golden crucifix hanging around his neck, pressed against his chest by the guitar strap as Tate slung it over his shoulder. Tate gave the house one last look and sent a silent well-wish to the other children before turning on his heel and disappearing into the night.

He wandered to the chorus of the peepers until their cacophony was broken by the sound of an approaching car. A man that looked too drunk to be driving sat behind the wheel of the pickup truck, an older boy with sunken in features in the passenger seat beside him. Tate didn't notice the boy in the truck bed until the vehicle veered, hurling him against the side. When he lifted his face in search of a handhold, Tate recognized the boy who knocked him out. He caught Tate's eye as he readjusted himself, nodding in acknowledgment as the truck swerved again.

Tate followed the truck until it swerved out of sight, and then he followed its tracks in the dirt road. Why he was following the boy who knocked him out, he had no idea, but Tate couldn't think of anywhere else to go, and at least the kid had shown him mercy by only hitting once.

Eventually, the tire tracks veered up a hidden driveway that emerged to reveal two precarious structures. The first was what Tate assumed to be the house, a little too slanted to be considered stable. The second was to his right, but the flames caught his eye before he could get a good look at it. Generally, Tate avoided fire at all cost, but the boy contained it in the fire pit as he sat alone in the night. As Tate approached, he was astounded to find the boy unscathed, despite the number of fights he was in that night.

"Hey." Tate tried to ease himself into view so as not to startle. "We never officially met. Tate."

The boy was shorter than Tate as he stood, but he was all muscle. Tate's throbbing left eye could confirm that. "Max." He examined Tate's eye with a grimace as if he could feel the pain of it himself. "Damn," he muttered, close enough now to see the pulsing of swollen skin.

"The purple brings out my eyes."

Max ignored him as he examined the rest of Tate's face. "Damn," he repeated as he took in the deep cranberry scars that slithered around Tate's cheek and mouth. "I didn't think I hit you that hard."

"Oh…no." Tate tried to turn away, but Max held his chin as he continued to examine. "That was already there." Max nodded, satisfied, and gave the swollen eye a gentle poke. Tate flinched and swatted his hand away. "What happened to not hitting again?"

"Can you see?"

"Enough."

Max did not look convinced as he gestured for Tate to sit down next to the fire before descending the hill and disappearing into the house. It was actually more of a shack, with a listing wooden frame and screen doors that slammed shut behind you like a flyswatter. A cluster of wooden steps was built into the hillside, connecting the two structures. Directly to Tate's right sat an old screen house, no bigger than the inside of an SUV.

Tate removed his guitar and laid it in the grass beside him. The crackle of flames made him uneasy, and he took several distancing steps backward. The only reason he was even in the proximity of this fire was because of Max. Well, that, and Tate was too exhausted to think of another place to go.

The screen door slammed again, and Tate heard the wooden steps creak as Max returned with a frozen bag of pizza rolls. Tate looked at him, confused. "You know most people cook those first."

Max rolled his eyes and pressed the frozen bag against Tate's swollen eye. "Five on, ten off."

"Right." Tate tried to ignore the intensified pain the bag caused as he pressed it against his eye, but eventually, it all went numb. "Too bad, I'm starving."

Max was gone again before Tate could say anything else, returning a minute later with two boiled hotdogs on a napkin. He handed one to Tate and sat down at the fire. Max watched Tate flinch as the logs settled, and he suffocated the fire with a handful of sand. When it became nothing but embers, he gestured again for Tate to join him on the log. The two boys sat in silence, aside from the ravenous attack on their hot dogs. Tate had shed his ice pack to eat, and the skin around his eye was turning a watercolor mixture of blues and purples.

"Sorry, by the way," Max said, nodding at Tate's eye. "Gotta throw at least one."

"Right." Tate took another bite of his hotdog, eyeing the embers as if they were about to jump back to life. Max layered another coat of sand on the logs.

"Broke my rib my first fight," Max said with a mouthful of bun.

Tate raised an eyebrow. "Guess I'm luckier than I thought."

Max shook his head as a roar of drunken frustration came from the shack below, followed by clattering of pots and pans and then the slam of a bedroom door. "Losing doesn't tame the beast. Or his boot."

"Damn." Tate couldn't even fathom the thought of his own father kicking him in the ribs. "And you still fight?"

"Every weekend. Only way to keep him from beating me." Max looked down the hill at the shack with what looked to Tate like disgust. "Pretty ironic."

Tate was a little surprised Max was sharing so much, but it didn't feel wrong. Honestly, it felt like they had done this a million times, sharing a log on this hilltop, confiding in one another. "You must be pretty good then."

Max smirked and handed Tate the frozen bag of pizza rolls. "You tell me."

"Well yeah," Tate said, smacking the bag against his bruise. "I meant against actual fighters. You must be good."

Max shrugged. "Good enough."

"But you're not very big."

"And you're not very subtle."

Tate grinned at that. "It's one of my many endearing traits."

"Right." Max seemed amused for a minute before his face returned to solemn indifference. By this time, they had both finished their dinner, so they let the peepers fill the silence. Tate replayed the night in his head. The abandoned barn in the middle of nowhere. The money changing hands faster than his eyes could follow. The winners, bruised and broken, gearing up for another fight. The losers, led to the woodline by people they should never have to meet.

Nobody knew about it, and nobody would ever stop it.

"Does he bet on you?" Tate asked. "Your father?"

Max rested his elbows on his knees. "All the time. Drinks away the winnings, though. I keep a little and bet behind his back to buy food."

"You bet on yourself tonight?"

A grin flashed across Max's face as he nudged Tate's knee. "Guaranteed win."

"Right," Tate laughed, his eye pulsing with the effort. "So your brother fights too?"

Max scoffed. "Kid's a string bean."

"And your dad's just fine with that?"

"Water seeks its own level."

Tate glanced down at the shack, the disgust from Max's previous expression creeping into his own face. "Sounds like a couple winners."

"Never really fit in with either of them."

Tate knew how that felt. "And your mom?"

Max picked up a stick and began poking the buried embers. "I was eight when she left." He didn't look up but paused long enough for Tate to know he was reliving something.

Tate didn't know what to say, but he knew from experience what it was like to lose someone you loved, so he let Max have his moment. "My mother died in childbirth," he said, trying to connect.

"Sucks." Max said nothing for almost a full minute before bursting out in an anger Tate hadn't realized had been building. "Old man shoved me in the stall the next night. Bastard." Tate watched Max prod the sand with a vengeance before finally relinquishing the stick. "What are you doing here, anyway?"

Tate shrugged. "Had to check on you. Make sure you're still standing."

"Right." Max continued to stare expectantly.

"No one's looking for me." Tate paused. "Foster father didn't really take to me anyway."

"Your endearing traits?" Although he was solemn in nature, his humor was quick-witted, and Tate enjoyed it.

"I want more, you know?" Tate paused, turning his dream over in his mind like a gemstone in his hands. "Apparently that's license to get thrown in with you to get my ass kicked." He shrugged as if it was a normal occurrence, which he guessed was true for Max. Tate couldn't imagine going to the barn every weekend without the smell of blood and the loathing spirit of evil men lingering on you forever.

But he didn't see any of it on Max. Instead, he saw dependability. A dependability filled with strength and goodness that connected them; two souls determined to come out of it all still standing.

"Damn." Max leaned back. "Guess they got what they wanted then."

Tate flashed a crooked grin. "I'm not exactly what you would call mellow. As long as the government checks keep clearing, I think they'd rather have me gone." Max snorted at this as if Tate had just revealed that the sky was blue.

"Your dad?" he asked.

"Dead. In 9/11." Tate had to focus on his words to keep his voice from cracking.

"Man. Sorry." Max looked like he understood better than any adult who had ever claimed to.

"Right." Tate stared at the ground for a minute before ditching the pizza rolls and grabbing his guitar. It was the only possession he had aside from the clothes on his back and the chain around his neck, and Tate began to strum it absently as if he was talking to an old friend. It soothed him, the strings beneath his fingers, the melody floating in the air.

Max looked up, surprised. "All right, music man."

"Definitely my most endearing trait," Tate said, breaking the guitar into a full chorus.

"Not bad." Max found another stick and began drumming along on the log next to him. He kept pace with Tate throughout the song, switching beats and tempos as if they had written it together.

"Wow," Tate said when they were done, letting the guitar rest against his thigh. "So those hands are good for more than knocking me out." For the first time all night, Max didn't look completely pissed off for more than five seconds.

"What can I say? I'm good at hitting."

The two sat together for another hour or so, looking up at the night sky, listening to the sound of the peepers, and absorbing the start of what felt like a solid friendship. Tate's body felt heavier with each passing minute, and by the time Max stood, he felt like he weighed three hundred pounds. Max grabbed the guitar and walked over to the screen porch, setting it inside as he entered. He motioned for Tate to follow. "You can crash out here," he said. "Screens keep the bugs out."

Tate nodded as he closed the screen door behind him. "Right. Thanks." The screen porch sat atop the hill, but it was at the edge of the property and much more secluded than the fire pit. It had a sereneness about it as if it was put there to watch over the dilapidated shack below. Max moved around it fondly, as if there was a reverence about it that connected him to who he was.

"What about your brother?" Tate asked, leaning against the waist-high wooden rail that ran along the entirety of the screen porch.

"He's stoned more than he isn't. Just say you're crashing for the night. He won't know the difference."

"But I am just crashing for the night."

Max ignored him. "There's a sleeping bag under the day bed. Thermal or whatever."

"Dude, it's like seventy degrees out." Tate felt his hair sticking to the back of his neck as he spoke.

"Tonight, yeah." Max held eye contact with Tate long enough to imply something that neither of them wanted to actually say.

"Seriously, it's just for one night," Tate repeated. "Two, max."

Max paused. "Right." And with that, he exited the screen porch and started toward the makeshift staircase in the hill.

"What about your dad?" Tate eyed the shack below, wondering what a man who bet on his son would do it he found Tate stowed away on his property.

Max looked amused and gestured to the wooden planks before continuing down them. "Why do you think I built these?"

CHAPTER TWO

"For God's sake, Cameron, take that hideous shirt off." Cameron's mother clicked around the house in her stilettoes like a possessed ballerina in pointe shoes. Her pastel green dress matched his father's pastel green blazer, which matched his sister's pastel green sundress, which was supposed to match the pastel green button-down Cameron wasn't wearing. Instead, he wore his black Simple Plan t-shirt, an apparent disgrace to their entire family name. Cameron loved the band, but their punk rock persona wasn't something his mother would be caught dead having her son wear anywhere, let alone to an end of the summer yacht party with the city's finest.

It amused Cameron whenever she said that, like their city was Uptown NYC instead of a middle-class suburb in New Jersey. His parents and their friends liked being big fish in a little pond, although Cameron's parents were definitely the smallest of the big fish. They acted as though they were miles above the blue-collar people that comprised the majority of their city, when in actuality, they were quite careless with their money, using it in ways that increased their social status rather than their longevity. The lot of them were slightly higher than well-off in terms of socio-economic status, but what did it matter when the money burned a hole in their pockets? Secretly, most of them were traipsing through rivers of debt with their noses in the air and Gucci rain boots on their feet. Even tonight, four families pitched in so they could afford to rent the yacht and act like they owned it.

"Cameron, now!"

His green button-down was laid out on his bed, crisp and freshly pressed from the dry-cleaner. Cameron didn't understand why they couldn't wash their own clothes, but of all the battles to wage with his parents, that was not high on the list. He started to take his t-shirt off before deciding to put the button-down over it. He hid his personality a little more with each button he threaded until he was a vision of misery masked in pastel luxury.

Cameron heard his mother yapping at his sister about her hair in the next room, so he grabbed the hair gel and spiked his bleached blonde strands a little higher than usual just to spite her. For the most part, he followed their rules (more out of fear than compliance), but he had his minor rebellions. Like the skateboard and guitar hidden beneath his bed.

"Even fashionably late has a deadline!" his father boomed from the foyer, and Cameron hurried down the stairs behind his mother and sister.

"We're a vision in pastel," his mother crooned, taking one final look at everyone as they walked out the door. *That's us*, Cameron thought as he climbed into the private car. *A semblance of luxury.*

The other families were already on the yacht when they arrived, and as much as his father griped, Cameron knew his parents loved nothing more than making a grandiose entrance. They all but floated aboard, introducing Cameron and his sister as if it was the first time anyone had met them before immediately dismissing them to play with their friends. Cameron's sister darted off in a posse of pigtails while Cameron meandered his way above deck, where his friends were sitting at the bow of the yacht.

Well, his assigned group of friends.

Despite his efforts, they never truly accepted Cameron, his meek nature and extensive vocabulary the butt of every joke. The boys were lounging on the boat furniture smoking cigarettes, and Cameron's nerves kicked in before he even reached them.

"Cammy!" Wilson flicked his cigarette overboard and stood up, dragging Cameron into the seat beside him. He laughed at Cameron's visible discomfort, Bruce and Brian following suit. They almost exclusively acted in either reaction to or direction of Wilson.

"Cigarette?" Bruce offered a pack that looked as though it'd been through a hurricane. "Nabbed them from my dad's squad car." Cameron shook his head.

"When are you going to stop being such a lightweight?" Wilson asked, shoving Cameron into the seat across from him. Although he did not appreciate the shove, Cameron was grateful to have his own seat, settling into it in his own awkward way.

"You'll never make it in high school," Bruce laughed. Cameron thought this odd since none of them had actually been to high school yet. They were slated to start the week after next, and Cameron was nothing but nervous.

"You can say that again," Brian agreed, taking a big drag on his cigarette that sent him into a coughing fit.

"Unless," Wilson purred. "You stick with us." His smile dripped of ulterior motives, the Cheshire cat with a New Jersey accent.

Cameron was anxious to make new friends in high school, but if he was honest, he was just as anxious about keeping the friends he had now. He tried to distance himself a couple times over the years, but their families ran together, and like his parents, a small part of Cameron longed for full acceptance into the group. He took refuge in being the best speller in the area, starting competition at a young age at his teachers' encouragement. Unfortunately, the spotlight had been short-lived, and Wilson's parents quickly pushed him into the world of spelling as well, where he reveled in throwing Cameron off his game. Wilson was a good speller, but he didn't have Cameron's vocabulary or natural ability. He didn't integrate the words into his daily life, so he easily forgot them. There was an unspoken animosity between them ever since Cameron won the regional spelling bee a few years ago, kicking Wilson out of the running and off the throne. Eventually, it became too uncomfortable for Cameron to take, and he had thrown every competition to Wilson since.

"Yeah, Cammy," Bruce said, accidentally flicking ash on his own pants. "Stick with us." Cameron didn't like being called Cammy, which was most likely why they continued to do it.

"All right, guys, listen to this." Wilson leaned back and put his feet on the glass table, a king on his throne. Bruce and Brian leaned forward like their lives depended on whatever Wilson was about to say. "I been busy this summer." Cameron shifted in his seat, cringing at Wilson's illiteracy. "I been going door to door pitching myself to our fellow freshman classmates, and it's a done deal. You're looking at the new freshmen class president." Bruce and Brian applauded as if he had been awarded the Nobel Peace Prize.

"But the election isn't until the end of the first week of school." Cameron had been reading the weekly summer newsletters to incoming freshmen. "How can you be certain?" He knew he was the least socially adept of the group, but even they couldn't predict the outcome of an election that had yet to happen.

"Cammy, Cammy, Cammy." Wilson reached into his pocket and snapped a twenty-dollar bill in Cameron's face. "Incentives, my friend." Cameron's cheeks burned with shame; the last thing he wanted was the inside scoop on Wilson's cheating. Bruce handed Cameron a ballot card, Wilson's name already scrawled across it in neat black letters.

"First order of business?" Brian asked, ignoring Cameron's discomfort.

Wilson looked smug. "Make sure people know their place around here." His eyes bore into Cameron as he spoke, and Cameron snapped his gaze to the ground before excusing himself to the restroom. He splashed cold water on his face and blotted it dry with a paper towel, but the pink hue of embarrassment did not fade from his cheeks.

Looks like I'm in for a harrowing year.

. . .

"First day of band camp, and you're best friends with the drum major. How do you feel?" It was the week before school began, and Tate and Max sat atop the risers in the band room like knights ready for battle.

"Star struck." Max mocked, but Tate puffed out his chest in pride anyway.

The drum major last year was a senior, as were the majority of the section leaders. With such a new group coming in, the band director had recruited Tate and Max from their middle school band to be drum major and drumline section leader, respectively. It was Tate's job to lead the parade, and Max's job to be the rock of the group.

Typical.

Band members began pouring into the room, and Tate nudged Max off the bench behind the drum set. "Oh, here goes the hot-shot," Max said as Tate took a seat.

"I've got to make a first impression, and my baton is still MIA." Tate picked up a drum stick and spun it between his fingers. It was the main skill he learned from Max over the years when it came to drumming.

"I'd love to see you do that with your baton."

The band director gave Tate the baton to practice over the summer, and Tate smirked as he recalled all those days by the screen house, him throwing and Max retrieving when it landed anywhere but in hand. Although Tate eventually mastered it, he managed to disfigure it when it careened against the screen porch roof, and they were still waiting for the band director to repair it.

"That was sensational!" Tate turned and matched the voice to a boy about their age. His blonde hair and tall stature gave him a gawky appearance, and his words were like a kid's on Christmas. He was dressed for choir practice in khakis and a button-down, while Tate and Max were dressed for the skate park in tattered jeans and punk band t-shirts. He sidled up to the risers to watch Tate spin the drumstick again as if he were a circus act.

"Hear that, Max?" Tate spun on the stool to face the kid. "I'm sensational!" Max rolled his eyes and sat down on the edge of the riser, one foot swinging over the edge. "Check this out." The boy took a step forward, his saxophone clanking against the riser as it dangled from his neck strap. Max casually repositioned his foot to buffer it from impact as Tate picked up another drum stick and began to spin one in each hand.

"How do you do that?" the boy asked, mesmerized. In a smooth motion, Tate tossed him a stick, which hit the boy in the shoulder and clattered to the floor. He looked stunned, then embarrassed, and Max snatched the other stick from Tate and handed it to the boy. Tate leaned over to adjust his grip.

"Start between your pointer finger and your middle finger, and flip the stick around." The boy let Tate guide the stick around his fingers with palpable concentration. "Yeah, and when you get to your pinky, send it back the other way." Except once he got there, the stick wobbled off the boy's hand, shooting out and hitting the bass drum with a distinct thud. He colored pink with embarrassment.

"Sounds better than when Tate plays it," Max said. Tate gave him a mock smile and pulled the pen that was academically positioned behind the boy's ear.

"Here," he said. "It's easier to start with a pen." Tate gave it a quick spin through his own fingers to demonstrate.

"Teacher of the year," Max added.

"Learned from the best." Tate winked. Max had taught him how to spin sticks using a pen years ago. He went to toss the pen to the boy, thought better of it, and instead extended it out like a sword to a knight.

"Right." Max stood and nudged Tate out of his chair behind the drum set. The band director called the class to attention and asked everyone to take their seats on the risers. The boy smiled at Max and Tate before he snatched the pen and scampered off. Tate collected the fallen drumsticks and tossed them back to Max. In one motion, Max caught a stick in each hand and began spinning them both. He held Tate's eye as he tossed one in the air and the other behind his back, catching both with a wink. Tate held his hands up

29

in surrender as he walked down the risers to join the band director in front. Leave it to Max to put him in his place.

As drum major, Tate was like the captain of a sports team, and it was his job to help the band director use band camp to get the members acquainted and ready to play. The band director introduced Tate before starting in on his expectations and what the year would hold for all of them. They had been invited this year to march in the Macy's Thanksgiving Day Parade, and they had a lot of preparation to do before that date quickly arrived. Tate saw Max give him a nod and felt his stomach twist with anticipation. Tate spent most of last year begging the band director to nominate them to march in the parade, and the band director had finally given in. He told Tate when he recruited him they had been selected, hence Tate and Max's relentless practice over the summer. Marching in that parade meant more to Tate than anything else, and Max supported him every step of the way.

As the band director continued on about lockers and sheet music memorization, Tate couldn't help but notice the boy at the end of the saxophone section, slowly spinning the pen in his hand.

. . .

Max and Tate ran into the boy again the next day in the instrument closet. Apparently, they were all running late because they were the only three that weren't outside yet.

That's what happens when you skate scared.

Max taught Tate to skateboard a while back, and although he could hold his own, he never quite mastered it. Then again, Tate was not coordinated like Max, except with the baton.

The boy smiled shyly as they entered before returning to piecing his saxophone together.

"Saxophone, huh?" Tate smiled.

"Just when I march," the boy said.

"And the rest of the time?"

"Guitar." Tate's surprise was short-lived as he began to clamor around the band closet in search of his baton. Supposedly it was ready, but the janitors moved it when they sanitized the room, which left Tate on the hunt. Max told him he would help him look after practice, but he should have anticipated Tate couldn't wait that long.

"The heart of the band," Max said with an approving nod. "Nice." The boy lit up like a Christmas tree before checking himself and returning to the assembly of his mouthpiece.

"Not really. Can't march with it," he muttered, mostly to himself.

"I meant heart of a real band," Max said. He and Tate loved marching band, but as they grew older, their skateboarding, messy-haired hearts were punk rock. "Like the All-American Rejects."

"Or My Chemical Romance!" Tate added as he attempted to squeeze himself behind the first row of cubbies. Max rolled his eyes as he slipped on a shoulder pad and careened into a pile of mallets.

Just as spastic as the day I met him.

"Or Simple Plan," the boy said. Max shot Tate a surprised look as Tate righted himself amongst the chaos.

"Don't tell me you're into Simple Plan." Tate sounded skeptical, and the boy smirked before turning to face them, a music festival t-shirt featuring Simple Plan peeking out from his unbuttoned dress shirt.

"No shit," Max said. "Never seen them."

"Neither have I!" Tate called, although he had worked himself so far behind the pile of extra music stands, they could no longer see him.

We haven't gone to much of anything, actually. He and Tate weren't exactly rolling in the money, and Max would rather keep his jaw bone intact than go to a concert.

"Technically neither have I," the boy confessed, returning to the assembly of his mouthpiece. "But I wanted to, and I love their music, so I bought it online." He paused as if mustering up the courage before turning to Max and extending his hand. "I'm Cameron King."

"Max." He was surprised by the formality but shook hands anyway.

"Tate! Nice to meet you, CamKing!" Again, they couldn't see him, but they heard him clattering around amongst the equipment as he voiced his introduction. Cameron laughed at the nickname while Max surveyed the closet for the other drum stick he haphazardly tossed through the door the afternoon before. Cameron spotted it first, reaching behind Max's head to pull it from its wedge between two open locker doors. He gave it a spin around his hand before presenting it to Max.

"Hey," Max said, shoving his now paired sticks in his back pocket. "Not bad." Max could tell by the grin Cameron masked he wasn't accustomed to getting many compliments.

"So you guys are section leaders?" Cameron asked, sliding into his neck strap and fastening it to his now assembled saxophone.

Max nodded. "I play sna–" His sentence was cut off as Tate made a lunge for what he thought was his baton. Music stands crashed to the floor as he emerged with the butt of a color guard flag.

"Damn!" he said before tossing the flag aside and disappearing again behind a second row of cubbies. Max bit his lip to keep from laughing.

"Snare," he finished, patting the sticks in his back pocket. "I just lead drumline."

"Heart of the band," Cameron said. Max liked that it already felt like an inside joke, and he could tell that Cameron did too.

"He's the one that holds us all together!" Tate echoed from God knows where. Another crash as he clattered out from the cubbies, tugging on the end of his baton.

"And you're the drum major." It was more of a statement than a question, and Max could hear the admiration in Cameron's voice.

Just what he needs, an ego boost.

There had always been something inside Tate that knew he was destined for more, and Max envied it the smallest bit.

"Yeah," Tate said as he untangled the remainder of his baton from a pile of cymbals with a final yank. "I lead. But when it's not marching season, I play percussion with Max."

"Certainly makes enough noise for it!" Max yelled over the cascade of crashing cymbals. Tate gave him a friendly shoulder shove.

"My real instrument is guitar, but I'm in the same boat as you. No room for that in a band like this."

"Superb!" Cameron said. "I can't believe I am acquaintances with the drum major and the drumline leader!"

"Hear that, Max?" Tate said as he headed out of the closet. "I'm sensational *and* superb."

"As if his head wasn't big enough already." Max nudged Cameron, and Tate turned back in mock offense. It was the first time Cameron saw Tate head-on, his eyes lingering just a moment too long on the patch of discolored scar tissue on the left side of Tate's face. Max pretended not to notice, but he knew Tate did.

"It's a burn," Tate said matter-of-factly.

Cameron snapped his eyes to the ground. "I didn't mean to—"

"Forget it," Tate cut him off before giving him a solid pat on the shoulder. Cameron stumbled forward from the force, and Max made a mental note of the boy's fragility. "No sense wondering all year." Tate had never been ashamed of his scar, and Max didn't even notice it anymore, but Cameron still looked embarrassed.

"Cool it with that acquaintance stuff," Max said, pulling Cameron's attention. "Try friends." Cameron smiled before he could catch himself, his cheeks flushing as he tried to swallow his excitement. Max couldn't help but smile at the kid. He was so genuine, and Max put his arm around him as they exited the closet.

"And while we're at it," Tate said, his arms around each of their shoulders as he wedged between them. "Max doesn't have pink eye. Despite his questionable hygiene."

Max was slightly taken aback by Tate's bluntness but turned anyway so Cameron could see his right eye. It was permanently bloodshot, the part that should have been white replaced by a soft shade of pink. Cameron examined it for a second before once again snapping his eyes to the floor. "I thought it was cool," he mumbled, and Max liked him for it. "That's an exceedingly rare birth defect."

"Nah," Tate started as he began to twirl the baton.

Bad idea.

A second later, the baton caught the edge of the risers and fell to the floor with a clank. Tate gathered it as he continued. "It's not from birth."

"Then what is it from?" Cameron looked like he wanted to swallow the question as soon as he asked it, but it was already out there.

Max rolled his eyes at Tate and his flair for the dramatics for the seven-hundredth time that day. "A punch." Cameron's expression shifted from shocked, to confused, to embarrassed again, all in the span of about five seconds. Max felt bad for the kid; it wasn't his fault for being curious. He probably would be, too, if the situation was reversed. Luckily, even though Tate didn't think before he spoke, Max could always count on him to break an awkward silence.

"Put my right side with his left, and together we almost make one decent looking dude." Cameron loosened up at Tate's joke, as did Max. Tate pushed the limits, but he always seemed to know what Max needed when it came down to it. Since the day they met, the two had been on the same wavelength, and surprisingly, Cameron seemed to fit right into their flow.

"And for the record," Max said, grinning over his shoulder as he led the way out of the band room. "My hygiene is sensational."

. . .

"I don't remember seeing you in middle school band." Tate nudged Cameron's foot to make sure he was still alive. The three of them were sprawled out in the grass, taking an overdue water break after two hours of marching. Cameron sat up, face flushed, and took a swig from his insulated water bottle.

"I wasn't. My parents are sticklers for using school time for academics."

"But you play." Tate propped himself up on one elbow and nodded toward the saxophone lying in the grass.

"Private lessons." Cameron sounded a bit annoyed with his answer. "At home, on the weekends. Good for college applications."

"Guitar too?" Max asked. A stream of water darkened the front of his shirt as he drank from his beaten up water bottle. Tate was spread eagle in the grass, eyes closed, and Max took the opportunity to douse him with a stream of water. He mustered up a kick in Max's direction for good measure before closing his eyes again and letting the water cool him.

"God, no," Cameron laughed. "That I taught myself." Tate thought about how difficult it was for him to learn guitar, even with his father's help, and he mentally applauded Cameron for learning on his own. "My parents don't even know I have one." Cameron didn't strike Tate as the rebellious type, and he sat up as Cameron continued. "I purchased it at a garage sale," he explained. "I practice at night. Perks of an empty house, I suppose."

Must be rough living in a mansion.

Tate pushed the thought away when he heard the loneliness in Cameron's voice. Alone was alone, regardless of where. "So how'd you swing it this year?" Tate asked, gesturing to the marchers and instruments surrounding them on the field.

Cameron shrugged. "I convinced them it was good for my socialization."

"Hanging out with Tate isn't good for anyone's socialization," Max laughed. Tate made sure the kick landed this time, and Max fell back into the grass before rolling athletically back up.

"Plus, when I told them pre-calculus and chemistry overlap, it left me with an open period for"—Cameron paused as the band director blew his whistle—"socialization." Tate scampered to his feet as the whistle blew again.

"Wait," Max said as he donned his chest harness. Cameron helped him snap his snare drum into place before grabbing his saxophone, and Tate smiled at the comradery of his band. "Pre-calc isn't running during chemistry. I'm taking both."

Cameron glanced over his shoulder and grinned as he headed toward the other marchers. "Oops."

. . .

"CamKing!" Tate's voice carried over the crowd from the back of the risers, where he sat leaning against the bass drum, legs outstretched and tired. Max sat beside him, one leg hanging off the risers, as usual. He handed Cameron a cupcake as he sat down, back against the safety rail. It was the last day of band camp, and they were having a potluck in the band room.

"Thanks!" Cameron always seemed happy to talk to them, and Max was really starting to enjoy having him around.

"Ready for classes on Monday?" he asked.

"I don't mind school, really," Cameron confessed with a mouthful of cupcake. "It beats a summer of pretentious parties." Max was still trying to figure out how to navigate Cameron's obvious disdain for his luxurious lifestyle, especially when he had next to nothing. He was grateful when Tate changed the subject.

"Who's your homeroom?"

"Brightly."

"We have Burton." Max surveyed the room full of marchers. "Actually, I think everyone in here does. At least all the freshmen."

"How'd you get Brightly?" Tate asked. "Homeroom's based on clubs so we can coordinate rehearsals." Max could see the drum major wheels turning in Tate's head with homeroom marching plans. Cameron tore at the edges of his cupcake wrapper.

"I'm in spelling bee club too. My parents' preference was Brightly." Cameron spat out the word "preference" like it was something stuck in his teeth.

"Spelling bee club?" Max hadn't even heard of it, let alone known anyone in it.

"Yes." Cameron's cheeks turned pink. "I won regionals a few years ago."

"Impressive," Max said, but the pink did not leave Cameron's cheeks.

"I know you probably think it's a preternatural hobby for a teenager."

Max had absolutely no idea what that meant, but Cameron was clearly embarrassed, so he sent his elbow into Tate's rib to keep him from making a joke. "It's sensational." Max made sure to hold Cameron's gaze long enough to show he was serious.

"Superb," Tate added. Cameron stopped attacking his cupcake wrapper, his shoulders visibly relaxing against the safety rail of the risers.

"What about you guys?" Cameron asked, eager to change the subject. "What do you do in your spare time?" Max kept his eyes on the fallen wrapper, but he could feel Tate look at him for just a moment too long.

"Guitar, mostly," Tate volunteered. "Not my own stuff, though. Just covers."

"He sings too." Max hated it when Tate sold himself short; everyone else already did it enough. Tate wasn't embarrassed by the comment, but he wasn't arrogant about it either. That's one of the things Max liked about him. Although Tate always had stars in his eyes, they had never blinded him from accepting the reality of how things were.

"I would love to hear sometime," Cameron said, tossing his cupcake wrapper onto the riser next to him. Max and Tate both smiled at the pureness of their new friend. "What about you, Max?" Cameron asked, shifting his body and attention.

"Can't sing a lick." Although he was not ashamed of his past, Max certainly wasn't proud of it, and it embarrassed him that he couldn't come up with something other than a used-to-be fighter to define himself. He wanted to be more than a fistful of problems, but the punches over the years each knocked a little bit out of him, and to this day, he was still trying to piece himself back together.

"Max is a whiz at math," Tate said. "Like crazy good." Cameron picked up on the awkward pause before Tate's interjection but let it go.

"You can help me in pre-calc then." Cameron nudged Max's foot with his own.

Max gave a small smile, reserved but sincere. They sat in silence, taking in the comfort of each other's company. Max felt bad he wasn't being completely real with Cameron. After all, Cameron had shared the spelling with them, despite his embarrassment. He felt the urge to tell Cameron something more. Something meaningful.

"Honestly," Max wrung his hands together as he spoke. "Mostly just trying to survive, I guess." A lifetime of problems and struggles passed between them as he locked eyes with Cameron.

"Aren't we all," Tate said, and Max could hear the weight in his voice.

"Yeah." Cameron leaned his head against the safety rail, examining the ceiling. "Aren't we all?"

CHAPTER THREE

Max and Tate were surprised when Cameron slid into Burton's homeroom just as the bell rang. "Hey, CamKing," Tate whispered as Burton took attendance. "What gives?" He looked genuinely concerned Cameron was accidentally in the wrong place.

Confirmation that I'm in the right place.

"Isn't this homeroom for the band?" Cameron whispered back, followed by "Here!" when Mr. Burton called his name. Once he finished attendance, Mr. Burton turned them loose to talk amongst themselves.

"Glad you're here," Max said, turning his desk to face Cameron's. "Do you have your schedule?" Cameron pulled his out, shocked that someone actually cared if they shared a class as Max compared Cameron's to his. "Hey, we do have pre-calc together," Max confirmed. "Sweet."

Cameron couldn't help but smile.

"Buncha geniuses over here," Tate laughed, brushing their schedules into their laps. "More importantly, we all have band together!"

Tate slapped his schedule on the desk, his pointer finger thrust at the only class he cared about.

Cameron examined Tate's schedule. "You're taking intermediate piano?"

"We can't all be math whizzes."

Max looked skeptical. "You don't even know beginner piano."

Tate shrugged as he sat on his desk. "How hard can it be?"

"Cammy!"

Cameron winced at the voice before following it to the doorway, where Wilson and Bruce were dressed for a country club luncheon. "I think you're lost," Wilson said, stepping into the room. "You're in Brightly with us."

"Is this homeroom or English as a second language?" Bruce snickered, taking in Max and Tate's darker complexion. Cameron's cheeks turned seven shades of magenta as he stared at the desk in front of him, wishing they would leave, while Max and Tate exchanged a look.

"Seriously though, Cammy," Wilson said. "What the hell are you doing in here?"

"This was my assigned homeroom," Cameron mumbled, sending Wilson and Bruce into a fit of exaggerated laughter.

"Get real," Wilson said. "You know we can do whatever the hell we want." His face hardened as Cameron made no move to get up.

"Why would you want to be in Burton anyway?" Bruce asked, looking at Max and Tate like rotten fruit.

"Tutoring." Tate's answer shocked Cameron. Wilson and Bruce seemed surprised he spoke English at all.

"Sí," Max added.

"Tutoring?" Wilson raised his eyebrows.

"A little early in the year for volunteer work, Cammy," Bruce said. "Even for you." Cameron glanced at Tate and Max, unsure how to proceed without offending his new friends.

"We talked about this at the party Cammy," Wilson said as he watched the exchange. "Hanging with the...wrong crowd." His eyes focused on Max and Tate as he spoke the last words.

"So what?" Bruce said. "You're out of the bee now?"

"No!" Cameron said, frustration mounting. "I'm just in a different homeroom."

"You better not be out of the bee," Wilson said. "We have unfinished business."

Max's head snapped up at the threatening tone, his eyes giving away nothing as he examined Wilson.

"I'll beeeeee there," Cameron said mockingly. Tate choked on a laugh as Wilson and Bruce glared at each of them in turn.

"Whatever," Bruce sneered as Wilson shoved him out the door. "Enjoy your projects."

"See you in pre-calc, Cammy." Wilson paused on his way out. "Unless you switched out of that too."

"*Adiós!*" Tate called after them, Max's eyes daggers on the spot Wilson had stood. It took all of Cameron's courage to look them in the eye after what just happened.

"You didn't have to do that."

Tate spun a pen around his fingers. "Do what?" Cameron snatched it from his hand and put it on the table. "So they're idiots." Tate shrugged. "Can't control your friends." He smacked Max lightly on the shoulder for confirmation, breaking him from his trance.

"You're not my projects," Cameron said.

Tate climbed off the desk as the warning bell sounded. "Time for intermediate piano!" He nudged Max on his way out the door. "See you guys in band."

Max tucked his schedule away before grabbing his backpack. Cameron watched him take a deep, calming breath. His fists unclenched as he released the air, the frown lines disappearing from between his eyebrows. "Ready for round two?" Something about the way he said it made Cameron feel safe, protected.

He nodded, slung his backpack over his shoulders, and followed Max into the sea of students to pre-calc.

. . .

Tate went to the band room first, assuming the band director would be teaching intermediate piano, only to be greeted with a group of wide-eyed freshmen incorrectly holding their guitars. Tate had to recheck his schedule before modifying his course to the chorus room. Although he had never played the piano, he was confident his guitar background and drum major experience would give him a leg up.

How hard can it be?

His question was answered with a cacophony of pounding keys and wrong notes as he entered the chorus room. It was smaller than he expected, but much like the band room, it pulsed with creative energy. Two foot risers formed a half-circle to his right that bent around a large piano. Behind that was the teacher's desk, tucked away in the back right corner of the room. To his left was the source of the noise: twelve keyboards, six face to face with six others. Ten of the seats were already occupied, leaving the two seats closest to the teacher's desk the only vacant spots.

The teacher was hunched over her computer as if mining for gold, completely unaffected by the chaos ensuing to her right. Tate assessed his options. Three seats in sat a guy the size of a linebacker, hands the size of oven mitts as he pounded the keys three at a time. He had more stubble than a high schooler should, and he raised an eyebrow as Tate approached. The last thing Tate wanted to do was offend someone who could squash him, so he slid into the seat next to the guy, leaving the seat closest to the teacher for the poor sap that came in last.

"How's it going, man? I'm Tate."

"Samson," the guy grunted. "Nice face," he added, gesturing at Tate's scar.

"Nice shoulders," Tate said, patting Samson's enormous collarbone, praying it wouldn't get him hurled at the wall.

"Touché," Samson laughed, and Tate exhaled.

"You ever played one of these things before?"

"Nope." Tate couldn't believe Samson hadn't broken a key yet as he continued to batter the keyboard in front of him.

The door opened a final time, and a girl rode the warning bell into the classroom, taking the empty seat next to Tate. She had one of those side shoulder bags that looked like it weighed about thirty pounds, confirmed by its audible clunk as she tossed it down by her feet.

"Hi." She said it so casually, Tate wasn't entirely positive she was talking to him. But seeing as there was no one to her left, and the boy across from her was ensnared in his headphone cord, Tate made the assumption.

"Hey," he said and was relieved when she gave him a quick smile as she unpacked a blank notebook and a pen. If she noticed his scar, she didn't show it.

Her hair was in a golden braid that fell over her right shoulder just past her collarbone, a couple shorter strands escaping to frame her face. Although against the dress code, her white tank top was tasteful, and she gave off such an heir of class and self-respect, Tate doubted anyone would even notice. Her jeans were pretty standard, cuffed at the bottom so she wouldn't step on them with her white sneakers. Max's strategy to shorten jeans was to saw off the extra length with a pocket knife to keep them from getting caught in the wheels of his skateboard. Tate made a silent thank you that he was just tall enough to avoid that fashion statement.

Before he could ask her name, the teacher erupted like a bear fresh out of hibernation. "Lyle!" she boomed. The girl next to Tate was the only one who didn't jump out of her seat. "I have your sheet music for select!" Tate understood now why those two seats had been empty and felt slightly guilty for leaving the worst one to this girl.

However, the girl seemed unfazed, all eyes on her as she rose to retrieve the sheet music. If she was embarrassed, she didn't show it, smiling politely as the teacher handed her the music before returning to her seat. Tate's guilt morphed into relief that he opted for the seat next to Samson, especially since the teacher seemed to like this girl.

Lyle.

She opened the sheet music and began to waltz her fingers across her keyboard, and although it wasn't turned on, it was obvious from the way she was swaying that she was riding the melody in her head. "Looks like you've done this before," Tate said.

"I accompany the choruses." As she spoke, she smiled at him, the tension he didn't know he had releasing under her attention.

"Plural?"

"Mixed chorus and select chorus. I accompany them when they compete."

"Nice," Tate said like an idiot who didn't know how to talk to a pretty girl. He was surprisingly thankful as the teacher rose from her chair at the final bell.

"I am Ms. Godllub," she roared. "And this is intermediate piano." Ms. Godllub was about as wide as she was tall, and every word she spoke came from her toes. "You are going to learn how to play a song on the keyboard!" Lyle was the only one unbothered by Ms. Godllub's boisterous nature; some students snickered to one another while others looked stunned, as if shot with a pellet gun. "Here are your lesson books for the term." She dropped two piles of books, one in front of Lyle and one in front of the now untangled boy across from her. Lyle quickly distributed them down their row before grabbing the other six and doing the same on the other side. "We have headphones for a reason," Ms. Godllub continued, waving Lyle's in the air. "Use them! I can't grade papers with you slamming wrong notes in my ear!"

Tate glanced at Samson, who was a deer in headlights. It was strange to see such a short woman instill fear in such a large guy. "Learn the song," Ms. Godllub finished as she returned to her desk and plopped back down into her chair. "You will be tested on the song at the end of the term."

"Singular?" Lyle whispered, flipping through the lesson book in search of more sheet music.

"Is she always this—?"

"No yapping!" Ms. Godllub squawked, eyes once again glued to her computer.

"—pleasant?" Tate finished, lowering his voice. Lyle didn't look up as she continued to flip through the lesson book.

"Pretty much," she said, rolling her eyes as she reached the song at the end of the lesson book. "Really?" She seemed doubly disappointed, once by the song and once by the lack of additional pieces to learn. By the look of the lesson book, Tate couldn't even imagine learning more than one song by the end of the term.

"Why are you even in this class?" he asked. Clearly, she knew this lesson book inside and out, while the double staff and multiple key signatures overwhelmed him. The thought of splitting his brain to simultaneously play two different key signatures with two different hands was insane to him, and looking around the room, he could tell he was not alone in this thought.

Lyle seemed frustrated as she snapped the book shut. "I was hoping it would be a little more...challenging." Tate didn't even want to know her definition of challenging sheet music. "I learned how to play this when I was little," she added, holding up the book. Tate couldn't tell if he was embarrassed by his newfound musical inadequacy or impressed by her musical prowess, but whichever it was made his face hot.

"Yeah," he managed before turning to Samson in an attempt to hide his lameness.

"Can I practice the select piece on the main piano?" he heard Lyle ask Ms. Godllub before collecting her things and relocating herself to the piano facing the foot risers.

Damn.

Tate was left with no choice but to turn his attention to the keyboard in front of him until the bell rang. He thought he caught Lyle look at him once across the room. Or maybe it was the other way around. Either way, he certainly didn't mind.

He was still thinking about her on the way to his next class, although his journey from the chorus room to the band room was a short one. He joined Max and Cameron atop the risers by the drum set as people around them christened their camp friendships into real ones.

"Alright guys, take your seats, please," the band director said, tapping his conductor's baton. The room hushed as everyone bustled into whatever seat was closest. "Looking around, I see all of you were in marching band camp last week. Although this class is technically concert band, the parade is before the winter concert, so we will be spending four of our five weekdays on marching music." The room nodded in agreement, Tate glad they were taking the opportunity as seriously as he was.

Well, almost.

"A couple announcements before we get started," the band director continued. "First, please make sure you keep the instrument closet clean and organized. There's a lot of money's worth of instruments in there that we want to protect. So if you happen to move or knock something over"—his eyes danced on Tate for a moment before returning to the class—"please put it back." Cameron stifled a giggle as Max elbowed Tate in the side. Tate shrugged apologetically as the director continued. "The other thing I want to talk about before we get started is the logistics of the marching trip. Everyone will need to hand in a signed permission slip from their legal guardian no later than next week in order to attend." Tate's body was rooted to the risers. "In addition, there will be a cost to each of you that will cover your hotel, transportation, and food in New York City. I know we are not far, but it is tradition that the marching band spend the weekend in the city, and we're not about to stop now."

"How much?" someone in the front row asked.

The band director hesitated. "Five hundred dollars."

Tate and Max's jaws hit the floor.

The band director was quick to continue. "I am telling you this now so you can all do whatever you need to do to raise the money. The principal has assured me the incoming class presidents will be required to provide a fundraising opportunity for each grade, so if that is something you are interested in, please go talk to your new class president once they are elected on Friday." Tate's entire body felt like it weighed a thousand pounds. "Okay, we don't have enough time today to get outside or run the songs, so talk amongst yourselves and get organized for an intense couple of months." The band director returned to his office, the room exploding with conversation in his wake.

"Legal guardian." Max's voice sounded hollow. Although Tate had mastered the art of forging his foster father's signature, Max was always hesitant to forge his father's, worried he would find out and suffer the consequences as a result.

"Five hundred dollars." Tate sloshed the words around in his mouth, trying to find a way to reorganize them into something else.

"Class president," Cameron squeaked. The three of them stared straight ahead in silence until the warning bell sounded.

"Shit," Max said.

It felt as if the floor dropped out from under Tate, and he couldn't find anything to grab onto as he fell. He couldn't afford that kind of money, and he knew Max couldn't either. But he had to march. He had to find a way. "Shit," he echoed.

"Preposterous," Cameron stood, pulling Max, then Tate, to his feet. The boys exited the band room without their usual theatrics, the weight of technicalities heavy on their minds.

. . .

Lyle grabbed Aariz's arm to steady herself as the bus rumbled across the bridge. At four thirty, they were lucky to find two adjoining seats in the back. This ride was so familiar to Lyle, she didn't bother looking out the window. Aariz, on the other hand, was leaning across her to take in the New York City skyline. He rarely found his way out of New Jersey, and by the looks he got from their fellow passengers when they boarded the bus, Lyle didn't blame him for staying close to home.

"How was your first day?" Aariz asked, adjusting his robe that had been jostled on the bridge.

"It was fine."

"Spoken like a true high schooler."

Lyle smiled. Aariz was her grandfather Rawel's best friend, a member of the family as far as she was concerned. He and Rawel bought their retail duplex together many years ago, Aariz living above his carpentry shop, Rawel and Lyle living above their dry-cleaning business. Aariz was there through it all, but in an observatory kind of way, sticking to the sidelines until Lyle needed him. He was more of a friend than a parental figure, keeping her company in the store during Rawel's late nights at the fire station.

Rawel had originally bought the dry-cleaning business for his wife and daughter-in-law, but Lyle's grandmother passed away when Lyle was just one. As for her mother, Rawel was forced to take on more than the business after the terrorist attack. That included parental responsibilities, so he switched to the night shift at the station and spent the weekdays running the business. Now that she was older, Lyle was able to take on an evening shift after school to help them make ends meet, and although they did their best to spend time together on the weekends, it never seemed like enough. Although they mostly saw each other in the mornings, Lyle loved her grandfather dearly, and Aariz was enough company to make her feel like she wasn't alone.

"School was good," she elaborated. "I have pretty good classes, and I didn't get lost trying to find them."

"Can't ask for much more than that. What's your favorite?"

Lyle thought for a minute. "Intermediate piano."

Aariz smiled. "I'm glad you decided to take it."

"The music is really easy, and we're only learning one song, but I can use the time to practice accompaniment, so it's nice."

Aariz nodded. He knew not to press the subject of piano with her, but she could tell he was glad to see her back doing what she loved. "And your classmates?" Lyle didn't know why the boy from intermediate piano popped into her head first, maybe because he was the only person who actually introduced himself.

What was his name again?

Lyle stood as the bus rolled to a halt at the stop across from the prison. She wove through the crowd of passengers, noting their expressions as Aariz followed. They seemed unsurprised he was getting off here, and although he held his head high, Lyle knew he noticed. The bus moaned away just after their feet hit the pavement, Aariz forcing a smile he had to muster from within. He was always trying to be her rock, but sometimes Lyle wondered who his rock was.

"Most of my classmates are terrified of their own shadow." She rested her head on Aariz's shoulder as they waited to cross the street. He snapped out of his disheartened state and became her trustworthy confidante again.

"Oh, come on, there must have been someone you connected with."

Tate.

51

The name came to her like the first drop in a bucket, quick and loud before getting swallowed up by everything else. She thought she caught him looking at her, his hair all dark and unkempt.

"Yeah," Lyle said as they started across the street. "Maybe someone."

Although the prison guards knew Lyle, they took special precaution screening Aariz, patting his robe like he was stashing a herd of elephants. She almost said something, but a shake of his head left Lyle stewing in silence until they finally gave Aariz his pass and led them into the communication room.

She had visited too many times to count, yet the dim lighting and mustard grey of the walls always made the air feel thicker. Most families went to the visitors' room, where they sat at tables with their loved ones and talked face to face. It took Lyle a while to accept she would never be allowed to do that, but hope was a weird thing in here. No matter how much Lyle tossed it away, it ricocheted off the cement wall back at her, just out of reach. Rawel used to bring sanitary wipes to clean off the receiver before they used it, but when he decided they weren't visiting anymore, Lyle felt too dirty from sneaking around to care about the germs.

Until today, Lyle never told Aariz where she snuck off to, but from the occasional looks he gave, she assumed he knew. Lyle even caught him covering for her a couple times when her grandfather started asking questions. Rawel didn't have a mean bone in his body, but his bones seemed heavier with each visit until he was weighed down by a mixture of shame, regret, and whatever other sour emotions came from being hopelessly stuck in a bad situation. Eventually, he hit his breaking point and cut the cord, telling Lyle it was best for both of them, but after a while, Lyle found herself needing to go. Needing to share her life with someone who was supposed to know everything about her. Needing to believe the person she loved was still in there, that there was a way out of this mess.

Per usual, they were alone in the narrow communications hall. The occasional grieving grandmother wept to her grandson, begging him to tell her where she went wrong, but other than that, there was never anyone in here. Lyle thought it best to have some time before Aariz joined, so she motioned for him to sit one cubicle over as she took her usual seat in cubicle four. He obliged, looking at her like a caged butterfly. Rawel had looked at her the same way when he came, but Lyle didn't feel like a butterfly. She felt more like a baby kangaroo fallen from its pouch, a little too cold and a little too turned around to find her way alone.

The bell echoed off the concrete walls, reverberating back at Lyle as it introduced the prisoner's entry. The light above Lyle's cubicle glowed red to mark its occupancy, casting her in its gentle shade like a photographer's development room. Sometimes it felt that way, as if Lyle was viewing photos of her life rather than living it, trying desperately to develop them into a prettier picture. Unfortunately, the effort was futile, and it always left her feeling like she failed in some way.

The prisoner clanked in, hands and feet chained, and sat across the glass from cubicle four. The officers unchained the handcuffs and gave the signal, the light overhead changing from red to green. Lyle and the prisoner picked up their receivers simultaneously like some sick dance. "Hi, Mom." Lyle's mother sat before her, a vision in orange. Her long blonde hair extended almost to her waistline, and she had somehow managed to acquire mascara for the occasion. Not that she needed it. She was a natural beauty, like a songbird people admired from a distance for fear of startling it. Lyle liked to think she looked a little bit like her mother.

"Hi, baby." Her mother's voice dripped with honey, and Lyle let it envelop her. "How was your first day of high school?"

"It was good. A lot to take in, but I think it will be a good four years."

"Any boys?"

Lyle's cheeks flushed. "Mom."

"That means yes," her mother laughed. She could be very perceptive when she wanted to be; sometimes, it felt like her mother could see right through her. "Tell me about him."

"Mom, there isn't a boy."

"Honestly, Delilah, you're cute as a button. There has to be a boy." Lyle could see Aariz look up from the cubicle beside her. He hadn't heard anyone call her Delilah since, well, since her mother was sentenced. "Who are you looking at, baby?" Her mother's eyes looked excited, expecting Lyle to present the boyfriend she didn't have.

For a second, Lyle was full of panic, her eyes darting from Aariz to her mother and back again. She was dreading this all afternoon, but Aariz had insisted on coming. He put a calming hand on her shoulder and shifted himself into view. Lyle had never seen her mother's eyes go dark so fast, all light extinguished by the cruel boot of hatred.

"What are you doing here?" she yelled loud enough for him to hear through the glass. Aariz remained standing, easing the phone from Lyle's white-knuckled grip.

"Hello, Marianna." At the sound of his voice, her mother's entire body went taut with adrenaline. Her eyes narrowed as if everyone else in the room had disappeared.

"How dare you come here with her." She motioned to Lyle. "What will people think?"

"Honestly, Marianna, I don't care what people think. And I'm not here to talk about Lyle."

"Delilah," her mother corrected, unaware Lyle had shunned her full name years ago. "Of course you don't care. None of you care about anyone but your own!" Aariz inhaled the remark, holding it in for a moment before exhaling it from his body.

"I'm here to tell you that I forgive you."

The statement took Lyle by surprise. If she were Aariz, she didn't know how she would forgive her mother. Then again, she was the one that continued to visit.

Does that mean I already have?

"Forgive me? I did everyone I love a favor." Losing two people she loved in a span of days didn't feel like a favor to Lyle, but she said nothing.

"I'll never understand why you did it," Aariz continued as if her mother hadn't spoken. "And I'll never understand how so much hatred found its way into your heart, but I cannot carry this burden with me any longer, this burden of hatred. I have to let it go now." Aariz paused, doing his best to swallow. "I have to let her go now," he added, more to himself than to Lyle or her mother.

"My husband is dead!" Lyle's mother shrieked, lunging against her ankle restraints. "You were probably all in on it." She looked at Lyle, wild-eyed. "And if that wasn't enough, she tried to take my Delilah from me."

Aariz had heard this all before, and Lyle could tell as he stood that he wasn't interested in changing her mother's mind. "Goodbye, Marianna. I hope your heart finds peace someday."

Her mother glowered at him before reeling back and spitting on the glass. Lyle jumped, Aariz unflinching as he watched the spit slide down the barrier. "I'll be outside," he said, patting her shoulder before handing her the receiver and exiting the hall.

Lyle couldn't take her eyes off the spit as it continued down the glass. The vision of her mother blurred behind it as she returned the receiver to her ear. "Delilah, baby." Her mother's voice snapped back to a croon as soon as Aariz was out of sight. "Delilah, you shouldn't have brought him here. Those people aren't safe…"

Her mother continued on, but Lyle didn't hear the rest, the blurry trail between them made blurrier by the tears welling in her eyes. She felt as though every prisoner was staring at her from one side, each of their victims staring at her from the other. Both sides bore a hole until they met in the middle, crushing her heart between them.

Her mother tapped on the glass. "Delilah?"

Lyle slammed the receiver back on its hook and rushed from the room without waiting for the red light. As she and Aariz rode the bus home in silence, the gap in the skyline where the Twin Towers used to be brought back memories Lyle wished she could forget.

. . .

"Delilah, you can pick from these three," her mother said. There were so many pianos in the showroom it looked like a museum, and Lyle was hesitant to touch anything. Technically her seventh birthday had been yesterday, and although her parents had thrown her a party at the store, they hadn't been able to make it into the city until today. It was a great party, Aariz and Yalina even came over from next door to sing to her, but today Lyle was ready for her piano.

She grew up surrounded by her mother's piano music in their apartment above the business, and sometimes just before closing, Lyle could hear Yalina's piano from their own apartment. She had been begging anyone that would listen for a piano since she was three years old, and she had woken her mother up at the crack of dawn to arrive exactly at eight when the showroom opened.

Lyle turned her attention to the starter pianos her mother was pointing at. Although she longed for a grand piano big enough to crawl inside, Lyle understood their financial limitations and was happy with anything. She examined the starters, immediately eliminating one, but after that, she was at a loss.

"Can I?" Lyle asked, her hands hovering over the keys as she shimmied onto the stool.

Her mother smiled. "You can't buy a piano without a test run."

Lyle played the scale her mother had taught her, swaying as her fingers danced around the keys.

"Sounds like you found your match." Her mother raised her hand to get the salesman's attention. "We've decided on this one," she said as he approached.

"Congratulations, young lady!" he boomed, shaking Lyle's small hand in his bony one before turning back to her mother. "Where would you like it delivered?"

"The Carry Out dry-cleaning. Ask for Rawel; he's the owner." Although there was a space in her room, Lyle and her grandfather decided to put the piano in the lobby so she could entertain the customers while they waited. "Thank you so much for your help," her mother finished. "Lyle, what do you say?"

"Thank you," she said to the salesman as her mother paid. "And thank you!" she added as they exited the showroom. Her mother pulled her against her hip.

"Your very own piano. Are you excited?" Lyle grinned, her tongue poking through the gap where her two front teeth used to be. "I am too." Her mother gave her a squeeze. "Plus, we're just in time to meet Daddy for your birthday breakfast."

They only ate in the city on special occasions, and Lyle couldn't wait for her father to arrive. "Daddy should be here by now," her mother said. She tapped her foot beneath the table and looked down the street, waiting for him to emerge from the crowd of passersby.

Lyle grabbed a purple crayon from the box at the table and began drawing. "Maybe he's cleaning the firetruck," she offered. It was her favorite thing to do when she visited her father at the fire station. They came out so shiny and bright, and sometimes he even let her turn on the siren when they were done.

"Maybe." Her mother sounded preoccupied as she dialed her flip phone. Lyle heard the beep and her mother began to leave a message. "Hey, Leon, it's me. It's almost 8:45, just wondering where you are. We've got a table near the window. You'll see it when you walk in. Okay, love you."

"Look," Lyle said, holding up her drawing of music notes.

"That's great, baby."

Her mother was examining the picture when they heard the bang. It shook the restaurant, the room buzzing with people trying to figure out where it came from.

"Mommy, it's raining paper," Lyle said wide-eyed, pointing out the window at the white pieces wafting from the sky. Her mother's head snapped to the window where Lyle was pointing, white office paper drifting down from the sky to coat the street.

"Oh, my God," she breathed. Lyle didn't know what was so scary about paper, but her mother looked as if she had seen a ghost. "Delilah!" Lyle barely made it out of the booth before her mother grabbed her hand and dragged her outside. Everyone was emerging from the surrounding buildings to see what caused the commotion.

Papers blanketed the pavement like the first fallen snow, and Lyle wanted nothing more than to draw on all of them.

She considered going back inside for her purple crayon, but her mother had her hand like a vice as she stared up toward the sky. Lyle followed her gaze down the street to the Twin Towers, where smoke billowed from the top of the one on the right. Everyone was staring, trying to figure out what was going on.

"There must be a fire inside," Lyle heard someone say.

"A bomb?" someone else called.

"No, I saw it," another person said, eyes wide. "It was a plane."

"Oh, my God," her mother repeated. A sea of people began flowing down the street away from the towers, and her mother pulled Lyle along to join them. A siren sounded around the corner, and the sea parted as a firetruck shot past them in the direction of the smoke.

"Maybe that was Daddy," Lyle said. It was a joke her mother had started when Lyle grew old enough to miss her father. Every time they saw a firetruck, they pretended it was him visiting her throughout the day.

Lyle waited for her mother to laugh like she always did, but instead, she stopped dead in her tracks, her face stone cold. If she looked like she saw a ghost before, her mother looked like she just saw an entire army of monsters now. Without a word, her mother took off running in the direction of the fire truck, Lyle tripping behind her by the hand.

CHAPTER FOUR

The rest of the week came and went, the boys no closer to a solution to their problems. The fundraiser was their only option, and by Friday, they were more than anxious to vote on their class president. The election was scheduled in place of homeroom, so Tate waited for Max and Cameron in the auditorium doorway before they slid into three empty seats near the aisle. Max and Cameron were always together in the halls, Tate baffled by their ability to consistently find each other in the madness of students.

He saw the piano girl, Lyle, across the aisle a few rows up. He recognized the girls next to her from the chorus room, and although she was friendly with them, he could tell by the way her eyes roamed the room they were more acquaintances to her than friends. Tate watched her scan the rows, entranced by her mannerisms, until he realized she was now observing him observing her. "What?" he asked, turning to Max as if he was trying to get his attention.

"Huh?" Max said, turning in his seat.

"Forget it."

Max shrugged one shoulder before returning to his conversation with Cameron. "My money's on the girl from the robotics club." Max paused. "Well, it would be if I had any."

Cameron shook his head. "It'll be Wilson." He seemed uncomfortable, but even in conversation, Wilson seemed to have that effect on him.

The faculty advisor called the auditorium to order, and the speeches began. The robotics girl went first, listing off great ideas about supporting the community and how that relationship could be reciprocated to help support extracurricular activities.

"Good shit," Max said, clapping as she exited the stage. Cameron smirked, and although Tate wasn't quite as enthusiastic, he agreed with Max. Band was technically an extracurricular activity, and her mindset was exactly what they needed to get to the parade.

The gears were already grinding in Tate's head about fundraising when Wilson took the stage. He looked like a Brooks Brothers model with his suit and leather dress shoes, and Tate resisted the urge to roll his eyes.

"I, of course, am Wilson," he began, "and I am here today as your class president. Oh, my apologies," he corrected, "potential class president." Cameron inhaled sharply, and Tate didn't hear him let it out. "Our class is full of many different types of people." Max glanced at Tate. "And as your president, it is my job—excuse me— *would be* my job..." Max huffed at the convenient correction. Tate was pretty sure Cameron was still holding his breath. "...my top priority, to make sure that everyone finds the place where they..." Wilson's eyes focused in on Cameron as he finished, "...belong."

Cameron finally exhaled as Wilson exited the stage, and Tate reached around Max to pat him on the shoulder. "You okay, CamKing?"

Cameron nodded, trying to control his breathing. Tate didn't understand why the guy had such a hard-on for Cameron, but whatever the reason, it was starting to get annoying. He could tell from the way Max bristled in the seat next to him that he felt the same.

One by one, the auditorium rows approached the stage to cast their votes. Tate saw a bunch of students shuffle around their pockets or backpacks as they reached the front of the voting line, and he cursed himself for not remembering to bring a pen. However, when he reached the front of the line, he was greeted with a plethora of paper and blue pens strewn across the stage. Tate scribbled his vote for the robotics girl and returned to his seat. Despite the students' odd rummaging when they would reach the front of the line, the whole thing took no longer than fifteen minutes.

"Is it just me?" Tate asked once they were all seated again. "Or was that really fast?" Max nodded, and Cameron sat completely still, saying nothing. Tate stole a glance across the aisle, and Lyle's brows were knit in a suspicious way that mimicked his. Her eyes landed on what he thought was him before realizing she was looking at Cameron. He followed her line of sight to Cameron's feet, where his backpack was not quite zipped all the way.

Hanging out the side was a ballot that read *Wilson* in dark black sharpie.

For a moment, Tate was proud of Cameron for changing his vote until he remembered the pens on the stage had been blue. He glanced at Lyle to confirm his suspicion, but her attention was redirected to the stage. "You okay, Cam?" Max asked as Cameron's leg bounced up and down like a chisel.

"Me?" Cameron squeaked. "Yeah, copacetic." Tate was about to say something when the faculty advisor took the stage.

"The votes are in, and your freshman class president is…" She paused for dramatic effect, and Tate thought Cameron was going to keel over. "…Wilson!"

All the khaki and leather in the auditorium whooped and hollered, the rest of the students settling for a round of applause. As Wilson took the stage, Tate glanced at Cameron, the unused ballot crinkling in his hand as he crumpled it. The warning bell saved them all from a grandstand acceptance speech, and the boys headed for the doors.

"The robotics girl was the obvious choice," Max grumbled, rounding the bend and walking smack into her.

"Well, thank you," she said, sounding equally pissed off. "I agree."

"Max," he said, extending his hand.

"Zana."

"For the record, I voted for you."

"I'll remember that," she said as the crowd of students carried her away down the hall.

Tate stole a glance over his shoulder at Cameron, who tossed his crumpled ballot in the trash can without breaking stride. "Rich people always find a way," Tate said, matter-of-fact. He and Max were used to this, but he was surprised to see Cameron nod in agreement before letting himself fade into the crowd.

Max and Tate stayed shoulder to shoulder as they raced to beat their new president to pre-calc. "Wilson!" Tate called, spotting him just ahead. Miraculously, Wilson heard him in the crowded hallway, stepping to the side just outside the classroom door as they approached. "Congrats on the win."

"Thank you." Wilson shook Tate's hand with the caution of someone touching an unsterilized needle before turning to Max expectantly. It was more of a power move than anything, and Tate was not surprised when Max made no motion to shake hands.

He's never been a bullshitter. Why start now?

A smirk danced across Wilson's face as his hand slapped against his freshly pressed pants, expecting nothing less from someone of Max's culture.

"So," Tate said. "We wanted to talk to you about the fundraising opportunity." Wilson looked at Tate as if he was speaking Spanish. "You know, for extracurriculars? The marching band?"

"Oh, yes, of course. The marching band." Wilson's eyes latched onto Max's. "Cameron really seems to be enjoying that."

Tate hoped to never be on the receiving end of Max's glower, but it did nothing more than amuse Wilson. "We have a great fundraising opportunity we are going to finalize this afternoon." He pulled a flyer out of his leather backpack and handed it to Tate.

"A talent show?"

Wilson switched on a newscaster smile that made Tate want to slap him. "What better way for the extracurriculars to get exposure? Cash prize at the end would cover any trip." A one thousand dollar cash prize was highlighted yellow in the middle of the flyer. Max snorted as he read over Tate's shoulder.

"But there would only be one winner," Tate said, weighing their chances in his mind. He was starting to understand Max's blatant disdain for this kid. "The whole point of a fundraiser is to help everyone raise money."

Wilson heard the attitude in Tate's voice and sprinkled a little into his own. "The entry fee money will be collected by the class officials and distributed as we see fit."

"As you see fit." Max made no effort to feign politeness. "Right."

Wilson took what was supposed to be a threatening step forward, but Max did not flinch nor break eye contact.

You have no idea who you're dealing with, buddy.

"There are a lot of clubs and resources our class needs fundraising for. We have to make sure that money ends up…" Wilson paused, looking Max up and down like cattle for auction. "…where it belongs. We wouldn't want to be discriminatory, would we?" Rage flashed across Max's eyes as he clenched and unclenched his fists at his side. It was more of a calming mechanism than a threat, an invisible stress ball.

"Are you always this charming?" Tate's step in front of Max forced Wilson back a step. His pompous expression showed he thought Tate was protecting Max, but Max certainly didn't need Tate's protection.

It's for your sake, dude, not his.

The sight of Tate, Max, and Wilson in the same place stopped Cameron in his tracks as he approached. Students flooded around him into the classroom as his eyes darted from one boy to another, red flooding his cheeks and neck. His presence was enough to snap Max out of his trance, stepping from behind Tate as he pulled a crumpled piece of paper from his back pocket. He did not look at Wilson again as he positioned himself to block Cameron.

"Want to compare answers before class starts?"

It was so casual, it took Cameron off guard, but he nodded nonetheless and let Max guide him into the classroom with the warning bell. Tate knew he would be late for intermediate piano, but he didn't care, returning his attention to Wilson. He was not a fighter like Max, but Tate certainly wasn't intimidated by this prepschool punk.

I'm a real punk with real problems.

Faint contempt crossed Wilson's face before he settled into his Cheshire cat grin, tapping the flyer in Tate's hand. "Make sure you check the requirements on the back." And with a wink, he disappeared into the classroom with the final bell, leaving Tate staring at the entry fee until he was the only student left in the hallway.

He was late to intermediate piano, but he was so preoccupied with the entry fee money Tate hadn't even tried to flirt with Lyle. He stewed through most of band, too, unable to show Max and Cameron the surprise twist until the end of class.

"One hundred dollars to enter? That's excessive." Cameron's shock was evident as the boys entered the band closet. Just as they were the last to set up, they were last to clean up too.

Tate nodded and leaned his head against the wall. "And we can't use any of our band songs to compete."

Cameron snatched the flyer hanging at Tate's side and skimmed the rules on the back. "That's conveniently disadvantageous."

Tate couldn't keep up with all of Cameron's words, so he just shrugged and went to put away his baton. He knocked over a guitar in the process, catching it just before it hit the ground. Tate breathed a sigh of relief as he casually thumbed a couple of chords. Max was wiggling out of his harness while Cameron continued to stare at the regulations as if they would change into something better if he looked long enough.

Tate continued to strum as his eyes went from the guitar to Max's drums, to Cameron's Simple Plan t-shirt.

Holy shit.

"Holy shit," he said aloud as he put down the guitar. Max was used to his antics and did not look up, but Cameron looked startled. "A band!"

"Band songs are against regulations, remember?" Cameron waved the flyer as if Tate hadn't read it a million times in the past hour and a half.

"Not *the* band, *a* band," Tate emphasized the distinction as he pointed to Cameron's t-shirt, his excitement building. "You and I can play guitar, and Max can do drums."

It took Cameron a few seconds to catch on to Tate's plan. "What about vocals?" he asked.

"I guess I can do that too. And you guys can do backup." The grin Tate was trying to contain broke out across his face, and he slung an arm around Cameron as the two of them relished in the solution. Only Max remained quiet.

"But wait," Cameron said, snapping out of their celebratory lull. "What about the astronomical entry fee?"

This is probably the first time he has had to worry about money in his entire life.

"Where there's a will, there's a way," Tate said, patting him on the chest.

"I'm going to be in a band." Cameron's grin was growing by the minute as he headed out of the band closet. Max smiled as Cameron passed before going pensive again.

Tate's excitement diminished as the reality of the situation set in.

How are we going to get the entry fee money?

One look at Max was all Tate needed to know what he was thinking, and he didn't like it. "We can find another way," he said.

"A band sounds cool."

"We can find another way," Tate repeated. A million words passed between their dark eyes as Max looked up.

"What other way? You and I both know no one's going to hire people like us."

"Cameron's got money. Maybe he could get it."

"Cameron's parents have money," Max corrected. "Cameron doesn't see any of it. They're in debt anyway."

Tate waited as Max stared at nothing for what felt like an eternity. "I could get a hundred bucks in a night."

"Yeah, we could."

Max raised an eyebrow. "Since when is fighting '*we*'?"

"Since I met you." Max smirked at the irony. "Seriously." Tate grabbed him by the shoulders. "We can find another way."

Max shook his head, his mind already made up. "I'll go tonight."

"We'll go."

"Tate. You suck, okay? You could get hurt, even out of the stalls."

Tate's mind flashed back years ago to his almost run-in with those men at the woods line. "It's always been us against everything. Why stop now?" If there was one thing Tate was, it was stubborn, and Max finally gave in with a nod. Tate pulled him into a quick hug before heading for the door. "Besides, someone's got to put you back together after."

He was joking, but only partially, and they both knew it. But even so, Max couldn't help but smile the smallest bit as he followed Tate out of the closet.

. . .

Things changed in the years since Max was at the barn. Its siding was reinforced, as was the roof, no longer threatening to collapse on its occupants with every gust of wind. The muddy grass parking lot was filled in with crushed rock, as was the walking path from the lot to the barn. Only the path leading to the clearing remained the same: abandoned.

An abandoned snowmobile trail.

Abandoned morals.

Abandoned childhoods.

Abandoned boys who abandoned hope for something better.

Boys like me.

Max paused as he entered the barn, taking in the changes. The front four stalls visible from the hayloft were re-sided and numbered with crisp white signs. The rusted chain-link fence that once separated the top halves of the stalls was replaced with thick black netting. What used to be the hayloft, where Max and the other fighters would retrieve new hay to replace the batches saturated in blood, was now a sort of viewing lounge. The ladder that once threatened the lives of many inebriated men was now a metal spiral staircase, whose railing extended around the perimeter of the loft to form a safety railing. Behind the railing sat two rows of padded chairs, the second slightly elevated to avoid obstruction of view.

Just when I thought this place couldn't get any more screwed up.

Even with this new addition, the most shocking change was the clientele. Or lack thereof. The front four stalls stood vacantly immaculate, as did the loft. Never in his life had Max seen it so empty.

"Whoa." Tate spun in a complete circle as Max shook his head and led the way to the back half of the barn. The difference was night and day, an affluent neighborhood separated from the projects by a set of railroad tracks. The familiar crowd had migrated to the last four stalls beneath the hayloft, where the scene was more or less the same as Max remembered. Every surface still threatened a splinter. The men were still dirty, drunk, and greedy. The fighters were still scrappy and scared.

The familiar stench of alcohol-infused sweat filled their nostrils as they glanced in one of the stalls. Two boys no older than twelve were going at each other, and Max could see Tate remembering the night they met. They had been about that age.

Don't think about it.

The horrifying crack of bone echoed through the stall as one of the boys took the other to the ground, followed by a scream of pain. He was down for the ten count before being hauled out of the barn, clutching his broken rib. The boy left standing limped out of the stall to a taller man Max assumed to be his father. The man was busy collecting money from the surrounding viewers but took time to grab the boy by the jaw and give him a quick once-over before patting him on the cheek and shoving him onto a nearby bench. The boy sat, recuperating, awaiting his next fight.

Max remembered how awful that feeling was, the disgusting adrenaline that made you feel like you were on top of the world and the scum of the earth at the same time. Tate was still staring in the direction of the first boy that had been dragged out, and Max put a hand on his shoulder before giving him a reassuring nod and stepping into the now vacant stall.

"I'm up." He wasn't speaking to anyone in particular; he didn't really want anyone to recognize him. He just wanted to get the money and get out. Max kept his eyes down as he waited for someone to step up. Blood from the last fight stained the hay at his feet.

Or maybe it was the fight before that.

Or the one before that.

The gate clicked shut as a boy stepped into the stall, and Max was relieved to see a boy his age, instead of a boy that had no business being in an abandoned barn at night.

Not that we do either.

As usual, the boy was taller than Max; the snarl on his face was meant to intimidate. Only Max wasn't looking at the snarl. Instead, his eyes searched the crowd until they landed on Tate. Once upon a time, Tate had been his saving grace in here, cheering him on late into the night until the fighting was done. But as he stood there now, Max saw nothing but fear in his friend's eyes.

Max stopped fighting years ago, and he could see the guilt written all over Tate's face for bringing him back to this life, even just for a night. The cowbell rang, and Max returned his attention to the task at hand, just in time to sidestep his opponent's first punch.

Here we go again.

It came back to Max like breathing. And that was what scared him. He always wanted to be more than a fighter, yet here he was, moving through opponents like some sick dance his body wouldn't let him forget.

Tate's hands patted Max's body as he exited the stall of his third victory, searching his extremities and torso for breaks or bruises. Max wondered if Tate even realized he was doing it.

"How many more?" All the life seemed drained from Tate's body, as if he spent the entire two hours donating blood. Tate could handle a lot, but he had never been able to handle it here, and Max envied him for it.

What kind of monster does that make me?

They had bet on twenty-dollar stints all night, but Max could see Tate was losing his stomach, so he took two crumpled twenties from his pocket and put them up for bid. The collector nodded and gestured toward the stall closest to the back of the barn. Max put a reassuring hand on Tate's shoulder. "One should do it." Tate nodded and gave him a pat on the back as Max entered the stall yet again.

This time there was someone in there waiting for him. He was bigger than Max, but they all were. The bigger the wager, the bigger the guy, but Max didn't care. His only thought was to get the money and get Tate out of here as quickly as possible.

The bell sounded, and it wasn't until he saw his own blood splatter across the splintered wall that Max became concerned.

. . .

"Oh shit." It wasn't the first time Tate saw Max take a hit, but it was definitely the first time he saw Max go down at the hands of someone other than his sad excuse of a father. Tate pressed his face against the netting, the blood from Max's nose staining the hay. "Max!" He wasn't knocked out, but another hit would probably do it.

Max responded with a groan as he rolled to a sitting position, clutching his nose. Most guys didn't go for the nose shot around here because of all the cleanup, but apparently, his big shot opponent didn't get the message. The guy paced the back of the stall like a caged animal, waiting for Max to make a move.

"Max!" Tate yelled again. Max raised a bloody thumbs-up to reassure him.

Mistake.

Tate's eyes shot to his opponent, the thumbs-up his green light to finish Max off. Tate knew the look in his eye, the merciless look that left boys seriously injured. The same vile look those two men gave Tate years ago when he was lying in the grass. No one ever stopped these fights. No one ever helped these boys.

His opponent heaved like a bull in heat as he squared off. "Duck!" Tate was screaming now, and Max looked up from his waterfall of a nosebleed just in time to roll beneath the roundhouse kick that would have punted his head down the road. His opponent landed awkwardly, the uninterrupted force of his kick leaving him unbalanced with one leg stretched too far in front. Blinking through the pain in his nose, Max swung his foot against the poorly positioned leg. Tate was surprised at how naturally the moves came to Max, as if his body acted without thinking.

His opponent crumbled on contact, falling to one knee as if in prayer. Without hesitation, Max sprang to his feet and landed a final punch to the temple.

Knockout.

Tate snatched their winnings from the collector just in time to catch Max as he hobbled out of the stall. He maneuvered one of Max's arms over his shoulder to support his weight, his nose gushing. He had never seen Max like this after a fight, limp and unsteady. Tate hobbled them out the backdoor of the barn without a word, the only trace of their presence tonight a trail of little red droplets in their wake.

"Jesus," Tate said as he hauled Max down the exit road.

"My shirt," Max moaned, clutching his nose with his free hand.

"Why the hell would you up the money to fight someone like that?" Tate knew the answer as soon as he asked the question, and he hated himself for it. *For me.*

"My shirt," Max repeated, muffled by his hand.

"I told you we could have found another way. Didn't I tell you that?"

"My shirt."

Tate dropped Max's arm as he wheeled to face him. "What the hell is wrong with your shirt?" Max teetered there, barely able to stand on his own as he looked down at himself. What had once been a white t-shirt was now almost completely saturated crimson. Tate swallowed at the sight of the blood before playing it off. "Forget it. We'll clean it at home."

"At home?"

It took Tate a minute to understand the look in Max's eyes. Then he got it.

Fear.

No way Max's father would believe this much blood was from a skateboarding accident. And when he realized Max was fighting again and holding out on him, a bloody nose was nothing compared to what he would do. Especially after all Tate went through to get Max's father to let him off the circuit in the first place.

"Dammit." Tate resituated his shoulder under Max's arm as they reached the main road. "What the hell did you wear white to a fight for?"

Max flipped him off with his free hand before letting his weight fall on Tate a little heavier. He was losing steam. They would attract too much attention walking down the street like this, so Tate practically dragged Max through backyard after backyard until they emerged onto the main drag of the city. Most of the store lights were off by now, but one sign remained lit.

The Carry Out. Dry-cleaning and laundromat.

Okay, new plan.

Tate redirected what was left of his energy toward the yellow illuminated letters. He felt the whole situation sucking the life out of him, and a dry-cleaner was the best Tate could come up with right now. The only thing he had ever seen Max truly afraid of was his father, and Tate had to do something.

The dry-cleaner was sandwiched between a carpentry store and an alleyway. The sign on the door listed the hours of operation for Friday: 9 a.m. – 11 p.m. Tate had no idea what time it was and tried the door, whispering a thank you to whoever was supposed to be listening as it swung open with a soft tinkle. After the night they had, a bell was the last thing Tate wanted to hear right now, wincing as it rang above them.

The store was empty as the boys hobbled inside, the wooden door with the glass frame closing gently behind them with another tinkle. Two sets of stackable washers and dryers huddled together in the front right corner of the store. The rest of the right wall was occupied by a long wooden bench with the craftsmanship of a church pew.

"Hello?" Tate pulled Max toward the counter at the back of the store, behind which looked to be a carousel of clothes. It reminded him of a luggage claim at an airport, belongings rotating in and out of sight into some unseen back room. The clothes were all designer brands, pressed to perfection and hung in plastic clothing bags.

Fancy clothes for fancy people.

Shit.

A rich store owner would do nothing more than report them to the police for trespassing. Maybe even fine them for dripping blood on the floor, which Tate didn't realize they had been doing until he glanced behind them. The last thing they needed was the police asking questions when Max was soaked in blood and Tate had a hundred dollars' worth of bills wadded up in his pocket. "Somewhere else, Max," Tate muttered, turning him around to go. "Hang in there." Max didn't have any energy left in him to argue as Tate led him to the door.

"Can I help you?"

The voice stopped Tate in his tracks, propping Max against the doorframe before whirling around. He was met with the smiling face of the last person he expected to see tonight. "Lyle?"

Her hair was tied back with what looked to be a white piece of cotton cloth, knotted at the top like a messy headband. Her cheeks were chapped from hours of cleaning hot dryer vents.

"Tate?"

"Yeah, hi." He stood there like an idiot, as casual as if this were a normal day in intermediate piano.

"Hi." She looked at him expectantly, but Tate was too busy choking on everything he wasn't sure he should say. "What are you doing here?" she prodded.

"I need your help." His embarrassment gave way to adrenaline as Tate grabbed Max by the elbow and spun him around to face Lyle, supporting most of his weight in the process. Lyle gasped at the blood that coated Max's face and shirt. His nose was still dripping, albeit not as much, but they could see the color draining from his tired and wounded face. Tate stared at Lyle, urgency radiating through his entire being. "*We* need your help."

CHAPTER FIVE

Dabbing a shirtless boy's nose with a Q-tip while her classmate mopped up his bloody trail was not what Lyle expected to be doing five minutes before closing. Luckily, no customers came in, and she could spread out on the wooden bench Aariz had made.

"What happened to him?" Lyle asked. The boy tensed as she disinfected the cut inside his nose.

Tate did not slow his mopping. "Skateboarding."

Lyle wondered how hard this poor boy had fallen to be this bloody, especially since he had no other cuts or bruises on him, but it wasn't her business. The boy didn't even seem to notice her; he just stared across the room and let her work. The air in the room felt heavy, and none of them said much until Lyle broke the silence again as she glanced at the wall clock.

"Can you turn the sign on the door and switch off the outdoor light?" She had gotten the boy's nosebleed to stop, but her bloody gloves rendered her useless on all other fronts. Tate nodded, dropping the mop as he headed for the door. Lyle bit her lip to keep from laughing as he switched the lobby into total darkness before flipping it back on. It took him a couple tries to find the right one, and she expected Tate to crack a joke like he did in class. But instead, he returned to the mop with laser focus, shooting a concerned glance at his friend every few seconds.

In class, he was confident, sure of himself. But tonight, Tate looked as though he carried the weight of both the duo's worlds on his shoulders, and Lyle felt sorry for him.

"Did the bleeding stop?" Tate's friend asked. It was the first time he spoke since they arrived, and Tate was next to him in two bounds.

"Yeah, man. It's looking better. You feel okay?"

The boy nodded, then noticed he was shirtless. "My shirt?"

"Yeah, it's…" Tate looked to Lyle to explain how that much blood was going to come out of a shirt.

"I'm taking care of it," she said matter-of-factly. "Do you feel dizzy?" The boy shook his head but swayed with the effort. Tate took a seat on his other side to steady him as Lyle stood up. "One second," she said, disappearing behind the counter. She grabbed a bottle of water from the mini-fridge and started for the lobby before turning back to grab another. Lyle handed a bottle to Tate, who immediately unscrewed the cap and held it to his friend's lips.

"I'm fine," he sputtered as Tate poured the water into his mouth.

"Right." Tate closed the boy's hand around the open water bottle. "Drink."

Lyle smiled and nudged Tate with the butt of the other water bottle. "You too." He seemed surprised, like he had forgotten about his own well-being as he drank it in a daze. She watched them for a minute before closeting the discarded mop and bucket. When she came back, they were on their feet, trying not to look at the bloody medical supplies strewn across the bench. The boy stood on his own, but Tate hovered close by, ready to catch him.

"You probably want to get home." Tate sounded embarrassed as he eyed the door. "Sorry we kept you after hours."

"Oh, don't worry about that," Lyle said. "Glad I could help." Tate gave her a weak smile and headed to the door, his friend a shirtless zombie behind him.

Crap.

"Wait a sec!"

The boys paused, Tate the only one with enough strength to look over his shoulder. Lyle felt his eyes on her and couldn't get her hands to cooperate as she fumbled below the counter, finally grabbing what she wanted and jogging across the lobby. The front of the shirt read "The Carry Out," the back listing other local businesses they supported and that supported them. Her grandfather got together with the surrounding businesses last year and ran a promotion to increase sales for everyone. This was the last shirt left over.

"Thank you?" Tate looked confused as he took the unexpected gift, and Lyle felt awkward.

"For him." She motioned to his friend's shirtless body that was about to wander down the main street.

"Oh, right." Tate pulled the shirt over the boy's head, leaving him to do the arms himself. "Thank you," Tate repeated, sincere this time. His eyes were so intense, his gratitude palpable, that it made the darkness of the night seem like a bubble lifting Lyle away from reality.

"Anytime," she said, although, for Tate's friend's sake, she hoped they didn't make this a habit. The bell tinkled overhead as she held open the door, and the boys stiffened as they stepped into the night air.

Tate's friend dropped his water bottle as he wrestled his arms through the t-shirt. It took a couple bounces on the sidewalk before settling against the building. Tate had to squat down to grab it, shoving it in the back pocket of his friend's jeans rather than his own. They were a few steps down the street when Lyle noticed he had dropped something. She couldn't make it out in the dark, but as she bent over to retrieve it, she saw it was a crumpled wad of money.

"Wait!" she called after them, snatching the bills off the sidewalk. "You dropped…this." When Tate saw what she was holding, he was at her side so fast she stumbled back a step. He grabbed the money from her outstretched hand and crammed it into the back pocket of his own jeans without explanation.

"Night," he muttered without looking at her. With that, Tate and his friend hurried off into the night without a backward glance. As quickly as they had come, they were gone, and Lyle watched them for a minute before returning to the store and locking the door behind her. Her mind took off as she disposed of the first aid supplies.

Why was Tate carrying around a wad of cash?

Where did he get it?

Did it have anything to do with his friend's injury?

Skateboarding, Lyle reminded herself as she shut off the lobby lights and headed for the back room. She armed herself with soap and bleach and went to work on the bloody shirt, which until this point had been soaking in a tub of cool water. As she worked, she thought, and the night didn't quite line up in her mind.

But where were their skateboards?

The story didn't match the hour, or the injury, or the urgency in Tate's eyes. The thoughts continued to tangle in Lyle's mind long after she ascended the back stairs and fell into a fitful sleep.

By the time she reached intermediate piano the next day, Lyle had concocted a hundred theories. She was surprised to find the Tate she was used to seeing. Confident. Smiling.

Wearing The Carry Out shirt.

She gave a shy smile as she took her seat beside him. He looked like he was about to say something, but he was cut off by the final bell.

"Today is a practice day!" Ms. Godllub yelled from her desk.

Like we've ever had any other kind of day in this class.

Lyle didn't really know what to say to Tate, so she collected her bag with a sigh and relocated to the concert piano by the choral risers. For all she knew, he wanted to pretend last night never happened. She situated herself with her headphones and began to play. She was just getting into a rhythm when she glanced up, practically jumping off the bench when she saw Tate standing in front of her. She pushed off her headphones, winding them up neatly as she recomposed herself. "Nice shirt," she said.

He looked down and twirled in a circle, arms outstretched. "Like it?" Lyle hadn't noticed his crooked smile before, but she certainly noticed it now. "Here," he said, and Lyle's stomach lurched as he began to take the shirt off. It took her a minute of not averting her gaze to realize he had another shirt underneath as he held out the one she lent him. "Trade ya."

Lyle shook her head as she pawed through her bag for the clean t-shirt. "Keep it. We've been trying to get rid of them anyway."

"Sweet." Tate tossed the shirt beneath the piano for safekeeping as Lyle handed him the one she worked all night to clean. "No shit," he said, astounded as he searched for the bloodstains that were no longer there. "I'm lucky we ran into you."

"How is he?"

"Oh, he's all right. Always is." It surprised Lyle how casual Tate was acting about the whole situation. If he was still as worried as he was last night, he certainly knew how to play it off.

"I hope the skateboard made out better than he did." Lyle knew she shouldn't press the issue, but she couldn't help herself. There still seemed to be a piece missing from this whole fiasco, and it had been eating at her all night.

The comment seemed to catch Tate off guard. He ran a hand through his dark hair, which only seemed to make it more perfectly messy. Lyle thought about how the static of the clothes at The Carry Out made her own hair take on a life of its own and was thankful that she had discovered the headband trick before Tate wandered into the store. "Right," he said, before snapping back into his cool, collected self. He leaned his elbows against the piano top, examining her sheet music. "If you ever need help with this, I'm your guy."

Lyle laughed. "Oh yeah?"

Tate slid onto the bench next to her, and Lyle stayed for a heartbeat before standing up to give him space to play. At least that's what she told herself. "Yeah," he said. "Check this out." He pounded out the first couple measures of the class assessment song, some of it correct, some of it not, before running his hand down the length of the piano with a flourish. Lyle clapped in mock applause.

"Encore, encore."

Tate threw his hands in the air in surrender as he stood up. "That's all I got."

"It's a good start."

"I don't believe you." That crooked smile again.

"No, really," Lyle assured him. "It always starts slow. It'll come together in the end."

Tate nodded, holding her eyes with his. "Maybe you can help me out before then."

"Apparently, that's what I do now." She was surprised by her boldness and immediately worried her joke might offend him.

"Tate!" Ms. Godllub bellowed. "Less flirting, more playing!" Lyle was still holding her breath from her last comment but exhaled when Tate started to laugh.

"While you're at it," he said, slinging the clean t-shirt over his other shoulder. "How about helping me get on her good side?"

Lyle giggled as he returned to her seat. *I'm not even sure I'm on her good side.*

The bell rang too quickly, and Lyle watched as Tate strode from the room. When he was gone, she wondered why it never crossed her mind to charge him for the cleaning.

And why all the pieces from last night still didn't quite fit.

And why she suddenly didn't mind.

. . .

"N-A-I-V-E-T- E. Naiveté." Cameron didn't wait for an answer as he retreated to the side of the stage; he knew he was correct. Even though it was just a mock spelling bee with the bee club, Wilson was competitive, and the two of them had been going back and forth for the win for twenty minutes. Cameron was confident in his abilities, but his opponent's glare wore him down, and he always ended up throwing these spell-offs.

"Your word is sacrilegious," said a club member as Wilson took center stage.

"S-A-C..." Wilson paused, gears turning in his mind. He struggled with the last word too, and Cameron knew he didn't have many more left in him. After pondering for a couple of seconds, Wilson continued, his voice unsure. "...R-I-L-E-G-I-O-U-S. Sacrilegious."

"Correct."

Cameron breathed a sigh of relief, Wilson's entourage whooping in the auditorium seats in true pep rally form. He felt Wilson's eyes on his back as he approached the microphone, and Cameron knew the longer he dragged it out, the more volatile Wilson would become.

"Your word is acquiesce."

A-C-Q-U-I-E-S-C-E. The correct spelling shot through Cameron's mind before he even thought about it, his shoulders deflating at the realization that he knew the word. He stole a sideways glance at Wilson, whose foot was tapping at the speed of light. Cameron tensed each time it hit the stage, like hoofbeats approaching from a rival army.

"A-C-Q-U-I-E-C-S-E. Acquiesce." It upset Cameron to purposefully misspell a word. He never removed or added letters, only moved them around. It was how he convinced himself he wasn't technically misspelling the word, just tampering with it a little bit.

"I'm sorry, but that is incorrect. Congratulations, Wilson, you have won this spell-off." In the real bee, if one of the finalists misspelled a word, the other had to correctly spell that word in order to win. Cameron silently thanked whoever cut that rule from their makeshift spell-offs; he could tell Wilson didn't know it.

Wilson whooped as Bruce and Brian stormed the stage as if it was an actual competition. Someone killed the stage lights as the auditorium ones came on, illuminating the rest of the spelling bee club as they gathered their things to go home. "Stellar performance, Wilson," Cameron said, hand outstretched as he joined his friends.

"Don't you get tired of me embarrassing you, Cammy?" He swatted Cameron's hand away, his cackle echoing through the auditorium. "You better step up your game if you want to come in second place this year." Cameron joined in this time as they laughed, pretending they weren't laughing at him.

"Damn," Bruce said, watching the girl who had been calling the spell-off as she walked up the aisle to leave. Cameron followed Bruce's eyes, turning twelve shades of pink when his own eyes landed on the girl's bottom, swaying from side to side as she walked. He snapped his gaze to the floor, but not before Bruce caught him looking. "We need to have bee practice more often, huh, Cammy?" Brian jabbed an elbow into Cameron's ribs with a nod, sending him stumbling into Wilson.

"Sorry," Cameron muttered as he tried to regain his balance. Wilson shoved him aside to watch the girl, and it was silent until she exited the auditorium. Cameron was the only one who didn't look, supremely fascinated in his shoelaces.

"So." Wilson returned his attention to Cameron. "What do you think about the talent show?" Cameron didn't know why, but the question ticked him off.

"It's a little, uh…" Cameron searched for the right word. "Extortionate." He was met with three blank stares. "Expensive," he corrected.

Wilson rolled his eyes. "Oh, Cammy, that money's going back to the students."

"Like the band?" Cameron asked with more hope in his voice than he wanted it to have.

"Or the cheerleaders," Bruce said with none of the class their social circle claimed to have.

"The talent show will raise money for everyone," Wilson said, patting Cameron on the back a little too hard. "Besides, it's a great way to get to know the students."

"Right."

"Right?" Wilson raised an eyebrow. "That seems a little low for your vocabulary, Cammy."

"Never mind." They were the last four in the auditorium, and an idea struck Cameron as he surveyed the empty stage. "Are any of you privy to who schedules practice time in here?"

"More bee practice?" Brian whined. He was the worst speller of the bunch.

"No, not that." Cameron ran his hand along the stage as if seeing it for the first time. "A group of us are compiling a performance for the talent show, and this would be an ideal place to practice."

"Us?" Wilson asked.

Bruce smirked as he elbowed Brian in the side. "Guess he was able to teach them enough English to perform." Cameron stared at the ground, shifting uncomfortably from foot to foot. He could feel Wilson's eyes on him, and he kept his down.

"As team captain, I reserve the right for us to use this space every night of the week," Wilson said. "You never know when you might need to have a spell-off." Bruce and Brian nodded in agreement, a pair of bobbleheads, while Wilson put his arm on Cameron's elbow. "You wouldn't jeopardize our team, would you, Cammy?"

"Of course not." Cameron was ashamed they could even think that.

"Good." Wilson sent Cameron stumbling forward with another pat on the back. "Glad everyone knows their place around here."

And with that, the boys gathered their bags and exited the auditorium. Cameron lagged behind them, trying to condense the stack of library books he had checked out into his backpack. Wilson's words were still bouncing around in his head, and as Cameron stood alone in the auditorium staring at the empty stage, he had never been more confused about where his place was.

. . .

Tate was attempting to organize the marching uniforms when Max and Cameron walked in. He always beat them to the band room, given the chorus room was just down the hall.

"Need any assistance?" Cameron asked, eyeing Tate's place amongst the various marching pieces.

Tate gestured to the pile of marching overalls heaped at his side. "I haven't done those yet. Can you sort them by size?" Cameron nodded and dove into the purple mass.

Max scanned the rest of the risers, where Tate had already sorted the hats around the drum set and was now working on the jackets. "You had to do this in the percussion section?"

Tate winked at him. "Couldn't do it anywhere else. I'd miss you too much." Max swatted him on the back of the head as Tate continued. "Today is a cleaning day anyway. Since your drums are all set and Cameron keeps his saxophone pristine at all times"—Tate threw his arms out as if presenting them with a grand prize—"welcome to the world of marching uniforms." Cameron laughed, elbow deep in polyester pants, as Max gave in and began sorting the minefield of marching shoes scattered across the floor.

"Now that we're registered, what's next?" Cameron asked. Tate paid the entry fee in homeroom that morning, their place in the show solidified. He convinced Max to forge his permission slip, but begrudgingly.

Tate shrugged. "I guess now we need to find a place to practice."

"Auditorium?" Max asked, working at a tangled pair of laces.

"No!" Tate and Max stopped what they were doing, startled by Cameron's outburst. "I mean, it just doesn't present itself as a viable option."

"Who could possibly need the auditorium five nights a week?" Tate couldn't imagine anyone besides the theater club using it that much, and they didn't have a production until next semester. Cameron's eyes darted between them in a frantic state, and one glance at Max solidified Tate's suspicions on the culprit.

"It's for the good of the team," Cameron assured them, but he looked as if someone was about to sucker punch him in the face, and Max looked ready to sucker punch whoever that someone was.

Tate knew it was a power move by Wilson, but he didn't want to make Cameron feel worse. "Don't practice too much more," he joked. "If you use bigger words than you already are, you're going to have to start translating for me." Every muscle in Cameron's body visibly relaxed as Tate tossed a jacket at him.

"Agreed." Max removed the jacket from Cameron's head, balling it up before chucking it at Tate.

They stewed on the issue of practice space until about five minutes before the warning bell. By that time, they had adequately sorted the jackets, pants, and shoes by size and were now carrying them into an empty practice room for storage.

"Oh, I almost forgot," Tate said as Max approached with a stack of shoeboxes. He pulled the white t-shirt out of his back pocket and slung it over Max's shoulder, who looked equally surprised to find no bloodstains.

"Thanks." Max sounded distracted, and Tate hoped he wasn't thinking about the fight. Max continued to stare at the stack of shoeboxes as Tate and Cameron made several more trips to dump various marching attire.

"She has a stage, you know," Max said their fifth time around.

Tate lowered the last few jackets into a neat pile. "Who?"

"The girl from last night."

"Lyle?" Max raised an eyebrow, surprised at Tate's familiarity with her. "She's in intermediate piano with me," he explained, thankful when Max let it go without razzing him.

"Well, she has a stage."

"It was a dry-cleaner, Max. Why would she have a stage?"

Max shrugged. "I was staring right at it the whole time she was fixing my nose." Tate thought back, but he had been so worried about Max he hadn't noticed much. The only thing he remembered was the bench on the right side of the store.

But what was on the left side?

"Jeez," Cameron huffed, entering with an armful of marching pants. The pant legs dragged across his face as he lowered them to the ground. "I sincerely hope these have been sanitized since last year's march."

Max smirked. "Doubt it."

"Well, they should be." Cameron shuddered as he disentangled himself from another rogue pant leg.

"You know, CamKing," Tate said, glancing at Max as the bell rang. "That's not a bad idea."

By the end of the day, Tate had convinced Max to go along with his plan, and within an hour of dismissal, they were halfway down Main Street with the uniforms.

"Remind me again why Cameron couldn't help?" Tate's voice was muffled behind the stack of jackets he was lugging.

"Bee practice." Max was behind him, bent over and using both hands to push the pile of marching pants stacked atop his skateboard. "He said he'd be here later."

"How convenient." Tate readjusted the jackets to keep them from falling. "How'd I get stuck with the armful?"

Max bumped his pile into the seat of Tate's jeans. "Feel free to switch views anytime." Tate ignored him as the yellow sign came into view.

He barged into the storefront without waiting for Max, dropping the armful of marching jackets in the corner. The smell of sawdust filled Tate's nostrils, and he looked around for its source. There was an old woman to his right removing her delicates from one of the dryers and folding them into neat piles on the wooden bench.

Not from her.

Tate looked to his left, forgetting the smell as his eyes landed on a rundown stage.

Max was right.

The stage opened up to the lobby of The Carry Out, and after a closer look, Tate saw it opened up to the lobby of the adjoining store too. The source of the smell became clear as Tate realized The Carry Out shared its wall and stage with a carpentry store, handcrafted wooden furniture strategically positioned throughout the adjacent lobby. The store was separated from The Carry Out by the stage and a wooden half-wall. It was a strange setup, the way the stores were connected, and the stage certainly needed some work, but Tate was in no position to be picky. The faint buzzing of an electric saw reached his ears from somewhere out of sight.

Max staggered in with an armful of pants, dropping them atop Tate's jacket pile before exiting and returning with another armful. "See?" he said, gesturing at the stage as he walked over. "Told you."

Tate nodded as he examined the stage. It appeared to be hollow underneath, three wooden steps leading up from both lobbies. The stage itself was large enough for the three of them, along with their instruments and equipment, but Tate was worried about the weight. The floorboards were splintered and cracked, some even broken or fallen in to reveal the floor below. The first step creaked loudly beneath him as Max put weight on it, raising his eyebrow at Tate.

"Right," Tate said, pulling Max off the step before it collapsed. He turned his attention to the back counter, where an affluent couple was huddled together. The woman's large fur coat obstructed his view, but Tate was excited to hear Lyle's voice as she responded from the other side of the counter.

"I cannot let you try on someone else's coat, ma'am."

"How could I possibly know if I would like to buy one for myself if I have never tried it on?" The woman gestured to a large fur coat hanging on the carousel behind Lyle.

"These coats are very expensive," the man said. "We need to be sure it is top quality before purchasing one. I wouldn't expect you to understand."

The muscles in Tate's arms tensed at the man's rudeness, but Lyle stood her ground. "I actually do understand. If you would like, we can start a community rack in the lobby for everyone. Ma'am, would you like to donate your coat?"

"And let the immigrants try on *my* clothing?" The woman put her hand to her forehead as if ready to faint. "How dare you!" At the woman's shrieking, a man appeared behind Lyle, his long black beard full of sawdust. A yellow robe wrapped around his body, and he put a gentle hand on Lyle's shoulder as he spoke.

"Everything okay here?"

"*And* you have a terrorist working here?" the man boomed. This time it was Max that tensed up. "Who is your supervisor? I would like to speak with him." Tate moved a little to his left so he could see Lyle, surprised at how calm she looked.

"All set," she murmured to the Muslim man with a reassuring look. He waited a moment longer before nodding and disappearing through a side door in the back. Tate assumed the door connected their shops.

The smile Lyle gave the rich man and his wife dripped with sarcasm, and Tate bit his lip to keep from laughing. "He's not here at the moment," she said, scribbling a number on a piece of scrap paper and handing it to the man. "But if you call his direct line and leave a message, he will get back to you as necessary." The man snatched the paper from Lyle's hand and stuffed it in the breast pocket of his suitcoat before gathering a pristine pile of dry-cleaned gowns from the counter. The woman clutched her purse to her body as she hurried past Max and Tate, eyeing them until she was out the door.

Tate gave Lyle a minute to decompress before approaching the counter, but she seemed perfectly composed as she turned her back to the lobby and continued to tag garments. He cleared his throat to get her attention.

"Tate?" she said, surprised as she set the tagging supplies on the counter. "What are you doing here?"

"Hey," he managed. She looked at him expectantly, then over his shoulder when he didn't continue.

"Hi," Lyle said to Max, who hung back a few steps. "How's your nose?"

"It's better," he said, stepping forward next to Tate. "I never officially thanked you."

"And I never officially met you." Lyle waited for an introduction, and Tate snapped out of his nervous trance.

"This is Max." Lyle gave a small wave and a smile. "Max, Lyle." Tate was surprised when Max smiled back, considering he hardly ever smiled.

"Oh gosh," she said, noticing the pink in Max's right eye. "I didn't realize you hurt your eye too."

"Oh…no," Max said, unsure of how to explain. "It's not hurt."

Tate was trying to think of a way to transition into why they were here when the phone rang on the counter next to them. Lyle checked the number on the caller ID, smirking as she let the phone continue to ring. "We don't mind waiting if you want to ans—" Lyle cut him off with a raise of her pointer finger, so the three of them stood there for two more rings before the answering machine came to life.

Hello and thank you for calling The Carry Out, an older man's voice said. *This is Rawel. I am not available at the moment, but if you want to leave a brief message, I will get back to you as necessary. Thank you!*

The machine beeped, almost immediately followed by the voice of the rich man that had just exited the store. Lyle put her finger to her lips to quiet the boys, even though they weren't talking. "Rawel," the rich man said. "I had a very unpleasant experience at your store today. A female employee was very rude to my wife when all she requested was to sample a fur coat. The girl suggested that my wife leave her coat for the riffraff to try on. There were even two Hispanic boys in the lobby eyeing my wife's purse." Max and Tate stole a glance at one another before returning their attention to the answering machine. "Not only that, there was a Middle Eastern man that approached in a very threatening manner when the girl became argumentative. I am sure I speak for the entire community when I say we do not want terrorists in our midst. I will be available for the remainder of the evening to discuss these matters by phone."

The answering machine clicked off after the man left his number, the flashing red button indicating a new message.

"Tough crowd," Tate said. The man had insulted everyone he had come into contact with in the last five minutes, minus the old woman and her delicates.

Lyle reached over and deleted the message. "No kidding."

"What about your boss?" Max asked.

She motioned to a photograph framed on the counter, where a little girl was sandwiched between two men, smiling from behind a seven-candled birthday cake. "I think I'm all set." One of the men looked like a younger version of the Muslim man, but Lyle pointed to the other, who looked a lot like her. "The answering machine said my grandfather would respond as necessary." Lyle's voice was firm as she continued. "Listening to racist garbage certainly isn't necessary."

Max nodded, impressed.

"Well, I'm sure you *riffraff* didn't come all the way down here to swipe a lady's purse. So what's up?"

Tate liked her humor. It was quick-witted but also kind. "We have fifty-four marching band uniforms that really need to be cleaned." Tate pointed to the pile in the front corner of the lobby.

"Sure, but it will take some time." Lyle thought for a minute. "A week, maybe?"

Tate nodded, and he and Max retrieved the pile from the corner and reconfigured it behind the counter. Lyle watched, amused. "Oh sure, right there's fine."

"Um, how much?" Max asked, unsure of how to respond to her sarcasm.

"Oh, pay at pickup." Lyle jotted down a few notes before handing Tate a receipt, which he shoved haphazardly into his pocket.

"So..." he said after an awkward silence. "What's up with the stage over there?" He pointed to his left as if she didn't already know where it was.

"Hasn't been used for a long time." Her voice was still polite, but her smile faded, and Tate wondered if he said something wrong.

"Would you be open to letting someone use it?" he ventured.

"For free," Max added quietly, almost ashamed.

Lyle looked confused. "Why would you want to use that? It's caving in on itself."

"Max and I can fix it up," Tate said, nudging Max in the side. Max nodded in agreement, but his skepticism was visible. "Our band is competing in the talent show," Tate continued. "And we've run out of places to practice."

Lyle looked like she was somewhere else entirely, staring at the stage as if it could come to life and attack at any moment. Her voice became defensive as she continued. "I've turned down anyone who asked to use that stage for the past seven years. Why would I help you out?"

Tate leaned against the counter with a half-smile. "Apparently, it's what you do now."

He saw a smile dance at the edges of her mouth, and Lyle stared at him for a minute, evaluating his motives. "All right," she said. "But it's not only up to me. Wait here." When she disappeared behind the counter, Max turned to Tate.

"'Max and I can fix it up'?"

Tate shrugged. "Maybe more Max than Tate."

"What will Your Highness be doing?"

"Serenading you," Tate said with a grin.

Max rolled his eyes. "Can't wait."

Tate was about to counter when Cameron burst through the door, looking like he had just run a marathon in a weighted vest. His freckles danced around his face as he heaved air in and out of his cheeks. "Am I too late?" he gasped, staggering over to the counter.

"Lose a button, Cam," Max said, unbuttoning the top button of Max's dress shirt so he could breathe better. "Did you run all the way here?"

"Had to." Cameron's words were short as he caught his breath. "Practice ran late."

"Another spell-off?"

Cameron nodded and began breathing through his nose, getting himself under control.

"Great," Tate said sarcastically. "Did you win?"

"He never beats Wilson in spell-offs," Max said.

Tate looked at Cameron, confused. "Why?" Lyle saved Cameron from answering as she returned with the Muslim man.

"This is Aariz," she said, brushing a few pieces of sawdust from the man's beard. "This is Tate, Max, and…" Lyle paused, her finger pointed at Cameron as she noticed him for the first time. Cameron stared at her like she was about to smite him. "Cameron," she finished, and Tate wondered how Lyle knew his name.

"Nice to meet you all," Aariz said. "I heard you're interested in using the stage."

"Yeah." Tate hadn't expected to be dealing with this man. "We want to use it to practice for the talent show."

"'We'?"

"Our band." Tate motioned to Max and Cameron. "We can fix it up."

"And we can help out around here to pay for the time," Max added, reinforcing once more his dislike of handouts.

"That won't be necessary," Aariz said, taking in the boys one by one. Tate was trying to portray enough confidence for the three of them, but Max seemed hell-bent on adding manual labor to the equation, and Cameron was still staring at Lyle like the cat that ate the canary.

"So we can use it?" Tate asked, urging the conversation along.

"I have one condition."

"Name it," Max said, and Tate shot him a look. Something about this man giving them ultimatums didn't sit well with him.

"Once the talent show is done, I would like your band to put on a concert here as a fundraiser for my mosque. We raise money every year to fund a scholarship for a promising young member of our community, and we use the leftover funds to give the mosque a facelift."

"A facelift?" Cameron asked.

Aariz hesitated. "Let's just say we seem to be a popular target of the...riffraff." He looked from Tate to Max on the last word before cracking a smile; he must have been able to hear the answering machine. Max smirked at the joke, but Tate did not find the humor in the situation. They needed this stage, and this man was not making it easy.

"So," Aariz said to Tate. "Do we have a deal?"

"No noise restrictions," Tate said, staring at Aariz's outstretched hand. "No time restrictions. No cost."

Aariz raised an eyebrow. "Just the fundraiser." He glanced at Lyle. "And I expect it goes without saying that you three conduct yourselves as gentlemen, supervised or not."

Tate didn't like the insinuation—like he would ever dream of taking advantage of Lyle—but it wasn't enough to dissuade him from the stage. He shook Aariz's hand, quick and hard. "Deal," he muttered.

Max practically football-checked him aside, taking Aariz's hand and shaking it as he spoke. "Thank you so much for this opportunity, sir."

Sir?

When was the last time Tate heard Max call anyone "sir"?

Aariz smiled. "It'll be good to hear some music in these walls again." And with that, he gave Lyle a kiss on the forehead before disappearing from the direction he had come.

"Sweet." Max gave Tate a bear hug from behind as Cameron jumped up and down with excitement. Tate plastered on a smile, fist-bumping each of them before Max and Cameron went to examine the stage. Tate leaned against the counter, processing the deal he just made and who he had made it with.

"So I guess I'll be seeing a lot of you guys then." Lyle's voice dragged him away from his thoughts.

"I guess so."

"Just do me one favor," she said. Tate raised an eyebrow. "Stay away from the keyboard." Her smile melted away Tate's concern about the fundraiser, and he couldn't help but laugh.

"I'm more irresistible on guitar anyway."

CHAPTER SIX

Cameron felt out of place at The Carry Out the next afternoon. Max was hitting it off with the store owner Aariz about the renovation logistics, and Cameron didn't exactly consider himself a handyman. He could help Tate with instrument tuning, but Tate was at the counter with Lyle, and Cameron was too ashamed to approach her. Her impression of him had to be negative, and honestly, he didn't blame her.

Unlike Tate and Max, Cameron had been to The Carry Out before. Every week, actually, to pick up his family's dry-cleaning. His parents tagged along once or twice to complain to Lyle or her grandfather about a wrinkle or an imperfect crease. Although Cameron had always been embarrassed by his parents' entitlement, he never acted on it. In all the years he had been coming here, Cameron was polite but succinct, saying as few words as possible, getting in and getting out.

It didn't help his conscience that Lyle and Rawel were nothing but nice to Cameron his entire life, congratulating him when his picture was in the newspaper for the spelling bee, giving him candy canes during the holiday season. They even hid his band t-shirts in his stack of folded polos so his parents would not see them. They were kind people, and Cameron didn't deserve it. Not then and certainly not now.

"Hey, CamKing!" Tate called, leaning against the wall with his guitar. "Want to tune yours?" Lyle was nowhere to be seen, working somewhere in the back, so Cameron nodded and slung his guitar over his shoulder. They didn't have an amp set up yet, but he could still hear as Tate strummed. He twisted his strings accordingly, matching pitch each time to test the correction. "Perfect," Tate said once they were all tuned up.

"Much appreciated," Cameron said. "How did you accomplish perfect pitch in the absence of a tuner?"

"Piano," Tate said. "Lyle helped me today in class."

"Ms. Godllub almost kicked you out for it." Cameron hadn't heard her return, but he caught Lyle's eye before snapping his gaze to the strings of his guitar. He could feel Tate studying his reaction, but thankfully he didn't say anything and returned to strumming his guitar.

"So Cameron," Lyle said, leaning her elbows on the counter. "How's spelling bee prep going? You feel a win this year?"

"I cannot be certain," Cameron murmured, eyes trained on his strings. Tate's strumming stopped, and Cameron could feel his eyes.

"Well, I'm sure you will," Lyle said. Cameron shrugged almost imperceptibly.

"You okay, CamKing?" Tate's voice sounded suspicious, but at least it didn't sound offended. The last thing Cameron wanted to do was offend any of them.

"You know," Lyle said, rounding the counter as she spoke. "It doesn't have to be awkward between us." Tate's eyes snapped from

Cameron to Lyle, back to Cameron. The unspoken question was written all over his face.

"Oh, no, no, no," Cameron said to Tate, waving his hands between them. "We were never acquainted…that way." Lyle raised an amused eyebrow at Tate's concern. Cameron searched for the right words, his vocabulary's accuracy failing him when it came to social situations. "This is my dry-cleaner," he finally said, motioning around to the store.

"You dry-clean Simple Plan t-shirts?" Tate looked amused and annoyed at the same time, and Cameron didn't know what to say.

He must think I'm a rich snob.

"It's not like that," Lyle jumped in. "Cameron's family has been coming here for years." She smiled at Cameron. "We've known each other for a long time."

"Oh," Tate said, relieved. "So you're friends. Then why would it be awkward?"

"We're not friends," Cameron blurted out, surprising even himself. Tate glanced at Lyle, who looked more intrigued than hurt by the comment. Cameron didn't want to hurt her feelings, but this needed to be said, so he soldiered on, the words falling out of him in a rush. "We're not friends. She and her grandfather do a great job with our dry-cleaning, and they have always been supportive of me." He paused. "Sometimes more supportive than my own kin. But my family does not treat them with dignity." Cameron paused again, embarrassed. "I am also guilty of that mistreatment by not saying anything. Friends stand up for each other. And I did not do that." Cameron was out of breath by the time he finished. He hadn't planned on saying all that, but the guilt carried it out of him like a leaf floating down a river.

No one said anything, and Cameron didn't know what to do. How could he expect Lyle to accept him if his family never accepted or respected her? Finally, Tate broke the silence. "Lyle, why do you wear that rag in your hair?" He pulled on the torn cotton piece Lyle used to tie her hair back, the bow untangling as it slid off her head. She reached instinctively to catch it, but it was already in Tate's hands. He waved it in the air like a worm on a hook. "Don't you have any real headbands?" Lyle looked confused and angry at the same time, and it angered Cameron.

"It was a real headband until you untied it," Lyle said, making a grab for the piece of cotton. Tate snapped it just out of her reach.

"Looks like scraps to me."

Cameron didn't realize he had shoved Tate until Tate hit the wall, his guitar reverberating in its belly from the contact. He looked stunned as Cameron snatched the piece of cotton from his hand and handed it to Lyle. She took it and wordlessly tied it back into her hair as Cameron turned back to Tate. He had extracted himself and his guitar from the wall and was standing there smiling.

Smiling?

"I don't know what's funny," Cameron said, wishing he understood modern humor. "But she doesn't deserve that." He paused to examine Tate's attire, gesturing to the bottom of his torn jeans. "Her headband is far superior to your frayed pant legs."

Tate continued to smile at Cameron long enough to make him uncomfortable before patting him gently on the shoulder. "Looks like you stand up for her to me." And with that, he shot Lyle a crooked grin and headed to the stage, strumming his guitar.

Cameron turned to say something to Lyle, but before he could, she was hugging him. He didn't have much experience with hugging; his family wasn't particularly affectionate. But hers felt warm and welcoming, and before he knew it, his arms were around her too.

She pulled away after a moment, holding him at arm's length. "You're a good person, Cameron King. No matter where you came from." She sounded so sure that Cameron actually believed her.

"I'm sorry," he said, trying to encapsulate his embarrassment over the last few years into one sentence. She smiled and released his shoulders.

"That's the only sorry you get. It's off your chest now, and we're going to start fresh." Her smile was gentle, and it made Cameron feel like she believed in him. "Friends?" she asked, holding out her hand, more like you would to a child than to a business partner.

Cameron couldn't help but smile as he nodded, putting his hand in hers. "Friends," he said, his face pink for God-knows-what reason this time. A customer walked in then, and Lyle gave his hand a squeeze before returning to her post behind the counter. Cameron stepped to the side to give them room. When he looked up, he saw Tate watching from the corner of his eye. He gave Cameron an almost imperceptible nod before returning his attention to Max's renovation instructions.

The rest of the night, Cameron did not feel out of place. In fact, he felt more at home with Max, Tate, and Lyle than he had ever felt with his other friends. Not only were they supportive, but they were kind. Cameron's rich friends simultaneously tried to fit in with one another and outdo each other, but these three didn't seem interested in that. They were comfortable in their differences and supported the uniqueness of one another. They didn't even make fun of him for his expansive vocabulary, although they did ask him once or twice what a couple words meant. Cameron enjoyed the dynamic, and for a minute, he forgot what it was like to be so unsure of himself.

Cameron's back was to the door as he helped Max pry nails from the stage's rotten floorboards when he heard Lyle's voice behind the counter.

"Hi, Mr. and Mrs. King."

He dropped the hammer, head snapping to the front door in disbelief. His mother wore a stark white pencil skirt and matching hat, his father's blindingly polished dress shoes and diamond-encrusted watch reflecting the sun around the lobby. Both looked as if they had just eaten a lemon, their eyes squinted and their lips pursed in disapproval as they took in Cameron's surroundings. They completely ignored Lyle's greeting, but a quick glance her way told Cameron she had meant it as an announcement of their entry.

"Cameron!" His mother's voice squawked as they crossed the lobby. Cameron turned to hide the hammer, which was no longer in front of him, but under Max's knee. Max gave nothing away as Cameron met his eye, so much so that he questioned if Max had hidden it, even though he knew he had. Tate was nowhere to be found, his hammer strewn with some rusty nails near the back of the stage.

"Cameron," his mother said again as she reached him. "What on earth are you doing…here?" Her emphasis on the last word ticked him off, acting like they were above this place or these people. Thinking about the headband incident, he wanted to tell her off, but for some reason, he didn't have it in him. "We came looking for you after bee practice," she continued. "We need to get your suit fitted for the spelling bee. Wilson said you were here." Cameron had to physically restrain himself from rolling his eyes. He wished he hadn't mentioned it to Wilson, but Cameron had been too excited to contain himself.

What kind of friend sells the others out?

"Well?" his father cut in. "What do you have to say for yourself?" Cameron was standing now, and although his mouth was open, no words came out. It aggravated him that the only time his parents gave him the time of day was when it related to appearance. He almost exclusively took the bus to and from school, but with the announcement that the upcoming spelling bee was to be televised on the local news, you better believe they were going to take him to spend some 'quality time' being poked and prodded in some fancy dressing room. Max continued to pry up nails, watching from the corner of his eye.

"Hey, Cameron?" Cameron was surprised when Tate immerged from behind the stage, even more surprised he called him by his full first name. He thrust a notebook in Cameron's face, a math problem scribbled on the wrinkled paper. "Did I get it right this time?" Cameron looked at Tate, then at the problem. The first half of the problem was done in Max's handwriting and was completely correct. The second half, written in what Cameron assumed to be Tate's handwriting, was scribbled gibberish, a compilation of mathematical numbers and symbols that made no sense whatsoever. Cameron was visibly confused as Tate turned to his parents. "Your son is a great tutor."

"Wouldn't understand it without him," Max added, waving a pre-calc textbook he grabbed from Cameron's backpack. Cameron's parents examined Tate, then Max, as if deciding if a street beggar was scamming them. Finally, they turned to Cameron with a look of pained satisfaction.

"That's my boy," his father said, giving him an audible smack on the back. Cameron stumbled forward into his mother's arms, who began flattening his spiked blond hair.

"I don't know where you got such a big heart," she crooned as she began to part his hair down the middle in the most unattractive way possible. "All this money and status, yet you still make time to volunteer with the less fortunate." She glanced at Max and Tate before continuing. "Although, you really do need to spend time practicing for the spelling bee, and don't you think there are more…" She paused and glanced around the store. "…appropriate locations to tutor the minorities?"

Cameron snapped away from her nagging fingers and gave Max and Tate a look that said he had absolutely no idea what to say or do. He didn't want to play along anymore, not with his mother talking about them like that. Max could see his reserve and gave Cameron a nod that was supposed to make it okay for Cameron to continue to play the part. His awful, rich boy part.

"Two birds with one stone, Mother," Cameron muttered after a minute, glaring at Max for letting him go through with it. "Dry-cleaning and volunteer hours." He turned to Lyle at the counter, hating himself even more as he continued. "When will our dry-cleaning be ready for pickup?"

"Tomorrow." Lyle looked sorry for him as she answered, but the last person Cameron felt sorry for in this moment was himself.

"Well, that's more than enough tutoring for tonight," his mother said, snatching the textbook out of Max's hand and attempting to shove it into Cameron's backpack on the steps of the stage. Cameron grabbed both from her and turned his back to them, giving Tate and Max his best apologetic look before zipping the bag and throwing it over his shoulder.

"We expect our dry-cleaning to be pressed and creased," his father said to Lyle as they herded Cameron toward the front door.

"Of course," Lyle said. Cameron stole a glance back at his friends and immediately wished he hadn't. Tate and Max were looking at each other in a way that suggested they were used to being treated the way his parents just treated them.

Like dirt.

Lyle gave Cameron a small smile as she adjusted her headband, as if reminding him that he had already redeemed himself today in her eyes. But shoving Tate over a headband hardly seemed to balance out acting as if the three of them were beneath him.

It had always been hard to go anywhere with his parents, hard to go where they went and do what they did. Hard to play the part. But it was just Cameron's world then; there had never been another world, another self, to leave behind.

And now that there was, it was almost unbearable.

Cameron lagged behind his parents as they clicked down the street and ran a hand through his bangs to spike them back up.

I'm almost unbearable.

. . .

Tate, Max, and Lyle spent the majority of the rest of the evening in silence, the boys working on the stage, Lyle on the dry-cleaning. Tate knew Cameron came from a different world, they all knew, but experiencing it first hand was a little hard to swallow. He saw how conflicted Cameron had been, trying to hold on to the past and move forward at the same time.

Believe me, I know the feeling.

The three couldn't help but feel uncomfortable about the subject, but talking about it felt like a betrayal to Cameron. After all, you couldn't control the family you were born into. So instead, Tate went about his business pulling up nails from rotting floorboards as Max began kicking in the ones ready to be replaced.

Tate didn't realize how late it was until Lyle flipped the signs at the front door. He thought she might ask them to leave, but instead, she grabbed an old broom from the closet that looked like a bird's nest on a stick and began sweeping the lobby. Max gathered up the rusty nails they had extracted from the stage and put them in a bucket Aariz had given them.

"Lyle, where do you want me to throw out these nails? I don't want you to cut yourself on them when you grab the trash." Max always seemed to know what could become a potential hazard in life, and most of the time, he knew how to avoid them. He'd saved Tate's sorry ass more than once on a skateboard, pointing out a pothole in the road or reminding Tate to cuff his jeans so the frays wouldn't get caught in the wheels.

Lyle motioned to the lobby of the other store. "Aariz has a disposal behind the counter for sharp objects. Just be careful in the dark." Max nodded as he catapulted himself over the wooden half-wall into Aariz's lobby, and Tate laughed to himself at Max's idea of careful.

"Aariz usually goes to bed after his evening prayer unless he has a project to finish," Lyle said in explanation of his pitch-black lobby. "I, on the other hand, am a night owl."

"Right there with you," Tate laughed. "I'm always keeping Max up."

"You live together?"

"Yeah, for a while now."

Lyle pondered his answer. "And your parents are okay with that?"

Tate was silent long enough for Lyle to regret her question, so she returned to sweeping. "You know, eventually we'll stop making such a racket and get to playing," Tate said, the sound of falling nails echoing from the darkness as Max dumped them into the disposal.

"Judging from your piano playing, I don't think there's much of a difference." Her sarcasm still caught Tate off guard sometimes, and he wondered how many people never heard it because they couldn't get past the pink-cheeked smile of innocence.

"Ha, ha." He feigned laughter, motioning toward the broom in Lyle's hands. "Need some help?"

"I'm all set." She struck Tate as someone who took pride in being self-sufficient.

"How about some company?" Tate didn't know why, but despite the hour, despite how tired he was, the only thing he wanted to do was stay.

Max hurdled back over the wall before she could answer, placing the empty bucket under the stage steps. "Thank you," he said. "Tate, you ready?"

Tate most definitely was not ready, but he knew Max didn't like getting home past midnight. Max's strategy to avoid drunken confrontation with his father had always been to be what he called invisibly present. Get home before his father got home from the bar, go about his business as silently as possible, retreat out to the screen house, and sleep there with Tate.

Out of sight, out of mind.

Out of reach.

"Yeah," Tate said as Max opened the front door. "Be right there."

"Night, Lyle." Max paused long enough to give her a polite nod.

"Night," she said sweetly as the door tinkled closed behind him.

Tate didn't know what to say now that they were alone again. He couldn't tell if she was nervous or indifferent as she continued to sweep, but either way, she wasn't giving him much to work with. He tapped the toe of his shoe on the floor.

"Listen," he started. "I hope I didn't upset you earlier." He looked at her until she met his gaze. "The whole headband thing."

Lyle looked at him like a puzzle she had already solved. "It was really nice, what you did." Her answer surprised Tate. "That and the whole tutoring thing. You're a good friend to him." The deep blue of her eyes rooted Tate to the floor. It was like he was looking at the earth, the rich blues of the ocean shaped into two breathtaking globes.

"Thanks," he managed. She returned her attention to sweeping, releasing Tate from the hold of her eyes. She was methodical, pushing the dirt into a thin line the length of the lobby before reaching the wall and pushing the line back another broom length. Tate was glad she hadn't let him help; he would have moved haphazardly in a circle until the dirt was mounded in the middle. "And thanks again for letting us use the stage." He almost didn't continue but felt like he should. "Even though you might not have wanted us to."

Lyle stood the broom up and leaned against it. "It's not that I don't want you to." Tate could see the same hesitation in her face that had been there during their initial conversation. "There's just a lot of history there."

Tate felt bad for pressing. "We can stop pulling it up if you want."

"No." She stomped the broom on the ground to get the dirt caught within. "Sometimes history needs a facelift." Same word Aariz had used earlier.

They must spend a lot of time together.

Max knocked on the window from the outside, tapping his wrist where a watch would have been.

"Right." Tate grabbed his guitar from the stage. "Night." His hand was on the door when Lyle's voice stopped him.

"Hey." She moved the broom back and forth at her feet like a Disney princess absentmindedly cleaning her forest cottage. "Do you really hate my headband?"

Tate immediately felt guilty, especially after seeing the gentleness of Lyle's face as she asked. He had been trying to prove a point to Cameron, not be a jerk. Especially not to her. "No," he said, and Lyle's body relaxed just the slightest bit. Tate started to push the door open, then let it close again as he turned back to her. "Do you really think I'm riffraff?"

"Of course not."

A half-smile immerged on Tate's face, and he gave her a small wave as he pushed the front door open again. Tate waited until he heard her lock the door behind him before grabbing his skateboard from Max's grip.

"Took you long enough," Max said, one foot on his skateboard, one foot on the concrete, both eyes on Tate. He could feel Max studying him, but Tate didn't have the energy to debrief the night's happenings. Instead, he dropped his skateboard at his feet with a clatter.

"Right." Tate pushed off down the street before Max could respond.

. . .

Lyle came downstairs the next morning to find a plethora of wooden planks leaning against the stage. They were sanded and cut perfectly to size to replace the rotted planks the boys had removed yesterday. She met her grandfather behind the counter, where he was balancing the register before opening.

Rawel gave her a kiss on the forehead. "Do you know what's going on?"

"Some guys in my class are renovating the stage so their band can use it to practice." Lyle shrugged. "I didn't know Aariz was donating material, though."

"Some guys?" Rawel stiffened. Lyle had always marveled at how her grandfather could look intimidating and inviting at the same time, even though she had long since stopped seeing the former.

"They're nice guys, Grandfather. Don't worry." Rawel didn't look convinced. "They even offered to help me clean up after closing."

"They're here after closing?"

Lyle rolled her eyes. Rawel had always been protective, but he had always trusted her judgment too. "Don't worry," she said again, grabbing his shoulders with her hands. "Plus, Aariz met them, and clearly he likes them if he gave them all this free wood." She knew Aariz's approval of the boys meant something to Rawel, and it should. They had been best friends her entire life. "Cameron's one of them," Lyle added, hoping his non-threatening demeanor would put her grandfather at ease.

"Cameron King?" Rawel asked. "In a band?"

"I was surprised too."

Rawel sighed and threw up his hands in surrender. "Far be it for me to stunt the musical education of the youth." Lyle smiled and gave him a kiss on the cheek. "Just promise me you'll be responsible?"

Lyle nodded. "Have I ever been anything but?"

Rawel looked at her with a hint of sadness she didn't understand. "You certainly haven't." Lyle grabbed her bag from behind the counter and gave him a quick hug before heading toward the door. "Hey, Lyle." Rawel's expression was both serious and gentle as he looked at her. "Enjoy the music." Lyle gave him a quick smile as she headed out the door and began her walk to school.

He used to say that to their customers when Lyle sat at the piano all those years ago. *Enjoy the music.* Lyle hadn't played the piano in a long time, but she knew Rawel missed the days when the lobby was filled with the notes of her beautiful music. He would whistle the tunes long after Lyle had pushed in the stool, swaying in time to a melody that was no longer there but hung around like the décor. It had become part of their daily routine, until one day it wasn't. And that day was followed by years of silence until the memory of the music was just vague enough for them to miss it.

She hadn't planned on signing up for intermediate piano. It had been freshman orientation, and some overzealous advisor was giving them a long-winded tour of the building. By the time they got to the music wing, the students had been standing for two hours, and everyone was exhausted. They began plopping themselves down wherever they could, some on the floor, and some on the choral risers.

Lyle on the piano bench.

The advisor droned on about musical safety, fire exits, and whatever other nonsense they would all forget as soon as they left the building. It was a digital piano, and she had turned the volume down as she started to play. Before Lyle knew it, her hands were weaving a musical cocoon, so quiet it held the melody close enough for only her to hear.

That is, until the chorus teacher came up behind her. Lyle jumped a mile and snapped the cover of the piano shut, but Ms. Godllub slammed it back open, demanding that Lyle stay behind as the rest of the freshmen were dismissed. Lyle obliged, and the next thing she knew, she was leaving the building as the choral accompaniment and a student in intermediate piano. Ms. Godllub was very…persuasive. Or terrifying. Either one worked.

Rawel was thrilled when Lyle told him she decided to take the class, and although Lyle enjoyed playing again, she still could not bring herself to touch the cold ivory of her own piano. She could tell Rawel and Aariz were slightly confused when she did not immediately pull it out of retirement. It had gathered dust for years in the lobby since Lyle had stopped playing, and eventually, at Lyle's request, it had been moved into the back room. It now sat in the middle of the oval carousel used to hang and rotate customer clothes once they were dry-cleaned. When the carousel was full, Lyle couldn't even see the piano, and sometimes, she forgot it was even there.

Out of sight, out of mind.

Out of reach.

Lyle knew if she could reach it, she would play, and everything she had been working so hard not to feel all these years would come rushing back, circling her faster and faster until there was no air left for her to breathe. As she walked down the sidewalk, Lyle wondered if someone else's music dancing through The Carry Out would make her feel that way too.

I guess I'll find out.

The boys were just as surprised when they found Aariz's donation propped against the stage after school. "I can't believe he just gave us all this wood for free," Max said, holding a plank in place while Tate nailed it down. It was the third time he said it, and Lyle could tell it was getting on Tate's nerves.

"It's not that I'm not grateful," Tate said to her as he went to the counter for some water. Lyle handed him a mini bottle, which he drained in a matter of seconds. "I just don't want to talk about it the entire night."

"You know Aariz woke up insanely early to cut those for you, right?" For someone who needed a stage to practice on so badly, Tate didn't seem very grateful for the help.

"Right," Tate said. "I didn't mean it like that." He looked at Max before turning back to Lyle, stumbling to find the right words. "I just want to get playing, that's all." Lyle nodded as she returned her attention to the dry-cleaning. After Tate realized she was done talking, he retreated to the stage to help Max.

Lyle understood he was eager to play, but a little gratitude went a long way in this world. Not that Aariz had done it with the expectation of recognition. If he had it his way, Lyle knew Aariz would have done it anonymously, but it was difficult to be anonymous when you owned the carpentry shop next door. Nevertheless, something about Tate's reaction struck Lyle as odd.

She didn't have long to dwell on it as Cameron walked through the front door. The bell announced him, and he looked up at it as if it had given away his position in a military raid. Lyle smiled, but Cameron averted his gaze as he hurried over to the stage. She could hear most of his conversation with Tate, given Tate was a loud talker.

"CamKing!"

"Hi."

"Get your suit okay?"

"Yeah."

"Yeah? You're not going to beat Wilson with words like that."

"Affirmative."

Tate gave Cameron a gentle pat on the back before leaving to grab another plank. Lyle watched Cameron shift his weight from foot to foot, avoiding Max, who was hammering at his feet. To Max's credit, he didn't push the subject, and finally, Cameron sat down on his own. Max talked quieter, so Lyle only got bits and pieces of their conversation.

"Hey, Cam."

"I'm sorry about…"

"No need…"

"…She hates me?"

"Doubt it…"

"…You?"

"Couldn't hate you if I tried," Max said the last sentence louder in reassurance. Cameron still looked sheepish, but Max seemed to have a comforting effect on him, and soon enough, he was smiling and joking with Tate as the three continued to work. There was something about Max that contrasted so heavily from Tate, a kind of stoicism and control that made people feel safe. It fascinated Lyle that they managed to be such good friends. Two opposing sides of a balancing act.

The afternoon went by without a hitch, customers in and out in a steady stream of hurried errands. The boys made quick work of the floor, the majority of the new wood nailed into place. Evening arrived in the blink of an eye, and although Cameron made no move to leave, they all knew he could only excuse his absence to his parents for so long. The sun shone more squarely through the front window as it sank deeper in the sky, and still, Cameron stayed, holding and hammering with no regard to the time. Lyle could see Tate and Max stealing glances at him, more so as time continued to tick by.

"What's for dinner tonight, Cam?" Max finally asked. Lyle and Tate both turned their attention to Cameron, expecting him to jump up, realizing he lost track of time. But Cameron just shrugged.

"I suppose I can scrounge up some leftovers when I get home." Max turned to Tate with a look that said he was tapping out before returning his attention to the stage.

"What time is it anyway?" Tate asked casually, looking around the lobby until his eyes found a clock mounted on the wall. "Holy crap, almost six?" He turned to Cameron. "Aren't you usually home by six?"

Cameron surprised them all by jumping to his feet in anger. "Can you all refrain from the preferential treatment?" He was speaking loudly, the loudest Lyle had ever heard from him.

"We treat you the same way we treat each other," Tate said, finding his way to his feet.

"No, you do not," Cameron said as Max rose as well. "You treat me like I'm aristocracy, and I don't deserve any of it." Max put a hand on Cameron's shoulder as he continued, quieter now. "I'm not part of them. I don't want to be." Lyle's heart went out to Cameron. She knew better than anyone that you couldn't choose your parents.

"Sure you are," Max said. Although Cameron was taller, he looked at Max like a wise older brother. "But you're part of us, too. That's the part you get to choose."

"And we're glad you chose us," Tate said. Cameron smiled a little, running the toe of his shoe in a small circle on the floor. "But now you've got to get home before your parents lose it." Cameron nodded and started for the door.

"Wait," Lyle called from behind the counter. "I have your dry-cleaning." Cameron begrudgingly took the pressed dresses and suits from her hands. "The thing is," she said before he could turn away, "with all the business we've been getting and the high quality your parents request, there's just not enough time in the day for me to get it all done." She was not surprised by Cameron's look of confusion. In all the years his family had been coming to The Carry Out, Lyle had never once been late with anything.

"Th-that's okay," Cameron stammered, unsure of how to respond. He clearly didn't want to offend her by asking why, and Lyle appreciated him for it, especially since she was making it up as she went.

She gave Tate a look that was enough to draw him over to the counter as she continued. "I think you'll have to start coming twice a week to pick it up." Her eyes bore into Tate as she paused, willing her plan into his head.

"All right," Cameron said, turning to leave. He made it halfway across the lobby before Tate finally got the message.

"Oh yeah," Tate called. "And Max and I might need a little more tutoring time."

Cameron turned, still confused. "But I don't actually tutor you gu—"

"Between the two of us," Tate cut in, "I'd say three times a week ought to do it. Max?"

Max, who had been observing this encounter from afar, turned his attention directly to Cameron. "Yeah, I could use some help with pre-calc." Lyle knew for a fact that wasn't true. She overheard Cameron and Max earlier chattering as they worked about their quiz scores from pre-calc. Cameron got a ninety, Max got a ninety-nine. She watched as Cameron processed what was happening, his face softening as Max continued. "Twice a week should do it for me."

"And once for me," Tate added.

Max joined them at the counter. "Does that work?"

Cameron looked around the room at each of them as if he were emerging from years in a cave and finally basking in the sunlight. The toothy smile broke out on his face before he could stop it. "Unequivocally." He didn't stop grinning his whole way out the door.

Max and Tate returned to the stage as if nothing had happened. Lyle didn't quite understand their relationship, but it seemed like they were always on the same wavelength, even when things got complicated. She wished she had a friend like that. But at least between the three of them, they were able to give Cameron a week's worth of alibis.

A couple hours later, Tate and Max ducked out to grab pizza across the street, returning with a greasy slice for Lyle that was loaded with meat and vegetables and whatever else didn't belong on a pizza. Lyle didn't have the heart to tell them, so she quietly picked off the toppings as the boys ate, pushing them to the edge of her plate until she was able to enjoy a plain slice of cheese. She was careful to throw her plate away upside-down when she was finished to hide the discarded toppings.

They continued after dinner, securing the last floorboard just as it hit closing time. Lyle began her usual regimen of switching the signs and sweeping the lobby. "And…done!" Tate said as Max hammered the final nail into place. The two hopped off the stage and stepped back to admire their work, inadvertently scattering some of the dust Lyle had piled. She didn't mind, though, not after seeing the looks on their faces. Max had the smallest smile on his, arms crossed as he nodded in satisfaction at his handiwork. Lyle was glad to see his typical pensive expression replaced by one of pride.

She thought Tate would be elated, jumping for joy like his usual rambunctious self. But he was silent, one thumb hooked in his front pocket, his other hand running absentmindedly through his hair.

He wore a look of hopeful awe as if this renovated stage surrounded by dryer lint could make all his dreams come true. She had never seen him look so vulnerable, but as quickly as Lyle noticed it, it was gone, Tate's crooked grin flashing across his face as he patted Max on the back. "We did it, man."

"Right. We."

Tate shrugged, jabbing Max with his elbow and catapulting himself onto the stage with one hand. "More or less." He stared out over the empty lobby as if he were surveying the audience of a full auditorium. Lyle was surprised how long he stood there, but Max just rolled his eyes and grabbed his sweatshirt and books from the steps. He seemed used to Tate's shenanigans.

"Can you thank Aariz for the supplies?" Max asked Lyle. He seemed hesitant as if he didn't want to interrupt her sweeping.

"Sure." She glanced at the stage, where Tate was still taking it all in. "You're quite the handyman."

Max shrugged. "Not really. Just floorboards." He was on the shorter side, just taller than Lyle, but he was sturdy, with muscles just visible enough to show that he shouldn't be messed with. And yet, he was reserved, with few words and simple actions. Lyle wondered if he was like that all the time or if he was just embarrassed about their first bloody interaction. "Tate, you ready?" he asked, pulling Tate out of his reverie.

"Max, we just finished." Tate jumped off the stage and joined them in the middle of the lobby. "Don't you want to test it out?"

Max looked at Tate like he had three heads. "Tomorrow. I'm beat."

"Oh, come on." Tate grabbed his guitar from the steps. "You can drum on the new floorboards." Max looked at the clock on the wall, then at Tate, as if to remind him of some unspoken curfew.

"I'm heading out." He turned to Lyle with what looked to be apologetic eyes. "Thank you again." Then to Tate. "You coming?"

Tate looked from the clock to the stage, to Lyle sweeping the floor, to Max. "I'll see you at home," he finally answered. Max seemed surprised by Tate's answer, but he also seemed too exhausted to argue.

"Right." He tugged his sweatshirt over his head as he pushed open the door. "Night."

"Night," Lyle said, but he was already gone.

"Don't mind him," Tate said. "He's got a curfew."

"And you don't?" Lyle tried to make sense of it. "I thought you lived together."

"We do." Tate paused before shaking his head. "It's complicated." She had more questions, but Tate already found his way back to center stage, this time with his guitar slung over his shoulder.

"All you need now is a spotlight."

"You got one?" That crooked smiled again. Lyle redirected her attention to sweeping as Tate continued to revel in his nonexistent fame. He still hadn't moved when she put the broom away and ducked behind the counter to balance the register, and she wondered how long he would stand there as she went about her business. It was only when he strummed a few cords that he caught Lyle's attention. The notes flew at her like arrows shot by an archer, and she looked like a prairie dog as she popped up from behind the counter.

"Whoa," Tate said, startled by her reaction. "That bad?"

"Oh, no." Lyle felt herself flush, but she recomposed herself as Tate set down his guitar and hopped off the stage. "It was better than your piano."

"Told you I'm irresistible on guitar."

"All the girls tell you that?"

Tate raised an eyebrow. "Apparently not all of them." He leaned casually against the counter as Lyle finished with the register. She could feel his eyes observing her as she worked, almost as if he could sense something was off.

"I thought you were going to play," she said in an attempt to divert his attention.

"What do you want to hear?"

Lyle shrugged. It was a hard question for her to answer. Deep down, part of her never wanted to hear music coming from that stage again. But even deeper down, part of her really did.

Tate studied her a moment longer before returning to the stage, one leg dangling off the edge as he sat with his guitar. He began to strum, Lyle listening as she collected rogue coat hangers that seemed to scatter themselves throughout the day. The music made her tense at first, but she vaguely recognized the song and became distracted until she finally placed it.

"Isn't that a song for piano?"

Tate smirked. "Nobody wants to hear me try to play the piano tonight." Lyle smiled a little before returning her attention to collecting the hangers. She was just beginning to fall into the lull of the song's chords when Tate started to sing. His voice was gentle, the way velvet felt, and Lyle let it envelop her. It swirled through the store, intermingling with the air until Lyle was breathing it in like she needed it.

For a long time, music had felt intrusive in The Carry Out, but hearing Tate strumming and singing a familiar melody, Lyle remembered how well it fit. She put the hangers down and leaned her elbows on the counter, letting his low voice surround her like a warm coat. Tate grinned as she caught his eye, and all at once, Lyle realized how much she had missed the music.

"Well?" he asked after he strummed the final chord, setting his guitar down beside him.

"A step below irresistible," Lyle said as she put the hangers in the storage closet.

"Don't worry." Tate picked up a hanger she dropped along the way and handed it to her. "I'll get there."

Lyle thought about that, a lobby filled with Tate and his music instead of silence and loneliness. "We'll see." She locked the front door and turned out the lobby lights, and it took a second for their eyes to adjust. The faint light from the back of the store spilled out just enough for them to find their way.

"Well," Lyle said, realizing she was out of mindless chores to do. "I guess I'll see you tomorrow."

"I'll walk you home," Tate said as he followed her behind the counter. The clothing carousel extended to their left, its light guiding their way as they maneuvered through the narrow space to the back doors, one of which was marked with an exit sign.

"You already have."

Tate looked confused until she pushed open the other door, revealing the staircase to their apartment. "You live here?" Tate laughed. "And to think I felt guilty about not walking you home yesterday." Lyle didn't know what to say as she switched off the final light above the carousel, keeping one hand on the doorknob as the two of them stood in almost complete darkness.

"Me and grandfather." Tate nodded, looking up at the ceiling as if he could see her room through the floorboards. The green glow of the exit sign played on his scar as he moved, like moonlight dancing on the ripples of a river. It was the first time Lyle let herself notice it, the way it wrapped around the left side of his mouth and bled into the corner of his lip, mesmerizing in a way that made her stomach feel light.

"Well," he said awkwardly as he motioned to the staircase. "Safe travels."

"Night." Lyle found herself wondering what he was going home to. What his room was like. Was it full of instruments? Did it have posters of bands? What color were the walls?

"Hey, Tate!" she blurted out, stopping him halfway out the backdoor. "What color is your room?"

He paused for a breath before answering. "Black." The darkness swallowed him as he disappeared into the alley, and Lyle listened to the wheels of his skateboard scraping the sidewalk, waiting for it to fade into silence.

"Thanks for the song," she whispered before ascending the stairs and retreating to her room. She pulled on a pair of white pajamas, thinking about Tate's answer as she climbed into bed.

Black.

She tried to imagine what it would be like to have black walls, darkness closing in from every direction. Darkness that left you with nothing but yourself as company, a treacherous crowd if you had memories to escape.

But the more she thought about it, the more enticing the darkness began to sound. She imagined the walls of her bedroom morphing from white to black, the darkness stripping away the outside noise, leaving her with nothing but her inner voice and the courage to listen to it.

Kind of like music.

Lyle let the thought tuck her into bed, the memory of Tate's voice lulling her to sleep.

. . .

Ever since he had stopped fighting years ago, Max had slept in the screen house with Tate. To this day, he wasn't sure what happened. One weekend his father was betting on him, throwing him into seven or eight stalls a night. Then the next, his father suddenly didn't want to go anymore, saying that Max was a sad excuse of a fighter and that he was embarrassed to be seen with him in public. Max was relieved to no longer have to wash someone else's blood off his hands or have his blood on someone else's. He was also thankful Tate no longer had to sneak to the barn with them, witnessing Max brutalize other children for money. It made him feel unworthy as a friend. But even with Max's relief, something always felt off about how it all went down, as if his father resented Max for the decision, even though he had been the one to make it.

Unfortunately, when Max's life became safer staying out of the barn, it became more dangerous at home. More verbal abuse, which he ignored, and more attempts at physical abuse, which Max had become accustomed to dodging or fighting off.

Unless he was sleeping, of course. One night was all it took to inspire his big move to the screen house with Tate. But even spending their nights outside, Max could not escape his father's rage if he arrived home after hours. His father always stumbled in at midnight, dropped at the doorstep by some regular at the bar who shouldn't be driving. He was a piss-poor excuse of a betting man, losing money to pool sharks and con artists that targeted him because he was too drunk to realize he was being duped.

When his father was drunk, which was always, he got it in his head that Max was to blame for his monetary losses, even though Max was pretty sure the dime bags lined on his brother's bedroom floor were funding his father's habits just fine. The last time Max lost track of time and got home after his father, he had been accused of fighting behind his father's back and keeping his winnings for himself. Obviously, that was not the case, but Max had long since resigned himself to the fact that it was impossible to reason with an unreasonable man.

Rather than endure the verbal lashing and drunken attacks that came with arriving home after his father, Max had adjusted his routine to his father's drinking schedule. Getting home before midnight allowed Max and Tate the time to get in the house, catch a shower, and cook up something to eat. Tate would usually retreat to the screen house after that, giving Max some time to get some school work done under the kitchen light if he was lucky. When Max heard his father working on the doorknob, he would gather his textbooks and sneak out the backdoor up the hill to the screen house. There, he would spend the rest of his waking hours chatting with Tate and finishing his homework via lamplight before falling asleep to the sound of the crickets.

In all the years Tate had lived with them, Max's father had only gone after Tate once. It was the only time Max ever hit his father, punching him square in the face and knocking him to the floor. His father never laid a hand on Tate after that, and Tate could have showered after hours without fear of getting beat over the head with a whiskey bottle while he shampooed. But what Max's father didn't do to Tate physically, he made up for verbally, grumbling about how Tate was a freeloader and that they weren't running an orphanage. Max had long since learned to block it out, but Tate wasn't so good at it, Max's father's words bruising him more than a punch probably would have, which was why Tate had always stuck with Max, getting in and getting out before his father walked through the door.

It was not a normal routine, but it was their routine, and Max and Tate had grown accustomed to it. That was why Max was surprised when Tate returned to the screen house around twelve-thirty in the morning with a giant smile on his face. "Hey," he said, as casually as if he were walking into homeroom.

"Hey," Max said from his spot on the daybed, where he rested his exhausted body from his work on the stage. "Later than I thought you'd be."

"Yeah." Tate stripped down to his boxers before crawling into his sleeping bag on the mattress on the floor. When Max was little, he and his mother would sometimes come out to the screen house to spend the night, her on the daybed and Max on the pullout mattress that was now Tate's. Max supposed he could have claimed it, but a part of him liked being on the daybed where his mother once was. It made him feel closer to her, especially when he started feeling farther away.

"What'd you do, run through an entire set?"

"No." Tate shook his head before laying back and staring at the ceiling. "Just one."

"One?" Max asked, rolling on his side. "Must have been a long song." Tate continued to stare at the ceiling, in no hurry to answer.

"I may have walked Lyle home."

Max raised an eyebrow. "Yeah?"

"Yeah." Tate paused before rolling over to face Max. "You know she asked me what color my bedroom is."

Max smirked as a breeze blew through their screen walls. "What'd you tell her?"

"Black," Tate said, motioning to the four screens surrounding them, where the dim glow of Max's lantern met the darkness of the night. Max switched the lantern off, and the two laid back down in almost complete darkness.

"Right." Max let the pitch black of the night surround them. He used to be wary of the dark, but fighting had pretty much nullified any fears that did not involve immediate self-preservation. Tate had always liked the dark, though. Max remembered the first time they officially met, how Tate had been so skittish around the bonfire, how he had welcomed the darkness of the screen house like a sanctuary. Max never asked Tate why he was scared of fire, but it made sense that he was comforted by its antithesis: the darkness of the night. "What about her?"

"What about her what?"

"Her room," Max said. "What color is it?"

Tate was silent for a moment. "I didn't ask."

"Maybe you should."

"Right," Tate said absently, as if his mind was playing the night over again. "I will tomorrow." A long silence embraced them before Tate spoke again. "What do you think it is?"

Max let the darkness speak for him as he lost himself in thought, and for some reason, he found himself thinking about his mother. About her long sundress, the one that flapped around her ankles when they used to walk to church. About the sheets she used to hang out on the clothesline, billowing in the wind like the sails of a ship. About the prayer candles she used to place all over the house. About his right eye, the color it used to be when she was still here. About the stars they used to look at together, illuminating the darkness just enough for him to see her face.

Before he lost his faith in God.

Before he slept in a sleeping bag.

Before his father smashed the candles on the kitchen floor after she left.

Before her face began to blur in his memory just enough to scare him.

Max thought about her smile, the way it had made him feel like he was safe, like someone actually cared about him.

The same way Lyle's does.

"White," Max whispered into the darkness, but Tate was already asleep.

CHAPTER SEVEN

"Extracurricular."

"E-X-T-R-A-C-U-R-R-I-C-U-L-A-R." Even though pre-calc had finished early and they were sitting in the back row, Cameron still whispered for fear of disrupting someone. "Speaking of, I hope we're not marching next period." He motioned out the classroom window at the storm clouds looming low in the sky.

"Me too," Max said. "Penumbra."

"P-E-N-U-M-B-R-A. Are you certain these words are hard enough? Maybe I should memorize more before the bee tonight."

Max rolled his eyes. Cameron was already a human dictionary, yet he was always convinced he didn't know enough words. "Neurosis."

Cameron smiled sarcastically before correctly spelling the word. Max was about to ask another when Wilson approached from his throne. He always sat in the front like some kind of prodigy, but Max suspected he bought his way onto the honor roll based on his incorrect class participation.

"What's up, Cammy?" Wilson grabbed the chair from the desk in front of them and straddled it backward, chin resting on the back of the seat.

"H-hi, Wilson." Cameron shot Max a look that screamed, *save yourself!*

Yeah, right.

Instead, Max planted himself firmer in his seat, deadpan as he stared at Wilson. The last person he was intimidated by was some rich boy that messed with his friends.

"Ready for the moment of truth tonight, team captain?" Wilson made Cameron so nervous, he seemed incapable of responding.

"Emissary," Max said, redirecting Cameron's attention.

"E-M-I—" Wilson started, his knuckles whitening as Max cut him off.

"Why don't you let the emissary of the bee team answer?"

"E-M-I-S-S-A-R-Y." Cameron's eyes were the size of dinner plates, looking between the two like a puppy caught peeing in the house.

"Correct." Max made a point to stare at Wilson as he said it, whose foot was tapping in what Max assumed to be rage.

I've got more, buddy.

"Yeah, well, too bad you can't keep that up on the stage, huh Cammy? Considering I beat you every spell-off."

"I think Cameron's got a good shot this year," Max said, putting a supportive hand on Cameron's shoulder.

"You know, I hope you're right." Wilson kicked the chair away as he stood and leaned his palms on Cameron's desk. "I would hate for you to do something that you or your new friends might…regret."

Max stood and put a protective hand between the two, unblinking until Wilson backed off. He knew a threat when he heard one, and this punk wasn't going to threaten Cameron on his watch. In an instant, Wilson went from menacing bully to poster boy class president, a fake smile worming along his face. "I know you'll do the right thing, Cammy."

"Good luck," Cameron blurted as Wilson walked away. For a second, Max thought he was being sarcastic, but looking at Cameron's sheepish expression, it seemed sincere.

"Quandary," Max said, and Cameron's face immediately shifted from white as a sheet to red with...what was it? It wasn't until Max remembered his nights in the stalls that he understood.

All the practice spell-offs Cameron lost to Wilson.

All the eagerness Cameron had to be accepted by Wilson and his buddies.

All the words Cameron suddenly forgot how to spell in the last rounds of the bees in years past.

Shame.

"Q-U-A-N-D-A-R-Y," Cameron mumbled.

"Correct." Max softened his expression. "And you'll be correct tonight, too." Cameron smiled, but it was sheepish, weighed down by his secret. "Even in the last round," Max added, holding Cameron's gaze long enough to communicate that he knew what was going on.

"You must think I'm a loser," Cameron said with that shameful expression.

"No." Max thought back to the first time he met Tate. "I know what it's like to not want to win." Although he had been too scared of his father to go through with it, Max had seriously considered letting Tate win that night. "Especially for your friends."

"You guys are my friends." He emphasized "*you,*" but Max knew deep down, Cameron thought of Wilson and his posse as his friends, too. And he didn't want to do anything to jeopardize that friendship, however one-sided it may be. Cameron had grown up with them, and Max could only imagine the pressure his family's social circle put on the poor boy to fit in. He understood better than most how powerful parental pressure could be, even if it made you go against everything you thought you were.

The bell rang, Cameron avoiding eye contact as they gathered their books. "Want to swing by The Carry Out before the bee to get Tate?" Max asked as they squeezed past Wilson out the door. Cameron nodded as he busied himself adjusting his backpack, and Max felt bad Cameron was trapped in the middle. "Exuberant," he said as they descended the stairs. They were an odd pair: Cameron slender, pale as a sheet, and dressed for success; and Max, stouter, darker, and wearing his same worn jeans and white t-shirt. But despite their differences, Cameron and Max connected, and Max could see in his eyes that Cameron valued their friendship.

"E-X-U-B-E-R-A-N-T."

Max put his arm around Cameron as they headed down the hallway toward the band room. "Which is exactly what Tate and I will be when you're on stage tonight."

. . .

They got to The Carry Out about an hour before the spelling bee, where Tate was strumming a few chords as he stared at the finished stage.

"Hey," Max said, grabbing Tate's attention.

"CamKing, tonight's the night! You ready?"

Cameron broke into a smile that morphed into a grimace. It was difficult for him to act excited when he knew he wasn't going to win, especially since Max and Tate were going. They were the first people who believed in him, and the last thing Cameron wanted to do was disappoint them. But he didn't want to disappoint Wilson, either.

Who would have thought, me of all people, juggling two groups of friends?

"I certainly hope so," Cameron said.

"You ready to go?" Max asked.

"Do you care if I bring Lyle?" Tate patted Cameron's shoulder. "The more support, the better, right?"

"Right," Cameron answered, but not quite wholeheartedly. The more support, the more disappointment when he didn't win, and Cameron had already caused Lyle enough strife. But Tate had already made his way to the counter, repeatedly ringing the little handheld bell until Lyle emerged from the back.

"What?" she said sharply, putting her hand on top of Tate's to stop the ringing.

"Want to come to the spelling bee with us to watch CamKing?" Lyle looked a little surprised at the invite, and she looked over his shoulder to Cameron for confirmation. Cameron was too embarrassed to do anything but look down and turn red, but he saw Max nod in affirmation out of the corner of his eye.

"I want to," Lyle looked around the lobby at the couple of customers folding their laundry. "But I have to man the store."

"Oh, come on," Tate said. "It'll only be an hour. Two tops."

Lyle chewed on that a moment, and Cameron hoped she was thinking of an excuse. "Hey, Aariz?" Aariz appeared after a moment, his dark beard, as usual, covered in sawdust. "Would you be able to watch the store while I watch Cameron in the spelling bee? I won't be long."

"Absolutely," he said. "I'm going to be in the back working the sander, so just tell them to come to my lobby and ring the register bell for assistance. It's rigged to flash a light in the back so I can see when someone needs me." He smiled at Cameron. "Spelling, that's a great talent to have. Good luck, son." Cameron shifted at the word son. Whenever his parents wished him luck, it was more of a threat than a well-wish. They were more concerned about Cameron's picture in the paper than his actual success. They weren't even coming tonight.

But they found time to pick me out an outfit.

Aariz gave Lyle a quick kiss on the forehead, brushing the sawdust off her shoulder that fell from his beard. "Have fun, love. Be safe."

Lyle smiled. "Thanks again. I won't be gone long." Aariz disappeared to the back of the woodshop, and Lyle scampered behind the counter to put up a sign that stated exactly what Aariz had just said.

"I take it you do this often?" Tate asked, examining the sign and handing her his guitar, which she tucked away behind the counter for safekeeping.

"I try not to, but yeah, sometimes. I cover him, too, when he needs to pray."

"Ready?" Tate rushed them all out the door, a parade of support for Cameron he was about to purposefully disappoint. As they left the building, Cameron was acutely aware of their tank top, t-shirt, and frayed jeans that stood in stark contrast against his full suit.

Their high school auditorium was almost full, far more people than he anticipated. Cameron tried to avoid Wilson before taking the stage, but Wilson stalked him like a lioness, positioning himself in line behind Cameron backstage. "Where you been, Cammy?" His breath carried the faintest scent of alcohol, and Cameron turned away. "You missed the pre-bee party."

"I was at The Carry Out."

Wilson peeked around the curtain and found Max, Tate, and Lyle settled in the audience. "Oh yeah, to pick up your fan club." Cameron blushed and said nothing. "Glad to see they dressed for the occasion," Wilson said, and Cameron hated himself all over again for thinking the exact same thing forty minutes earlier. "She's pretty." Wilson's eyes lingered on Lyle just long enough for Cameron's stomach to drop into his toes. "Too bad she's going to see you lose." Cameron laughed nervously, thankful when they were ushered onto the stage. Wilson was always nicest in the spotlight.

Cameron listened attentively as the principal did a quick introduction and review of the rules before taking his seat with the other judges. Cameron had little apprehension as he stepped up to the microphone. The beginning was the easy part. "Your word is alliance."

"A-L-L-I-A-N-C-E. Alliance." Cameron didn't even have to think as the letters raced out of his mouth.

"Correct."

Tate whooped from the audience as Cameron returned to his seat, and he smiled in spite of himself.

"See you in the last round," Wilson whispered as he headed to the microphone.

The following rounds were a blur, Cameron spelling words correctly with ease as his competitors dropped one by one until only he and Wilson remained in the sea of vacated folding chairs. Wilson struggled the last couple rounds, discretely writing the words in the air with his fingertip, taking a long time to give his answer. He became more intense with every correct spelling. His intensity was at an all-time high as the principal returned to the stage to announce the final round. If one of them misspelled a word, the other had to spell that word correctly to win. This was the part Cameron hated the most. Throwing the bee felt like being repeatedly punched in the gut afterward, but in a way, he deserved it for being a sellout. Wilson's trash talk was now a silent glower Cameron felt boring into the side of his head as he approached the microphone.

"Your word is savvy."

"S-A-V-V-Y. Savvy." Cameron liked going first in the final round; it gave him the opportunity to spell at least one word correctly before tailoring his performance to second place. Cameron took his seat as Wilson approached the microphone, intentionally brushing shoulders as he passed.

"Your word is bombastic."

"B-O..." Wilson paused, scribbling the word in the air at his side. "M-B-A-S-T-I-C. Bombastic?"

"Correct."

A sigh of relief escaped Wilson as he and Cameron switched places. "Your word is artifice."

Cameron usually gave in at this point, but he felt compelled to spell one more word correctly before relinquishing the title. Maybe it was for Lyle, who he saw smiling at him from the audience. She and The Carry Out had always supported his spelling, even before they were friends, and she had taken the evening off from work to come watch him. Didn't he owe it to her to spell one more word correctly?

"A-R-T-I-F-I-C-E. Artifice."

"Correct."

"What the hell, man?" Wilson hissed as he passed. "End it already." And by end it, he meant throw it. The irony of the matter was this was just a preliminary bee to determine eligibility; both of them and whoever had gone out third had already qualified for the next round. Wilson just wanted to be the best. He approached the microphone, his walk more pissed off than nervous.

"Your word is sovereign."

Cameron could tell by Wilson's face that he didn't know it. "S..." Wilson held out the letter to buy time to think. "...O-V-E-R-E-G-N. Sovereign?" The bell dinged below, indicating a misspelling, the entire auditorium exhaling in disappointment as Wilson returned to his seat.

The entire auditorium except three.

Cameron searched for them as he approached the microphone. Tate leaned forward, elbows on knees, ready to spring into celebration. Lyle's hands were pressed together against her mouth as if praying for his success.

"The word is sovereign," the reader repeated.

All Cameron had to do was switch the E and the I, and Wilson would be the winner.

Again.

That was the way it worked in Wilson and Cameron's world. You did what you had to do to save face. Even if it meant throwing something that was important to you to keep a friend. "Sovereign," Cameron said. "S-O-V-E-R..." His eyes searched the rows again until they fell on Max. Unlike Tate and Lyle, he was not tense. He was the only one who knew what was coming, and Cameron was surprised that he didn't look upset. Instead, Max gave him the smallest nod indicating he supported whatever decision Cameron made, and all at once, Cameron realized he didn't have to throw the bee to keep a friend. "E-I-G-N. Sovereign." The correct spelling spilled out of his mouth before he could stop it, and it tasted sweet, like saying I love you for the first time.

"Congratulations, Cameron, you are the winner of the first round of the spelling bee."

Tate and Lyle leaped into the air, cheering and whooping. Max stood, clapping hard and sure, a smile dancing across his face as he held eyes with Cameron. He couldn't help but smile back, but his exuberance was short-lived as the principal joined him on the stage. "And congratulations Wilson and Brian, who also qualified for the next round of the bee. Boys, join Cameron center stage." Wilson and Brian obliged, sandwiching Cameron between their Brooks Brothers suits. Wilson wouldn't look at Cameron, staring straight ahead like a drill sergeant hoping for rain to make the basic training course just a little harder on the new recruits.

"Congratulations," Cameron said, extending a hand. People were watching, so Wilson took it, shaking it up and down as he leaned in so only Cameron could hear him.

"Your friends look happy for you. Any regrets?" Cameron could hear the sneer in his voice, but Wilson's face lit up like a politician's as the cameras began to flash. Cameron's stomach felt like a balloon someone had poked a hole in as the boys exited the stage, a slow deflation that was far from over. Wilson was met by a crowd of classmates, crooning about how great he was and how much he deserved the win. Cameron wove his way through them, jostled here and there as he went.

Even when I win, I'm invisible.

"Cameron!" He followed Lyle's voice to the back of the auditorium, her arms around his neck in a hug as soon as he got close enough. Cameron stood stiff for a moment, unsure of what to do, before wrapping his arms lightly around her waist until Lyle let go. A part of him lit up inside, and Cameron realized he was glad she decided to come after all.

"Way to go, CamKing!" Tate was boisterous as ever, grinning as he patted Cameron on the back. Cameron couldn't keep the grin from spreading to his own face. "We have to celebrate," Tate declared. "Let's take a victory lap."

Cameron didn't know what that meant, but seeing as none of them had money to do anything else, he just went with it. Tate grabbed him by the hand and dragged him outside into the cool night air. They went around the building and down the hill until they reached the track, where Tate finally released him and took his place as head of the parade. Lyle fell into step behind him as Tate began to march on the spongey surface around the soccer field. Every now and then, he would whoop or chant Cameron's name, Lyle giggling at the absurdity of it all; she hadn't been as exposed to his antics as Cameron and Max had.

"Congrats, Cam," Max said, falling into step next to Cameron, his hands in his pockets. He looked proud, and Cameron felt it patch the hole in the balloon of his stomach.

"Thanks." Tate and Lyle had gotten ahead, laughing and joking as they walked side by side now. Cameron and Max were comfortable falling behind, taking the lap at a more casual stroll. "Couldn't have done it without you."

"You didn't need me to practice. That was all you."

"True," Cameron said, thinking about that morning in pre-calc. "But I needed you to win."

Max nodded but took no credit as they continued. "What did he say to you?" It took Cameron a minute to realize Max was talking about Wilson and was surprised he noticed the onstage exchange at all. It was becoming apparent that Max didn't miss much.

"Asked if I had any regrets."

"Do you?" The question wasn't leading or presumptuous. It just sat there in the moonlight, bobbing along like a balloon attached to Cameron's wrist as they continued to walk. Cameron thought about all the time he wasted at his parents' parties, hiding his band t-shirts, sitting second fiddle to Wilson for the sake of a friendship he was beginning to realize was never a friendship at all. It had taken true friendship for Cameron to see the difference, and as he strolled the homestretch of the track with Max, he let the milky comfort of the night soften his worries. They met Tate and Lyle at the finish line, where Cameron took a round of high fives from everyone.

"I have to get back," Lyle said, looking at the time on her flip phone and starting back up the hill.

"We'll walk you," Tate said. "It's not that far." Lyle nodded as the four of them followed the school parking lot to the road, walking down the sidewalk up the steep incline that separated The Carry Out from the school. Main Street was still awake when they reached it, the florescent signs of local businesses guiding their way. They were just about at the door of the The Carry Out when Cameron finally answered.

"No," he said, catching Max's eye as they followed Tate and Lyle through the front door. "I don't."

And he meant it too. Until he bumped into Tate's back, who stood frozen to the floor. Cameron followed his eyes to the stage, and what was left of the air in the balloon of his stomach deflated on the spot.

· · ·

Everything in Tate's being wanted to scream, but for some reason, he couldn't. Couldn't speak. Couldn't move. He just stood rooted to the ground, staring at the demolition of his dream. The stage was ravaged; there was no other way to describe it. The new floorboards were broken and smashed, caving in with shards scattered across the lobby. The steps had been ripped off and were currently on their side, nails protruding from what should have been the bottom.

Lyle gasped as she slid in behind him, and he saw her take a quick survey of the lobby as he felt Cameron bump into his back. Luckily, nothing else was vandalized, which made it all the more clear to Tate that this was personal. His suspicion was reaffirmed as he read the words written on what was left of the stage, squirrely but legible in runny red spray paint.

Still sovereign?

Max and Cameron were silenced as well, Max clenching his fists at his side, Cameron's jaw on the floor. They all knew what it meant. And they all knew why it happened.

"Oh, my God," Lyle said, alarmed. "Where's Aariz?" She scampered to the adjoining lobby and disappeared behind the front desk. Tate had not noticed the faint buzzing sound until it stopped, Aariz hurrying behind Lyle back to the lobby. By his shocked expression, it was easy to see he had not been aware of the vandalism.

"Goodness," he breathed, his hand playing at his beard as he took in the devastation. He turned to the boys, who were clumped together just inside the door. "Boys…I'm so sorry. You worked so hard."

"You're sorry?" Tate felt the rage bubbling up inside him. He knew they shouldn't have trusted Aariz. "How could you let this happen?"

"Tate!" Lyle said, taken aback by his outburst. Aariz seemed surprised as well, but Tate couldn't stop.

"You were supposed to be watching the store!" Tate felt Max's hand on his arm and whipped around to face him.

"We can fix it."

"Fix it?" Tate practically screamed. "There's nothing left to fix! It's destroyed!" He whipped back to face Aariz. "HE should have been watching it."

"Tate." Max took a step forward to look Tate in the eye. "Stop." His voice was firm, but Tate was having none of it.

"No." Aariz's voice surprised everyone as Tate ripped his arm from Max's grip. "Tate's right." Lyle looked at Aariz like he was claiming pigs could fly, and he put a hand on her shoulder. "I agreed to watch the store. I shouldn't have been running the sander, or I would have heard the commotion. The fault is mine." Everyone was shocked as Aariz stepped forward. "And if you would have me, I would like to help you rebuild."

Tate glared at Aariz's outstretched hand. If he had done what he was supposed to, they would still have a place to practice. Now they were left with nothing, and he had the nerve to try to make amends? Tate worked hard his entire life to make his dream come true, and to be honest, he didn't have much forgiveness left in him.

Max saw Tate had no intention of shaking hands, so he offered his own. "Thank you," he said as they shook. "Start Monday?" Tate couldn't believe what he was hearing. Max knew they were on a time crunch, and he wanted to wait until Monday?

"I'll be here." Aariz made eye contact with each boy before walking back toward his counter, pausing a moment to read the red words. "And congratulations, Cameron," he said before disappearing behind the desk of his own lobby. Tate heard Cameron try to answer, but nothing came out but a strangled grunt of recognition.

As soon as Aariz was out of earshot, Tate turned on Max. "Monday?"

"Yes, Monday."

"But—"

"Maybe," Max cut in, pulling Tate to the side of the lobby. "You have more important things to worry about this weekend." He jutted his jaw sideways to where Lyle was trying to comfort a visibly distraught Cameron. Max stared Tate down, deep into his soul, until Tate deflated under his gaze. Resigning himself to the fact that the stage was Monday's problem, he started in the direction of the door.

"This is all my fault," Cameron was saying over and over, his eyes wide as the clock on the wall.

"It's not," Lyle said, one hand on his arm, the other rubbing his back. "You didn't do anything wrong."

"I knew I shouldn't have done it."

Lyle looked confused. "Shouldn't have done what?"

"Win."

Lyle's eyes begged for assistance as Tate and Max approached.

"You didn't do anything wrong, CamKing," Tate repeated, patting Cameron halfheartedly on the shoulder.

Tears welled in Cameron's eyes, sniffing as he looked at Tate. "I should have lost like I always do." Tate's gaze darted to Max, whose expression gave away nothing.

Tate didn't know what to say, and he was grateful when Max swooped in and nudged Cameron out of Lyle's grasp. He ushered him out the front door, where they plopped down side by side on the sidewalk. Tate couldn't hear what they were saying, but after a couple seconds of back and forth, Cameron's shoulders stopped convulsing with sniffs, and he seemed to relax as the two sat there, Max's hand on Cameron's shoulder.

From the corner of his eye, Tate saw Lyle also watching the pair, her look of concern replaced by one of relief. "Who knew Max had a way with words?" Tate said. Lyle looked at him for a moment but said nothing before retreating to the closet and returning with a broom and dustpan. "Oh, let me," Tate said, reaching for the broom, but Lyle ignored him as she began to sweep the scattered splinters of wood into a pile.

"Are you always this rude to people?" she asked without looking up.

"What?" Tate felt off-balance as he answered. "No. I was just upset."

"We're all upset, Tate, but you're the only one that yelled at Aariz."

Tate couldn't believe she didn't understand. "I just thought—"

"Thought what?" Lyle's voice rose with frustration. "That he should stare at the stage from the second we left to the second we returned? That it's his fault some jerk at school has a vendetta against you for stealing his friend?" Tate had never seen Lyle like this before, and he tried to backtrack.

"Listen, I didn't mean—"

"You're the one who wanted to take a victory lap, remember? Wilson obviously didn't do this while he was on stage losing. If we had come straight back like you said we would when I agreed to go with you, this wouldn't have happened!" Her knuckles were white on the broom as she fixed her eyes on him for the first time since Max and Cameron had gone outside. "He said he'd help you fix it, even though it wasn't his fault to begin with. So don't go blaming your problems on other people. Especially people who are trying to help you!"

"I'm sorry," Tate mumbled, feeling about three inches tall. He hated that Lyle was mad at him, and he hated even more that what she said was true. The whole point of this was to make his father proud, but he certainly wouldn't be proud of how Tate was treating the one girl he cared about.

"I'm not the one you should be apologizing to."

"Right." Tate put a hand on her shoulder. "I'll talk to Aariz tomorrow." Lyle seemed satisfied as she continued to sweep. Tate picked up the dustpan and squatted as she swept the massive pile of splintered wood. "I'm glad you came tonight," he said, hoping it didn't sound like a line.

Lyle sighed as if she had been restraining herself from saying something. She propped herself against the broom and looked down at him. "Why is this stage so important to you?"

"So we can practice for the talent show." He thought the answer was obvious.

"But why does that matter so much?" Lyle pressed. "It's just a talent show." Tate brushed a few rogue woodchips into the dustpan with his hand.

"We need the money to march."

"March?"

"Yeah," he said as he stood. "Marching band. In the Macy's Day Parade." He felt Lyle examining him as he dumped the contents of the dustpan into the trash. It was past eleven now, and Tate took the broom from her hands to finish sweeping so she could turn the signs. Max and Cameron stood as she bathed them in darkness, coming inside with the tinkling of the bell.

"I'm sorry," Cameron moaned, his emotions flooding back as he caught sight of the stage again.

"Cameron," Lyle said, pulling him into an embrace. "Stop." Cameron pulled away so he could blow his nose, tugging a crumpled tissue out of his pocket and stuffing it back once he was done. "You were great." She glanced at the clock. "But you should probably get home before your parents lose their minds."

"I'll ride with you," Max said.

"We're proud of you," Lyle reassured him as they stood in the open doorway.

"Thank you for coming," Cameron said, blushing the slightest bit.

"Congratulations, spelling bee champ," Tate called from the lobby. Cameron had not met Tate's eyes until that moment, and he seemed relieved Tate didn't want to pound him. Lyle raised her eyebrows, surprised by Tate's thoughtfulness.

"Thank you," Cameron said, exiting with an awkward wave.

"I'll swing back to pick you up?" Max asked, halfway out the door. Tate looked at Lyle, who gave him no indication that she wanted him to leave or stay.

"Nah," he said finally. "I'll see you at home."

"Right." Max looked from Tate to Lyle as he let the door swing shut behind him. "Night, guys."

"Night," Lyle said before clicking the lock into place. Tate dumped the dustpan once more before returning it and the broom to the closet. When he emerged, Lyle was at the counter, his guitar in her hand. He was overcome by relief that he hadn't left it on the stage. She was holding it out as if daring him to take it. No one had ever held his father's guitar before, and Tate was surprised he didn't feel the urge to snatch it away from her.

"I really am sorry," he murmured, knowing she deserved better than what he had given her tonight. Lyle reached out to put a hand on his shoulder but thought better of it and placed it on the neck of the guitar instead. She looked at him as if he were a wounded soldier in a medical ward.

"I know. It's okay."

"And I'm glad you came tonight." Tate was relieved to see a hint of a smile and paused to enjoy it before continuing. "How can I make it up to you?"

Lyle lifted the guitar the smallest bit, still holding it close to her white tank top. "Play me a song."

He smiled a little as he reached for it, his fingers brushing against hers as he took the guitar from her grasp. He wanted to look down in embarrassment, but he looked at her instead, her eyes staring back at him like two perfect worlds he could escape into. She didn't look away either, and they stood like that for a moment, frozen in time. "What do you want to hear?"

"Whatever you're feeling." Tate thought about that for a moment, trying to come up with a song that would sweep her off her feet, or impress her, or at least let her know that he was sorry. But in the end, the song just came to him.

Lyle slid to the floor, her back against the side of the counter. Tate killed the lobby lights and lowered himself down next to her. He began to strum, the chords weaving a thin but strong blanket around them in the darkness. Lyle looked exhausted as she rested her head against the wooden base of the counter, weighed down by a million little troubles. Tate did his best to sound soothing as he began to sing the first song that came to mind. Something about it made him feel vulnerable, exposed, and in that moment, he wanted Lyle to see that side of him. To truly understand him for who he was beneath everything life threw at him.

He leaned his head against the wood of the counter as he strummed the last chord, letting his hand fall between them. Although silence could be suffocating, sometimes it communicated everything that couldn't be put into words, and that's the kind of silence that surrounded them as they sat on the dark floor of The Carry Out.

"You seem much more…passionate about it than Max and Cameron." Lyle chose her words carefully so as not to pop the balloon they were floating on.

"Music has always been my escape."

"And marching?"

Tate felt his little finger brush against hers as he fingered his guitar pick. "I guess it's the closest I can get to where I want to be." He didn't think that made a lot of sense, but he didn't feel like he needed to. He let his hand fall open, his pinky overlapping hers. The guitar pick clicked against the wooden floor as it slid from his grasp.

"What color is your room?" he whispered, overwhelmed in that split second with the urge to know everything about her.

"White." Her voice sounded wispy, like strands of a paintbrush tickling his skin. She let her head rest against his shoulder as she spoke. Her blonde flyaway hairs tickled his scar as Tate leaned his cheek against the crown of her head, and he tried to remember the last time he let someone touch his scar. His flirting attempts felt foolish now as he sat drunk on the kind of moment that couldn't be planned.

"I understand if you don't want us to use the stage anymore." After all the work Tate put in to find a place to rehearse, he couldn't believe what he was saying. Everything was a part of the process, an integral piece that got him one step closer to his goal. But as they sat together, her outstretched right leg against his left, Tate didn't want to think like that. For a minute, he didn't want to plan. He didn't even want to think. He just wanted to live in that moment. With her.

"I want you to," Lyle answered.

He nudged her foot with the toe of his worn-out Vans. "So you're okay with music in the store?"

"I guess you're just irresistible," she murmured, letting the moment fill her up a little more before propping his guitar against the backside of the counter and leading him to the back door.

Tate felt like he was floating as he skated through the night air, and he made it all the way home before noticing he forgot his guitar pick.

. . .

Lyle was relieved when Tate walked through the door the next morning, skateboard under one arm as he approached the counter. It was a busy Saturday morning at The Carry Out, Lyle manning the front while her grandfather rushed around the back. When she did have a free moment, she spent most of her time apologizing to Rawel and trying to convince him the boys weren't trouble. After seeing the stage, he questioned her judgment for leaving her post and allowing these boys to cause trouble at the store. It was now up to Lyle to persuade him that they weren't trouble.

When Tate walked in with his scarred face and a skateboard under one arm, Lyle knew she had her work cut out for her.

"Hey," he said.

"I'll get Aariz." She didn't give him time for pleasantries as she disappeared to Aariz's workshop. Lyle was relieved he showed up, but it didn't diminish the reason for his visit.

"Hi, sweetheart," Aariz said. He was sanding an oversized board, blowing the dust off before brushing them off himself.

"Tate's here."

"On a Saturday?" Aariz raised a playful eyebrow. "You must have a date."

"No," Lyle stumbled. "He wants to apologize."

"It's not his fault the stage got vandalized. You should forgive him."

"Not to me. To you."

That caught Aariz's attention. "You didn't have to put him up to this."

"I didn't—" Lyle started but was cut off by Aariz's look of skepticism. "Okay, maybe I did, but you deserve an apology for the way he spoke to you."

Aariz sighed as he stood from his stool. "Lyle, a forced apology carries the same weight as no apology. But if you insist on doing this, let's get on with it." He followed her back to The Carry Out counter, where Tate was leaning against the side wall like he wanted to disappear into it.

"Aariz." Tate straightened up and gave a quick nod in Aariz's direction.

"Good morning, Tate." There was no anger in his voice, and Lyle didn't understand how Aariz managed to forgive so easily. True, she forgave Tate the night before, but Aariz hadn't seen the side of him that she had. Nevertheless, it wasn't in Aariz's nature to hold a grudge. He always said people who acted with prejudice had an issue with themselves, not with him or his people. Even so, Lyle never found it in herself to be quite as forgiving, and she took wrongdoings to heart.

She waited, the pressure on Tate to break the increasingly awkward silence. "I wanted to apologize for last night." Lyle cleared her throat, and Tate glanced at her before making eye contact with Aariz. "I may have come off a little strong."

"I would have done the same thing," Aariz said, but Lyle knew that wasn't true. In her entire life, she had only seen Aariz raise his voice one time, and it had been at her mother. He was not as quick to anger as Tate seemed to be. Although the more Lyle thought about it, Tate was more of a pressure cooker than a short fuse, doing his best to go about his business, unable to control himself when someone turned the heat up too high. "Apology accepted." Aariz extended his hand over the counter, and Tate eyed it as if evaluating its motives. For a minute, Lyle thought he might not take it, but to her relief, Tate gave it a single pump before dropping his hand to his side.

"Recruiting a new apprentice?" Rawel asked, emerging from the back.

"No, Grandfather," Lyle said, motioning in Tate's direction. "This is one of the boys I told you about. From the band."

"One of the good guys." Rawel emphasized the last two words enough for everyone to note his sarcasm.

"Sir, about the stage, I didn't mean..." Tate trailed off, unsure of what to say next, intimidated by Rawel's presence. Lyle didn't blame him; Rawel's body was concrete solid with sharp edges, strength from years of firefighting radiating from his being. Although he looked intimidating, Lyle didn't see the sharp edges, but rather the valleys between them where she snuggled in for comfort and safety.

"Actually, he was just apologizing for the mishap," Aariz said, patting Rawel on the arm. "Not that he or his friends had anything to do with it. Quite the opposite, they were doing a great job renovating the stage until those other boys came along." Lyle saw her grandfather's face soften the slightest bit. Aariz was his oldest and dearest friend, and Rawel valued his opinion greatly. Aariz did not linger, making quick work of disappearing back to his workshop.

"If you would have us, sir, we would love to renovate the stage again. Fix it for you."

"And use it to practice," Lyle added. Tate nodded sheepishly, as if afraid that piece of information would negatively sway Rawel's decision.

"Mm-hmm." Rawel's eyes lingered on Tate's scar long enough for Lyle to feel uncomfortable, a minuscule twitch of Tate's mouth indicating he noticed. Finally, she felt compelled to interject.

"They are good guys, Grandfather. Tate even stays behind afterward to help me close."

"Afterward?" Rawel's eyebrows lifted in the way only a protective grandfather's could.

"He just helps me sweep," Lyle said.

Rawel exhaled a few breaths before turning to Tate. "If you are here after hours, I expect you to conduct yourself with the utmost respect in the company of my granddaughter." Rawel leaned forward. "No exceptions."

"Yes, sir." Tate managed to hold eye contact until Rawel finally backed off.

"Make sure none of this disrupts the business," he said, returning to the back of the shop.

"Don't worry," Lyle called after him. Tate's exhale was audible when they were finally left alone, and Lyle leaned her elbows on the counter with a smirk. "Now, was that so hard?"

Tate answered with a sarcastic smile.

"Thank you for apologizing to Aariz." Lyle thought about what Aariz had said. "Did you want to?"

Tate looked confused by her question. "Sure, why?"

"I don't know, you want to use the stage so badly. I just wanted to make sure."

"I didn't apologize for me."

"Then who'd you apologize for?"

Tate's eyes leveled with hers as if asking why she was pushing the envelope so far on the subject. "You." He dinged the bell on the counter in front of her and walked out the front door without another word.

Lyle mulled over his answer as she returned her attention to tagging clothes.

Why would he apologize for me and not Aariz?

Maybe he just cares about me more.

Does a heartfelt apology count as sincere if it was heartfelt to the wrong person?

Lyle's thoughts spun with the carousel as she continued to tag, each rotation contradicting the previous until she was so tangled up in her own head, the only thing she could unravel from Tate's visit was the crooked smile as he left.

CHAPTER EIGHT

Constructing a new stage proved much more difficult than renovating an old one, but Max enjoyed the challenge. Although they tried, Tate and Cameron were little help, while Max reveled in the mathematics behind it all. By Wednesday, he had mentally constructed and deconstructed three different frameworks, drawing big x's in his notebook through the sketches that failed in one way or another. He was limited in his designs due to their materials, which consisted of nails and screws scrounged from the dirt of a construction site and rotting wooden planks from a collapsed fence.

"Damn," he said, crossing out his fourth plan of the week. Cameron had gone home hours ago, leaving Tate to watch Max brainstorm.

"What's wrong with that one?"

"Don't have the supplies."

"Sure, we do." Tate motioned to their pile of junk in the corner of the lobby. "We can make it work." He put his hand on the page to stop Max from turning it.

"This will never work with that wood."

"But couldn't we just—"

"Tate." Max was getting annoyed now. "It won't work."

Tate shoved himself out of his squat and threw his hands in the air. "Why don't we just practice in the middle of Main Street then?" The only reason Max cared about the talent show was because of Tate, and the last thing he needed right now was a fifteen-year-old temper tantrum. "I'm going to get a slice." Tate motioned to the pizza place across the street. "Maybe they'll have some wood worthy of Your Highness's plans." Max rolled his eyes as Tate jerked open the door and stalked across the street.

"Well then," Lyle said from behind the counter. "That was exciting."

Max shrugged. "He's fine. Just not very—"

"Patient?"

"Yeah." Max understood what it felt like to lose a parent, but he wondered how long Tate's past could excuse his behavior. The lack of emotional control, the outbursts, the tunnel vision. They were both weighed down by the losses of their pasts, but Max was the only one who found a way to deal with it.

Or at least suppress it.

"What's he all worked up about?"

"I had to scrap another plan." Max pointed at the now crossed out scribbles on his notepad, and Lyle knelt beside him as she examined it.

"It looks like it would work to me. What's wrong with it?"

"Materials. We don't have the quality wood to support this framework like last time."

"Aariz does." Max gave Lyle a look, which she returned. "Seriously, he would love to help you."

"We don't have the money."

The night they met passed between them like an electric current: the bloodied shirt, the first aid kit, the wadded bills Tate dropped on the sidewalk. Although Lyle wasn't from his world, Max could tell she was trying hard to understand it. And for her own sake, he wished she wouldn't.

"I'm sure you can work something out," she said as she took the pen from his hand and drew a star in the upper corner of the page. She traced over it a couple times until it was too bold to ignore. "I think he's still in his workshop." Lyle's hand was gentle on his shoulder as she stood and returned to the counter, a ghost of a memory that was blurred at the edges but still whole enough to fill in all the places Max felt cracked.

The bell announced Tate as he fumbled through the front door with three slices of pizza, one in each hand, one balanced on the crook of his elbow. "They were about to close, but since they were going to throw out the leftovers anyway, they let me have them for free." Tate paused in front of Max, who was prepared to catch whichever plate took a tumble. "We good?"

Max nodded as he followed Tate to the counter. They had never stayed mad at each other for long, and what better peace offering than a free slice of pizza after a long day? Max inhaled the sweet aroma and realized how hungry he was, salivating as it filled his lungs.

"They only had two loaded pieces, so someone's stuck with cheese," Tate said. "And since I was a jerk, I'll bite the bullet." Lyle bit her lip and leaned against the counter as he set a loaded slice in front of her.

"I'll take it." Max removed the cheese from its balancing point. Tate gave no objection, too preoccupied with his own slice to notice Lyle tearing off and nibbling a piece of crust from her own. "Napkins?" Max asked.

"Right," Tate mumbled, mouth full of pizza. Max waited until Tate turned to his back pocket, subtle as he masked his movements with a stretch.

"Thanks," he said as Tate presented him with a crumpled napkin. "I'll be right back." Max took his slice with him as he headed across the lobby, Lyle listening as Tate started in on some marching band story. She didn't notice Max had switched their slices until she went to tear off another piece of crust. Her eyes shot to Max as she took a savory bite of plain cheese, and Max held his piece up in recognition before hurtling into Aariz's lobby, the darkness masking the smile he had attempted to conceal.

A dim ray of light from behind the counter lit Max's way as he maneuvered around the various carpentry items. He knocked on the wall of the doorway of the workshop, where Aariz was staining by lamplight what looked to be a sign. Max couldn't make out what it said, but it was longer than the workbench and hung off the sides.

"Max." Aariz sounded happy to see him as he ushered him in. Newspapers scattered the floor to catch the rogue drops of stain, and they crinkled under Max's feet as he entered. He approached the worktable, careful not to step on what he assumed to be a prayer rug. It was woven in beautiful shades of red and orange, and it was positioned not quite square against the wall. "We face Mecca when we pray," Aariz explained, Max nodding as his eyes bounced around the rest of the room.

"Wow. You've got a nice setup here."

Aariz let his eyes roam affectionately over the various pieces of equipment. "I am very proud of what I have built here, carpentry and business-wise."

"You do beautiful work." Max examined the intricate carvings on a finished nightstand to his left. It had that unique look to it, something that could only be done by someone who cared about their craft.

"You flatter me," Aariz said, using a dirty rag to wipe the stain off his hands. "What brings you back here?"

Max never asked for help, but in this little workshop tucked away, he felt as though his weakness could be kept secret from the outside world. "I've been trying to redesign the stage, and I have a plan that will work…" He trailed off, notebook dangling at his side.

"But?"

"We don't have the wood." Max thought a moment before correcting himself. "At least not wood that could support this structure."

"Do you mind?" Aariz motioned to the notebook, and Max handed it over before finishing his pizza in two swift bites. "Interesting," Aariz said, flipping through the pages. Max cracked his knuckles against his leg, waiting for the critiques. "I assume this is the plan you are referring to?" Aariz held up the page with the bold star.

Max nodded. "But all we have is some partly rotted fence wood."

"I see." Aariz looked at the plan again. "You're right; that definitely won't support this framework." He looked around the workshop before motioning for Max to follow him to a door on the back wall. Inside the closet was a storeroom of materials, different types of wood in various shapes and sizes leaning against the walls and stacked on the floor. It smelled of possibility and accomplishment, and Max paused a moment to let it fill his lungs. "Something like this would work great." Aariz motioned to a pile near the corner. Max nodded, lingering in the doorway before retreating to the workbench. Aariz followed him out, returning to his seat on the stool in front of the sign.

"I can't pay for that," Max confessed.

"Consider it a gift."

"It was a gift the first time." Max's voice was serious.

"Then consider it my way of repaying you for what happened."

Max clenched his fists, aggravated that Tate's outburst over the vandalism was still fresh in Aariz's mind. "You don't owe us anything. If anything, Tate owes you an apology."

"Actually," Aariz said. "He came by last weekend and apologized."

"Tate?" Max couldn't believe what he was hearing.

"Yes, Tate." Aariz chuckled before leaning forward and lowering his voice. "But between you and me, I think it was more for Lyle." Max rolled his eyes inwardly.

He doesn't even know what kind of pizza she likes.

"So," Aariz said, pulling Max from his thoughts. "How long are we going to go back and forth before you accept my materials?" He gestured toward the sign on the workbench. "Because this beauty needs more work."

Max was caught between needing the help and not wanting it. "I can't accept it for free."

Aariz thought about that for a moment. "I could use someone to clean up around here after closing, and I see Tate's been staying late anyway."

Max's mind ran through every possible scenario in which he could help Aariz and still beat his father home. But after turning the problem over in his head, no solution presented itself. "I'm sorry," he said, the words heavy. "My dad..." He trailed off, but he saw Aariz glance at his permanently pink eye and nod.

"Yes, of course." He didn't look sympathetic, and Max was grateful. Instead, Aariz looked pensive as he ran his hand along his beard. "Max, have you given any thought to what you want to be?"

"Be?"

"In life. What do you want to become?" The question made Max uncomfortable, and he shook his head as he silently examined his beat-up sneakers. Aariz let the silence hang for a moment before continuing. "Well, then let's start with this. What don't you want to be?" Those answers came quicker, flashing through Max's head like cars on a highway.

Too poor to afford any food except pizza rolls.

Too scared to go home every night.

A drunken failure.

A fighter that hurts other people to save himself.

Alone.

Finally, one solid answer danced into his head that seemed to encompass all that he was feeling. "Nothing." Max's answer was almost a whisper. "I don't want to be nothing."

Aariz held out Max's notebook, pointing to the starred page. "Let me be the first to tell you, someone who was nothing would never be able to design a plan like this."

Pride buzzed through Max's body, quickly replaced by embarrassment. "It's just a design."

"So was this sign," Aariz said, nodding toward his masterpiece in progress. "Are you in woodshop at school?"

Max nodded.

"What about mathematics?"

"Advanced pre-calc," Max muttered, wishing he sounded more modest.

"Have you ever thought about going to college?" At first, Max thought he was joking, but Aariz's features remained serious.

"Not really."

Aariz handed him the notebook. "That's how you can repay me for the materials."

"By going to college?" Max could barely afford the clothes on his back, let alone a college education.

"By considering it."

Max raised an eyebrow. "There's not much to consider."

"You know, that abandoned stage was supposed to be for open mic nights for a coffee shop before it went bankrupt, and Rawel and I bought the place." Aariz pointed to the design in Max's notebook. "Now look what it could be."

Max thought about his propensity for clenching his fists. "It won't change, though. It'll still be a stage."

"It doesn't have to change." Aariz nodded knowingly. "Just become what it was meant to be all along." He winked at Max as he returned to his stool. "Think about it, and I'll have the wood ready for you tomorrow."

"Thank you," Max managed. He felt disoriented, as if he were standing on a pile of rugs being ripped from beneath him. He turned to leave, reaching the edge of the lamplight before turning around. "I'm sorry about what Tate said."

Aariz sat up a little straighter, offering a smile that made Max feel like he was worth something. "Other people's actions do not define you." He picked up the stain and started working on the sign again. "Unless you let them." Max let his eyes linger on Aariz's masterpiece a beat longer before he stepped into the darkness of the lobby.

Aariz's words echoed in Max's head as he and Tate laid in the screen house that night. He stared into the darkness, thinking of all the things he wanted to be.

Someone with integrity.

A hard worker.
A good friend.
Successful.
Loved.

His mind chased away the possibility of sleep that his body was trying to catch as he thought. Could he actually go to college? He could get out of here, make something of himself. Become a carpenter, an architect. Someone worthy of the company of kind-hearted people like Lyle. Someone his mother would be proud to call her son.

Max rolled over, smirking as he pulled his pillow over his head to stop his thoughts from racing.

Aariz is already getting his money's worth.

. . .

Tate was still stewing two days later as he entered the chorus room. Every time he turned around, Aariz was giving them a hand-out. At least Max insisted he worked out a deal this time, so Tate had that to hang his hat on. "How's it going, big guy?" he asked, taking his seat next to Samson. Over time, it became clear he was more of a giant teddy bear than anything, and the two had bonded over their mutual failure at anything related to the piano. Samson's face was paler than usual, his eyes wide as he looked at Tate.

"Playing quiz," he hissed.

"This morning?" Tate asked. "Shit." Although they practiced daily, Tate spent at least half his time distracted by Lyle. Samson stared at the keys as if they were ready to attack as Tate began to wrestle with his headphones.

Lyle gave him a strange look as she walked in on the wake of the warning bell. "Doing okay there?" she asked as she sat down, Tate knocking his sheet music to the floor in the process of disentanglement.

"Just great."

"Playing quiz today," Samson grumbled again.

"It's not your entire grade, is it?" Lyle asked.

"Fifty percent of it."

Tate nodded. "If I fail this quiz, I'll fail the class." His hands found their way into his dark mass of hair. "No band without a passing grade." He glared into the black notes of the sheet music as the embarrassment rushed to his face.

Music ruining my chances at music. How ironic.

Lyle put a hand on his shoulder. "I've seen you practicing."

A flash of heat darted through Tate's stomach at the thought of her watching him. "But I still suck."

"You don't suck."

"Yeah?" Tate unplugged the headphones from the jack so she could hear as he attempted to play the assessment song, his fingers hitting every note but the ones he was trying to play. Lyle tried to hide it, but he saw her wince at least once. "What do you call that?"

"A work in progress." She was so kind, but he let himself slump deep into his chair anyway. There was no way he was going to pass this quiz.

Lyle stood so fast she almost knocked over her chair as she hastened to Ms. Godllub's desk. Tate couldn't make out what they were saying, but after about a minute of back and forth, Lyle returned to her seat.

Samson groaned as the final bell sounded. Lyle placed her sheet music up in preparation, but Tate knew it was only to make him feel better.

At least someone's going to pass.

"Class!" Ms. Godllub cawed from her desk. "Due to her lack of preparation, Lyle has requested I dumb down the playing quiz." Lyle kept her eyes down. "The quiz will be at the end of class, and it will be one hand only."

Tate snapped straight up in his seat as the entire class sighed in unison. He watched in awe as Lyle played the assessment song without pause or flaw on her keyboard, the volume low enough for only the two of them to hear. Her hands were like two doves kissing the ivory keys. "Lack of preparation?" he asked.

"Something like that." Her look was mischievous as she finished. "This is actually the first song I ever learned on the piano."

Tate grinned at her wit, then slumped at his own lack of preparation. "So now what?"

"Guys," Lyle said as she stood. All heads turned as if she were Ms. Godllub, who was engrossed with her computer, as usual. "If anyone wants help preparing for the quiz, I'll come around. Practice with headphones like you always do, and when I get to your keyboard, just unplug so I can hear you play, okay?" The class nodded in collective agreement, one organism dependent on Lyle for survival. Everyone dawned their headphones except Tate, who was still waiting for an answer. Lyle leaned in, her voice making the hairs on the back of his neck stand up. "Try starting with the right hand." And with that, she made her way to the other side of the classroom to help her first student.

"Right hand," Samson echoed, dropping his left into his lap. How had it never occurred to either of them to learn the song one hand at a time? It allowed Tate's brain to focus on hitting the correct notes without getting jumbled with the left hand, and after about five rounds, he was actually starting to sound decent.

By the time Lyle got to Samson, Tate had almost fully mastered the right-hand portion of the song. He could tell Samson was still having issues hitting multiple notes at once, and Tate slid one side of his headphones off his ear to eavesdrop on Lyle's corrections. "See how your hand is hitting all these notes at once?"

"I have big fingers." Samson sounded ashamed as Lyle repositioned his meaty hand with her small one. "See how your hand is lying flat? Hold it up like this and curve your fingers down, like you're holding a lacrosse ball while you play. Then the only thing hitting the keys will be your fingertips." Samson looked skeptical as he tried the song again, but he and Tate were both amazed to hear only one or two excess notes. "So much better!" Lyle said, leaving him with a big smile as he plugged in his headphones to continue.

Tate tugged his back into place as she approached and unplugged his headphone jack. "Save the best for last?" Tate let his headphones slide to a resting position around his neck.

"Something like that," Lyle said, motioning toward the sheet music. "Let's hear what you have."

"Honestly, I thought you'd start with me." Tate positioned his hand on the keyboard, careful to hold it like Lyle had instructed Samson, although every ounce of his being wanted to hold it wrong so she would take his hand in hers. "Since helping me is what you do now." Despite the nerves he felt playing in front of her, Tate was shocked when he played through the song without a mistake. He dropped his hands in his lap after hitting the last note, staring at the keys in awe, as if they had accepted him as one of their own.

"Time to quiz!" Ms. Godllub roared, rounding her desk with gusto.

"Only when you need it," Lyle whispered before pulling her chair back into place in front of her own keyboard. Tate watched out of the corner of his eye as Lyle played her quiz perfectly. He probably should have run his song through once more, but when she played, he was entranced. "The extra time really helped," Lyle said as Ms. Godllub marked her score on a clipboard.

"Next," she barked, and Tate jumped in spite of himself. Lyle stifled a giggle, and he shot her a sarcastic smile as he began to play. His hand moved across the keys with a confidence he didn't have twenty minutes ago. He stole a glance at Lyle near the end, her proud look worth the two-point deduction he got for missing the last note. "Not bad," Ms. Godllub mused, marking his score on her clipboard as she moved on to Samson. Lyle leaned back in her seat to steal a glance at his score.

"Ninety-eight," she mouthed, holding her hand down below the keyboard for a quiet low-five. Instead, Tate took her hand in his, caressing her cold fingers long enough for her cheeks to turn the faintest shade of pink. At The Carry Out, Tate could never tell if she was blushing or if it was just the heat from the dryers. But here, as they sat hand in hand in the middle of the classroom, there was no doubt.

"Thank you," he mouthed back, giving her hand a squeeze before letting it drop.

"I passed!" Samson said, grabbing Tate by the shoulders and shaking him forward and backward like his favorite ragdoll.

"Way to go, man." They both turned to Lyle. "We have a great teacher." She tried to hide her smile as she proceeded to the choral piano to practice. Tate heard the faintest melody of her accompaniment drift across the classroom, and he left his headphones draped around his neck to listen, trying his best not to stare until the bell rang.

Tate spent most of the evening following Max's instructions on the stage. He was so exhausted by the end, he only picked a couple chords while Lyle swept, and he was eager to spend some more time with her in class the next day. As always, she rode the warning bell into the room, but rather than taking her seat next to Tate for attendance, she made a beeline for the choral piano. After the final bell, Tate abandoned his keyboard and made his way to where Lyle was practicing. She looked more frustrated than usual, running her hands through the flyaway hairs of her braid and stopping several times mid-song to sigh in exasperation.

"Hey." Tate leaned his elbows against the back of the piano, but Lyle didn't look up.

"Hey."

"Sorry I couldn't stay last night. Max worked me into the ground." Again, she didn't look up. "Um, you okay?"

She smacked the sheet music with the back of her hand, bending it over the back of the music stand with a thwack. "I would be if this didn't sound like the worst thing ever."

Tate pulled the sheet music taut again, checking and confirming it was the same song he had listened to her play for weeks now. "This song? It sounds great."

"Not this part," Lyle huffed, flipping to a couple of measures marked up with pencil and highlighter. Tate noticed how cute her handwriting was, then kicked himself for categorizing anyone's handwriting as cute.

"Let me hear it."

Lyle shook her head. "I can't even play it. This one part"—she held up her hands, two parentheses indicating the starting and stopping point of her angst—"is ruining the whole song." Tate walked around the piano and slid onto the bench beside her, pressing his shoulder against hers to make room for himself.

"Please?" He pouted his lips the smallest bit, and Lyle rolled her eyes and slammed her hands down on the keys. She muddled through the troublesome couple of measures, her hands striking the notes like two cinderblocks attached to her wrists.

"Maybe you should hit it harder."

"You're so helpful."

"Seriously, you're playing like you have a deep hatred for those keys."

Lyle leaned her head against his shoulder. "Sometimes I do."

A blonde braided beauty sharing a piano bench with a Hispanic bad boy. Tate wondered if people would shun her, make the racist remarks they made to him and Max when no one else was listening. It was one thing to be seen with him at The Carry Out, but it was another to be seen by the entire student body. He didn't want that burden for her.

He pulled away, even though every ounce of his being objected. "One of my favorite parts of the day is hearing you play. If you quit, I'll melt into a puddle of angst."

Lyle smirked. "You're already a puddle of angst."

"Imagine what I'd be without your playing?" Tate counted her smile as progress, even if it didn't reach her eyes. "You really are good, you know." His hand cupped her knee beneath the piano. "Why are you so wigged out about this song?"

Lyle deflated, her entire body sinking a visible inch. "I don't want to be the reason the select chorus loses. They don't need live accompaniment to compete. They chose to, and if I mess up, everyone's going to hate me."

The sound of thudding keys without melodies filled the room like footsteps in the sand, each student walking on their own musical journey. "First of all, no one could ever hate you." Tate stared into her eyes for a moment for emphasis. And because he couldn't bring himself to look away. "Second of all, I've watched you play this entire song from memory, minus this part, without messing up once."

Lyle gave him the side-eye, adjusting the straps on her tank top. "Oh, have you?"

"You're the only one who plays without headphones," he said, trying to swallow the foot he just put in his mouth. "The point is, you'll get there."

"How?"

Tate rounded the piano, leaning on his elbows until his army green eyes were pierced by her deep blue ones and flashing her a grin. "Try starting with the right hand."

. . .

The dismissal bell sounded, and Cameron made his way to the auditorium. The bee club voted on extra practice time to keep their qualifiers sharp, but it was nothing but a revenge scheme for Wilson. Cameron knew Bruce and Brian did most of the dirty work when it came to vandalizing the stage, but there was no doubt Wilson had been the one to spray the message. He always found a way to get the last word. Cameron teetered on the fence between standing up for his new friends and pleasing his old ones, his footholds shrinking by the minute.

He was in no hurry to get where he was going, the house lights dimly lit in a dreamlike haze by the time he arrived. The stage lights were in full force, buzzing with the effort as they illuminated the spell-off that was about to take place. Wilson, Bruce, and Brian slouched in the front row, knees sprawled wide enough to leave a seat between. "Took you long enough," Wilson said.

"You didn't have to wait," Cameron said.

"But we wanted to."

Cameron gave a contrite smile. "Congratulations on advancing, Brian." Although the two didn't talk much, this was the first time Brian made it past the qualifier, and Cameron felt the need to acknowledge it.

Wilson certainly won't.

"Thanks." Brian stole a glance at Wilson for reassurance, whose attention was still focused on Cameron. His powder pink dress shirt was unbuttoned one too low, revealing a measly tuft of chest hair unworthy of display.

Lyle would hate that.

The thought of Lyle stiffened Cameron's body in a defiance he wasn't used to. "You shouldn't have done it."

Wilson's voice sounded like ink spilling across a desktop. "Done what?" Cameron had avoided him since the qualifier, and he had to take a deep breath to keep himself from deflating.

"They're my friends."

"I was under the impression we were your friends." The Cheshire cat smile on Wilson's face made Cameron uneasy.

"You are—"

"Then as your friend," Wilson interrupted, "I think you owe me for your little stunt during the qualifier. Don't you agree?" The possibilities of what it would take for Wilson to forgive him scared Cameron, and he hated himself as he nodded in agreement. "Good," Wilson said. "I'll let you know when I think of something."

A clap on the back sent Cameron stumbling toward the stage, the rest of the club assuming their positions as spectators. Although Brian also qualified, he took his seat behind the table to lead the spell-off. That left Cameron alone with Wilson onstage, where he proceeded to spell every single word wrong. With each misspelling, he clawed his way back into Wilson's good graces, and as the competition continued, Cameron wondered if last week's victory had been the right decision after all. Was being the best really worth being the outcast? As Cameron continued to rearrange his spellings like an anagram machine, he wasn't so sure.

Max and Tate were almost finished with the stage by the time Cameron got there. Two-thirds of the floorboards were hammered into the frame, and Max was working on the final third. "Hey," Cameron called over the hammering. Lyle gave him a wave from the counter.

"Hey, Cam," Max said, wiping a couple beads of sweat from his brow as he stood. He pulled his t-shirt away from himself in an attempt to fan his sweating torso. "How was practice?" Cameron felt like a double agent, shrugging as he tossed his backpack next to the stage. "Any trouble?"

"Nope." Cameron knew he didn't believe him, but Max let him change the subject anyway. "Where's Tate?"

"He and some guy from his piano class are bringing over the drum set." Max took a sip of water before pouring the rest of the bottle over his head, closing his eyes as it soaked his white t-shirt. Cameron thought he saw Lyle watching from the corner of his eye, but she was gone when he turned to look.

"It looks exquisite," Cameron said, motioning to the stage beneath them.

"Just a few more boards. Hand me the nails, would you?"

Cameron gathered a handful and took a seat next to Max. They were quiet for a while, the rhythm of the hammering soothing to Cameron. For the first time all day, he felt like he could relax, and he was almost disappointed when Max broke the silence. "You ever think about what comes after this?"

Cameron surveyed the almost completed stage, unsure why Max was asking him for renovation advice. "We practice?"

"No." Max continued to hammer between sentences. "After all of this. After high school."

Cameron thought about it for a minute. "College, I suppose."

"What would you go for?"

"Probably something in the sciences. My parents would love that."

Max glanced at him out of the corner of his eye. "You hate science."

Cameron had been pushed and pulled by so many people throughout his life, he never stopped to think about what he actually wanted. "Advertising, maybe?"

"You certainly have the vocabulary for it."

"What about you?"

Max hesitated, hovering the hammer above a poised nail. "I don't know." His hand hovered there for what felt like an eternity before he snapped out of his reverie and pounded the nail into place. "I'm not really the college type."

"Are you jesting?" Cameron saw Max smile the smallest bit at his choice of words. He was the first friend Cameron ever had that didn't make fun of the way he talked. "You're the best math student in our grade. And probably the school. How is that not the college type?"

Max looked himself up and down, and Cameron got the message. People made assumptions when they looked at Max. Unfortunately, none of those assumptions included college graduate. Or mathematician. Or musician. Or friend.

There was a long pause before Max broke the silence. "I could never afford it, anyway."

"What about your parents?" He watched every muscle in Max's body tense up as he hammered a little harder.

"What about them?"

Cameron tried to backtrack from the line he just crossed. "Would you go if you could?"

"I'll never be able to afford it, Cam." There was a longing in Max's tone, just faint enough to line his sentence without coloring it hopeful.

"But if you could," Cameron pressed. "Would you?"

Max sat on his heels, exhaling as the hammer dangled at his side. There was something different about him that Cameron couldn't place, and he watched as Max's expression morphed into something almost hopeful. "Yeah, maybe." But as quickly as the hope had filled him, it drained twice as fast, seeping from his body until the weight of reality settled itself firmly on his shoulders. "That'll be the day," he muttered, more to himself than to Cameron.

"If anyone can find a way, it's you."

"Yeah." Max stared at the final nail for almost a full minute before pounding it into the wood with one swift hit. He seemed lost in thought, and Cameron wanted to be lost with him. He wanted to be the kind of friend Max could count on, confide in. But then again, did Judas deserve that kind of friendship? The stage felt like hot coals beneath him, only he wasn't the one getting burned. He was the one burning everyone else.

The crash of a cymbal tore them from their thoughts as it ricocheted off the front door. "A little help?" Tate called, setting it in the lobby before disappearing out the door with a broad-shouldered boy that looked more like an uncle than a student.

Cameron scampered over, reaching for everything but grabbing nothing as Max, Tate, and the other boy lugged in the rest of the drum set.

. . .

The amps buzzed behind Max as he sat behind his assembled drum set, begging to be filled with sound. Tate's buddy didn't stick around, but it was helpful to add another set of muscles to the effort. Customers filtered in and out during setup, but no one remained as Tate and Cameron tuned their guitars onstage in front of him. Even with the empty lobby, Max felt bad playing here. They were loud enough individually, and Max worried how loud they would be combined.

Lyle didn't seem concerned as Max stole a glance. Her hip jutted out to one side as she thumbed through a wad of bills from the register. Her lips moved almost imperceptibly with her hands, keeping count before punching the number into a calculator and moving to the next wad.

"Check. Check." Max bobbled the stick he was spinning as Tate's voice boomed from the speakers, quick to divert his attention straight ahead. "Ready, CamKing?"

Cameron nodded, looking like a model buck naked at a fashion show. He had never performed with his guitar before, let alone practiced in front of a pretty girl. Tate's voice echoed through the room as he chose their first song, and Max hit his sticks together four times to count them in. He thought he saw Tate wink at Lyle before belting out the opening verse.

He expected their first rehearsal to be a train wreck, and Max was genuinely surprised by how good they sounded. He didn't dare another glance at Lyle, so instead, Max tried to imagine watching them from her perspective. Tate looked fragile, his entire body leaning into the music as if it were carrying him through life. Although his hands caressed the frets like an old friend, his voice carried a hint of angst as he sang away every emotion he didn't know how to feel.

Cameron was a contrasting combination of excitement and rebellion. Max did not peg him as the rebellious type, but his fingers flew around his guitar at hyperspeed, his spiked hair a bleached blur as his head banged to the beat. Although there was a newfound edge about him, his goofy grin remained, as if he had waited his entire life for this release.

Lastly, Max turned his attention inward, trying to picture himself from Lyle's big blue eyes. Small, bruised, and brooding was what she saw, but he was tired of being that way, tired of feeling that way. Instead, Max tried to focus on what else he felt. He hit the drums harder, trying to drown out the voices in his head telling him he was nothing more than a fighter.

But those voices weren't Lyle's, and his arms got goosebumps as her soft voice swirled through his mind, telling him he was not a product of his circumstances, telling him she believed in him.

Then Max heard his own voice as a plan formulated in his head, telling him there was a way, telling him he had to become someone he didn't like to become someone he did. He felt the tension of that thought stretching him like taffy until his moral compass was hanging on by a thread.

Max squeezed his eyes shut until the only voice he could hear was Tate's belting into the microphone. And he hit the drums. He hit them over and over, the veins in his arms pulsing with the energy of the song. It buzzed between the three of them, an electric current that came from being a part of something, as the song forged on. They hit the final note in unison, careful not to hold it out for fear of ruining the moment. The three breathed heavily as they exchanged the same look.

We actually have a shot at winning.

A single pair of clapping hands broke the silence, the boys turning to Lyle in thanks. Although her expression was proud, her hands remained occupied counting bills, the clap continuing to echo until Aariz emerged from behind the counter of his lobby. "If I knew you boys were that good, I would have asked you to play two fundraisers." He continued to clap as he meandered to the front of the stage, positioning himself front and center like a teenage groupie. Cameron gave him a geeky wave, his rebellious streak dissipating by the minute. Tate's fragility was once again masked with gruffness, giving Aariz nothing but a small nod of recognition.

Max tried his best to avoid eye contact, but he could feel Aariz's eyes on him across the stage. When they did lock eyes, it felt as though Aariz was reading his mind, and Max tried to push his plan out of his thoughts. There was no judgment in his eyes, just a pained understanding as he mentally prepared himself for what Max was planning to do. Aariz let out one final clap before disappearing into his workshop, Max staring after him as Tate and Cameron began to pack up.

"You okay?" Max hadn't noticed Lyle approaching the stage, and her voice startled him from his reverie. She looked concerned, seeing right through his tough façade, but Max ignored her as he hopped off the stage and flipped the speakers off.

"That," Tate said, plopping himself down on the stage so his legs dangled between them, "was a damn good first rehearsal." Max nodded, putting some proximity between himself and Tate's legs.

"You guys are great." Lyle's excitement was genuine, but her concern for Max was still tucked into the corners of her eyes.

Cameron joined them, but his movements were hesitant, as if he wasn't sure whether or not he belonged in their circle. "Good playing, Cam." Max put his hand out for a low-five, forcing Cameron to join them. Tate patted Cameron on the shoulder once as he stepped forward.

"Who knew the spelling bee champ had a punk side?"

Cameron turned his usual shade of red, staring down at his shoes. "You ready?" Max asked him, sticking his drumsticks in his back pocket as he leaned toward the door. Cameron nodded, bumbling around as he collected his backpack.

"Just one song?" Lyle asked.

"No need to ruin a good thing," Tate said, flashing her a grin. "See you at home," he called across the lobby as Max held the door for Cameron. Max nodded, feeling Lyle's eyes on him as he grabbed their skateboards and exited the lobby. But he didn't look back.

If Max looked at her, he'd lose his spine, and he needed it twice over for what he was planning to do. Just thinking of the concerned shades of grey swirling in the blues of her eyes made him question his plan, but as he rode home with Cameron, he was reassured. The houses grew larger with each passing block, and Max vowed that he was not going to spend his entire life in a screen house, nursing his wounds.

Just tonight.

By the time Max got to the barn, darkness had more than set in. The fancy vehicles crammed into the parking lot indicated he made the right decision to wait. Although many things changed over the years, one thing remained certain.

The scum bags still come out at night.

It was much easier to keep a low profile without Tate trembling with anxiety. Besides that, his scar had always tricked people into thinking he was a hardcore fighter when in actuality, Tate had just been in the wrong place at the wrong time. The last time he came here may have been for Tate, but this time, Max was here for himself.

He slid through a side door hidden behind some old barrels, emerging into the crowd of ruffians with his hands in his pockets and his head down. The place was packed, making the divide even more noticeable. Max's end looked the same: alcohol-stained shirts and the stench of bloody sweat that sat in your nostrils for days. All four stalls were filled, groups of men of various sizes and shapes massed together to watch boys lose the light in their eyes.

Max kept moving until he reached the divide, again surprised by its emptiness. Although there was a set of boys fighting in each of the renovated stalls, there were no bystanders, no cheering and jeering. He hugged the wall as he stepped into unknown territory, examining the fights. The boys on this side had no cuts or bruises on their faces, no blood in the hay at their feet. They all wore shirts with designer fitness logos, and their hair looked styled by someone who actually cared what it looked like.

A boy in the first stall, the one farthest from Max, went down like a ragdoll, a buzzer sounding from the hayloft to end the fight. Max inched from beneath the loft as he followed the sound, surprised to find every seat above him filled. Even more surprising than the attendance was the clientele. It was all shiny dress shoes and expensive suits, clean-shaven men that still looked dirty to Max. Their shirts and pants were crisply pressed, as if on their way to the ballet.

I wonder how many of them send their dry-cleaning to The Carry Out.

Even in his thoughts, someone as kind as Lyle didn't belong in a place like this, and Max rushed to push her out of his head. The victor appeared unharmed as he strode out of the first stall, his large stature suggesting football as a pastime. He ascended the spiral staircase to the loft, where he collected his winnings one by one from the outstretched hands. After totaling his winnings, a man to the side placed his total on what looked like a leaderboard next to a name Max couldn't make out. Doing the math in his head, it looked to Max as though each onlooker bet their desired amount twice to two separate pools of money. One pool went to the winner, the other divided into the still outstretched hands of the lucky few that chose the winning fighter.

The big guy took a bow before shoving the money in a gym bag and descending the staircase. His feet were bare, but his footsteps clanked with each step as if he wore work boots. With his facial stubble and defined broad shoulders, he resembled a college football player, and by the looks of the loser wincing in the corner, he fought like one too. He returned to the first stall, arms folded as he waited for his next victim. Max couldn't believe his eyes, the scoreboard above totaling in real-time as the men began to place their bets.

$300

$550

$825

$1200

$1475

$2500

Damn, they've got deep pockets.

Max retreated beneath the hayloft as the number continued to increase, hovering where the renovated stalls met the ratty ones so he could watch the high roller from a distance. A taller boy entered the stall, closing the gate behind him. His persistent acne advertised him as a high schooler, but still older than Max, maybe a senior. His build was more basketball than football, but nevertheless, he had a threatening stride. A buzzer sounded, and the reigning champion attacked, taking the high schooler to the ground in one tackle. From there, he positioned himself on top, taking shots at the guy's ribs, stomach, and chest. The high schooler landed a couple knees to the beast's abdomen, giving him the perfect opening to land a hook on the jaw.

But he didn't take it. Instead, he tried to roll to the dominant position, only to be slammed back down by his shoulder blades and finished off with a swift kick to the groin. Max couldn't believe his eyes.

"'Ey, Max!" The collector from the old part of the barn approached with the same peg leg gate he had years ago, his grin exposing two fewer teeth than the last time Max saw him. "I thought I saw you in here the other day. Couldn't stay away, huh?" Max nodded as imperceptibly as possible, trying to trick himself into thinking he hadn't. "Changed since you last been here, huh?"

"Are there still step-up fights?"

"Yeah, we got all that over here," the collector said, trying to usher Max back into the life he once lived.

"What about them?" Max jutted his chin toward the renovated side of the barn.

"Come show these young kids how a legend fights." The man tried to usher Max back to his old life, but Max remained still and expressionless until the collector gave in. "Some suit came in last year and fancied it up. Couldn't keep us from hanging around, though, so he left our side as is." He spat into the dirt at their feet. "For part of the profits, of course."

"They do step-ups?"

The collector hesitated. "Yeah, but rules are different over there."

"So are the bets."

"Big bets for big boys."

Max rolled his eyes. "Different how?"

"Betting system is all different. Too complicated if you ask me. Challengers get harder as the stall numbers get smaller. Shirts required. No shoes. No headshots."

"No headshots?" Over half the punches Max had taken were headshots.

"Nope. Too obvious. Wouldn't want the world to know their nasty little habit."

Max pondered that for a moment, watching the football player from the first stall collect his money yet again. "What's up with him?"

"QB? College football star."

"Then what's he doing here?" Max would give anything to trade this shithole for college.

"Daddy owns the barn." A look of contempt worked across the collector's face as he jabbed a finger into Max's side. "Look, you been out of the game a long time. Word of advice? Stay away from QB. Shady shit goes on over there."

Max wondered what could possibly be considered shady to a collector with bloody bills weighing down his pockets. The familiar cowbell sounded to their left, and the collector gave Max a gummy grin before limping back to the dilapidated side of the barn. Max stood neutral for a moment, one foot on either side of the barn. He could do this the old-fashioned way, twenty bucks at a time, trying to hide his bruised face from Tate. Or he could go to this new side, where the money flowed from deep pockets, and no one would ever see a bruise.

Tate never has to know.

Max slipped off his torn sneakers and entered the newly renovated fourth stall before he could change his mind.

It was weird fighting without headshots. Twice he had to stop his fist in midair when the kid left himself exposed. Max's fighter stance had always held his hands by his jawline, but after a few hard punches to the ribs, he shifted to protect his vital organs. The kid tried to take him to the ground with a leg sweep, but Max was able to catch his foot with his own, knocking him off-balance before landing a hard punch to the stomach. The air audibly whooshed from the kid's lungs as he fell to the ground, gasping for air.

Max counted ten seconds, but the buzzer didn't sound until twelve. He didn't know what the protocol was over here, so he exited and did what he saw QB do. He clanked up the spiral staircase, careful to be surefooted but not memorable. The betting men looked at him like a sewer rat loose in their house, but they paid up nevertheless. Max walked down the line, his eyes on the money being transferred from manicured hands to his grimy ones. He could feel his blood pressure rising as he mentally calculated the sum of his winnings exchange by exchange.

Holy shit.

"Total?" asked the man next to the leaderboard, who looked more like a car salesman than a high roller.

"Eight hundred dollars." Max could hardly believe his answer. It would have taken him dozens and dozens of fights to make that kind of money on the other side of the barn.

The car salesman raised his eyebrows before writing the amount next to a blank space. "And your name?"

"Max."

"Well, Max, not bad for a walk-on."

And that was when it clicked. Max's reputation hadn't crossed the status line. These people bet so much because they thought Max was going to lose. No one knew who he was or how he fought. He wasn't sure if that was good or bad, but as Max stuffed the wad in his pocket and returned to the floor of the barn, he was leaning toward the former. He walked back into the fourth stall to face off against a new opponent.

The onlookers were more cautious the second time around, betting conservatively to see if Max's first win was a fluke. A couple of back and forths to the ribs and a buzzer later, Max collected another two hundred dollars, his reputation starting to form around him. The glow got brighter with each win until the onlookers couldn't help but pay attention. Max wasn't one for showboating, but he needed to keep their attention. So he skipped the third stall completely and entered the second stall to take on the basketball player that lost to QB.

And he immediately regretted it.

. . .

"One song's not much of a rehearsal," Lyle repeated as the door swung behind Max and Cameron.

Tate shrugged. "More of a sound check, really. Now that we finally have somewhere to practice." Lyle locked the door and turned the signs, eyeing Tate as he sat with his guitar. His left foot dangled off the stage as he finger-picked a few notes. They sounded great as a band, but Lyle liked it best when Tate played quiet and solo. "Hey, did anyone around here turn in a guitar pick?" He patted his empty pockets and shrugged. "Lost mine."

"How did you play without a pick?" Although Lyle already counted the money, she was so entranced by the band that she felt the need to thumb through the last stack again.

Tate held out his left thumb to reveal a single grown out nail. His grin was lazier than usual but still there, and Lyle lost count of the money. She flushed, averting her eyes to avoid getting lost in his. "You know," he said. "I might have one more song in me." He motioned her across the lobby, and Lyle abandoned the stack of bills after losing count for the third time. She let her legs dangle off the stage in rhythm as he began to strum, stealing a glance at him every now and then. There was a hint of sorrow tucked away in his expression, as if it had been there long enough for him to be used to it. His voice was softer now, more velvet than metal. It became rawer with each verse, his layers peeling back like an onion. Lyle inched close enough to feel his shoulders sag, rising and falling with the words like a sob trapped in a song. She wasn't sure where he was, but as he closed his eyes, his mind was not in the lobby with her. Tate swallowed to compose himself before singing the final line, but his voice cracked anyway.

The final strum was slow, each individual string sounding off apart from one another until they faded into silence as one. Lyle felt as though she was intruding on a personal moment he didn't want to share, so she waited until he set his guitar aside and rested back on his elbows. "How's the chorus song?"

She mimicked his motions, leaning back until her head rested against the smooth wood of the stage floor. "It's okay. How's the assessment song?"

"Definitely not as good."

She ran her fingers along her knee, tapping the complicated sequence she had been practicing. "That one part's still choppy, but it's better."

"Too bad you can't practice here. You'd have it nailed in a night."

Lyle shifted, her eyes examining the exposed ductwork of the ceiling. "Yeah, in all my spare time."

Tate lowered himself down the rest of the way, rolling his head to face hers. "Do you ever have time for yourself?"

"When I do, you interrupt it with first aid or renovations."

Tate rolled his eyes. "Seriously."

Lyle thought about it for a minute. "I guess, right now."

"And you're spending it staring at the ceiling with me?"

A smile played at the edges of her lips as their eyes locked in that intense way Lyle was still trying to get used to. "I'm just here for the music." Tate knew she was joking, but she sensed he also knew a small part of her wasn't. Despite Lyle's initial wariness of their music, she was getting swept away by it as she had all those years before.

Lyle sat abruptly, sliding off the stage and grabbing the broom from the closet. Tate propped himself up on his elbows and watched her for a moment before returning his guitar behind the counter for safekeeping. "Thank you."

"For what?"

Tate gestured around vaguely. "This. All this." Lyle nodded as she swept a couple of loose coins from under the lobby bench. "From Max and Cameron too. We are all very..." Tate paused, his eyes shifting around in search of the right word. "...lucky." Lyle offered him a shy smile as she gathered the coins and stuck them in her back pocket. Although they felt heavy, they did not compare to the weight of Tate's guitar pick tucked into her other back pocket.

"Well…" Tate rocked from his toes to his heels. "I should probably get back."

"Will you be here tomorrow?" Lyle surprised herself with the question as Tate followed her past the carousel to the back door.

He shook his head. "Can't jailbreak CamKing on the weekends."

"See you Monday, then." The space was cramped, and Lyle had to reach around Tate to unlock the backdoor. His arms wrapped around her before she had a moment to think, pulling her into a hug long enough to surpass friendship and short enough to avoid something more. He wasn't bulky, but Lyle felt the muscles of his arms caress the small of her back. She surprised herself by leaning into him, her hair brushing against his lips until she pulled away.

"See you Monday," he murmured, dragging his eyes away from hers before disappearing into the night.

After two more attempts, Lyle managed to close out the register before heading to the back. She could still feel the way his lips pursed against her hairline, not quite a kiss but not quite something else either. Although it was just a hug, the energy passed between them felt like something more, as if they knew the other was struggling with something and needed a way to hold each other together.

Lyle clicked the lobby lights off and was about to head upstairs when she heard the tapping. She figured it was Aariz and some new tool of his, so she ignored it. Two steps up the stairs to her apartment, it came again, too inconsistent and faint to be a machine. Lyle glanced at the clock, ruling Aariz out completely when she saw it was after midnight. She descended the steps again, checking the carousel motor, then the steam press before spinning in a complete circle. The third time the tapping came, Lyle was able to follow it to the back door. Tate had been gone for over thirty minutes, but her stomach knotted anyway as she opened the door. "Got one more song in y—?" Lyle stopped mid-sentence as Max's face emerged from the shadows.

"Hey." He was slumped against the brick wall of the alley, his knuckles poised for another knock. He let them fall to his side as he shoved himself to a stand. "Can I...come in?"

Lyle had to blink twice to make sure she wasn't seeing things. "Of course." She held the door open as Max hobbled in. He wasn't limping per se, but his breath was shallow as if each inhale pained him. Lyle let the door click shut behind him, Max folding and unfolding his arms in an attempt to get comfortable. "At least you're not bloody this time," she joked as she switched the back lights on.

Max smirked, glancing down as he tugged up the bottom of his t-shirt with one hand. "How about bruised?"

Lyle's jaw dropped open. What were supposed to be uniform ribs were swollen into uneven bruised lumps the size of fists. Crimson colored veins twisted in and around the bruises, flushing them in deep, painful shades of plum and navy. "Oh, my God, Max."

"It's not as bad as it looks." He let his shirt fall back into place but winced as Lyle pulled it up again.

"You need to sit down." She spun around, looking for a place for Max to sit. There wasn't much back there besides equipment, and they were usually too busy to sit down anyway. He couldn't lift himself up onto the washers, nor could he lower himself onto a crate. Max stumbled to get out of her way, grabbing a hanging plastic garment bag to catch himself. It slid a couple inches under his weight, revealing a flash of deep black within the carousel.

The piano.

"Here." Lyle pushed the clothes aside, revealing her beautiful piano she had tried so hard to forget. Despite its hiatus, the image of the last person who sat on that stool remained fresh in her mind like a newly developed photograph. Lyle pulled the bench from under the piano and motioned Max over before she could change her mind.

"I didn't know you had a piano back here." He grimaced as he lowered himself onto the bench.

"What happened?"

"I just needed somewhere to catch my breath."

"You can't go home?"

Max rolled his eyes. "Dad isn't passed out yet." Lyle's gaze flicked to his permanently bloodshot right eye. "Plus, I have to wait until Tate's asleep." His voice lowered like a child admitting to breaking the vase. "I promised him I wouldn't do this anymore."

"What about your skateboarding accident?"

Max noted her emphasis on the last two words, too tired to keep up the story of the bloody nose. "One-time exception."

Lyle raised an eyebrow as he grabbed his side in pain. "Apparently not."

His eyes snapped up defensively. "He'd be worried sick if he knew I was back in the stalls."

"Then why are you?"

"Money."

"I thought you already entered."

"We did." Max ran his finger along a loose seam of the bench. "This is for something else."

Lyle rolled her eyes. "What could possibly be worth all this?"

"College." Max bit his lip as soon as the word left his mouth. Lyle moved to sit beside him but couldn't bring herself to do it. For the first time since she met him, Max looked scared as he looked up at her. "I can't become my father."

"My dad's been dead for years." Lyle didn't know why she said it, and she wished she hadn't.

"Damn. Sorry." A pained understanding rippled across Max's face. "My mom left when I was eight. No note. No goodbye. Just… disappeared." There was a reverence in his voice that didn't match the sadness in his eyes.

"Sometimes I wish my mom would disappear," Lyle muttered. Max took her hand and pulled her onto the bench beside him. She wanted to fight it, but there was a safety in his rough hand around her gentle one.

"Maybe you can hide her in the carousel, too."

Lyle laughed in spite of herself, Max pressing his side as he joined in to keep her smiling. Lyle felt instant guilt for making this about her when he clearly needed her support, so she retraced her thoughts to earlier in the evening. "I knew you looked off tonight."

Max nodded. "I saw you studying me."

Lyle flushed the smallest bit, thinking back to the pizza slices. *He doesn't miss much.*

"Where do you even do this?" she asked, motioning to his bruised body.

"Some shithole upstate."

Lyle shifted on the bench until she was perched on the edge, not fully committing to being on or off. "There has to be another way."

"Sure." The sarcasm dripped from Max's voice. "I could work construction downtown until my body's too broken to do anything else."

"As opposed to the awesome state your body's in now."

He gave her a look but said nothing. Although she wanted him to feel supported, Lyle felt obligated as his friend to speak up. "I really think you should find another way. I can help you—"

"Look," he interrupted. "I appreciate it." His soft brown eyes cradled her as he laid his hand over hers. "More than you know. But I made a thousand dollars tonight. One night, and I could already pay for the marching trip."

A lightbulb went off in Lyle's head. "So that's why you can't tell Tate."

"He's my best friend. I'd do anything for him. I really would." Max sounded adamant, as if he needed her to understand his reasoning in order to accept it himself. "But winning the talent show is his chance at living out his dream." He ran the palms of his free hand along his knee like a guilty man wiping away evidence. "This is my only chance at living mine."

Lyle sandwiched his hand between hers. "I see how you look out for him. And Cameron."

A sadness filled his eyes that broke her heart. "I try so hard…" Tears welled in his eyes as his voice trailed off, even though he fought to blink them back. "…But who's looking out for me?"

Lyle let herself settle back onto the bench, exhaling her own worries to make room for his. She put a reassuring arm around his shoulder, his muscles relaxing under her touch. "I am."

The bags of extravagant ball gowns and crisply pressed suits crinkled around them like a gossiping crowd. "Then who's looking out for you?"

Lyle thought about all the prison visits she hid from her grandfather. About all the hours she worked to keep the business afloat. About all the lonely nights she spent trying to fill a void that could never be filled. About the piano, tucked away in the carousel with the feelings she wanted to forget.

She thought about how often she wanted to scream, or cry, or even laugh, but didn't because she didn't want to burden someone else.

That's a good question.

CHAPTER NINE

"Where'd you end up last night?"

It was a casual question, but it set Max on edge as he walked into homeroom. The last thing he wanted to do was lie to Tate, but he wanted to go to college, and he wasn't man enough to admit he put his own dream before Tate's. He was careful not to grimace as he lowered himself into his seat.

"I stayed to quiz Cameron."

"At his house?" Tate feigned shock. "How were the inner workings of the elite?"

Max thought about the new side of the barn. "Not as different as you'd think."

Tate smirked. "Liar." A pang of guilt tore through Max's bruised ribs.

You have no idea.

"He probably needs my help all week," Max said, digging his hole of deception. "With the regional bee coming up."

"And your father?"

Max shrugged. "He has to sleep sometime, right?"

Tate looked as drained as Max felt. "Can't you just quiz him at The Carry Out?"

"And cut into practice time?" Max asked, playing shamefully to the one thing he knew Tate cherished most.

"No one else can help him?"

After all the late nights Tate spent with Lyle, Max didn't think he had room to talk. "We're not all as popular as you."

"Salutations," Cameron interrupted as he sat down.

Tate gave him a nod as the teacher took attendance. "You look more rested than your midnight oil companion here."

"Thanks…" Cameron looked at Max, confused.

"Spelling bee prep never sleeps," Max jumped in. "We're still on for tonight, right?"

"Yeah…" Cameron's eyes begged for the conversation to end before he said something to ruin it.

"Jeez." Tate spun a pen around his left hand. "How much spelling practice do you need?"

"A helluva lot if he plans on beating Wilson." Bruce's voice entered the room before he did, followed by Wilson.

"Again," Max said. Contempt flashed across Wilson's face, quickly replaced with his slimy smile.

"How goes the talent show prep?" Wilson's voice was like skates cutting into fresh ice.

"Couldn't be better." Tate fixed a glare directly between Wilson's eyes.

"I'm so glad you came up with the entry fee money." Wilson turned his attention directly to Max. "Maybe now you have a fighting chance." Tate shot Max a look, but Max remained stoic, unwavering as he held Wilson's stare.

"Too bad Cammy's parents couldn't pitch in," Bruce chided. "I'm sure they would have helped us." Cameron's shame was almost instantaneous; they all knew Bruce was right.

"At least we're performing," Tate said. "Let me guess. You're judging?"

"Sadly, our principal insisted on three neutral judges made up of teachers and the student body." Wilson showed no signs of defeat, but he puffed his chest out a little too far. "The student body that almost unanimously voted me class president."

"Almost." Tate's glare darkened as the bell broke up the lovefest of tension.

"Later," Bruce snarled. Tate's eyes followed him and Wilson out the door before speaking again.

"Great. What are the odds of those judges being neutral?"

"They could be." For once, Cameron sounded confident. "He seemed pretty perturbed about it." If Max trusted anyone to read Wilson's emotions, it was Cameron.

"Well, that's one point in our corner," Tate shrugged, his entire demeanor shifting as he bounced out the door. "See you in band."

I'd be happy too if I was heading to class with Lyle.

"Thanks for having my back," Max said as he and Cameron headed down the hallway.

"Anytime."

"Cammy!" Wilson caught them just outside the classroom door. "I almost forgot. Thursday night, my place."

Cameron looked panicked stricken. "I have practice."

"Then after." Wilson stared him down enough to send Cameron stumbling back, knocking the corner of Max's textbook into his ribs. Max tried to swallow his gasp, repositioning the textbook as the pain wound through his abdomen. His calculator clattered to the floor, as did his notebook.

"All right there, Max?" Wilson's voice was the last thing Max wanted to hear right now.

"All set." He winced as he squatted down to grab the notebook.

"Here." Wilson scooped up his calculator and held it out. "Pre-calc can really pack a punch." The comment hit Max like another blow, and he snatched the calculator as he pushed past Wilson into the classroom.

"You okay?" Cameron whispered as they took their seats in the back. "Don't worry about Thursday night. I'll still cover for you with Tate."

"Thanks." Max's mind was still buzzing from Wilson's comment.

"Where are you actually going, anyway?"

For a split second, Max wanted to tell him. But with Wilson's threat looming, he couldn't bring himself to burden Cameron with it. Max opened his notebook as the final bell rang. "Investing in my education."

. . .

As the day went on, possibilities for his Thursday rendezvous with Wilson piled up in Cameron's mind, each more horrifying than the last. "What was with Wilson before pre-calc?" Max asked when they got to The Carry Out.

"It was uncharacteristic of him to help you with your stuff," Cameron said, deflecting the attention onto Max.

"Thursday night?"

"Oh, just a bee club thing." The only time Cameron lost his vocabulary was when he lied, and he saw the skepticism on Max's face as easily as Max saw the deceit on his.

"If you need me to go somewhere with you—"

"No!" Cameron interjected, Max's eyebrows raising in suspicion. "You already have plans. To invest in your education."

"You don't owe him for winning, you know."

"Hey, Cam?" Lyle's voiced drifted across the lobby like an answered prayer saving Cameron from the conversation. His steps were quick and awkward as he made a beeline for the counter, where Tate was milling about as Lyle worked. "Is it okay if I give you your dry-cleaning today? The chorus competition is tomorrow, and the day after I have…" Lyle paused a beat before continuing. "…a family thing."

"Sure." Cameron felt almost as much guilt about Lyle doing his dry-cleaning as he did lying to Max.

"I'll grab it," Tate said, turning toward the back. "Is it tagged?" Lyle gave him a look, and he threw his hands up in playful surrender. "Of course it is, of course it is."

"When are you going to stop being upset about me doing your dry-cleaning?" she asked Cameron.

"When you stop doing my dry-cleaning."

"But it's your cover, CamKing," Tate called from somewhere they couldn't see, the sounds of crinkling bags and screeching hangers preceding his return. He handed Cameron six pressed shirts and two long sundresses, along with a laundry bag full of delicates. Although it was more or less the same dry-cleaning every week, it felt heavier each time Cameron took it. "A disguise into your double life."

You have no idea.

Cameron's guilt clung to him as he set the clothes aside and followed Tate to the stage. He stole a glance at Max, who was stealing a glance at Lyle as he counted them in.

As Tate sang, Cameron contemplated telling them. How everything was his fault because he was too spineless to cut the cord with Wilson. He felt caught between who he should be and who he wanted to be, and the lines were getting so blurred he found himself aimlessly confused somewhere in the middle.

. . .

By Tuesday, the hug had taken on a worrying hue in Tate's mind, and it annoyed him. It was spur of the moment in the privacy of The Carry Out, where no one could see them or judge them. He wasn't ashamed of Lyle by any means, but he was ashamed of himself for her and how people would treat her if she was close and personal with him. But even with his worries, he couldn't shake the cotton-fresh smell of her hair or how every worry dropped out a trap door in his stomach when the butterflies fluttered in.

Stop.

The chorus room bustled with students Tate didn't recognize, milling around the risers and gabbing in a sea of claustrophobia. He jumped as the bell sounded, his eyes searching until he found Lyle combing through the visitors as she made her way to the choral piano.

Damn.

"What's up, savant?" he asked as he took his usual perch against the back of the piano. "Ready for tonight?"

"I hope so."

"What's with this?" He glanced over his shoulder at the full risers.

"Final rehearsal." Lyle ran her fingers along the keys without pressing down. "Want to hear it once through?"

Tate nodded and leaned down so he could hear at the low volume she selected. "Wow," he said when she was finished. "That part sounds way better."

"It's even smoother with a page-turner. Of course the hardest part of the whole piece is on the page break."

"Do you have one?"

"Ms. Godllub said she has someone for tonight, but they can't rehearse today." Lyle rolled her eyes. "Who knows who she's got lined up for this rehearsal."

"Well, in the meantime, I'll be your understudy."

Lyle didn't even try to hide her skepticism. "You can't even play the assessment song."

"Not for playing," Tate laughed. "For page-turning."

"That'd be great." She ushered Tate to her right, where he could reach across to turn the pages without obstructing her view. "I'll tell you when." Tate followed along measure by measure, turning the page without waiting for her cue. Lyle's fingers halted as she looked at him, surprised.

"Was that the wrong spot?"

"No..." Her voice trailed off as she started the song over. Tate liked to surprise her, and although he would love to attribute his timing to musical knowledge, it was mostly because he eavesdropped on her playing enough to know when she turned the page.

"That was amazing," he said once she finished, and she beamed in a way that made his heart hurt.

"Lyle!" They both jumped as Ms. Godllub's voice tore through the room. "Just because tomorrow is your birthday doesn't mean you get to flirt the entire period! That accompaniment better be perfect!"

"No pressure," Lyle muttered.

"It's your birthday tomorrow?" Tate couldn't believe she hadn't told him. "That's the family thing you were talking about?"

"Yeah," she shrugged, focusing her attention back to the sheet music.

"You don't seem excited."

"I kind of stopped caring a while back." Although she tried to make her voice sound light, Tate could hear the weight of it tucked away, and the curiosity ate at him.

"Are you celebrating at least?"

"Grandfather and Aariz will probably do a cake or something." A fondness embraced Lyle's features as she spoke of them, and Tate wondered if that same fondness appeared when she talked about him.

If she even talks about me.

"All right, lover boy!" Ms. Godllub waved her hands at Tate as she waddled over to the piano. "Shoo! We need to rehearse."

Tate raised a playful eyebrow at Lyle and took a couple steps back. The select chorus gathered into neat rows on the risers, all eyes on the piano. "Who's going to turn my pages?" Lyle managed.

Ms. Godllub waved a dismissive hand as she took her place in front of the director's podium. "Just turn your own for the rehearsal."

Lyle's eyes widened with apprehension. Tate knew how nervous she was to mess up in front of the select chorus, and now she didn't have a page-turner? "I'll do it," he said, stepping forward once again.

He could tell Ms. Godllub wanted nothing more than to say no and exile him to his seat, but she softened under Lyle's pleading eyes. "None of this googly-eyed crap." She waggled her finger with each word, and Tate raised his hands in surrender as he returned to Lyle's right.

"Thank you," she whispered. Her hands shook the smallest bit as she poised them over the keys. Ms. Godllub raised her conductor's baton, and Tate and Lyle took a simultaneous breath as they began. The instrumental introduction was flawless, but Lyle stumbled as the chorus joined in, lagging behind their tempo before stopping altogether.

"Sorry, sorry," she hurried. The eyes of the upperclassmen bored in on them, and Lyle swallowed back her tears as Ms. Godllub tapped her baton to restart.

"You've got this," Tate whispered as they started the song over. And this time, Lyle played it perfectly.

"Again!" Ms. Godllub commanded, Tate barely able to reset the sheet music before she counted them in. And again, Lyle played it perfectly. They repeated this process four more times, interrupted only by the warning bell. "All right," Ms. Godllub said, setting her baton on the podium as she addressed the group. "Everyone be here at least thirty minutes early tonight. And for God's sake, no weird hairstyles or piercings. We're looking professional here, people! And Lyle…" Tate held his breath, Lyle's shoulders by her ears as they braced themselves for embarrassment in front of the entire select chorus. "Nice job."

Lyle exhaled all the air from her lungs as the upperclassmen nodded in approval before dispersing. "Not bad for an understudy," she said, grinning at Tate in a way that made him want to grin too. Instead, he gave her a casual wink and headed for the band room to tell Max and Cameron their change in rehearsal for tonight.

They arrived early later that night, but choral groups from other high schools were already clumped in the auditorium seats, delineated by their matching costumes. The judges sat at a small table front and center, shuffling folders of paperwork in an attempt to get organized. Tate couldn't see the risers very well from their spot at the outer edge of the front row, but he could see the piano perfectly, and that was all he cared about.

"This isn't an optimal vantage point," Cameron observed.

"It works," Max said, his eyes on the vacant piano as he lowered himself down beside Tate.

Cameron fidgeted in his seat like a toddler. "So this isn't a real competition?"

"It is, but it's a performance too," Tate said. "They just get scored individually instead of ranked."

"If there's no winner, then it isn't a real competition."

He didn't know why Cameron was so angsty today, but Tate canceled band practice so they could support Lyle, not criticize her. "Just like your adult spelling bee isn't really Scripps?"

Cameron puffed his chest in defense. "I aged out of Scripps, and colleges like to see continued extracurricular activity on applications, and joining the adult spelling bee is the only way—"

Max put a hand on Cameron's chest to stop him from plunging into his adult spelling bee rant for the hundredth time. "We know. He's screwing with you." Cameron slouched back in his seat like a child at the opera as Max turned to Tate. "How are they scored?"

"Lyle said it's like a medaling system? So they get bronze, silver, or gold."

"Or platinum." Lyle's knee-length black dress swayed to and fro as she approached, the neckline beaded and sparkling in the auditorium lights. "I'm so glad you guys are here," she said, starting with Cameron as she gave each of them a quick hug. It was rushed, nothing like their moment the other night, but it made Tate's heart pound all the same. "I've gotta run; we're second in the lineup." They watched her retreat backstage as the auditorium lights were replaced by the blinding stage lights. The first group to compete sounded alright, but they didn't have piano accompaniment.

Lyle could have played that better than the recording.

The boys clapped as the group exited the stage, Ms. Godllub leading the charge as the select chorus took the stage. Lyle brought up the rear as she took her seat at the piano, and Tate could tell by the look on her face something was wrong. She was as nervous and frantic as ever, her eyes boring into him as she repeatedly opened and closed her sheet music.

Shit.

"She doesn't have a page-turner."

"What?" Max's eyes darted from Lyle's forlorn expression to Tate, desperate to understand. But Tate was already on his feet, hustling to the base of the stage.

"What happened?" he whispered up at her.

"They didn't show," she hissed. She looked like a deer in the headlights of an eighteen-wheeler. The biggest performance of her life and her page-turner skipped out? Tate looked around frantically for another option, but everyone else was competing for another school.

Shit.

"Loverboy!" Tate didn't think it was possible, but Ms. Godllub's voice was even more terrifying in a whisper-scream. She held her baton at her hip, stabbing it toward the piano. "You're on." Tate looked down at his worn jeans and faded t-shirt, an alarmingly stark contrast to the black dress clothes of the rest of the group. He looked at Ms. Godllub helplessly, motioning to his clothes. She shook her head, giving a final stab at the piano with her baton. "Now," she whispered, so low and menacing that Tate pulled himself onto the stage without another thought. He stayed low as he made his way to

Lyle's right-hand side, trying to hide his street clothes behind the piano as he set the sheet music.

Ms. Godllub turned to face the audience with a crocodile smile, her arms outstretched as she accepted their applause. Tate felt every eye in the auditorium scrutinizing him: his clothes, his skin, his relationship with Lyle.

Lyle.

It only took one look at her terrified face for Tate's insecurities to melt away, his one and only thought in this moment supporting her. Ms. Godllub turned to face them, tapping the baton on the podium as the select chorus assumed their positions. The baton thrust at Lyle like an arrow at a target as Ms. Godllub led it through her four-count cue. "Just enjoy the music," Tate murmured, his left hand on her shoulder in reassurance. Lyle closed her eyes and took a deep breath, Tate's hand falling to his side as she began to play.

The rest of the competition took over three hours, Max and Cameron lasting half the time before bowing out to help Cameron prep for the bee. When it was all over, Tate and Lyle sat side by side on the piano bench, watching the last of the crowd and performers bustle out of the auditorium. It was hard to find the right words in times like this, so they sat in silence. Her legs swung beneath the bench, and the wooden stage echoed with the tap of his foot. "Sorry I wasn't better dressed."

"Your chain really caught the stage lights." Lyle fingered his golden cross before letting it fall to his chest.

"How did it feel playing again? Like really playing."

"I don't know." Her answer was quiet, and Tate watched her cycle through a range of emotions before resigning herself to feeling conflicted. "Play me something," she said, resting her head on his shoulder. "NOT the assessment song," she added as Tate readied his hands on the keys. "I'm starting to hear it in my sleep." The only other song Tate even remotely knew wasn't flawless, and he hadn't planned on sharing it with anyone until it was ready. But at that moment, all he wanted was to give Lyle the world, so he played it anyway, careful to keep his left shoulder still so as not to disturb her. He flinched at his own missteps, the wrong notes jarring them out of their reverie. "What is it?" Lyle asked.

"A song I was going to play at the talent show."

"On the piano?" Again, the kind of astounded tone that reminded Tate he did not have a future as a pianist.

"Just until the jerk."

"The jerk?"

"Yeah." Tate swiveled to face her, excited to share the song with someone. "The opening is really soft and slow, only a handful of notes. Then there's the jerk." He lurched his body as if startled. "The audience jerks as the entire band joins in, and the rest of the song is loud and angsty."

Lyle laughed. "Sounds like your kind of song."

Tate thought about how special this song was to him and how wrong it sounded when he played it. "The intro would sound better if you played it."

"But I don't know the s—"

"It's just a handful of notes," Tate cut her off before rattling the notes aloud by memory. If only he could get the message from his mind to his hands, he'd be in good shape.

But she can.

Lyle tapped her fingers along the notes without pressing them down before she began to play. Her first run through sounded a million times better than Tate's best, and on her second, he began to sing the intro. It was the first time he sang the lyrics in front of anyone, and he put his hands on hers to stop them before they reached the jerk. He swallowed his emotions as the silence overtook them again, longing for Lyle to understand him. "Why didn't you tell me you had a piano at The Carry Out?" He hadn't planned on bringing it up, but he was tired of being the only one with secrets. "I saw it when I grabbed CamKing's dry-cleaning."

Lyle ran her fingernail back and forth, making a faint clicking sound as it went from key to key. "I kind of wanted to forget it was there."

"Why don't you just throw it out?"

Her gaze was at her feet now. "My mother gave it to me."

"Why won't you use it?"

Lyle looked at him, her eyes fogged with a conflict Tate did not understand. "Same reason."

"All right, lovebirds!" Ms. Godllub's voice boomed across the stage, the moments of whisper-screaming long gone. "Time to fly the coop!" Tate hopped off the stage, offering Lyle a hand as she attempted to do the same in a dress. The lights faded off before they reached the door, but Tate saw Ms. Godllub waving from the stage as they dimmed.

"I think you're officially on her good side," Lyle laughed. The cool night air nipped at their cheeks and hands as they stepped into the night. The moonlight bounced off the white parking lines with authority, claiming the deserted parking lot after dark.

"It only took platinum to do it," Tate said.

Lyle threw her arms around his neck, almost knocking him over as the little warmth the night air hadn't stolen held safe between them. "Thank you."

When she pulled away, Tate kept an arm around her shoulder, not wanting to let go. "Not bad for an understudy, huh?" He rubbed his hand up and down Lyle's arm to keep her warm as they started their walk toward The Carry Out, but as he rode his skateboard back to the screen house, all he could think about was Lyle's mother and the hidden piano.

. . .

They were a few blocks from the Twin Towers when Lyle's mother finally stopped running. Two police cars formed a barricade nose to nose across the street, preventing pedestrians from interfering with the firemen. Lyle stumbled more than a couple times trying to keep up, but her mother hadn't broken stride. "Mommy," she said when she caught her breath. "What happened?" Her mother stared as more firetrucks poured into the blocked off-street. Lyle didn't recognize anyone, but it was hard to tell when they were all dressed the same. They were organizing themselves into groups at the base of the towers, each group leader yelling out instructions.

"Excuse me," her mother said, leaning over the hood of one of the police cars. The police officer closest to them turned, the radio on his shoulder crackling non-stop. "My husband is a firefighter. I need to get in."

"Sorry, ma'am. No one past the barricade."

"You don't understand." Her mother sounded agitated now. "I need to see my husband." The policeman said something back, but Lyle couldn't hear it over the buzzing. It sounded like a box fan on turbo speed, and she looked around in search of its source. She looked to the sky as her mother continued to argue with the police officer, where she saw a plane flying low like a video game.

"Mommy!" Lyle yelled. Her mother and the police officer stopped mid-sentence as the buzzing became a roar, the plane picking up speed as it crashed directly into the second tower.

"Oh, shit!" the police officer screamed as the second bang reverberated down the street. Lyle covered her ears and put her head to her knees. When she stood up, her mother was no longer next to her but over the barricade and sprinting toward the firetrucks. "Lady!" the policeman yelled after her. "Get back! Are you crazy?" The crowd grew around the barricade to see what happened, and Lyle crawled beneath the hood of the police car unnoticed. Embers fell from the sky as Lyle found her mother in the chaos, asking random firemen where her husband was. When no one could help her, she started screaming Lyle's father's name.

"Leon! Leon!" Lyle could barely hear her over the whine of more approaching sirens, and she doubted her father could either. It was like she forgot Lyle was there, and twice Lyle lost her in the crowd before hooking her finger through the belt loop of her mother's jeans.

"Marianna?" Lyle followed the new voice to her grandfather, Rawel, dressed in full fire gear as he emerged from the smoke. The patch on his jacket indicated his status as chief of the unit; Lyle remembered watching as he sewed it on. "What the hell are you doing here?"

"Rawel!" Her mother pounced on him, grabbing his jacket in both hands. "I have to check on Leon. Where's Leon?"

"You can't be here right now. It's not safe!" Rawel scooped Lyle into his arms and set her down on the edge of a nearby ambulance, kissing her cheek before turning to her mother. "Marianna, how could you bring Lyle here? It's dangerous for anyone, let alone a little girl!" Lyle's mother was forlorn with worry, and Rawel softened a remarkable amount for someone in such a chaotic situation. "Leon is doing what he does every single day. The bridges are closed, so stay here and I will come back and get you." His firmness left no room for argument, Lyle's mother sliding onto the back of the ambulance as Rawel disappeared into the crowd.

Time passed like molasses until the ambulance driver shoved them inside and slammed the doors. Lyle hugged herself as dust and smoke engulfed the ambulance, nothing but heavy darkness visible through the little windows as the building collapsed. Her mother's screams bounced off the inside of the small space, coming at Lyle from a different direction every time. "My husband!" she screamed, pounding on the doors. "My husband was in that building!"

Eventually, their surroundings rematerialized through the back windows, the two of them peeking out the pane of glass at where the first tower used to be. The doors opened without warning, sending Lyle cascading into the arms of a paramedic, who quickly carried her to the passenger seat of the ambulance. Lyle's mother was like a caged bull as she hurled herself to the pavement and took off running. "Leon!"

"Shit," Rawel said as he hustled to the open doors. Lyle watched him from the side mirror. He was shirtless and carrying what looked to be a lump of fire gear. He handed the lump to the waiting paramedics, whose fear showed in their eyes but not their work. Once they took over, Rawel rushed to the passenger side, opening the door and pulling Lyle into a hug. "Sweetie," he said. "The paramedics are going to take you to the hospital."

"But I'm not hurt."

Rawel's smile was pained as he took her little hand in his. "I know. But it's safer there. Do you remember the emergency phone numbers I taught you?" Lyle nodded. "Good. Go to the front desk when you get there and call Aariz. Tell him where you are, and he will come get you."

Lyle's eyes welled with tears. "But what about Mommy?"

Rawel grimaced as if he had just stepped on a thumbtack. "Sometimes grownups don't always do the right thing." Rawel gave her hand a squeeze. "Mommy will be fi—" He was cut off by a scuffle in the back of the ambulance, where his giant fire coat was trying to escape. "I love you. Call Aariz." And with that, Rawel closed the door and rushed back to help.

Lyle examined the ash left on her hand from her grandfather's. It was like making shapes out of clouds, only sadder. She deemed the shape a grand piano as the second tower collapsed with an earsplitting roar. The ambulance driver flipped on the siren as Rawel shut the back doors and gave them a pound with his fist. The ambulance driver buckled Lyle's seatbelt before speeding away in an attempt to outrun the smoke.

Lyle watched in the side mirror as her grandfather ran back into the smoke, and for the first time that day, she began to cry.

. . .

The cake was decorated with white icing, little white flowers piped onto the edges. Lyle had refused a birthday party every year since 2001, but that never stopped Rawel and Aariz from getting her a cake. Aariz lit the candles, and they were just about to start singing when the bell tinkled at the front door.

"Tate?" Lyle wasn't expecting him, especially since he canceled band practice again. He barely acknowledged her in intermediate piano, pouring over his keyboard with his headphones firmly in place. Was he mad at her for making him go on stage last night?

"I didn't mean to interrupt…" Tate's hands were shoved deep in his pockets as he hovered in the middle of the lobby.

"Nonsense!" Aariz said, waving him over. "We were just about to sing." There were a few people sitting on the lobby bench waiting for their clothes, and Rawel raised a hand for them to join in as he started the song with a deep, tenor voice. Rawel and Aariz's voices were so loud Lyle could have heard them across the street.

But not Tate's.

She stole a glance at him, and although Tate was mouthing the words, Lyle heard his voice enough to know he wasn't singing. Nor was he at the counter, hovering back a few steps until Lyle blew out the candles.

"Every year I am more proud of the young lady you are." Rawel pulled her into a bear hug. "I'm sorry I have to go back to the fire-house tonight."

"It's okay. It's just a birthday." Lyle immediately felt bad for the comment as her grandfather flinched the smallest bit. This time of year wasn't easy for him either, but she never knew how to console him when she could barely console herself.

"Well, at least take the night off," he said, ruffling a hand through the blonde strands that had escaped her braid. "Aariz agreed to watch the store."

"Go have fun," Aariz said with a wink.

Rawel eyed Tate a beat longer than he should have before turning back to Lyle. "Don't stay out too late." Lyle slid off the stool as he kissed her on the forehead. "I love you."

"Happy birthday, sweetheart," Aariz said, following suit with the forehead kiss before grabbing the stool and retreating to his workshop.

When she was sure they were gone, Lyle turned to Tate. "You weren't singing."

Tate took her hand without a word and led her to the back of the store. The clothing bags crinkled in defiance as he pushed them aside to reveal the hidden piano. He lowered himself onto the bench, pulling Lyle down beside him before she could object. "I wanted to do it myself." His dark skin was a stark contrast to the white ivory as, to Lyle's astonishment, he began to play "Happy Birthday." His fingers moved smooth and sure as he accompanied his own voice. No one had played this piano in seven years, and Lyle wasn't sure how to feel about it. It sounded the same as it had back then as if no time had passed.

Tate's hand slipped into a wrong note as he stole a glance at her, hitting the right note before pausing mid-song to look into her eyes. The clothes hanging all around them became a protective barrier, a waterfall hiding a cave of wonders. No one and nothing else existed except the right side of her body pressed against the left side of his, his hands suspended over the keys as they shared this moment together. She let herself get drunk on it, the feeling of celebrating without waiting for the other shoe to drop. His voice wrapped around her like a fleece blanket that you couldn't help but snuggle into as he sang the last verse, hitting the final note with a flourish of his hand.

Lyle felt her neck and cheeks flushing pink, and it took her a minute to find her voice. "And here I was thinking you were upset with me in class today."

"Hardly."

She leaned into Tate a little more, catching a glimpse of his crooked smile. "Not bad for an understudy."

"Happy birthday," he murmured as his lips found her cheek. They were cool against the warmth of her blush, and her braid tickled his nose as he pulled away. They were suspended, halfway between floating into the clouds and crashing back to reality, and although Lyle's mind clawed upwards, the eighty-eight keys she had tried so hard to forget beckoned her down.

"Will you come somewhere with me?" she asked abruptly. Tate examined her a moment, concerned by her sudden change of demeanor, before nodding and following her out the back door to the bus stop.

Lyle's mother's voice was audible even before she picked up the receiver. "Delilah! I knew you'd come see me today!"

"Hi, Mom." Lyle hadn't planned on visiting the prison on her birthday, and she certainly hadn't planned on bringing Tate.

"Happy birthday, baby. Did you celebrate?"

"Grandfather got me a cake. And the afternoon off."

"And you came to spend it with me?" Her mother pressed an open palm to the heart of her orange jumpsuit. "You're such a good daughter." Lyle shifted in her seat, trying to hide her discomfort. Out of the corner of her eye, she could see Tate's confusion from where she had planted him a couple cubicles away. "How's your grandfather?"

"Good," Lyle said, trying to lighten her tone. "Always keeping busy."

Her mother hesitated, running her finger in slow circles around the bottom of the receiver. "Does he talk about me?" Her voice wavered like a soundwave in the city, and Lyle could hear the longing in it. The longing for someone that had abandoned her to come make everything okay again.

I know the feeling.

Unsure of how to answer, Lyle motioned for Tate below the counter. "Mom, this is Tate." Tate stumbled as she pulled him awkwardly into view.

"Well, aren't you handsome." Her mother raised a perfectly plucked eyebrow, her lips pursed.

"Nice to meet you." Tate started to extend his hand before realizing his own stupidity and dropping it against his thigh.

"Situational hazard," her mother said, brushing off the glass between them like a few raindrops on an otherwise sunny day. Tate glanced at Lyle before pulling up another stool and taking the receiver from her outstretched hand. "Did you join in the celebration this afternoon?"

"Yeah, a little."

"I see." The smile in her mother's voice was not as well hidden as the one on her face, and Lyle averted her gaze in embarrassment. "Just the two of you?" Her mother loved nothing more than a good romance, and Lyle began to wonder if bringing Tate here was premature.

"No," he rushed. "Me, Rawel, and—"

"And a few customers," Lyle interrupted, snatching the receiver out of his hand.

Tate's hand remained suspended next to his ear, trying to understand what she wanted him to say. "Right," he managed, but the damage was done. Lyle watched her mother's eyes slide from her to Tate and back again, knuckles whitening as she tightened her grip on the receiver. A mask of hatred glazed over her eyes that Lyle was too used to seeing.

"He was there, wasn't he?" Her mother's voice was low, menacing.

"Mom—"

"You celebrated with *him* first? Your felon of a mother's just an afterthought, is that it?"

"No!" Lyle looked around desperately, as if the fingernail marks etched into the table in front of her could provide an answer on how to defuse the situation.

"He's just helping us with the stage." Tate grabbed the receiver and returned it to his ear.

How on Earth does he know we're talking about Aariz?

"My band," Tate continued, more confident now. "We practice at The Carry Out, and he insisted on helping with the stage." Lyle held her breath as her mother studied him for an indication of a lie. Finding none, she leaned closer to the glass, as if it would make a difference when they were talking through a telephone.

"Word of caution," she said, Tate's expression serious as he mirrored her motion. "Watch your back. You seem like a nice boy, and people like him will overstep."

"People like him?" Lyle asked.

"Delilah fights me on this. She doesn't understand. But you do." Her mother scrutinized Tate for an uncomfortable amount of time, Tate's eye contact unrelenting. "I can see it in those lily pad green eyes of yours."

"Yes." His answer was firm, and it took Lyle by surprise. "I understand." They seemed to be traveling on the same train of thought, a train to which Lyle lost her ticket.

"Good." Her mother leaned back in her seat like she just sealed a business deal. "Someone has to." Lyle was astonished by the ease with which her mother took to Tate but even more astonished by the way Tate took to her.

"You should have heard Lyle playing last night," Tate said, changing the subject as he read Lyle's face. "She was amazing."

Oh no.

"Playing?" Her mother sat bolt upright, the mask of hatred in her eyes replaced by a look Lyle didn't recognize.

"The piano..." Tate clarified, his words slow as he once again tried to figure out their dynamic.

"You've been playing again?"

"A little..." Lyle trailed off, easing the receiver out of Tate's hand.

"On *my* piano?" Lyle hadn't wanted to venture here. As far as her mother knew, she had given up the piano the day she was arrested. But here they were, and if the glass were a mirror, the look on her mother's face would be in Lyle's own reflection every time she visited this godforsaken place.

Hope.

Her mother hoped she would play that piano again, hoped it would connect them the way it was supposed to back then. The thought of them sitting at that piano together sloshed around Lyle's head like warm water, soothing the mental wounds she didn't know how to heal. But the claustrophobia of the concrete walls began to close in, the memory of why Lyle hid the piano in the first place sending jagged splinters of reality piercing through her thoughts of what could have been.

"I thought it was my piano," Lyle said through gritted teeth. She was tired of her mother's absence tainting the piano she had once loved. Tired of redirecting her mind when it tried to remember the happy times at that piano that bled into horrific times that led to its exile.

Her mother's eyes squinted into slits, as if she could read each thought as it pulsed through Lyle's mind. "Once upon a time, I thought so too." The accusation in her voice hit Lyle like a stone to the forehead, Tate barely catching the receiver as it slipped out of her hand.

She blames me.

"We better get back," Tate said, the cord stretching as he pulled Lyle to her feet. "Big pre-calc test tomorrow." Her mother was about to object, but something about the glare Tate fixed on her made her stand down.

She thinks it's my fault she's in here.

"Don't study too hard on your birthday." Her mother's forced smile turned to a real one as she pressed her hand to the glass. "I'll be out for the next one, Delilah," she said loud enough for Lyle to hear without the phone. Tate tapped her leg under the table with the butt of the receiver, offering it discreetly, but Lyle pushed it away. The light above their cubicle turned, casting them in a green hue as Tate and her mother hung up, both pairs of eyes on Lyle as she hurried from the room.

The bus was almost back when Tate finally broke the silence. "Delilah, huh?" Lyle's thoughts felt like a ball of yarn knotted by the paws of a cat, exhausted from the exertion of feeling so many conflicting emotions at once.

"She's the only one who still calls me that."

"It's pretty," Tate offered, daring to let their legs touch for the first time the entire ride. Lyle inched away, tucking her leg under herself as she looked out the window.

"She liked you." Her voice was monotone, and she could feel Tate's eyes on her as he searched her body language for insight.

"That's good, right?"

The bus screeched to a halt outside The Carry Out, the sign illuminating the otherwise dark night. Lyle rose without answering, squeezing past Tate's knees as she led the way down the bus steps and across the street.

"Back so soon?" Aariz looked surprised as they walked through the front door, but one look at Lyle's face clued him in on where they had been.

"Thanks for covering for me." Lyle rounded the counter and immediately began organizing piles of tags. Aariz touched her cheek with the outside of his hand, a pained understanding passing between them before he retreated to his workshop. By now, it was almost closing time, and for the first time in her life, Lyle strode to the front door and locked it early, flipping the signs off without a glance at Tate.

"Did I do something?" he asked, hovering in the lobby like a stranger. Lyle hurried past him and grabbed the broom from the closet, slamming the bristles on the floor and dragging them in a sporadic pattern.

"It's getting late," she said. Her mother blamed her for being in prison, she and Tate got along like bosom friends, and Lyle was left wondering where she fit into her own life. She was tired of putting on a brave face for everyone when all she wanted to do was scream at the top of her lungs until she was too hoarse to cry. "Thanks for coming with me."

Tate watched her irregular sweeping pattern, trying to piece together the night's events. "Do you mind if I practice one more song?" Lyle waved a dismissive hand, too mentally exhausted to care as she plopped herself down on the lobby bench. She moved the broom between her feet, dragging it in a square inch of space like a limp noodle. She heard rustling as Tate grabbed his guitar from under the counter, but instead of taking his usual perch on the stage, he settled himself next to her.

He reached instinctively to his pocket before remembering he no longer had his guitar pick, readjusting himself to strum with his thumbnail. Despite the night's confusion, the guitar pick felt like a comfort in Lyle's back pocket as her thoughts raced around her head like greyhounds on a track. It lifted her spirits, reminded her that not everything about reality was bad. She loved Tate's voice, the private concerts he did just for her. It made her feel special. Loved.

Vulnerable.

But with vulnerability came pain, and Lyle wasn't sure she was ready to brave both sides of the sword. How could she feel so close to Tate, so connected by the moments in which they continued to be each other's lifeline, and yet so far away from him at the same time? So distanced by his propensity to hold back pieces of himself, Lyle didn't realize they were hidden until they reared their dangerous heads in a prison visit.

Tate began to tap his foot to a beat that only he could hear, and Lyle let the broom still as he began to sing. His voice was foreign and right at the same time, like a love song in another language. The lyrics wound around her like a ribbon on a Christmas present, a perfect bow on an imperfect night. Lyle tried to hide the tremble in her hands as the goosebumps scattered across her arms. The emotions of the night were starting to take shape in her mind and heart, and she felt like a sponge that needed to be wrung out.

Loving was so much harder when you knew what it felt like to lose it, and Lyle didn't know if she could handle any more loss. She felt herself choking on the sobs she was fighting to suppress as Tate repeated the chorus a final time. And then she was in his arms, the broom and guitar thudding to their feet. Her shoulders wracked with sobs as he held her, tears staining the chest of his t-shirt. He did not speak, just rested his scarred cheek on the crown of her head, his arms a protective blanket around her. They stayed like this for a long time, Lyle sobbing out the confusion and the feelings that kept her up at night.

When she was finally able to gasp a few breaths of air, Lyle started to pull away to compose herself.

Only Tate didn't let go.

His left arm remained wrapped around her, light enough to let her know she could pull away if she really wanted to, but tight enough to let her know he didn't want her to. She sniffed herself under control as he reached beneath the neck of his shirt and pulled his golden cross over his head. He stared at it for a moment before extending it to her. "I know it's not much of a birthday present, but I want you to have this."

Lyle fought the urge to reach for it, to arm herself with another item of his to take away her pain. "I'm not religious," was all she could think to say.

"Neither am I." Tate rolled the crucifix back and forth between his thumb and index finger, savoring whatever peace of mind it brought to him. "I know what it's like to lose someone." He was not looking at her, but the entire lobby felt like a funhouse of mirrors, magnifying their emotions back at them until they couldn't help but understand each other. "All the love you are afraid to feel, all the vulnerability you want to hide away, you can hide it in here."

"Is that what you do?"

He nodded as he placed the gold chain over her head, the metal cold against her collarbone. "Then no one will ever know about it."

"Except you." Lyle brushed the cross with her fingertips, imprinting it the slightest bit on her pale skin.

"Yeah." Tate rested his cheek against her head once more, Lyle's mind too tired to want to be anywhere but exactly where she was. "Except me."

CHAPTER TEN

Max wasn't surprised when Tate cut school on Thursday, nor did he have any intention of trying to find him. One thing Max learned over the years was the last thing Tate wanted today was company. It was just as well, the way the week was going. Tate canceling so many rehearsals helped Max cover his tracks at the barn, although it didn't do anything for the guilt gnawing at his conscience. Not to mention Cameron was vacillating between pensive and argumentative, neither of which were characteristic for him; whatever Wilson was planning certainly had him rattled. On top of all that, Max missed Lyle's birthday yesterday. The only person he could be completely honest with, who really seemed to understand him, and he was too busy making dirty money to wish her a happy birthday.

He shook Lyle out of his head as he stepped into the second stall. One night was all it took for Max to adjust his defensive stance from blocking his face to protecting his torso. It was simple after that, dodging and punching his way back up the fighting ladder. He solidified his place in the top tier of fighters last night by defeating the basketball player who colored his ribs a few nights earlier. Max was now the fighter to beat in the second stall, the elite and their wallets intrigued by his lethal combination of low profile and high performance.

Suits continued to fill the loft as the moon rose higher in the sky, and the bets continued to climb as Max's opponent stepped into the stall. They all looked the same after a while, and Max made quick work of the fight as the bell rang. He went for the diaphragm rather than the ribs, a temporary hindrance that would, if done correctly, end the fight without causing injury to his opponent. Max even let the guy land a punch on his side before taking him down to keep him from being blackballed.

The collector from the loft leaned into the stall as Max's opponent hobbled out. His suit was outdated, a memento from the rat pack, the corner of the price tag peeking out beneath his fedora. He looked stuck between the two sides of the barn, a sellout that crossed over but didn't quite belong. "Hey, kid," he said. "We got a request for you in Stall One."

"I don't take requests."

"Look, kid. I don't know who you think you are, but when the owner makes a request, you do it." Max had no intention of facing the owner's son; he wasn't here for a dog and pony show. He just wanted to make a quick buck and get out. "Unless you want your flow of cash to dry up," the man added in response to Max's defiant expression. Max hated feeling like he could be bought, but if he didn't chase the money, he was here for the wrong reasons. Reasons that shaped the onlookers into the scumbags they were, and to Max, that was worse than being a sellout. "That's what I thought," the man said as he followed Max out of the stall and steered him to the left. "Stall One."

The QB wore compression shorts under his athletic ones, pale shoulders dotted with freckles, light hair perfectly coiffed. His expression was smug, and Max couldn't shake the feeling he looked vaguely familiar. Then again, all these preps looked the same: entitled, overconfident, and overdressed. Max wasn't scared to face him, but he wasn't stupid either. If Daddy requested his son go against the underdog on the rise, he had to have the upper hand; Max just had to find it.

"Special delivery," he said, lowering himself into his new fighter's stance as the stall door closed behind him. The QB was truly massive, his biceps and pecs bulging like balloons filled with water. His fighter's stance mirrored Max's, face unguarded to protect his torso of rock hard abs.

"Not me," the QB said. "Request came from"—he jutted his chin toward the hayloft as the bell sounded—"higher up."

Max stole a glance upward, then did a double-take, his entire body going rigid as his eyes locked on the front row. He didn't even see the left hook coming, his eye socket exploding with pain as he crumbled to the ground. The bell sounded again, and Max didn't even lift his head as the QB left the stall for his victory lap. The hay stung his nostrils as he breathed in and out like a bull that bucked its rider, the physical and emotional pain a lethal combination as they flooded his body. He understood now why he was summoned to the first stall tonight, and for the first time in his life, Max wanted to hit someone.

"Double or nothing!" Max's voice rose over the rain pummeling the barn roof as he pushed himself to his feet. He was talking to his opponent, but his eyes were trained on the hayloft.

On the QB's upper hand.

. . .

It was only fitting that it was raining. Tate spent the majority of his day wandering through it in a daze, and only after closing time did he find himself at the back door of The Carry Out. He wanted to be alone, but he wasn't strong enough, so he wanted to be alone with Lyle. Tate didn't wait long after knocking before trying the door, surprised to find it open as he let himself in from the alley. The back of the store was dark, the bags on the carousel ominous as their shadows lurked like the demons he was trying to escape. Tate hurried past them to the lobby, surprised to find Lyle wasn't there. A trail of water dripped in his wake as he grabbed his guitar from under the counter and found his way to the stage.

My father's guitar.

Tate was accustomed to referring to it as his own, but today it felt important to implement the mental correction. The absence of his gold chain weighed on his chest more than the crucifix would have, and Tate could hear his own heartbeat pounding in his ears. It connected him and Lyle on a deeper level, and he was grateful for that, but it didn't make it any easier when he reached for the chain and was met with nothing.

Tate sat in the middle of the stage, legs crisscrossed as he began to strum the guitar. The calluses on the fingers of his right hand moved around the chords with ease, years of playing hardening them against the pain.

Kind of like me.

Tate held his hand up and chose one finger, his middle, to raise. He stared at it, cursing the world that showed him nothing but unfairness, before pressing it against the skinniest string and running it up and down the neck of the guitar. Faster and faster he went until the pressure and friction finally cut through the callus. A thin line of blood gathered on his fingertip before overflowing down his knuckles. He pressed his finger harder against the string, the pain filling him up like an inhaler during an asthma attack. He wanted to feel it. Not all the time; he wasn't strong enough for that. But on this day, with his fingertip the only gateway to release the pain he buried inside, he wanted to feel it. He needed to feel it.

So with his bloody hand, he began to play. Tears stained his face, tracing the pattern of his scar like some sick reminder. His shirt clung to him like papier-mâché, as if it understood he didn't have much left to hold on to. He had wanted the rain to cleanse him, wash all the malice and treachery from his body and his mind, but as Tate began to shiver, he realized the only thing the rain did was make the world around him even colder.

For years Tate had tried to forget, tried to move on, tried to find a way to keep on living a life he never wanted. But the tragedy hung in his mind like a fog, clouding everything else in loneliness. His voice broke as he tried to imagine the next three years without his father. The next thirteen. The next thirty. Alone when he had children, or got married, or graduated. Alone when he won the talent show, or marched in the parade, or just needed someone to love him.

Although he finished the song, Tate repeated the chorus over and over, the anger and unfairness and loneliness pulsing inside him until he was screaming. Again and again, he screamed it, the blood rushing to his face as he hunched over his knees. Instead of sitting on his shoulders, the weight of the world felt like it was inside of him. Bursting at the seams, tearing him apart to find a way to escape the confines of his body, where nothing made sense and everything hurt no matter what he did. Tate's screams turned to sobs, and before he realized what he was doing, he had his father's guitar in both hands, raised over his head.

And he smashed it.

He brought the guitar down against the stage, again and again, his howls audible over the hollow thud of wood on wood. It was an electric acoustic guitar, and it held on, but after the second smash, the body of the guitar dented, and by the fifth, the entire neck gave way. The body hung limp as it swayed from side to side at his knees, the bloody strings the only thing connecting it to the neck clutched in Tate's hands.

"Tate!" Aariz's voice reverberated over the commotion, and for a split second, Tate wondered if he woke him before deciding he didn't care. Aariz took the steps in one bound, jerking the neck of the guitar out of Tate's hands, the body dragging behind it as he placed it by the drums. "Tate," he said again, placing a comforting hand on his shoulder.

Tate reared away as if he had been burned, slashing Aariz's hand away. "Don't touch me!"

"Tate, you're bleeding."

"I don't care!" Tate ran his hands through his hair until the blood caked in.

"I understand how you're feeling." Aariz's voice was low, controlled, like he was talking someone off the ledge. "Today is difficult for a lot of people."

"You don't understand!" No one could possibly understand, especially not Aariz. "I lost my father in that attack!"

"And I lost my wife."

At first, the comment stunned Tate, but it quickly morphed into anger. His mind felt like a rock show with strobe lights that had spiraled out of control. He was blinded by his own rage, his own suffering, his own pain he tried so hard not to feel. "She was probably flying the plane."

Aariz took a physical step back from the words, and Tate turned away. His chest rose and fell with an adrenaline he didn't know what to do with. He knew what it felt like to be hated because of how you looked, but after what happened to his father, how could he think any differently?

"The entire world isn't against you, Tate," Aariz said after a minute, collected once more as he squatted so they were face to face. "Please let me help you."

"Haven't you done enough?" Tate felt helpless, an empty bottle of wine drained by an alcoholic desperate for one last sip. Only there was nothing left for him to give.

At seven years old, he was torn from the life he was supposed to live, ripped away from the only reality he had ever known. At first, Tate was scared, overwhelmed by a world with no father to protect him. As time went on, his fear turned to frantic hope as he tried desperately to work his way back to the life he lost, pushing against the new reality he was forced into. But that desperation soon morphed into hatred as Tate realized he could never escape this new life that never seemed to have enough oxygen. The years continued, and Tate carried that hatred with him as long as he could cling to it because it made him feel strong. It made him feel worthy of his old life, like he was honoring his father's memory by fighting against the people that had taken him away.

But as Tate knelt here now, staring one of those people in the face, his hatred gave way to helplessness. His eyes pleaded with Aariz for mercy, begging him and everyone like him to stop the suffering he could no longer stand. "What more could you take from me?" Tate whispered, his body giving way as he sunk to the floor.

Aariz lowered himself next to Tate, his eyes trying to communicate support that his words couldn't convey. "My people are not against you, Tate." He grabbed Tate's chin, tilting his head until they were eye to eye again. "*I* am not against you."

Tate pulled away, holding his head in his hands as the darkness of the lobby and the darkness within himself bled together until he could no longer decipher where reality began and ended. "Please," he begged, his voice raspy. "Just leave me alone." He waited, expecting Aariz to continue, to try to pull Tate back to a reality he couldn't stand to live in a moment longer.

But he didn't.

It was silent for a long time until Tate heard rustling as Aariz pushed himself to his feet. He did not speak another word, the sound of his footsteps pausing as he reached the edge of the stage before descending the steps and fading to the back of his workshop.

Tate stayed like that for a long time, crumpled in a heap soaked with misery. He thought about his father. About how marching was the only way Tate could think of to make him proud. He needed it. NEEDED it. Because truthfully, Tate couldn't make it on his own. Hard as he tried, hard as he fought, he just couldn't. And he hated himself for it.

He pushed himself to his feet and walked over to examine his father's guitar. His ticket to the talent show, to marching, to making his father proud, laid at his feet, mangled and unrecognizable.

Kind of like me.

What was left of Tate's heart dropped into his stomach as he averted his eyes from the guitar, only to be met by two deep blue spheres piercing through the darkness at the foot of the stage. The horrified expression was debilitating, especially considering the source, and he couldn't stand it. He couldn't stand disappointing one more person he loved, so Tate tore his eyes away from Lyle's, leaped off the stage, and ran out the back door.

. . .

At seven years old, Tate was still able to perch atop the window-sill of a coffee shop, his back pressed against the glass as he looked over the sea of people at the parade. He watched the other kids smiling and laughing, watched their parents pull them into a warm embrace, and Tate wondered what his life would be like without that warmth. Would it feel cold? Or would he just eventually go numb, unable to feel anything until he finally froze to death?

At least then I'd get to see my dad again.

The crowd grew silent as the flag approached, the men and women holding it dressed entirely in black. Even their eyes looked dark, and Tate hoped the images lurking behind them weren't the same ones lurking behind his. But he knew they were.

They marched in silence, each gloved hand holding an end of the flag so that its face was toward the sky. It was as if they were showing all the people in heaven they weren't forgotten, that they were still a part of all this. The flag passed in silence, followed by a line of firetrucks. Their lights were flashing, but their sirens were silent, the firemen and families aboard solemn and still.

Tate felt the drumline beating in his heart before he heard it, gently breaking the silence with another patriotic tune. It probably put some people at ease, hearing their country's ballads played for the masses like some form of reassurance, but not him. The band marched in place behind the drum major as he halted and tossed the baton. It twirled in the air, a little too crooked, before clattering off his hand onto the pavement. The drum major caught Tate's eye as he collected the baton, immediately squaring off and tossing it again. This time it rotated perfectly, landing square in his hand in time with the music. The drum major gave Tate a wink as the band continued on, but Tate didn't care. The tears froze to his face as he thought about the drum major's second toss and about his father.

Some people don't get a second chance.

. . .

He can't be going again.
Please don't go again.

When Max got knocked out, his eyes had been on Cameron, but as he called for a rematch, they were locked on Wilson one seat over. Nevertheless, Cameron couldn't take his eyes off the bruises in various stages of healing that colored Max's ribs deep blues and purples. Off the swelling on his face from the knock out he just took. Off the betrayal in his eyes as he made a conscious effort not to look at Cameron again.

"Damn," Wilson said as the winner re-entered the first stall. "How many times does my brother have to kick this kid's ass before he gets the message?"

His brother?

The message?

Cameron's head spun as the collector with the tacky suit approached, clipboard in hand. "Bets up, Cammy." Wilson produced a hundred dollar bill from his pocket, snapping it taught five times before pocketing it once more. "Five hundred on the reigning champ." The collector marked the bet down on his clipboard before turning to Cameron.

"I don't have any more," Cameron lied, fingering the remaining two hundred in his suitcoat pocket.

"I told you to bring three hundred." Wilson had encouraged Cameron to bet a hundred dollars blind on the previous fight, where he proceeded to watch Max get his ass kicked. Cameron squirmed under Wilson's gaze until he couldn't take it, reaching into his pocket and producing his remaining two hundred dollars. "Atta boy, Cammy." Wilson turned to the collector. "Two more on the big guy."

"No," Cameron said. "The other one." It was a futile attempt to make himself feel supportive, but as Cameron basked in the glow of Wilson's approval, he felt like the one that got punched. The collector glanced at Wilson, who shrugged and waved him off. Cameron tried to convince himself he was staying to look out for Max, make sure he made it out okay, but even he knew that wasn't true.

Max refused to look up as he prepared himself, bouncing on his toes and throwing ghost punches like a prizefighter ready for battle. Wilson's brother was taken aback by Max's change in routine, a big bulk of awkward as he tried to shadow Max's movements.

Look at me.

Cameron willed Max to look up, even just for a second. He would see this wasn't Cameron's idea. That Cameron hadn't known they were coming here tonight. That he hadn't known Max would be here. That he didn't want to watch his best friend fight.

Wouldn't he?

But the more Cameron thought about it, the more he realized what Max would actually see. Cameron side by side with Wilson, staying to watch even though he didn't have to. Betting on the fight even though he didn't want to. Taking his proper place amongst the elite.

Cameron jumped at the sound of the bell, swallowing hard as the rematch began. His gasp was audible as Wilson's brother took a swing at Max's already bruised eye, but Max's fighter's stance was different this time, hands tucked in front of his face.

"Come on, Chester!" Wilson yelled to his brother. "Put him in his place!"

Max's body tensed at Wilson's voice, his muscles contracting tighter and tighter until Cameron could see every vein snaking through his shirtless torso. An anger radiated off Max that Cameron hadn't seen before, propelling his fist forward as he landed a punch square in the middle of Chester's nose. Blood shot in all directions as Chester's scream reverberated through the barn, but Max did not hesitate with another hook.

And another.

And another.

Crack. Crack. Crack.

Chester's head swiveled back and forth with each blow until he couldn't take it, knees buckling as he fell to the ground like a strand of cooked spaghetti. The entire barn was silent; all other fights paused as all eyes trained on Max. His chest rose and fell with adrenaline as he stared down at his opponent, fists clenching and unclenching as a mental battle raged within him. The bell sounded, announcing his victory, and Max's hands fell open, released from a role he didn't want to play.

He immediately took Chester's arm over his own shoulder, grunting under the weight as he lifted him to his feet. They exited the stall together, and Max propped Chester on a nearby bench before grabbing a towel from the hands of the wide-eyed fighter next in line for the first stall. Max helped Chester press the towel to what was left of his nose, but it quickly saturated a deep crimson. He took one hand off the towel, snapping his fingers behind him until another towel was produced for him to swap out. Max continued this process for what felt like eternity.

"Someone should call 9-1-1," Cameron squeaked, nauseous at the sight of all the blood.

"No!" Wilson practically yelled, although they were side by side. "What are you, an idiot? My dad would be ruined."

Cameron tried to process Wilson's words, but they darted around his head like firecrackers that wouldn't burn out. By the fourth towel, the blood finally began to speckle instead of saturate. Max placed Chester's hands in place of his own before gathering the discarded towels and piling them out of sight. He grabbed the shoulders of two onlookers and sat one on each side of Chester's, positioned to keep him from toppling. Max stepped back and did a final once-over, satisfied he did all he could for Wilson's brother. Only then did he ascend the stairs to retrieve his winnings.

He started in the back row, Cameron craning his neck to watch as Max walked down the line. His knuckles were raw, layers of skin stripped away by the punches as he collected the wads of out-stretched cash from a dumbfounded crowd. He kept his head down and he started down the front row. He did not offer a word nor glance as he snatched the money from Wilson, who was pink with rage and sputtering incoherently.

A million betrayals passed between them as Max finally looked at Cameron, his hand suspended mid-reach for the two hundred dollars trembling in Cameron's outstretched hand. Chester's blood was splattered across Max's face like a Pollock painting, his right eye more bloodshot than usual and practically swollen shut. They stood like that for a long time, Cameron's money outstretched, Max deciding whether or not he should take it. After all that happened, Cameron wanted him to. He owed Max for being such a terrible friend, and this was the only way he could think to make up for betting on him in the first place. "I bet on *you*," Cameron emphasized, raising the money a little higher to indicate he wanted Max to take it.

Max reared back as if Cameron had struck him, shaking his head as his hand fell against his thigh. Without a word, Max collected the remainder of his winnings and descended the spiral staircase. He did not look back as he exited the barn, leaving Cameron with two hundred dollars in hand that weighed two hundred pounds on his conscience.

. . .

Lyle never thought she would miss the sound of sirens, but as she stood atop the firetruck with her grandfather, she realized the silence was so much worse. Her mother stood behind her, a cardboard cutout of who she once was not but two months earlier. Rawel stood to Lyle's left, his arm protectively around her, but despite his best efforts, she could feel him shaking. Every now and then, he made a comment about the winter chill, but even at seven years old, Lyle knew it wasn't from the cold.

There was no one to her right, and Lyle felt the empty space like the missing arm of a chair. He was supposed to be there next to her like he always was. There were so many other firemen, paramedics, police officers, so many public servants who made it through September and were here with her today.

Why couldn't one of them be Dad?

Lyle swallowed the thought before it rooted in her head, turning her attention to the crowd as they passed by. Everyone did their best to be quiet, but the minutes of silent respect morphed into minutes of restless shuffling and mutterings about the upcoming balloons or performances. Lyle easily picked out the people whose families were directly affected by the September tragedy. An old woman in a folding chair, clutching a picture of her grown son to her chest. A man sandwiched within the crowd, his body so still it was as if someone paused the blood in his veins. A boy standing on the windowsill of a coffee shop, radiating loneliness as he lurked in the shadow of the awning.

She knew how that felt.

Lyle didn't expect the rest of the crowd to understand. How could they? It was one thing to be ravaged as a country, or even as an individual. But to be ravaged as a family? That took an entirely new toll. The loss of her father not only affected each of her family members individually, but it affected their relationships with one another, too. Despite the efforts of Rawel, Aariz, and Yalina, Lyle felt the void between herself and her mother growing larger with each passing day.

A tear froze to her face before she could stop it, and for the hundredth time that day, Lyle wished she stayed home with Aariz.

. . .

Lyle stood rooted to the foot of the stage, the image of someone she didn't recognize branded into her mind. She felt stunned, unable to move her body or mind past what she had overheard. She was keeping Aariz company as he worked overtime on his latest project when they heard the commotion. Thinking it was Wilson and his crew back for more, Aariz leaped into action, Lyle following behind in the shadows.

And she heard everything.

Aariz hadn't noticed Lyle when he left the stage, but as he emerged from his workshop now, one look redirected him up the stairs to his apartment. He flashed her a smile on his way that didn't quite reach his eyes, distancing himself from the situation under the guise of giving her some privacy. Lyle didn't blame him; one person could only feel so much emotion in one day. Being strong for others didn't leave much room to be strong for yourself, and today Aariz certainly needed all the inner strength he could muster. They all did. So they left each other alone, to heal themselves from inside the best way they knew how.

The lights were off, but Lyle knew the place by heart and wound her way behind the counter with ease. Tears trickled down her face in a nonchalant manner, as if trying to sneak out of her without her knowledge. She nearly jumped out of her skin as she rounded the carousel, surprised to find a shirtless and swollen Max sitting at the piano. His eyes looked lost and even more broken than his body, and he sat hunched with his back to the keys, elbows on his knees.

"Oh, my God," Lyle said, hastily wiping her tear-stained cheeks as she took in Max's swollen eye.

Max took his time looking up at her, his expression pensive. "Hey."

"What happened?" Lyle had grown accustomed to the colorful bruises spattering his ribs, but other than the night they met, she had never seen Max's face injured. Max didn't answer as she took his chin in her hand and turned his head toward the glow of the exit sign. It bathed his face in red, making his swollen eye socket even more menacing, and Lyle quickly let her hand fall away. "Max," she prodded.

"Headshot." He was studying her face too, red and swollen from tears rather than punches. "Are you okay?"

"What? Yeah." Lyle didn't want to talk about what she saw, so she sat down next to Max, motioning to his eye. "How did this happen?"

"I got…distracted." Max hesitated, as if weighing whether or not to continue. "Cameron was there."

"Cameron as in our Cameron?" Lyle asked. Max nodded. "Cameron King?" Max nodded again. "Fighting?"

Max shook his head. "Watching. With Wilson." Lyle tried to process this, wondering how Wilson even knew Max was fighting at all. "He bet on me." His voice was low and wavering, his eyes trained on his own torn-up knuckles.

"Cameron?" Lyle pushed Max's hair back to examine his swollen eye again. "Looks like he lost his money."

"Not the first round." Max's voice was bitter now.

Lyle dropped her hand in disbelief. "He bet against you?" Max did not answer, but the way he bit his lip was enough of an indicator. "And the second round?" she asked, trying to piece together the events.

Max rubbed his left hand along his right knuckles, tracing and pressing on the open skin in a way that looked painful. He was quiet a long time, his attention drawn inward. "I really hurt someone tonight."

"On purpose?" Although Max was tough, Lyle couldn't imagine him intentionally causing anyone pain. Even in an illegal fighting ring.

"I don't know what came over me. It was like I couldn't control myself." His muscles tensed as he sat up straighter.

"That's probably what Wilson wanted."

Max gave Lyle a look. "For me to break his brother's nose?"

"No," Lyle said, trying to keep the image of Max's fist smashing against someone's nose out of her mind. "For you to feel like this."

Max mulled that over. "Cam bet on me to win that round." His eyebrows were knit together but also raised, like he didn't know if he should feel angry or sad. "Like that's any better."

Lyle sighed. "You know how he gets around Wilson."

"How much longer can that be an excuse?" Max's voice boomed around the carousel. "How much farther does it have to go before it's too far?"

Lyle's mind flashed to Tate's comments to Aariz, how the lows with him were starting to outweigh the highs. "I don't know," she whispered

Max's body softened, his expression turning to one of concern as he studied her. "Why were you crying?" Sometimes Lyle wished he was a little less observant.

She thought about downplaying the situation, but she was tired of doing that. "I overheard Tate talking to Aariz." She paused, trying to think of how to best articulate what she was feeling. "And I wish I hadn't."

"Tate was here?" Max sounded surprised. "Today?"

Lyle nodded. "He basically accused Aariz and his wife of being terrorists."

"His wife?"

"She died." The more she thought about it, the more Lyle saw similarities between Tate and her mother. And she didn't like it. "How can people have so much hatred in their hearts?"

It was a rhetorical question, and they sat in silence as they tried and failed to come up with an answer. "Come here," Max finally said, clasping her hand as he led her out the back door. The rain had stopped, but the pavement of the alley glinted wet in the moonlight. He pulled his skateboard out from behind an empty garbage can and dropped it on the ground between them. "Get on."

Lyle looked at him like he had three heads. "Max, I don't know how to skateboard."

"I'm going to teach you."

"Why?" The last thing Lyle felt like doing right now was falling on her butt in a puddle.

"Because." Max tugged her forward onto the skateboard. "We both could use some fun right now." He left no room for objection as he took Lyle's hands in his and began rolling her down the alley.

"Max!" she cried as they hit a bump, her hands flailing around in an attempt to stay balanced.

"You're all right." Max reached for her hands and settled them on his shoulders. "There you go, hold onto me." Lyle clasped her hands together at the base of his neck, his hands steady on her hips like a slow dance. With the extra inches from the skateboard, they were about eye to eye as he continued to roll her around the alley. He let her go a couple of times, prying her hands from the nape of his neck and jogging along beside her as she skated solo. The smell of recent rain was thick around them, leaving no space for them to go but closer as he slowed her roll, gently pushing and pulling her the length of his arms.

"My father died in that crash too," Lyle said, trying to make sense of the last couple hours now that her mind was quieter. "And I don't hate Aariz."

A fond smile tugged at the corners of Max's lips. "You don't hate anybody." His lips were darker than hers, an intriguing magenta, and Lyle wondered whether or not they were swollen. "But Tate isn't as strong as you."

"And Cameron isn't as strong as you," she shot back, tired of everyone defending Tate's actions.

"Touché." His hands pushed firmer on her hips as he stopped her from rolling, his eyes on her white sneakers perched atop the skateboard. "Look, I'm sorry you have to deal with all of this…with all of us." His expression shifted to something softer than usual as he lifted his eyes to meet hers. "You're so selfless, Lyle, and so good. You don't deserve it." There was guilt in his voice, and the whole thing sounded almost like an apology.

"What you did tonight doesn't make you a bad person," Lyle said, pushing a strand of hair off Max's swollen eye.

"I didn't take his money."

"And I didn't confront Tate."

Max paused, and she could tell he was fighting an inner battle. "But did you want to?"

Lyle thought about it a moment. "A little. Did you?"

"A little." She could feel the muscles in his neck and shoulders relax at the thought of someone finally understanding him. "I'm sorry I wasn't here for your birthday." He stepped a little closer so his hands met at the small of her back, something strong for Lyle to lean into.

"You're here now."

"Yeah," Max said, the first real smile of the night gracing his face. Lyle rested her head on his right shoulder, heat from his swollen eye radiating inches away from her face. A breath of air escaped Max's lips as she placed the lightest of kisses on his traumatized eyelid, and he pulled her body closer to his in an embrace that neither of them wanted to release. Lyle stood there with him on the skateboard for a long time, each of them the only thing holding the other one together.

And for the first time all day, she no longer felt unsteady.

CHAPTER ELEVEN

The makeup Lyle smudged over his eye in the bathroom during homeroom felt clumpy and strange on Max's face as they set up for rehearsal. Flits of bruised blue peaked through as it wore off, but from a distance, Tate wouldn't notice, and Max's day had revolved around keeping that distance. Judging from the way Tate was skirting around the lobby like a roach at a cocktail party, Max guessed Lyle spent her day doing the same.

Cameron, on the other hand, couldn't keep his eyes off Max, glancing toward and away from him as if watching a tennis match. He hadn't been in pre-calc, and Max was shocked to see him at rehearsal. There was a longing in his timidity, his eyes begging for Max to engage so he could apologize. But Max didn't have the strength to be everyone's rock today, so he took his seat behind the drums and clacked his sticks together to count them in.

Max was surprised Tate was singing without his guitar, and even more surprised he didn't know why. Once upon a time, he and Tate told each other everything, and look where they were now. Together, but alone. Max watched Cameron's bleached blond head bob with the music. The product in his hair probably cost more than the winnings of a fight. How could he understand what Max was going through when he had never faced a decision that cost more than popularity? How could they be friends when they came from two completely different worlds?

The red of his skinned knuckles flashed in and out of Max's vision like a warning sign as his hands flew around the drum set. Something came over him last night, made him lose control, and it scared him. Fighting wasn't who he wanted to be, but who was he trying to kid? He couldn't afford to make it to college, much less through it. His secret was driving a wedge between everyone. He and Tate were more distant by the day, he and Cameron crossed a line that was hard to come back from, and their late-night escapades weighed on Lyle in a way that gnawed at Max's gut. The drum sticks seemed to be the only thing left to hold onto, and Max clung to them with all his might, slamming them into the drums with all the frustration inside him as the song ended.

Maybe the only thing I should stop fighting is fate.

A clapping once again startled them as it echoed through the lobby, and Max perched up in search of Aariz. He needed his support right now. He needed someone who still believed in him. But Aariz was not there, the buzz of carpentry equipment vouching for his whereabouts. Instead, Max's heart dropped into his stomach as his eyes landed on the source.

"If I didn't know any better, I'd say you had a fighting chance tomorrow." Wilson continued to clap until he reached the foot of the stage, his choice of words not lost on Max.

"Do you need something?" Lyle asked, rounding the counter faster than a mama bear protecting her cubs. There was an attitude in her voice Max was not accustomed to, and he loved her for it.

"I need a pretty girl to be my date tomorrow night. I'm sure you'll find my company much more…" Wilson glanced at each boy in turn before taking a step closer to Lyle, "…civilized."

"Don't bet on it." Her voice was cold as ice, her choice of words lost only on Tate. Wilson's smirk faltered the slightest bit, but he recovered as the boys descended the stage.

"What do you want?" Tate asked, his voice tired.

Wilson stepped back to take them all in. "I just wanted to give you one more chance to back out. Save yourselves the humiliation."

"We don't plan on losing." Tate bristled as Wilson dropped a hand on his shoulder.

"Why don't you just quit while you're ahead? You already beat the odds. There's no way you're going three for three."

"Three for three," Tate repeated, the wheels in his head not quite turning fast enough.

"After Cammy's spotlight performance at the bee, and your boy's knockout performance last night…" Wilson's eyes wrapped around Max like an anaconda around its prey before slithering back to Tate. "…I'd say your luck's about run out." The confusion on Tate's face felt like a punch to the gut, and Max saw Lyle suck in a breath before fixing a glare on Wilson. "Oh, he didn't tell you?" Wilson pulled a cigarette from his breast pocket and an old-fashioned lighter from his khakis. "Not quite a big happy family, are we?" Tate flinched as the lighter clicked to life, and Wilson let the flame dance a beat longer than necessary, studying Tate's reaction before returning it to his pocket. For the first time since he arrived, Wilson fixed his eyes on Cameron, who squirmed under his gaze like a worm in a bait bucket. "Then again, that was evident last night when Cammy here bet against your boy."

"Screw you," Lyle spat.

"Want to?" Wilson did not hesitate as he took a threatening step toward her, and Max did not hesitate as he took a step between them, nudging Lyle behind him with his arm. Wilson whistled and raised an eyebrow at Tate. "Looks like you'll be losing the money and the girl." Wilson raised his hands in surrender as he returned his attention to Max. "I better take a step back. We've all seen what you're capable of."

Max could feel everyone's eyes on him, Tate's the heaviest as Wilson headed for the door. "Looks like you *friends* have a lot to talk about. I'll leave you to it. Oh, and Tate, do me a favor?" Wilson took one last drag from his cigarette before flicking it in Tate's direction. "Put this out for me? We wouldn't want it to get out of hand." Tate tripped over himself as he stumbled backward, barely holding his footing as Max stomped out the cigarette. Wilson watched from the doorway, the bell tinkling again as he let in the cold night air. "By the way," he said to Max, tapping a finger beneath his own eye. "You might want to reapply. Your secret is poking through."

Tate was the first to move in Wilson's wake, and Max did not pull away as he rubbed away the makeup to reveal the purple blossom of a bruise. "You're fighting again." It was a statement, not a question, a thought that needed to be spoken for Tate to process it. Max did not respond, just looked at Tate looking at him, the betrayal in Tate's eyes more painful than the bruise around his own.

Tate turned to Cameron, who had been stunned silent by Wilson's visit. "And you bet on him?"

"I didn't mean to—"

"You didn't mean to." Tate repeated the words slowly, as if feeling them in his own mouth would help him understand them better.

Cameron looked helplessly at Max, cringing at his own explanation, and Max felt sorry for the kid in spite of himself. "Wilson told me—"

"Oh!" Tate interrupted, all of them jumping at the boom of his voice. "Wilson told you! I forgot you can't have a thought for yourself." There was a menacing aspect of the last sentence that Max didn't like.

"Tate," he said, but Tate was on a roll Max couldn't slow.

"Don't you realize all of this trouble is because of you?" Cameron's eyes grew wider with each accusation Tate hurled at him. "The only reason Wilson has it out for us is because you jumped ship from his preppy cult. And while Max bent over backwards defending you, you scampered right back to them. You only use our friendship to heal your wounds before you crawl back to being a rich asshole!"

"Tate, stop!" Max had heard enough. "He doesn't know!"

"Doesn't know what?" Although Tate was still talking about Cameron, his volume was now directed at Max. "Doesn't know how to wash his own clothes? Doesn't know how to be a friend? Doesn't know how to stand up for you, or himself, or anyone?"

"I'm sorry." Cameron could barely get the words out as he hastened out the front door.

"Cameron," Lyle called as Max started after him, but Cameron did not turn around, his tears carrying him and his skateboard down the street.

"What the hell, Tate?" Max heard the anger creeping into his own voice as he turned back. There was no doubt he was hurt by Cameron's presence last night, but Max was beginning to understand Cameron hadn't wanted to be there any more than he had.

Tate looked astonished. "How could you defend him?"

"Someone has to!"

"Like he defended you at the barn?" The mention of the barn dropped a heavy silence between them, both boys boiling with a rage they fought daily to suppress. Tate's voice was low when he broke the silence, ready to pounce regardless of Max's response. "How could you be doing this again?"

"He needed money for college," Lyle blurted, realizing her mistake too late as a newfound confusion settled on Tate's face.

"You knew?" A disbelief lined his voice that matched the hurt in his eyes. Lyle knew better than to answer, still and unthreatening until Tate's gaze tore back to Max. "You told *her*?"

"You haven't exactly been around." Max kept his voice steady, matter-of-fact.

"Are you kidding?" Tate's arms flew around as he spoke, animating his frustration. "I've been here every night!"

Max squared off his shoulders and looked Tate dead in the eyes. "So have I." The comment had its desired effect, the weight of its implications passing through Tate like a kidney stone. His eyes flashed from Lyle to Max as if they had been reincarnated into people had didn't know at all.

"We had a plan," Tate finally said.

"What plan?" Max was starting to get annoyed. After all that just happened, all he just found out, Tate was still preoccupied with winning. "Losing the talent show? You know Wilson's never going to let us win."

"The plan to march!" The veins in Tate's temples protruded more with each response, his scar deepening in color as the blood rushed to his face. "Or has your mentor convinced you college is more important?"

"College *is* more important! The only reason any of us are doing this is for you!" Max heard his voice echo through the lobby, and for Lyle's sake, he was thankful it was empty. "I've stood by you for so long, but what about me? You're too mad at the world to want anything else, but I want a future!"

"Like you're not mad at the world?" Tate scoffed. "The only reason you're such a good fighter is because you're so angry all the time."

There was a bite to Tate's voice, judgment. He wanted it to sting. And sting it did. "You're coming at me now?" Their friendship felt heavy for a long time, a burden Max carried around in the name of loyalty. But what kind of loyalty was Tate showing now? "You're being an ass to everyone, and all any of us have done is try to help you! Have you ever stopped to think that you're not the only one around here who's lost someone this week?"

Tate reeled away from Max's comment before lunging back louder. "My father is dead!"

"And marching isn't going to bring him back!" Max screamed, honesty overpowering his need to protect. "Or being a racist ass to Aariz!" The mention of Aariz sparked a disdain in Tate's eyes, a disdain Max had excused for too long. "Or berating Cameron to make yourself feel stronger!"

"Why are you defending him when he bet on you?"

"He needs me," Max said simply, whatever grudge he held against Cameron dissipating as he came to his defense.

Tate jabbed himself in the chest with his index finger. "I need you! I've been busting my ass for weeks to win this money, and you've apparently had it the whole time!"

"I don't owe it to you!" Max's skin was radiating heat like a tea kettle longing for release. For as long as they had been friends, Max put Tate's needs before his own. It was time to think of himself. "This money is mine! My blood, my pain, my choice to save it for college. It's not always about you!"

"You don't think I'm there for you?" Tate asked in disbelief. "After everything we did to get you out of those stalls?"

"'We'? Don't pretend you had a hand in any of it!" Max's open palm thudded against his own chest as he continued. "I was the one that spared you that night when we were twelve. I was the one who took you in when you had nowhere to go. I was the one who agreed to this marching thing because it was important to you. I was the one that backed off your girl because you needed someone to lean on."

"You call sneaking around after closing backing off my girl?"

Lyle's eyes grew wide at being caught in the middle, but Max ignored the comment, determined to keep the conversation on course. "What have you ever done for me?"

"You stopped fighting because of me!" Tate was screaming now, although his voice held a tremor that hadn't been there before. "You think your greedy drunk of a dad would have ever let you stop if I hadn't found out the truth?"

"What truth?" If Max had known what Tate was about to say, he never would have asked.

A flicker of hesitation flashed in Tate's eyes, but his mouth had already started to answer. "He had your mother deported!"

. . .

Tate clamped his mouth shut in a futile attempt to take his words back. Max's spine went rigid, making him the kind of taller that came from uncertainty, not confidence. As though he was teetering atop stilts, the height making him vulnerable instead of strong.

Tate never intended to tell Max about his mother, and the next thing he knew, he felt the force of Max's hands against his shoulder blades. It was the first time Max laid a hand on Tate since the night they met, and Lyle gasped as Tate fell to the floor. "Lying about my mother isn't going to help you."

"I'm not lying. Your father is."

Max's breathing deepened, and Tate could see his mind churning adrenaline through his body as he tried to make sense of it all. Max took a threatening step forward, clenching his right fist as Tate lay between his feet.

"Max!" he hurried, raising his hands to protect his face. "She was going to tell! He was hitting her, and she was going to tell, so he used 9/11 as an excuse to have her deported."

"He hit her?" Max's grit was instantaneously replaced by sadness, a healed wound reopened that hurt now more than ever.

"I found polaroids in his safe."

"You broke into his safe?"

"That money belonged to you, not him." Tate grazed over his trespassing and continued. "She was going to report him, and he found out. The fake marriage license was in there too. She probably thought it was real." Max looked nauseated at the thought. One trip to Mexico and one fake marriage license was all it took for his father to have total control over his mother. "I threatened to tell if he didn't let you stop."

"You knew all this time." Max's statement was low, his words slow. "How could you not tell me?"

Lyle's arm found its way around Max's broad shoulders, her hand rubbing up and down his arm in a way that sent a fit of hot jealousy burning through Tate's throat that he couldn't swallow. "I guess now we're even."

"Tate!" Lyle's voice was shocked, but Tate's attention locked on Max. Max looked at Lyle's arm around him as if noticing it for the first time before gently shrugging it off. In an act of chivalry that both impressed and enraged Tate, Max grabbed him by the hand and pulled him to his feet before turning for the door.

Tate's stomach boiled with scalding water as he watched his best friend turn his back on him. "I was trying to protect you!"

"Protect *me*?" Max whipped around. "Or *you*?" Tate had seen Max fix that hateful glower on countless scumbags over the years, but this was the first time he found himself on the receiving end of it. "You took my mother away because you need me to need you." Both boys stared at each other for an eternity before Max was able to recompose himself. "See you at rehearsal tomorrow," he finally said, Tate's eyes finding their way to the floor as Max crossed the lobby. "You okay?"

Tate started to answer before realizing Max was speaking to Lyle, his hand grazing her upper arm protectively. Lyle nodded, and Max left without another word, leaving Tate wondering when he became public enemy number one. And where he was going to sleep tonight.

"Lyle..." He wanted her to understand him, needed her to understand him. Only Lyle was looking at Tate like he was a stranger, a stranger who hadn't turned her pages or accompanied her to the prison or cracked himself open to show her what was inside.

"How could you keep that from him?"

Tate's mind was still snagged on Lyle patching Max up night after night while the evils of the world slept. "You're going to talk to me about secrets?"

"Oh, my God! He was embarrassed to tell you."

Tate's heart didn't want another fight, but his head was reeling in search of answers. "Were you?"

Lyle bit her lip. Even in the thick of all this, it was evident she didn't want to hurt him. "I was being a good friend."

"To who?"

"To everyone! Which is more than I can say for you. The way you talk to Cameron, to Max…" Lyle fixed a glare on Tate. "…to Aariz."

Tate bristled. He was running out of reasons to hate Aariz, but he had to, so he settled on the incessant buzzing of some carpentry machine that had been running in the background for hours. All Tate wanted was to make his father proud, and not hating Aariz would be a disgrace to him.

Wouldn't it?

"This isn't about that."

"It all goes together, Tate!" His gold chain bounced against Lyle's chest as she yelled. "You're so convinced the whole world's against you, you're pushing away the only people who aren't."

"The world is against me!" Tate's fingertips found their way to his scar as he thought about the fire, about the night he met Max, about Wilson and the stage, and the constant uphill battles. "Have you seen what my life's been like? It's always been against me!"

The silence that fell between them was heavy, the air stuffed with too much of life's troubles for them to see each other clearly. Lyle fingered the chain around her neck. "If you truly believe that, then you need this much more than I do."

The gold chain felt like an anvil as Lyle dropped it in his hand, grounding him in a reality he no longer wanted. Tate glimpsed a tear rolling down her cheek before she turned away. "Lyle…" But she didn't turn around, quickening her pace as she headed for the counter. "Delilah!" The longing in his voice stopped her, but again she did not turn around. Tate held his breath as the two of them teetered on her next move, until she finally disappeared behind the counter and retreated up the stairs.

Tate hadn't noticed Aariz's machine stop, the silence overwhelming as he wandered to the stage. In thirty minutes, he managed to lose the three people he cared about most, and for the first time since his father died, Tate evaluated himself.

Am I the problem?

His question was answered by his father's guitar, perfectly reconstructed and propped in the back left corner of the stage; a newly sanded neck and body held together by six taught strings. Tate dropped to his knees, lodging his hands in his hair. The talent show was tomorrow, yet the only thing Tate could think about was what a failure he had become. Desperate for something to piece himself back together, Tate slipped the gold chain over his head and grabbed the guitar. The chords sounded through the lobby, and although the guitar was flawlessly repaired, playing it still felt wrong without anyone there to listen.

. . .

I shouldn't be here.

Cameron couldn't shake the thought as he stood in The Carry Out for their final rehearsal. The talent show was in an hour, and Rawel closed the store for the day so they could practice uninterrupted. As he looked around the lobby, Cameron took in all the reasons he didn't belong there. Lyle doing his laundry. Tate's vandalized stage. Max's eye.

I let it all happen.

Cameron should have been excited as Max counted them in, but he was too engrossed in his own guilt to care. Max struck the drums with such ferocity, Cameron began to fear for their integrity. His black eye made Max look like a raccoon, but the insides of his eyes were black, too, as if a dark smoke found a crack in his body and seeped in. Cameron strummed upwards, then downwards, in an attempt to stay on tempo, unable to make even the smallest of decisions. Tate's voice strained against the notes as they reached the bridge of the song, screaming more than singing, the pain audible in his voice. Cameron had never seen him so disheveled, so out of control. The song was too perfect for the sorry trio of underdogs, and Cameron found it ironic that the loneliness that pulled them together was the same thing tearing them apart.

They finished the song with as much turmoil as when they started—off-beat, off-key, and off-kilter—but Aariz clapped anyway. "I just wanted to wish you gentlemen luck tonight." His eyes paused as he noticed Max's eye, and Cameron wanted to shrink into himself.

I'm no gentleman.

"Thank you," Tate said earnestly, and Max nodded before averting his eyes.

"You deserve it." Aariz looked at each of them in turn, as if emphasizing his point. "All of you." Their collective smile was weak and convinced no one, dropping as soon as Aariz disappeared into his workshop.

"We should probably head over soon," Tate said to no one in particular. The boys began to gather their things, readying themselves for the night that felt like it would never come.

"What song are we playing?" Max's voice sounded distant, as if in a daze. The tinkling of the bell caught everyone's attention before Tate could answer.

"Sorry, we're closed," Tate said politely, his back to the door. When the bell didn't announce someone's exit, he turned to who he thought was a customer. "Man," he said when he saw who it was. "Get the hell out of here."

"Is that how you treat someone coming to wish you luck?" Wilson feigned offense to his henchmen on either shoulder.

Tate hopped off the stage and squared his shoulders, his voice pointed. "I'll let you know when I see one."

Cameron saw the anger slip into Wilson's face, but he was quick to mask it with a toothy smile. "Why don't you save us all the trouble and drop out now?" Wilson jutted his chin toward Max. "Your boy here's making more than enough for all of you." Max and Tate looked at one another before averting their gazes. There was a rift between them Cameron had never seen before, and Wilson noticed it too as he elbowed Bruce in the side. "I guess he's not sharing."

Bruce guffawed, giving Max and Tate the same once-over Cameron's parents had. "They're all stingy."

"Apparently." Wilson zeroed in on Tate. "No wonder your girl's not interested. Where is she anyway? I'm sure she's come to her senses by now about being my date." Tate's step forward was instinctive, protective, even though Lyle was nowhere to be seen.

"Here comes the tough guy," Bruce laughed, poking Brian in the side for affirmation. Brian obliged, but begrudgingly, looking at Cameron almost apologetically.

"Relax," Wilson purred, reaching into his pocket as he stepped to meet Tate. "Have a cigarette." The stick hung between them like a threat as the two's eye contact remained unbroken.

Until the flame clicked alive.

The fear that overtook Tate's entire body was deep-seated, and he stumbled backward into Max's hands that nudged him back onto his feet. Bruce, then Brian, snickered as Wilson flicked the flame once more at a skittish Tate, and all at once, Cameron had enough.

It angered him he was friends with these people for so long.

It angered him the way they treated his real friends.

It angered him that he had been too spineless to do anything about it.

Before he fully realized what he was doing, Cameron stepped forward, looked Wilson dead in the eyes, and punched.

. . .

Lyle stole the headphones from Tate's keyboard earlier in the day, and as she sat inside the carousel of clothes, she wasn't sure if they were blocking out the noise of the boys' final rehearsal or the noise of her own thoughts. The piano spread out before her, eighty-eight ivory memories she wished would disappear. But her fingertips rested on the keys, and within the shelter of the carousel, they all came flooding back.

. . .

When the piano was delivered, her mother tried to send it back. "We didn't order that," she said as two delivery men lugged a giant crate into the lobby.

"Yes we did, Mommy." It confused Lyle that her mother had so quickly forgotten their trip to the city only two weeks ago.

The delivery man double-checked his clipboard, puzzled. "We were told to ask for Rawel?"

"Grandfather!" Lyle yelled loud enough for Rawel to hear. Her call summoned Aariz as well, who hovered at the edge of the lobby.

Lyle's mother huffed her hair out of her eyes, but the blonde mass had taken on a mind of its own without a brush to tame it, and it fell forward almost immediately. "I'm not paying for this."

Lyle's heart sank at the thought of losing the only thing she was still excited about it. "Marianna…" Aariz said, stepping forward, his hand outstretched in a comforting gesture.

"Stay out of this," her mother snapped, Aariz nodding his head as if answering a question Lyle hadn't heart.

"It's already paid for, ma'am," the delivery man hurried, hoping the clarity would jog her memory. "With a credit card belonging to a Leon Kaminski. I just need a signature." Lyle's body felt like it weighed forty more pounds at the mention of her father's name. Her eyes sprang to her mother, whose face was hard as stone, the lack of emotion unsettling.

"Lyle, what's the prob—?" Rawel stopped short as he rounded the counter to find the piano crate, his eyes finding Aariz's as he processed the situation. "Marianna," he said after a moment. "I'll take care of this." Lyle was surprised when her mother allowed her grandfather to usher her up the stairs to their apartment.

Aariz stepped forward again as Rawel returned and scrawled his signature across the clipboard. "Over there is just fine," he said, gesturing to the stage between his and Aariz's lobby.

"Grandfather." Lyle tugged at his shirt sleeve as she watched the men move the crate. "I don't think…" She glanced over her shoulder to where her mother had retreated. "I don't think it should go there."

"Why not?" Aariz asked, sandwiching her between them. "I think that's the perfect place for everyone to listen to you." Lyle bit her lip as Rawel squatted down to her level.

"Your mother just needs time to heal." He squeezed her into a hug before straightening up and flashing her a grin that looked just like her dad's used to. "And what better way than listening to your beautiful music?"

"I couldn't agree more." Aariz gave her a loving nudge as his wife Yalina joined them. The sleek black and pure white hatched from the crate as Lyle watched the delivery men peel away the wooden exterior.

"Why don't you play us something?" Yalina asked as the door closed behind the delivery men. Lyle skipped over to the piano, sat herself down, and with three out of four of her favorite people watching, played the same scale over and over.

. . .

Yalina's feet rested on the ground as Lyle's swung forward and backward next to her. "Want to try again?" Yalina asked. Lyle nodded and let her fingers step across the keys in a double-handed C scale, followed by the three major chords. "Good!" Yalina put her arm around Lyle. "You picked that up quickly."

Lyle basked in the positive reinforcement. Although Rawel convinced her mother to keep the piano in the lobby, she refused to teach Lyle how to play it. Lyle tried to teach herself but quickly became frustrated by her lack of knowledge. Yalina had been nice enough to step in, and for the past three weeks, she and Lyle fit in lessons when they could. While her mother was in the shower, out running errands, already asleep. They weren't sneaking, but it was certainly easier when Lyle's mother didn't know.

Besides, Lyle liked working with Yalina. She was calm and caring, supportive, and interested in Lyle. Everything her mother wasn't. "Now that you're warmed up, why don't you try the song we've been working on?" Lyle began to play but stopped as she hit a wrong note, blushing into her hands. Yalina tugged the music book off the stand, thumbing through it absentmindedly until she landed on another song with a look of nostalgia.

"What?" Lyle asked, reading her expression.

Yalina pointed to a word in the title, her finger tracing each letter. "We almost adopted a little girl with this name."

"You did?"

"Yes." A fond smile played at the edges of Yalina's lips as she remembered.

"What happened to her?"

Her eyes clouded as they focused on something Lyle couldn't see. "There was a…complication with the adoption. We couldn't keep her."

"What kind of complication?"

Yalina tugged her hijab more snuggly around her face. "They didn't think Aariz and I were…the best fit to adopt right now."

Lyle knit her brow in confusion. "How could they think that? You'd be a great mom!"

She smiled sadly, running her hand up and down Lyle's back. "Well, thank you, sweetheart. Want to try it again?" Lyle nodded as Yalina flipped back to the previous title. She reached the last page of the song without a mistake before she was interrupted by the front door slamming, the bell above it ricocheting wildly against the doorframe.

"Unbelievable!" Lyle's mother stormed into the lobby, engrossed in a piece of paper in her hand. "My husband dies saving American citizens from terrorists, and I have to pay for his burial services! This is absolutely absurd—" She stopped short as her eyes landed on Lyle and Yalina at the piano. "What's going on?" She sauntered over to the piano in a way that made Lyle uneasy. "Having a little lesson, are we?"

"Lyle's learning her very first song for you," Yalina said. "Do you want to play it for her, Lyle?" Lyle leaped at the opportunity and began playing the song she had worked so hard on, but she was quickly interrupted by her mother yanking her hands from the keys.

"I don't want to hear anything you learned from *her*." Lyle tried to look at Yalina without moving her head, straining from the corner of her eye.

"Marianna, please. I'm just teaching her a song."

"You don't need to teach her anything!" Lyle's mother yelled. "You're not her mother!"

"You're right, I'm not." Yalina sounded aggravated now. "She wanted to learn from you, but you won't teach her."

"My husband just died! Your people killed him!"

"But your daughter is still here!" Yalina ignored the racist accusation. "And she needs a teacher. She needs her mother."

"Don't you tell me what she needs!" Lyle's mother tugged at Lyle's arm in an attempt to get her to stand. "Come on, Delilah, you're not learning from her anymore."

"No!" Lyle resisted, yanking her arm from her mother's grip. "I want Yalina to teach me!"

"You bitch," Lyle's mother said in a fierce whisper. "First my husband, now my daughter?" She was so close her words sent spit flying, Yalina rearing back as it struck her in the eye.

"Marianna. I wasn't trying to—" Yalina's words were cut off as her head snapped backward, a fistful of her hijab clenched in Lyle's mother's fist.

"Mommy!" Lyle shrieked, but her mother did not stop, yanking Yalina to the floor and sending Lyle and the piano bench tumbling to the ground. Lyle bumped her head on the bench leg on her way down, rubbing it in an attempt to keep the budding bruise at ease.

"You're all the same!" Lyle heard her mother scream, but she couldn't make out more than a sea of limbs and tangled hijab from her vantage point on the floor.

"Aariz!" Yalina screamed, but Lyle knew he was gone to the market with her grandfather. There was no one there but them. Lyle scrambled behind the piano on her hands and knees, letting it shield her from the horror of what was happening.

"Leave us alone!" Lyle's mother bellowed, and Lyle wondered why she was saying that when she was the one attacking Yalina. The crack that followed echoed through the lobby. Lyle covered her ears and clenched her eyes shut in an attempt to be anywhere but where she was. All she wanted was for things to go back to the way they were. When she finally opened her eyes and dropped her hands from her ears, the only thing Lyle heard was breathing. She spun herself around and inched upward until she could peek over the top of the sheet music.

Her mother stood at the foot of the stage, hair and eyes wild, her body heaving up and down like a rhino after a stampede. She smiled at Lyle for the first time in weeks, and Lyle was so swept up in it she almost didn't see Yalina.

Laying at her mother's feet.

Unmoving.

Her hijab disheveled and stained a deep burgundy.

CHAPTER TWELVE

Cameron crashed to the ground like a tree cut by a chainsaw as Bruce's fist collided with his eye. Max immediately jumped in, and although Max was a badass, Bruce was a big boy with a little conscience, and Tate worried as the two squared off.

Wilson found his way to his feet, seeing red as he lunged for a helpless Cameron. Tate was as much a fighter as he was the night he met Max, but he tackled Wilson with enough force to send them both flying across the room. Wilson grunted as the air left his lungs, his composed façade replaced by a hatred that fueled him. Even so, he and Tate were relatively evenly matched as they rolled around on the floor. Until Wilson pulled out the lighter.

He brandished it like a sword, and Tate felt himself thump against the half-wall separating the lobbies as he scampered back, nowhere left to retreat. Wilson flicked the flame on and off as Tate worked his way to his feet.

On.

Off.

On.

As the flame extinguished, Tate grabbed Wilson by the shoulders and yanked him forward. The two of them tumbled over the wall into Aariz's lobby, the lighter skittering across the floor as they fell. Wilson scampered to recover the lighter, and his ears perked up as a door slammed in the workshop.

Aariz. Shit.

In one motion, Wilson was behind the counter, out for blood as he stormed the workshop. Tate hurried to catch up, both grateful and confused to find Wilson alone in the room. A pile of newspapers with splotches of brown sat crumpled in a pile next to what should have been the back exit. Instead, it looked like a closet of sorts, an addition to the back alley Tate never noticed before. Tate prayed Aariz had turned in for the night, but the muffled clank of wood on wood sounded behind the closed door. It was so subtle Tate thought Wilson missed it, but following his eyes to the pile of newspaper, Tate realized too late what he was about to do. "Wilson, don't." But by the time Tate tackled him, Wilson had already dropped the lighter. He kicked the door open to reveal a surprised Aariz, who was piling select pieces of wood in front of the doorframe for his latest project. They crashed to the floor as the flame caught, the newspaper igniting in front of them. Tate clamored away from the flames, but Wilson stood calm, his look chilling.

"That ought to keep the two of you busy long enough for me to have a chat with my pal Cammy." Wilson gave the flaming pile of newspaper a swift kick that sent it tumbling into the stack of wood blocking the doorframe. By the time he retreated to the lobby, the wood had caught, leaving Aariz and Tate face to face with a growing fire.

. . .

"You too good to fight me?" Bruce bounced around Max like a boxing kangaroo. He grew more agitated the more Max didn't engage, searching the room for something to provoke his opponent. Bruce's eyes roamed the lobby until they landed on the unaccompanied counter.

Shit.

"Your girl back there?" Bruce's words had the desired effect, Max's entire body flexing in defense. "Maybe I should go say hello. She's already hooking up with two of you. What's one more?"

Max hauled off and nailed Bruce in the kidney, knocking him to the ground and out of the way for the time being. He glanced at Cameron and Brian hovering around each other before booking it behind the counter. "Lyle!" Max felt his throat constrict when she didn't answer, realizing he had no idea where Wilson was or what he was doing. He hustled around the packed room, turning circles until he spotted her.

In the middle of the carousel, at the piano.

"Lyle!"

"Jeez!" Lyle jumped a mile as she removed her headphones. "What?"

"You need to get out of here."

Worry crept into her eyes as she took in Max's haste. "What's wrong?"

His answer was interrupted by the wail of a fire alarm, but it sounded muffled, like it was coming from outside.

Or next door.

"Shit," Max said, grabbing Lyle by the hand and pulling her toward the lobby. She resisted long enough to yank the fire alarm behind the counter, the sound intensifying as it echoed all around them. Cameron and Brian stood together now, eyes wide as they tried to figure out what was going on. Bruce stirred at the sound but remained unthreatening in a heap on the ground. Max craned his neck as Wilson rematerialized from Aariz's lobby, but there was no one behind him.

Lyle's eyes darted around, landing on Max when she too couldn't find what she was looking for. "Where's Tate?"

One look at Wilson's wild grin answered her question, a stone dropping into the pit of Max's stomach as he bounded across the lobby. With his disheveled hair and menacing New York accent, Wilson sounded nothing but amused as he looked at Max. "Who you gonna choose, Rocky?" He brushed past Max, his steps slow and methodical as he closed in on Cameron.

Lyle scampered to the broom closet, returning with a mini fire extinguisher. Max prepared himself to catch it, but instead of tossing it, Lyle clicked the pin and brandished it like a bazooka. "Go!" she yelled at him. Max leaped over the half-wall, Lyle stopping long enough to douse Wilson with a sea of foam before following him to the workshop.

. . .

The fire stared into Tate's soul, challenging him as it grew larger by the minute. Aariz's eyes were wide as the fire devoured the wood at his feet. The wood in the closet was already prepped for carpentry, which made it dry, sanded, and extremely flammable. "Hold on!" Tate yelled, although he wasn't sure for what. He spun around, knocking over tools and discarded wooden pieces in a futile attempt to locate a fire extinguisher. Finding none, his eyes landed on a bowl of water next to the prayer rug in the corner.

"Get out of here!" Aariz called, backing away to the rear of the closet. "Get help!"

Tate scooped up the bowl, water sloshing, and he rushed over to toss it on the flames. The fire laughed at his futile attempt, unrelenting as it continued to grow. Tate felt the blood pulsing through his body, urging him to run, but as much as he wanted to, he couldn't. They both knew by the time he got help, it would be too late. The flaming doorway looked familiar in a way that made Tate's stomach wrench, and despite his reservations, his mind dragged him back to an image he didn't want to remember.

. . .

The flames grew larger as Tate's father dragged him by the hand, desperately looking for a way out of the burning building. They were still too high to jump, but as they descended, each level of the tower proved more perilous than the last.

Tate wasn't even supposed to be in his father's office today, but he faked a stomachache to avoid a bully on the bus. The boy was older, a third-grader, and he made fun of Tate for his Hispanic skin. "They called me adopted," Tate whimpered earlier that morning. "They said you didn't love me because our skin doesn't match."

"Nonsense," Tate's father had said, kneeling down to his level. "I couldn't love you more. And I loved your mother just as much. She's where you get that wonderful heritage from, and I am lucky to be a part of it. They're just jealous they're only American, while you get to be American and Hispanic. See?"

As Tate strained to hear his father over the emergency sirens and alarms, his stomach began to hurt for real. Hope rose within them as they reached the third floor, but it was quickly extinguished when they rounded the bend to a crumbled staircase. "Shit." Tate's father eyed the walls like he didn't trust them to do their job as he dragged Tate through the side door into the third floor. The slickness of the floorboards proved the sprinklers went off at one point, but they hung motionless now, exhausted by the whole ordeal.

The entire building creaked as Tate followed his father through the chaos, dodging turned over desks, toppled chairs, and book-cases leaning precariously against other pieces of office furniture. The creak was deep and guttural, a mix between a freight train and a bass drum, and Tate felt it in his heart as his father yelled. "Come on!"

They were halfway to the opposing stairwell when the ceiling gave way. Tate was shoved away from his father, ricocheting off the wall and thumping to the ground as a cascade of flames and floorboards landed between them. "Shit!" someone yelled. The voice was not his father's, and it sounded farther away, like it was coming from heaven.

"Daddy!" Tate screamed, scampering to his feet. He used the wall to guide him around the room, the flames hot and threatening. He finally caught sight of his father on the other side of the flaming pile, bent in a position Tate had never seen a human body bend beneath what looked like a burned piece of the ceiling. "Daddy!" he called again. At first, his father said nothing, but he came alive as Tate shook his shoulders.

He struggled to pry himself free, but the pain that followed made him stop and cry out. The flames were expanding now, almost completely filling the room, and Tate could feel the heat of them on his face as he pressed his entire body weight against the wood, trying desperately to move it.

"Tate," his father croaked, grabbing him by the arm. "I need you to find the stairs."

"But what about you?"

"Find the stairs," his father repeated. "Get yourself out."

"Not without you!" The tears stung Tate's eyes even more than the smoke as he looked around in desperate search for something, anything to help. He was just about to try his weight against the wood again when he heard the voice.

"Anyone down here?" It was muffled through the smoke, but it was the same voice as before.

"Here!" Tate screamed, trying to figure out where the voice was coming from.

"Hello? We're firemen! Is anyone down here?"

"Help!" Tate screamed at the top of his lungs, following the voice to the other side of the room. The flames had engulfed the doorway of the opposing stairwell, but above them, Tate could make out two shadows, large and strong. "Help us!"

"You were right; there is a kid in there," the voice said. "Hey, buddy, can you hear me?"

"Yes! My daddy, he needs help!"

"We're coming to help you. I need you to step away from the doorway. Can you do that?"

Tate nodded and stepped back as a big boot emerged through the doorway, pulling back as flames bit the sole. Tate began to cough as the smoke nipped at his lungs, covering his nose with the crook of his elbow as he watched. The boot returned, the floor creaking threateningly as it planted on Tate's side of the fire. It was the same sound they heard before the ceiling gave way, and the boot disappeared again. "Okay, buddy, can you still hear me?"

"Yes!" Tate croaked.

"Okay, I need your help. I'm going to come through to help you, but I need to know where to step. Kneel down real low." Tate got down on his hands and knees, surprised to find he could see much better below the cloud of smoke. "Okay, now look at the door. Do you see the flames?"

"Yes."

"Okay. See how the floorboards are kind of bendy where I just stepped?" Tate examined the creaky floorboards, charred and sinking into a V-shape.

"Yes."

"Okay. Do you know your right from your left?"

"Yes."

"Okay, good, smart boy. I need you to look at the rest of the floorboards. Are there any that aren't bendy like that?" Tate was proud the fireman called him smart, and his eyes skimmed the area, landing on what looked to be firm floorboards.

"Yes!"

"Okay. Are they on your right or your left?"

Tate held up his thumbs and pointer fingers like his father had taught him to determine which way was left. "The right!"

"Okay, good. Now I need you to stay low, buddy, and don't move." Tate obliged, holding his breath as what looked like a fireman's coat dropped in the doorway, smothering the flames beneath it long enough for the boot to step where Tate had instructed, followed by the other. Tate felt the gloved hands lift him off the ground, and next thing he knew, he was face to face with a blue-eyed fireman.

"Great job, buddy," he said, settling Tate in his left arm. "Now, let's get you out of here."

"Wait, you have to help my daddy!"

. . .

The prayer rug.

Tate hadn't noticed its intricacy before, but then again, he hadn't noticed a lot of things about Aariz these past few weeks. Smoke clouded the room as Tate grabbed the tasseled edges, the red and orange thread resembling a flame rippling in his hands. "Get ready!" Tate managed, knowing he only had one shot. The smoke parted just long enough for Aariz to catch a glimpse of him, his expression forlorn and pained, as if Tate was about to smite him. His eyes clamped shut as Tate lifted the prayer rug over his head, a tear trickling into his dark beard as he turned away. Tate stood frozen, conflicted as he fought to make the right split-second decision.

He needed to save Aariz, but not like this. Tate lowered the prayer rug, careful to avoid the flames as he attempted to reverently toss it to the side. "Aariz!" he screamed, searching wildly for something else to smother the flames. Aariz's only answer was a series of muffled coughs. They didn't have much longer until the entire closet caught. "Help!" he yelled to anyone that would listen, doubling over as smoke lodged in his throat. Despair began to set in as Tate fell to his knees, gasping for air that was replaced by thick smoke and failure.

And then he felt it; the cool relief of foaming snow blanketed everything around him. The force of it was strong, and as the world around him turned white, Tate crawled to his right in an attempt to shield the prayer rug.

. . .

The fire extinguisher was more powerful than Max expected, whooshing past his ear as Lyle coated the room in fire retardant foam. His eyes searched wildly until he found Tate, coated and shivering, his body rounded around something Max couldn't make out. "You okay?" Max wiped the foam from Tate's face and grabbed him by the chin, turning his face this way and that before patting down his body in search of burns.

"Yeah," Tate croaked, leaning into the strength of Max's embrace before snapping upright, revealing a mostly clean prayer rug beneath him. "But he took in a lot of smoke."

Max followed Tate's finger to the closet, where Aariz's body materialized in a foamy heap. Max wedged himself beneath Aariz's arm and helped Tate drag him to the lobby, where they laid him flat on the stage. Lyle was already at the front desk, phone in hand. "I'm at The Carry Out dry-cleaners on Main Street. There was a fire, and people need help. Please hurry!"

Aariz's face matched Tate's, the skin beneath the foam smoke-stained and charred. "Got a pulse," Max said, pressing his fingers to the artery just below Aariz's jawline. No sooner did he get the words out, Tate shoved him aside, fervently and ineffectively starting chest compressions.

"Tate…Tate!" Max had to use all of his body weight to pull Tate off Aariz's unconscious body. "The paramedics are on their way." Tate eyed Aariz like a newborn he was responsible for, but Max only had eyes for Tate. There was something different about his eyes. Although they were bloodshot from the smoke, there was despair pooled within them. It was as if Tate resigned himself that no matter what he did, he would never make his father proud.

The anger burned in Max's stomach until every inch of his body pulsed with a rage he knew he couldn't control.

"All you had to do was drop out," Wilson said.

Tate looked up, forlorn. "All this because of a stupid talent show?" Max hopped off the stage without a sound, a leopard landing from its perch in the treetops.

Aside from his eyes, Wilson's mouth was the only thing visible amongst the foam on his face, and when he grinned at Tate, the whites of his teeth blended in. "That, and a spelling bee."

"We actually like Cameron!" Tate said. "All you want to do is manipulate him." His voice cracked as he continued. "Don't you see how pathetic that is?"

By now, Max had positioned himself between Wilson and Tate, silent as Wilson's expression shifted from taunting to menacing. He reached in his breast pocket for the lighter as he took a step toward Tate.

One step was all it took. The crack of Max's fist against Wilson's eye socket was audible even over the fire alarms, and Wilson dropped to the ground on impact.

Lyle's hand flew to her mouth as she knelt beside Aariz and Tate, but Max remained expressionless as he turned to Bruce and Brian. Bruce had found his way to his feet by now, but Max could tell by the way he stood his kidney was still smarting. Brian's eyes widened as the sirens approached, louder with each of their heartbeats. "Ready to stand by your fearless leader?" Max glanced at Wilson, who was moaning as he began to come to.

"The cops? Shit!" Bruce shoved Brian over in his mad dash for the front door, Brian unstable but close behind as they took off down the street. Lyle rushed outside to flag down the emergency vehicles: one firetruck, one ambulance, and one police car. Cameron scurried out of the way as the firemen rushed in, dispersing to secure the area. Once they determined the threat had been eliminated, the paramedics followed suit.

"Help him," Tate pleaded, coughing with the effort as he pointed to Aariz. Max tugged Tate off the stage to give the paramedics room to work.

"Delilah!" Rawel's voice entered before he did, dressed in full gear as he lumbered into the lobby and took his granddaughter in his arms. "Oh, my God. Are you okay? What happened?"

"I'm okay," Lyle reassured him. "There was a fire. Aariz…" Her voice broke as the paramedics buzzed around the stage with various pieces of equipment.

Rawel's eyes lagged on his friend before returning to Lyle. "They're doing everything they can. How did this happen?"

Her answer was interrupted as the police officer strode in, his eyes unrelentingly casual as he surveyed the scene. His expression shifted to one of confusion as his eyes landed on Wilson, who managed to right himself to his feet. "Wilson? What are you doing here?" Wilson's smirk was almost imperceptible as the policeman extended his arm. Max wracked his brain trying to figure out the connection between a stuck up rich boy and a New Jersey cop. "What the hell happened?" Wilson let his face melt into one worthy of sympathy as he allowed the policeman to wipe the remaining foam from his face. "Is Bruce here too?"

"No," Wilson muttered, perplexed by the thought of being abandoned by his posse. Relief flooded over the police officer as Max realized why Bruce was so keen to get away from the police.

"What happened to your eye?"

Wilson fixed his eyes on Max before turning to Bruce's father with a look of distress. "I came here to wish these guys luck at the talent show, and next thing I know, I get punched in the face!"

Wilson looked at Max as if scared of him. "As if playing with fire wasn't enough!" The policeman put his arm around Wilson before calling over a paramedic, who ushered him out of the building to the ambulance for examination. Wilson looked over his shoulder only once, Tate and Max feeling the weight of his accusation like anvils dropped from the heavens.

"Well?" The police officer turned to Max and Tate. "Who's the hot hand?"

"Excuse me," Rawel cut in as they stood in disbelief. "These boys were victims of an arson, and you're treating them like criminals?"

"Excuse *me*," the officer sneered, eyeing Max and Tate like it wasn't their first run-in with the law. "One of them assaulted a peer."

"It was self-defense!" Lyle cried, but the officer held up a hand to silence her.

"So you say." He didn't look like he was a fan of Lyle or her grandfather. "The fact of the matter is, girls your age will say just about anything to protect their boyfriend." Lyle bit her lip, her face red with anger, embarrassment, or both. "We take this kind of thing very seriously nowadays," the officer continued. "Especially on this side of town." Tate's head snapped up at the implication, as did Rawel's. "Unless there's an impartial third-party that can verify otherwise, one of you is under arrest for assault and arson." The policeman did a once-over of the empty lobby for witnesses, missing Cameron completely as he cowered in the corner. "So I'm going to ask you again." His eyes bore into Max and Tate. "Which one of you is responsible?"

Max's heart sank as thoughts of what could have been glistened in his mind for the final time. He would never be able to go to college now, not with a criminal record. He felt his entire world crashing down around him as he stepped forward, ready to accept his fate.

He shot a final glance at Tate in an attempt to convey forgiveness for their fight last night before opening his mouth to confess.

"I am," Tate said before Max could speak.

Max whipped to face him in disbelief. "Tate, the show..." He trailed off as Tate shook his head the smallest bit, gently pushing past Max as he stepped forward. The police officer wasted no time cuffing him, and although they all wanted to, no one intervened as Tate was led to the squad car. Max watched, dumbfounded, as his best friend rode away, giving up his lifelong dream so Max could have a chance at his own.

CHAPTER THIRTEEN

"No!" Lyle snapped to life as the squad car disappeared, yanking at Rawel's arm like she was trying to start a lawnmower. "You have to help him."

"I knew I shouldn't have left you alone with these boys." Rawel pulled his arm away as Cameron skulked over to join them. "First, the vandalism, then the late nights. Now this?" He motioned to the stage. "Look at Aariz!"

Their collective attention shifted as the paramedics propped Aariz into a sitting position to give him oxygen. Rawel rushed to the stage, and if it wasn't his touch that jolted Aariz awake, it sure seemed like it. Rawel did not hesitate to strip off the t-shirt beneath his fire coat, balling it up and placing it as a cushion behind Aariz. "Are you okay?"

"Tate!" Aariz scanned the room, suddenly full of energy. "Where's Tate?" His voice was hoarse from all the smoke.

"They took him away."

"Who did?"

"The police." Rawel looked confused at his friend's concern. "They arrested him for what he did to that boy." Rawel watched as Aariz struggled to breathe. "And to you."

"What *he* did?" Aariz sat bolt upright, cascading himself into a coughing fit. "That other boy started the fire. Tate was trying to save me." Aariz's eyes floated to Max. "As far as hitting someone is concerned, I supposed Tate was also trying to save someone."

Max bowed his head in embarrassment before turning to Rawel. "He was going for Tate. I had to hit him."

Rawel's eyes bounced from Max to Aariz before landing on Lyle, whose look of desperation softened his shoulders a bit. He was a big man and very strong for his age, but beneath it all, Rawel had always been a teddy bear at heart, especially for his granddaughter. "You three go ahead to the show. We'll meet you there."

"I'll stay and explain what actually happened to a real official," Aariz said. "Good luck to you all. You certainly deserve the win." Max and Cameron blushed as Aariz retreated to his office to speak to the other firemen.

Rawel dawned his fire coat and headed for the door. "The talent show is in an hour," Lyle called. He paused long enough to give her a kiss on the forehead and give Max a look that said no funny business, before climbing into his firetruck and pulling away.

Cameron looked at the clock, speaking for the first time in what felt like days. "We're never going to make it on time."

Max stared out the window. "Cam, how'd you get here?"

"Skated." The two of them headed for the back door without another word, Lyle close behind. As they mounted their skateboards in the alley, Lyle's heart sank as she tried to convince herself it was more important for them to make it to the show than her.

She started for the door when Max stretched out his hand. "Aren't you coming?"

"You know I don't know how to skateboard."

Max produced what looked like an amused grin, but it was different than Tate's. His lips pursed together as if too afraid to actually let himself enjoy something. "You don't need to. Just hang on." Lyle thought about all the ways this could go wrong as she stood rooted to the pavement.

"So after all this, you're not going to watch us?"

"I want to go…" Lyle trailed off.

"It meant a lot to me that you came to watch me in the spelling bee," Cameron said.

"And it will mean a lot to us if you come now." Max fixed his gaze on her, hand still outstretched. "Especially Tate."

Lyle's shoulder's sagged as the guilt convinced her, letting Max pull her onto the board behind him. "How do I even do this?"

"Don't move your feet and hold on." Lyle felt Max wince as she wrapped her arms around his bruised ribs. She loosened her grip, but he immediately pulled her arms tighter around his torso.

"Are you sure this is safe?"

The look Max shot over his shoulder made Lyle giggle in spite of herself. They had just been through a fistfight and a fire, and she was worried about riding a skateboard. "Lead the way, Cam," Max said, and the three of them took off toward the school.

. . .

They made it to school in record time, and although Cameron was comfortable on a skateboard, he had to skate faster than ever to keep up with Max. Stopping was a bit of a challenge for all involved, but by the grace of God, they made it in one piece. Cameron tossed his board into the bushes next to Max's and rushed into the auditorium.

"Holy cow," Lyle said. The auditorium was packed full, people standing in the back who couldn't find seats. Cameron felt the tiniest of knots tangling in his throat, and he knew it would only expand the closer they came to performing.

The three scampered backstage as a dancing duet was exiting, the principal taking the spotlight in their place. "Let's have another round of applause for that excellent routine." The crowd roared, and Cameron wondered how good the dancers were. "Before we introduce our last act of the evening, I want to thank you all again for coming to the first annual freshman class talent show. All proceeds will be distributed by the class officers to best suit the needs of the students in the grade level." Cameron felt Max's eye roll without turning around. "After this last act, our three anonymous judges will convene and decide on a winner. Not even the organizer of tonight's festivities knows who they are."

Cameron followed the principal's eyes to Wilson, who was waiting at the base of the stage. He had managed to shower and change his clothes, but the punch he took from Max was beginning to swell, despite his best efforts to mask it with what looked like his mother's makeup. "Speaking of, let's all take a minute to thank the man of the hour, freshman class president and organizer of this event, Wilson!"

Lyle clapped mockingly as Wilson took the stage, the applause from the audience thunderous and naïve. His grin was blinding as he feigned embarrassment, and it wasn't the first time Cameron wondered if Wilson had too many teeth in his mouth. Wilson accepted his accolades, but they weren't listening. The three had about enough of Wilson for one lifetime.

Lyle glanced at the clock backstage, fervently searching the sea of performers for Tate. "Where is he?"

Wilson caught their eye, his expression shifting from shock to taunting as he realized Tate was not with them. "And now, without further ado, I would like to introduce the final act of the evening."

"Shit," Max said. The knot in Cameron's throat felt more like a punching bag now, which was ironically appropriate, considering he let himself be Wilson's punching bag for so long.

"Folks, please give up for…" Wilson's voice trailed off, the four of them realizing simultaneously they did not have a band name.

"Wait!" Cameron heard his voice echo through the auditorium as he grabbed a microphone and strode onto the stage. Max and Lyle's jaws dropped as he sidled up next to Wilson, forcing him to share the spotlight. "Hi, everyone." Cameron waved at the audience with an ease he wasn't used to wearing. "I'm Cameron King, and I'm a good friend of Wilson's." Max's brow furrowed as he tried to figure out what Cameron was doing.

Wilson paused for a beat but quickly recovered as he plastered a smile back on his face and put his arm around Cameron. "Yes. Everyone, you remember Cameron. The underdog of the spelling bee. I've beaten him for years, and for the first time, he managed to get lucky and pull out a win on me." The crowd laughed along with Wilson as his grip tightened on Cameron's shoulder. Usually, a comment like that would embarrass Cameron, but in one gulp, Cameron swallowed the knot in his throat and painted on a fake smile of his own. He laughed along with Wilson and the crowd, Lyle and Max horrified in the wings. Wilson took advantage of the momentum as he continued. "Here tonight to try competing in something a little more in your wheelhouse?"

"Actually," Cameron glanced at Max for a split second, which was all it took for him to understand. He gave Cameron a firm nod of support as Cameron turned back to Wilson. "I thought it would be fun to give everyone an encore." Wilson's eyes bored into Cameron like he was trying to smite him, but Cameron didn't back down. "You've been so considerate announcing all these acts tonight, you've been unable to showcase your own talents."

"I think my talents were more than shown at the last spelling bee." Wilson's façade faltered the slightest bit as his voice began to shake.

Cameron turned to the crowd, shaking his head like the mother of a scholarship recipient. "He's so modest, our class president. Folks, wouldn't you like to see the man of the hour give a little encore performance for you?" The crowd roared in applause and cheers, wrapped up in what they thought was rehearsed banter. Cameron shot a grin to Lyle in the wings at Wilson's sudden helplessness before turning back to his so-called friend. "I challenge you to a spell-off."

. . .

Tate hadn't expected to be the only one in the jail cell, and as he sat trapped with his own thoughts, he wished there was someone else there to distract him. Some criminal to keep him on his toes, because otherwise, he was left with no one but himself for company. What would his father think of him now, sitting in a jail cell?

The heat from his adrenaline subsided the longer he sat, and he shivered under his shirt coated in fire retardant foam. The police officer made sure to take his gold chain when they locked him up but was generous enough to leave him with a drenched t-shirt. When his teeth began to chatter, Tate peeled the shirt off and balled it up on the bench beside him. He tried to picture himself from an outsider's perspective, shirtless, scarred, and alone in a jail cell. Despite his best efforts to fight against this life he was given, he still ended up looking like a criminal.

Murmurings and footsteps echoed down the hallway as Bruce's father appeared, not bothering to hide his smugness. Tate didn't look up as the keys jiggled in the lock, uninterested in whatever verbal berating the man had in store. "You've got a visitor, kid." The officer snickered as Tate looked up. "I was surprised too." When he finally managed to get the cell unlocked and motioned down the hallway, Tate was astonished to see Rawel's massive frame appear. He slid into the cell without a sideways glance at the officer, his eyes on Tate as Bruce's father locked them in and retreated down the hallway.

Rawel gestured to the bench, waiting for Tate's nod before sitting down. They nestled into the silence, staring straight ahead as if waiting for an explanation for how they ended up here. "Lyle thinks you're innocent." Rawel turned to Tate. "Is she right?"

Tate thought about Lyle's perfect combination of gentle support and harsh reality checks. "Usually."

"And yet here you sit." Tate felt Rawel studying him, suddenly self-conscious about his scar. "Why is that?"

"It was my fault."

"What was?"

"All of it. The vandalism, the fight, the fire—none of it would have happened if I had just listened." Tate shook his head. "She tried to tell me too, but even meeting her mother didn't get through to me. Now she probably hates me, and Aariz..." He trailed off as the image of Aariz's charred face filled his mind. A hot tear rolled down his cheek, the cell walls turning to mirrors as he finally turned the blame onto himself. "I never knew I had so much hatred in me."

It was silent for a minute before Rawel spoke. "I didn't know you visited the prison."

"She asked me to."

"How was Marianna, with Lyle?"

"Hot and cold." Tate lowered his eyes in shame. "She liked me, though."

"She likes Lyle, too."

"The good part of her likes Lyle." Tate forced himself to look at Rawel. "I think the bad part of her likes me."

"Did Delilah ever tell you what her mother did?"

Tate shook his head. "I never asked."

"She killed a Muslim woman. Aariz's wife, Yalina. Hate has a domino effect, and it can isolate us from everyone and everything we love if we let it." Rawel put a hand on Tate's thigh. "Aariz is fine, just a little shaken up. And someone so full of hatred wouldn't run toward the flames to save him." Tate's shoulders sagged with relief at the news of Aariz, but he said nothing. "You know," Rawel said, standing and pacing the cell like a lawyer in the courtroom. "I was wary of you boys at first. Especially you." Tate couldn't help but smile the smallest bit as Rawel continued. "But Lyle's changed since you've been around. For the first time in seven years, she seems…" He paused, his eyes grateful and sad at the same time. "…happy."

"That's because of the piano," Tate said, remembering Lyle's smile at the end of the chorus concert.

"You know why she started playing again?" Tate shook his head as Rawel faced him once more. "Because she feels safe. With you."

Tate scoffed. "I don't even feel safe with me."

"Accepting the wrath of your classmates to include a friend? Visiting a high-security prison on a moment's notice? Rescuing someone from a fire?" Rawel fixed his eyes on Tate. "Taking the fall for your best friend? I'd feel pretty safe with you too."

Tate bit his lip. "How do you know I didn't hit him?"

Rawel motioned to Tate's hands with a smirk similar to Lyle's. "Clean knuckles." He grabbed Tate's t-shirt off the bench as he called to Bruce's father, which had hardened into more of a sculpture than an article of clothing.

Bruce's father rounded the bend and unlocked the cell. "All set?"

"Actually"—Rawel put his arm around Tate as he pushed the door open—"he's coming with me."

"This boy has been accused of assault and arson. He's not going anywhere."

"Lucky for him, we found an impartial third witness. The shop owner, whom Tate saved from the fire that someone else started. Perhaps someone who didn't belong there in the first place."

The sneer morphed into defiance as Bruce's father stood his ground. "I'm not sure what you're implying here, but this witness has been through quite an ordeal. His judgment can't be trusted."

"His judgment, or his kind?" Rawel let his accusation hang in the air long enough for Bruce's father to squirm. "I suggest you retrieve this boy's belongings and drop the charges. Otherwise, I'll have to pull the tapes from my security cameras." Tate stood, astonished as Rawel went in for the kill. "And if I'm not mistaken, the boy who was assaulted has a few friends of his own. It would be a shame if they popped up on those videos, wouldn't it?"

The realization that Rawel beat him at his own game washed over Bruce's father, who did not make eye contact as he returned with the small plastic bin containing Tate's sole belonging. "You're free to go." Rawel snatched the bin without looking and strode past the officer, Tate on his heels.

The bite of dusk nipped at Tate's bare chest as they stepped outside, and he shivered in spite of himself. Rawel shrugged off his fire coat and draped it around Tate's shoulders, revealing a healed but dark scar tossed over his shoulder like a mechanic's rag. It almost resembled an upside-down kite, the tail snaking over his shoulder, the crisscrossed frame of a kite landing halfway down his back.

"You got burned too." It was more of a statement than a question, and Tate wondered if he shouldn't have said it. But something about it connected them, made Tate feel more understood than he had in a long time.

"Yes." Rawel made a beeline for the firetruck, the red gleaming bright despite the evening haze.

"How?"

Rawel opened the driver's side door, about to pull himself up when he realized one hand still held the plastic bin. He grabbed the contents without looking and tossed the bin into the cab of the truck. The gleam of the gold chain caught his eye as he held it out, catching Rawel's attention for the first time. Tate started to reach for it, but Rawel pulled it back, turning it over and over in his hands as he looked back and forth between Tate and the crucifix, his expression morphing into something Tate didn't recognize.

Tate was weary when Rawel extended the chain again, but Tate was able to tug it from his grasp before Rawel pulled it away again. He slipped it over his head and tucked it beneath the oversized fire coat, close to his heart where it belonged. No sooner had he done so, Rawel's big arms were around him. Tate couldn't remember the last time someone other than Lyle hugged him, and he leaned into it despite not knowing the reason.

After what felt like an eternity, Rawel pulled away, tears brimming in his eyes as he held Tate at arm's length.

"What?" Tate asked, confused by the sudden outpouring of emotion.

The clock outside the police station struck the hour, Tate's act for the talent show about to start. Rawel hauled Tate across the center console into the passenger seat before climbing into the driver's seat and switching on the emergency lights. "I'll tell you on the way."

. . .

"The first word is privilege." Max's voice boomed through the speakers as he crouched at the base of the stage, dictionary in hand.

"Privilege." Wilson lunged into the spotlight. "P-R-I-V-I-L-E-G-E." Lyle rolled her eyes from the wings at his eagerness for an easy ride, and Max confirmed the spelling as Wilson stepped back.

"Expendable."

Cameron stepped forward, his hesitation as slight as someone breaking free from the tendril of a spider's web. "Expendable. E-X-P-E-N-D-A-B-L-E."

"Correct." More applause from the crowd, and a sneer masked as sportsmanship from Cameron's unworthy opponent.

"Condescend." The sarcasm in Max's tone was enough to distract Wilson for the briefest of moments.

"Condescend. C-O-N-D-E-S-C-E-N-D."

"Correct." The boys switched places again. "Hypocrite."

Cameron cringed as the spotlight bathed him in what he once was. Max gave him the smallest of smiles and a nod that put Cameron at ease. "Hypocrite. H-Y-P-O-C-R-I-T-E."

"Correct." Wilson stepped forward again. "Judgmental."

"Lyle!" Tate startled her as he appeared from the depths of backstage, shirtless and panting from what appeared to have been a sprint.

"Thank God." Lyle gave him a quick hug as the crowd applauded another correct spelling. "Do you have a band name?" Tate didn't hear her, his eyes glued to Wilson center stage. "Tate."

"What? No." Tate paused. "I never thought of one."

"Errant."

"Was that Max?" he asked, and Lyle nodded as Cameron stepped forward.

"Errant. E-R-R..."

"What the hell are they doing?" Tate whispered.

"Stalling." Lyle dragged him by the hand toward the backdoor. "Come with me." Applause echoed faintly as the door shut behind them, and Lyle smiled at Cameron's advancement. They were alone in the wings, makeup, costumes, and props scattered about from the last show.

"What are we doing back here?" Tate asked as Lyle sifted through eyeshadow pallets.

"Helping you win. Now come here." Lyle hopped onto the makeup counter, mirror to her back as she tugged Tate forward between her knees. "Close your eyes."

"Haven't we had enough surprises?"

Lyle rolled her eyes. "Just close this one then." Her finger brushed the top of his left lid to close it, Tate still as Lyle applied purple and black eyeshadow.

"I'm really sorry," Tate said after a moment, his open eye trying its best to look sincere. "About everything."

"I know you are." Lyle tapped his shoulder, and Tate opened his eye, the green of it distracting as she smudged some purple beneath his bottom lashes. "Aariz is okay," she said.

"Your grandfather told me." Tate's voice sounded constricted as if his windpipe had shrunk tenfold. "Thank God."

"No," Lyle said. "Thank you." The blue and green of their eyes collided as their gazes met, and it felt like they were back at The Carry Out again, sitting in the dark behind the counter, filling the room with music and secrets. Despite everything that happened, Tate had redeemed himself tonight, and the connection they had was deep-seated in a way she couldn't explain.

His arms wound around her torso as he lifted her off the counter, their bodies against each other as he guided her feet to the floor. The pink of his scar entranced her as it traced his lips, so much so she didn't notice him reaching into her pack pocket until he held the guitar pick between them. "Can I borrow this?" That crooked grin made her knees buckle, blushing with embarrassment as Tate reached into his own pocket. "Here," he said, handing her a crumpled receipt. "Collateral."

Lyle pulled the receipt taut to read it, her own handwriting for a band's worth of uniforms staring back at her. "You kept this?"

"I still owe you, don't I?" Tate asked, his body against hers as he slipped the receipt into her back pocket.

"Just win," she breathed. And then he was kissing her. His forearms felt strong as they pulled them together, her fingers winding around the hair at the base of his neck. His left hand remained in her back pocket as his lips traced hers, breathless and weightless as she leaned in to what they both wanted since they met.

It took another roar from the crowd for them to finally pull away, her fingertips grazing his shirtless torso as they fell. "Wait," she said, taking a step back. "You're missing something." She scampered into the chorus room before he could pull her in again, reaching beneath the piano for the shirt that was balled up there for weeks.

She returned to the hallway and tugged The Carry Out shirt over Tate's head, taking longer than she should as she slid it down his tanned torso. His arms wound around her again, and she ran her thumb along his scar affectionately. "You ready to do this?"

In response, Tate lifted her off the ground, spinning her in a circle before grabbing her hand and leading the way as they returned to the wings.

"Vengeance. V-E-N-G-E-A-N-C-E."

"Correct," Max's voice echoed as Wilson stepped back.

"Max," Lyle hissed, loud enough to catch his attention as well as the two spellers. She pointed to Tate, who gave a sarcastic wave, and Max smirked before returning his attention to the stage. Cameron grinned and began to walk off stage, but Tate shook his head, motioning for him to continue. He gave him a nod of encouragement, and Cameron returned to the spotlight. This was his battle to finish.

"Reckoning."

"Reckoning. R-E-C-K-O-N-I-N-G."

"Correct." Cameron's chest swelled as he stepped back, unfazed by Wilson's glower. It was apparent that he expected Cameron to step down when Tate arrived, but Cameron only shrugged in a casual challenge.

"Infallible," Max said.

"Infallible." Lyle could tell right away Wilson didn't know it, his eyes darting around in search of a clue that wasn't there. "I-N..." He paused, tapping his fingers against his thigh before continuing as slow as he could. "F-A-L-L..." Another pause, this time his glare fixing on Tate, who was unintimidated as he raised his eyebrows expectantly. "A-B-L-E. Infallible."

"That is…" Max paused, his eyes flicking to Cameron. "…incorrect." A combination of gasps and murmurs came from the crowd as Wilson stood dumbfounded at center stage. When he finally stepped back, his legs were stiff as boards, as if unsure how to navigate this foreign terrain. His hand snatched Cameron's wrist as Cameron stepped forward, Tate and Max taut and ready to pounce in defense.

"Don't do this," Wilson hissed. He was trying to be threatening, but his eyes were a little too wild, his breathing a little too out of control, his voice a little too desperate. The three friends watched as Cameron faced Wilson, stoic and unwavering, his demeanor everything Wilson's wasn't. He didn't say a word, just stared, until Wilson finally released his wrist.

"Cameron," Max said as Cameron stepped into the spotlight. "Same word. If you spell this correctly, you win. Infallible."

A smile danced across Cameron's face. "Can you use it in a sentence?"

Max put the book down and turned his eyes to the stage. "Cameron King's friendship is infallible."

That one sentence was all it took to seal the deal. "Infallible. I-N-F-A-L-L-I-B-L-E."

"That is…" The entire crowd held its breath as Max held the microphone to his lips. "…correct!" The auditorium erupted, Max's voice barely audible over the roar. "Congratulations, Cameron, you won the spell-off!" Lyle cheered as Tate used his fingers to whistle, Max climbing onto the stage as Cameron turned to Wilson.

"Good game," he said, extending his hand at a slight angle so the crowd would see. Wilson recoiled, but the eyes of the crowd bore in on him, and he took Cameron's hand and shook it the smallest amount.

"Now that we've settled that," Max said into the microphone. "I think our president has one more act to announce." Lyle scampered onto the stage, pressing a piece of paper into one of Wilson's hands as Max clicked his microphone off, holding it up like a toast to Wilson's demise.

The principal stood at the base of the stage, nodding earnestly for Wilson to continue as Cameron and Max took their places behind him with their instruments. "For the final act, I would like to introduce…" Wilson sounded like he was reading his own death sentence, fixing a final, hateful glare on Tate in the wings before continuing. "The Shiners."

The crowd cheered as Tate strode to center stage, guitar hanging from his neck. His eye makeup matched the actual bruising on Max and Cameron, as well as the bruise on Wilson. "If you don't mind," Tate said, motioning to Wilson's unmoving feet in the spotlight. "I'd like to take my place."

Wilson's face turned to stone as Tate snatched the microphone from his hands. "Thank you, everyone! We're so excited to be here tonight. Looks like we have our first fan!" He pointed to Wilson's black eye, forcing Wilson to fake a smile before scampering off stage.

Tate pulled Lyle into a side hug as she brought him a microphone stand. "Enjoy the music," he whispered soft enough for only her to hear. Lyle nodded, the grin immovable as she retreated to the wings. Tate leaned away from the microphone as he said something to Max and Cameron, who nodded as Max began to click his sticks together. They strummed the beginning chords, and just like that, they were doing it. Tate, Max, and Cameron were actually performing in the talent show.

Lyle couldn't take her eyes off her boys. Cameron, sporting his punk t-shirt, looked more loose and confident than ever with a grin from ear to ear. Max stood as he continued to drum, kicking the stool away and smiling in his own stoic way. Tate strummed his father's guitar, singing his heart out as he raised a hand for the crowd to join in. And join they did. Even the principal felt the beat, although Wilson remained rooted next to him like a scarecrow that forgot how to dance.

The final words pulsed through the auditorium as they hit the final note, the three of them breathing heavily as the crowd exploded with cheers. Tate removed the guitar from his neck and stepped back as Max and Cameron approached, putting his arms around each of them as the three friends basked in their moment.

After an eternity of applause, the principal sauntered onto the stage and grabbed the microphone. "Well, that was nothing short of spectacular!" The crowd roared again as the boys gave a final wave as they exited, Lyle throwing her arms around each of them when they reached the wings, holding onto Tate just a breath longer. "Now," the principal said as the crowd took their seats. "I would like to introduce our three judges. They have been sitting apart throughout the night for the sake of anonymity. Judges, can you please join me on stage?"

They couldn't see much of the auditorium from their place in the wings, but Lyle saw the front row craning their necks as they searched the auditorium for the culprits. Cameron shook Max on the shoulders as the first judge came onstage: Zana, the robotics girl. "Hey, your girlfriend's on the panel!"

"Shut up." Max shrugged Cameron off, but the smile tugging at the edges of his lips gave him away.

They heard the second judge before they saw her. Lyle could not suppress a surprised laugh as the second judge meandered onto the stage: Ms. Godllub, the music teacher. "She's always got her nose in something," she whispered.

Tate's mouth dropped open, his hand finding Lyle's as the third and final judge crossed the stage: Samson, the lacrosse captain.

CHAPTER FOURTEEN

"I should probably get going," Cameron said. "My parents are going to wonder where I am." The four of them had returned to The Carry Out to return their instruments after the show, but they wound up lounging around the stage for over an hour.

Lyle gave him a hug. "I'm so proud of you."

"You kicked Wilson's ass twice tonight." Tate motioned to Cameron's black eye. "Thank you."

Cameron bowed his head. "Sorry it took so long."

"I'll ride with you." Max patted Cameron on the back, starting for the door before turning to Tate. "See you at home."

Tate grinned. "Right." And just like that, they were back.

The bell tinkled as the boys exited, and Tate returned to the stage, his legs dangling off the edge in slow circles. "For someone who just won the talent show, you don't seem very happy," Lyle said, climbing up next to him.

"I am." Tate put his arm around her like he'd been doing it for years. "Couldn't have done it without you." He pulled away to look into those eyes of hers. "Any of it." A smile danced across her face as she kissed his cheek, just low enough to graze his scar. Tate shuddered, wanting nothing more than to pull her to him and let the blackness of the night hide them from the world. But the drive with Rawel rang in his head, a secret he couldn't stand to keep. Even if it meant losing her. "Your grandfather drove me from the jail," he started.

"I knew he would." Lyle winked at him. "Just like I knew you would win." She reached across him and grabbed the neck of his guitar, plopping it in his lap. "How about a victory song?"

He wanted to tell her, so badly he wanted to tell her, but he was a sucker for those eyes. He strummed the chords as he started to sing. He should have felt perfect, singing to Lyle after winning the talent show, his dream of marching finally a reality. But it didn't feel anything like he imagined. How could he possibly find the words to crumble the world Lyle had worked all these years to rebuild?

The sadness of the lyrics leaked from his body like a spill Tate couldn't stop, the thought of losing her lodging in his throat. His voice broke on the next note, and he laid the guitar down in an attempt to maintain his composure. Lyle's expression shifted from one of contentment to one of concern. "Are you okay?"

"I have to tell you something." It came out in a hurry, and as Lyle leaned back to examine him, Tate found himself thinking of their favorite colors. Although black and white were opposites, they complimented each other in an unconventional way. He depended on her to brighten his world, but his darkness felt heavier the longer they sat, looming as it threatened to smother her light. Tate put a hand on Lyle's knee, willing her to feel how sorry he was as he took a deep breath and began.

. . .

"Wait, you have to help my daddy!" The flames had re-established themselves in the doorway, the fireman's coat only a temporary solution. Tate tugged at the fireman's shirt as he held him, urging him to listen.

"Where is he?"

"There!" Tate pointed to the heap of rubble and limbs that was his father, the thickening smoke almost completely shielding him.

"Sir, can you hear me?"

"Tate," his father mumbled. "Go."

"Tate. Is that your name?" Tate nodded as the fireman leaned over. "Sir, we have your son. Don't worry. We're going to get you all out of here."

"Get...Tate out." His father's voice came in rasps now, as if losing his energy to speak. The fireman nodded before he turned and began to carry Tate toward the doorway.

"Wait!" Tate screamed, craning his head to look back. "My daddy!"

"Let's just focus on getting you safe, buddy." They were almost to the door when Tate managed to wriggle free, falling to the floor and scampering to his father.

"Daddy!" Tate threw his arms around his father's neck. "Come on. We have to go!" The fireman was at his side now, his grip firmer as he scooped him up again.

"Listen to the fireman, Tate." His father stroked Tate's face as Tate leaned down from the fireman's arms. "I love you so much."

"No! Daddy!" Tate held on to his father as long as he could. When the fireman finally managed to pull him free, Tate latched onto the golden chain around his father's neck until it broke away in his hands. Tate clung to it as the fireman hauled him to the door, calling to his partner on the other side of the flames.

"Same thing with the coat! We have to get the kid out!" Moments later, a second fireman's coat fell to the floor of the doorway, once again temporarily suffocating the flames. The second man was older, his expression anxious as he examined the room. The fireman with the nice eyes passed Tate to him, and the second fireman motioned to the door. "Let's go!"

The younger fireman hesitated. "I have to get his father."

"It's too dangerous!"

A thousand words passed between them as the men stared at each other. Finally, the second fireman nodded, his eyes sad like Tate's father's were when they pulled Tate away. "Be safe," he said, stroking the younger man's cheek with his gloved hand.

The first fireman nodded as the flames began to overtake the coat again. "Get the boy out!" And just like that, he was gone, his blue eyes disappearing in a mix of flames and smoke. The second fireman hauled Tate higher into his arms as he began to descend the stairs. Tears streamed down Tate's face, and he couldn't tell if they were from the smoke, the flames, or crying.

The smoke thickened as they continued down the staircase, Tate's coughing more uncontrollable with each step. The fireman stopped, placing Tate on the steps just long enough to strip off his own shirt before scooping him up again. "Put this over your face," he instructed, the barrier of fabric making it a little easier for Tate to breathe.

Tate watched the stairs grow more numerous behind them as they continued down the stairwell, the chain dangling from his firm grip. As they rounded the last bend, flames licking at their ankles, the golden chain caught on the banister, ripping from Tate's grasp as it fell into the flames. "No!" Tate screamed, and before the fireman could stop him, Tate lunged from his arms.

Face-first into the flames.

Tate screamed as the skin burned on the left side of his mouth. The fireman ripped him from the flames, Tate clinging to the t-shirt as he used it to grab the metal chain hanging from where it snagged on the railing above the fire. The fireman hauled Tate over his shoulder as he continued down the stairs, crying out in pain as the hot chain dangling from Tate's hand dragged across his back.

They rushed from the building to an ambulance, where Tate was handed off to a team of paramedics. They immediately began to tend to his eye, asking stupid questions like could he see? Did it hurt? "My daddy!" Tate screamed. "Where's my daddy?"

The fireman, who had disappeared to the front of the ambulance, returned now as Tate tried to lunge out the back doors, pressing him back into the vehicle. "Don't worry. My son's going to get him." The words no sooner escaped his lips when the world exploded with sound. He and Tate watched in horror as the building they just escaped collapsed, floor by floor, until there was nothing left but a growing cloud of dust.

"Daddy!" Tate sobbed, confusion and shock overtaking his little body.

The fireman stared at the ruin for only a moment, wide-eyed and unmoving, before placing Tate deeper into the ambulance. "Get him out of here," he said, slamming the doors and pounding on them with his fist. Tate watched him through the back window as the ambulance drove away, but before he knew it, the fireman disappeared back into the black fog.

. . .

"Maybe I shouldn't have told her." It was Sunday night, Tate and Max in their usual places in the screen house.

Max rolled to face him. "She deserved to know."

"She probably hates me."

"She doesn't hate you." Tate and Lyle's onstage hug flashed through Max's mind. "Or have you not noticed?"

"It's my fault."

"You didn't kill her father, Tate." Max rolled onto his back, the two of them staring into the blackness. "And while we're at it, you didn't kill yours either."

"I might as well have."

"Why? Because you were scared of a bully like every other seven-year-old?"

Tate smirked. "Except you."

Max's eyes wandered down the hill to the house, where his father was either in a drunken rage or drunken stupor. "Don't be so sure."

Tate chewed on that for a moment before speaking again. "I'm the one that begged him to go back." The darkness of the night was beginning to feel more heavy than private. "To save my dad."

"Tate, he would have gone back anyway. That's his job."

"Right."

Despite his reassuring words, Max understood the guilt Tate felt. If Max had realized what was going on sooner, maybe he could have stopped his mother from being deported. Or maybe he could have convinced her to take him with her. Max could hear his mother in the back of his mind, sobbing and telling him she loved him that last night. He could feel her sitting in this very sport, hugging him close for the final time all those years ago.

Tate sat up, shifting to lean against the foot of Max's daybed. "I have to give the money back."

Max couldn't believe his ears. "To Wilson?"

"No." Tate rolled his eyes. "To Aariz."

"Why?"

"It's my fault his storage closet got demolished. Plus..." Tate trailed off, searching for the right words. "I sort of owe him."

"You're right. Rescuing him from a fire wasn't nearly enough." The sarcasm was a little stronger than Max intended, and he softened it as he continued. "He doesn't hate you, Tate. None of us do."

"Still." The skepticism in Tate's voice was clear.

Max chewed his bottom lip. After everything that happened, was going to college really more important than his best friend? He took a deep breath as he sat up, decided. "I'll give him my money."

"No." Tate's answer was immediate. "That's for college."

"This is more impor—"

"No, it's not," Tate cut him off. "Everyone keeps making sacrifices for me, saying the talent show is more important, marching is more important, *I'm* more important." A redness crept up Tate's neck as his voice rose, but a couple deep breaths allowed him to compose himself. "Well, I'm not. And if I realized that sooner, I would have saved everyone a lot of trouble." His look was solemn as he looked Max in the eyes. "I want to."

"Right." Max did not argue as they laid down once more, surrounded by their own thoughts. He was relieved Tate rejected his offer, and for the first time since they met, Max wondered if he was the one being selfish.

. . .

"Cameron, fashionably late does not apply to school." It amazed Cameron how his mother managed to get herself ready in the morning when she was so concerned with everyone else. He spiked his hair as tall as it would go just to spite her. "Oh, by the way," his mother said, her perfectly curled hair and made-up face poking into his bedroom. "We need you to pick up the dry-cleaning today instead of tomorrow."

"Why?" Cameron continued to gel his hair, refusing to look at her.

"I cannot go to a dinner party without my floral dress." She looked at Cameron's reflection like it had three heads, her eyes lingering on his growing spike.

"Well, I don't think it'll be ready on such short notice."

"Oh, I called the girl last night."

Cameron slammed the gel down as he turned to face her. "They're not even open Sunday nights."

His mother flipped her skinny fingers out to the side in exasperation. "Well, how else am I expected to get it the next day?" She brushed a bit of lint off her sweater and adjusted her pearls. "The girl was quite short with me, actually. Perhaps I should call the manager directly since she clearly didn't pass along my last list of concerns." Cameron was at a loss for words, no amount of vocabulary capable of educating ignorance in one conversation. His mother pointed her manicured finger at his Simple Plan t-shirt. "Don't forget your button-down. Wouldn't want to go to school in that hideous thing." And then she was gone, floating down the stairs in a fog of perfume and superiority.

Cameron fingered the sleeve of the button-down she had laid out for him before balling it up and chucking it across the room. He was tired of this façade, not only pretending to be someone he wasn't but pretending to be someone he didn't want to be. He adjusted his hair again and stomped down the stairs, guitar case in hand.

"Cameron, would you please go get dressed?" his mother chided as she adjusted his sister's hair bows.

"I am dressed."

His sister's eyes widened at his rebellion against the dress code. "You're not wearing that," his mother said, straightening up on her high heels. Cameron took a step forward, prying himself away from the outskirts of the family for the first time.

"Watch me."

"Cameron King," his father boomed as Cameron strode past them to the front door. Cameron stopped but did not turn around.

"What on earth are you lugging in that tacky case?" his mother asked.

"Oh, this?" Cameron raised the case as he turned to face them. "This is my guitar. I'm in a band, and we practice every day after school. The boy you think I'm tutoring in math is the drummer, and he gets higher scores than I do. And the other boy you think is such a bad influence? He's the singer and leader of the marching band. And the girl you think is so rude at The Carry Out?" Cameron sipped in some air, his temples pounding with adrenaline. "She is the kindest girl I know, and the reason they can't rush your order is because Wilson set their building on fire two days ago." He started to open the door before turning back to the shocked faces of his family. "Speaking of Wilson, I've been letting him beat me in the spelling bees because he's an asshole." Cameron was on a roll, and there was no stopping him. "I punched him in the face for the same reason."

The slacked jaws of his mother, father, and sister were the last thing Cameron saw as he slammed the door behind him and sauntered off to school, feeling more like himself than he had in a long time.

. . .

"Did you do it?"

Tate nodded as he and Max took the stage.

"Do what?" By now, Lyle was tired of surprises.

Max glanced at Tate before ignoring her and turning to Cameron. "Cam, you ready?" Something about Cameron was off today, but Lyle couldn't pinpoint it.

"CamKing," Tate repeated when he didn't answer.

"Oh, affirmative." Cameron gave Lyle an apologetic smile as he took the stage.

"Wait." Lyle placed a hand on his arm to stop him. "Before I forget." She scampered behind the counter and returned with his mother's floral dress, beautifully pressed in a garment bag. "I did your mother's dry-cleaning last night."

Cameron made no move to take it. "Last night?"

"Yeah." Lyle shrugged. "I was up anyway." She saw Tate bite his lip from the corner of her eye. Cameron stared at the dress a beat longer before yanking it from Lyle's hand and stalking to the front door. To her horror, he proceeded to unzip the bag and dump the spotless dress in a heap on the dirty sidewalk.

"You can keep the bag," he said, and Lyle took it because she didn't know what else to do. "Don't worry," he added. "I'll tell them I dropped it riding home." He gave her one of his shy smiles and headed onstage.

"Hey Cameron?" Lyle pointed to his torso, unclad with its usual button-down. "Nice shirt." Max and Tate nodded in agreement as the three began to practice for the fundraiser. As Lyle returned to the counter, she realized how quiet the lobby would be when they were gone.

Tate shot her an occasional glance as he sang but diverted his eyes as soon as he caught hers. He honored her request for space after they talked, and Lyle had spent the rest of the night trying to make sense of it all. She had always taken solace in the fact that her father died saving someone else, but she never imagined that someone was Tate or his dad. The more she thought about it, the more morbidly ironic it became, and although she knew it wasn't Tate's fault, a little part of her resented him all the same.

"CamKing," Tate said as their final note reverberated through the lobby. "I need a favor." He gathered something from the base of the stage as Cameron followed, extending his drum major baton as they reached the middle of the lobby.

"You want me to retrieve it?" Cameron readied himself to field Tate's practice throws.

"No." Tate handed him the baton. "I want you to throw it. Over and over until you can't miss." Lyle's head snapped to Max, who was doing his best to look everywhere but at her.

Cameron was tentative as he took the baton. "Okay…why?" Tate ignored him as he dove into a slew of instructions. The rest of the evening consisted of the baton clattering to the floor, Cameron pink with embarrassment as Tate urged him to try again.

"It's getting late," Max prompted as dusk approached. Cameron jumped at the excuse, shoving the baton back at Tate and gathering his belongings.

"Thanks, CamKing."

"See you tomorrow," Cameron said as he rushed out the door, snatching the ruined dry-cleaning from the sidewalk as he skated down the street.

Rather than joining Lyle at the counter, Tate and Max retreated to the stage and busied themselves winding up chords they always left unwound. "I'll just do it," Max murmured, tossing a drumstick and catching it behind his back.

Tate sighed, exasperated. "You have to lead the drumline."

"Well, I'll practice anyway." Max grabbed the baton from Tate's hand and headed for the lobby. "I'll help him practice during lunch or something." Tate nodded, spending the next couple hours rebounding Max's tosses.

"I have to sweep," Lyle interrupted when it was time to lock up.

"Right." Tate ushered Max to the side in a spastic attempt to get out of the way as Lyle brushed past to flip the signs. Tate was clearly caught between wanting to give her space and wanting that moment back before the talent show. Lyle wanted it to, her grief speckled with longing for the only lips and arms that seemed to hold her together.

"What is this?" Aariz was half speaking, half yelling as he stormed into the lobby.

Max did not look up as he climbed the stage steps. "What's what?"

"Don't give me the runaround." Aariz thrust his hand forward, overflowing with a wad of bills. "This!" Max dismissed himself from the conversation with a shrug, retreating to the back of the stage to idly adjust whatever he could get his hands on. Tate fingered the strings of his guitar before leaning it against the drums. "Tate." Aariz's voice was intense, forcing Tate to meet his eye. "I know you put this in my workshop." They stared at each other for a long time, Lyle doing her best to pretend she wasn't watching.

Tate shrugged, but his stare was serious. "Maybe it was the same person that fixed my guitar." His retort surprised Aariz long enough for Tate to turn his back and pretend to help Max. Aariz started to tuck the wad of bills into Tate's guitar strings, the largest one reverberating a low note as he accidentally plucked it. "It's just going to find its way back to you," Tate shot over his shoulder.

Aariz sighed as he snatched back the bills. "This is not your responsibility, Tate."

He extended the bills again, but Tate did not take them, his eyes sad but stubborn as he turned to face Aariz. "Then whose responsibility is it?"

Max and Lyle stood frozen, waiting for an answer Aariz didn't have, so after almost a full minute stare down, he stomped back to his workshop with the money. "That went well," Max said, Tate smirking as he grabbed the baton and hopped off the stage.

"Where'd you get all that money?" Lyle came on strong, gesturing to Max as she approached Tate. "Did you take him fighting again?"

"What? No." Tate was offended by her accusation, Max raising his hands as he once again removed himself from the conversation. "It's just to replace the wood."

"Where did you get it?" Lyle watched Tate finger the baton in silence until she pieced it together. "Your marching money."

"There's always next year." As soon as the words left his lips, a grief washed over Tate that broke Lyle's heart. He dropped his head as he found his way to the stage again, lowering down next to his father's guitar. He extended his fingertips several times but kept drawing them back, unable to bring himself to touch it. Max made himself scarce as long as he could, Lyle's eyes magnetically drawn to Tate as she attempted to continue sweeping. His body seemed to sag more with every glance until he was nothing more than a heap of misery. It amazed Lyle how well Tate had held it together in front of Cameron and Aariz, but it was obvious he didn't have much left. Max sensed it, too, grabbing his skateboard and heading for the door.

"See you at home," he said, attempting to give Tate and Lyle some privacy. Tate made no acknowledgment as Max started toward Lyle before thinking better of it and retreating to the door. The bell on the door dragged Tate out of his trance, and to Lyle's surprise, he pushed himself to his feet, grabbing the baton and his skateboard. "Hold on," he said to Max as he hopped off the stage.

"You're leaving?" Lyle asked, astonished. She felt torn, half of her chomping at the bit to place blame on him for something that happened years ago, the other half wanting nothing more than his serenading voice to help her feel okay again.

"I can't do this." His voice was as broken as Lyle felt, a tear escaping down his cheek as he turned away. "I'm sorry." Lyle swallowed a cry as she watched them go, the first night since the renovation Tate did not stay to sing.

She was still sweeping a half hour later when Rawel emerged from the back. "I thought you were working," she sniffed, hastily wiping at her eyes. He took the broom from her hands and rested it against the wall.

"This is where I need to be tonight." He pulled Lyle down next to him on the lobby bench, her head falling against his muscled chest. They sat holding each other for a few seconds, overwhelmed by everything that needed to be said.

"Why didn't you tell me?"

"You didn't need to know the details." Rawel paused, looking at the empty stage. "I didn't realize myself until we left the jail."

"He's the reason dad went back."

"Your father went back because that's the kind of person he was."

"How could you defend him?" Lyle exploded. "It's his fault my father's dead!"

Rawel grew serious as he turned to face her. "And I suppose it's your fault Yalina's dead?" Lyle's eyes widened at his words; they never brought up Yalina. Rawel's large hand engulfed her small one. "Being in the wrong place at the wrong time doesn't make you responsible."

A tear squeezed from the corner of Lyle's eye. "He didn't even stay to sing."

"Sounds like he's out of hope." Rawel patted her knee as he stood. "Maybe you could lend him some."

CHAPTER FIFTEEN

"Holy shit." Max had abandoned his spot behind the drums to watch the people come in.

"Yeah." Tate did not look up, monotone. "Good turn out."

"No, look." Max turned Tate's body to first Aariz's front door, then Rawel's, as people from all parts of the community and all walks of life were entering. The donation baskets quickly filled, the volunteers dumping them into a clear bin in the middle of the room labeled *scholarship* to make room for more. Above the bin was a velvet cloth covering something mounted on the wall. A golden rope was attached to the bottom, ready to reveal what Max assumed would be the total amount.

What a difference from the whiteboard at the barn.

The more Max watched, the more he realized everything about this day was different from the barn. A community coming together to support its youth, regardless of religion or status. Money given freely for a good cause. Laughter and easy conversation echoing around the rooms, rather than cries of pain and the crack of bone.

By now, Tate had returned his attention to tuning his guitar, but his eyes darted around the crowd at least once every thirty seconds. "I haven't seen her yet," Max said for the third time, patting him on the shoulder in support. Tate nodded as he went to help Cameron tune his guitar, a skeleton of the wreck he had been last night, Max unable to console him as he fluctuated between sobs and stone-cold stillness.

"Max!" He had to scan the crowd twice before he found Aariz, who was motioning him over to the counter. Max hopped off the stage, careful to be polite as he wove his way to Aariz, who was standing with a woman he did not recognize.

"Max, this is Aasimah," Aariz introduced.

Max shook the woman's hand politely. "Nice to meet you. You're a part of Aariz's mosque?"

"Yes." Her voice was a mixture of honey and sawdust, inviting and intriguing at the same time. "He's told me a lot about you."

"Not much to tell," Max muttered.

"Aasimah is an international advocate," Aariz said. "She helps our people come to this country legally." Max nodded, unsure why he needed to know this woman's life story. "She has contacts in over thirty countries." Aariz paused before continuing. "Including Mexico."

"Aariz told me about your…situation." Aasimah's smile was confident. "I would love to assist your mother in returning to the United States."

Max stared in disbelief, unable to formulate a complete sentence. "But she's not…you said your people…why would you…"

Aariz put his arm around Max's shoulder to silence him. "Aasimah is more than willing to help your mother." He squeezed

Max's shoulder affectionately. "Besides, I consider you boys my people just as much as anyone here."

"Th-thank you," Max stammered, shaking her hand more vigorously this time.

"I'll be in touch." Aasimah gave another pearly smile before adjusting her hijab and fading into the crowd.

Aariz turned to Max, a tinge of worry riding his brow. "I hope I didn't overstep." Max flung his arms around him, the unfamiliar peace of someone looking out for him filling his body with a warm tingle. The clock struck the hour, and Aariz gave him a final squeeze before motioning to the stage. "I think you've got somewhere to be." Max grinned larger than he ever had, reaching the stage in two bounds.

"What?" Tate asked, taking in Max's demeanor.

He wanted to share the news, but with Tate's defeated expression and still no Lyle, Max couldn't bring himself to do it. "Nothing, just ready to go." He took his place behind the drums, unaware he was still smiling until he saw Cameron grinning back at him.

"Hello, everyone." The lobbies quieted as Tate spoke into the microphone. "Thanks for coming today to raise money for your mosque. We're The Shiners..." Tate paused, feeling beneath his left eye where his makeup would have been if Lyle had been there to apply it. "And we're going to get started." Despite Tate's effort, Max heard the sadness in his voice, and as he counted them in, he watched Tate scan the room one last time as he started to sing.

They made it about halfway through before Tate's hand dropped to his side, his mouth opening and closing with no sound coming out as the second verse began. And just like that, Max knew Tate loved her. He could tell by the way he had shrunk into himself last night, wishing he hadn't left without singing. By the way he was now, unsteady and without purpose in her absence, a longing radiating from every muscle of his body.

Cameron glanced over at Max, who nodded as they ended the song early. Tate was still as the music cut out, a shell of the person he was three days ago with nothing left to give. "We're going to take a short break," Max said, leaning into Cameron's microphone. Rawel and Aariz got the hint, resuming the passing of fundraising baskets on either side of the stage as Max pulled Tate away from the microphone. "You okay?"

Tate shook his head, forlorn as he scanned the lobbies yet again. "Where is she?"

· · ·

She knew she didn't have much time if she wanted to make it back, so taking a breath of stale prison air, Lyle entered the empty communication hall. Something about her usual cubicle felt wrong for a visit like this, so she spun on her heel and planted herself against the wall in cubicle one. The bell rang as her mother jangled in, checking the usual cubicle before locating Lyle in the one nearest the door. "Delilah, I wasn't expecting you."

"Hello, Mom." Lyle's voice was heavy, sterile, and she clung to the weight of why she had come. "I needed to see you."

Her mother fluffed her hair like she had been cat-called by a passing car. "How nice."

"I wanted to tell you something."

Her mother seemed taken aback by Lyle's directness. "Anything, baby."

"I've decided to play my piano again."

Her mother's eyes lit up with a misunderstood joy. "I knew you'd come around."

"I haven't come around, but I have realized something." Lyle curled her toes to muster all of her strength. "It's my piano, not yours. It's always been mine."

"Well," her mother started, a little unsure where to step. "We did buy it together—"

"No," Lyle interrupted. "It was a gift. You were supposed to teach me, but you wouldn't."

"Your father—"

"Died, I know." Lyle was over the excuses. "But I still needed you." Her mother's sudden concern was infuriating. "Yalina was more of a mother to me than you were!" Although she hadn't planned on saying that, Lyle didn't wish the words back, even when her mother recoiled.

"They took everything from us," she growled.

"She was my friend!" Lyle lowered her voice. "She used to be your friend."

"They can't be trusted."

"You're the murderer, not Yalina."

"That's all you think I am?" Her mother's entire demeanor shifted, shaded by a moonless night hiding from a hopeless soul.

Lyle stared into her mother's eyes. "You didn't use to be."

Her mother looked around the empty room. "Where's that boy? He understood!"

"Tate related to your hatred because he was hurting. But you know the difference between you and him?" Lyle leaned in, her forehead inches from the glass. "He chose to be a good person anyway."

"Your father would be ashamed of you right now." It was the lowest blow her mother could muster, solidifying Lyle's purpose for visiting.

"No, he would be proud." The cord stretched as Lyle stood, but something about her mother's pain gave her pause. She had planned on storming out, but they both needed closure. So instead, Lyle leaned over, the receiver close to her mouth. "I will always love you, Mom, but I'm not visiting anymore."

"Delilah…" Her mother's voice faded into nothing as Lyle ducked out the door. The last thing she heard was her mother banging against the glass, but Lyle did not look back. It had taken her this long, but she finally understood. It wasn't her fault, it never was, and that realization made her feel ten pounds lighter and ten times faster as she rushed to make it back in time for the announcement.

. . .

Lyle was still nowhere to be found as they ended their third song, Tate fingering his guitar pick as he willed her to appear. He knew in his heart telling her was the right choice, but a part of him wished he could take it back to see her smiling face in the crowd, especially when he had nothing left to hope for.

"Let's hear it for The Shiners!" Aariz yelled as he joined them onstage. Tate didn't doubt his decision to give Aariz the money, but he wondered if, without marching, he would feel incomplete forever. Aariz caught Tate's elbow as he started to follow Max and Cameron offstage. "If you don't mind," he whispered away from the microphone. "I could use your help announcing the scholarship recipient. Tate nodded, but he felt wrong presenting such an honor to the members of Aariz's mosque; he didn't deserve their acceptance.

"As you all know," Aariz echoed. "We make a commitment every year to allocate some of our funds to the promising youth in our community. For the past eight years, we have chosen to do so in the form of a scholarship. This goes to a young community member who has demonstrated his or her efforts to unify varying religions and races within the community to foster acceptance for all." Tate hadn't noticed how many audience members were around his age, and he now understood why Aariz had wanted a band. He made a mental note to find the recipient afterward to talk about how he could become more accepting; it was the least he could do. "This year," Aariz continued. "We decided to rename the scholarship to recognize a valued member of our community." Tate glanced at Aariz, hoping he didn't expect him to announce that too. "Because of a young man who has proven that being yourself is the best path to acceptance, this scholarship is now the CamKing Scholarship of Acceptance."

Aariz smiled at Tate, who now understood why he had asked him to stay onstage. Tate scanned the crowd for Cameron, who was stunned stiff in the back. Tate descended the stairs and pulled Cameron onto the stage, planting him front and center as Aariz announced him. "Cameron King, everyone!" The crowd thundered its applause, Cameron's face pink with embarrassment as he grinned from ear to ear. He waved at the crowd, a tear escaping his eye as he scurried off the stage. Tate held his hands up as he started another round of applause, Max whooping as Cameron joined him once more near the back of the room.

"Thank you," Tate whispered to Aariz. More than any of them, Cameron needed this acceptance, and anyone willing to throw and take a punch in his defense was a friend for life in Tate's book.

Aariz smiled. "Are you sure you're good to announce the scholarship recipient?" Tate nodded, more comfortable after seeing Cameron's elation. "All right," Aariz said, raising his hand to quiet the crowd. "You've been voting throughout the event on the nominated individuals, and the votes were tallied during the last song." Aariz pulled an envelope from his robe and handed it to Tate. "My new friend Tate was kind enough to announce this year's recipient." Tate fumbled as he opened the envelope, letting it waft to the floor as he removed a folded piece of paper. As he began unfolding the paper, Tate's father flashed into his mind. He pictured him standing in the crowd, pale skin and green eyes at peace as he watched his son supporting the Muslim community.

He would be proud.

"And the winner is…" At first, Tate paused for dramatic effect, but as he read the name on the paper, his mouth couldn't find the words to speak.

"The suspense is too much!" Aariz prompted, the crowd giggling as they looked at Tate expectantly. His mouth felt dry as his saliva lumped in his throat, but Aariz's gentle hand on the small of his back encouraged him to continue.

"Tatem Rodriguez." It was so soft, the microphone barely caught it, but from the encouraging looks of the crowd, it was clear Tate was the only one surprised.

"Tatem Rodriguez!" Aariz boomed, the crowd clapping as Tate stood before them.

"Aariz…" Tate said, turning away from the microphone. "I can't accept this."

"Why not?"

A million reasons ran through Tate's mind. "I'm not part of your mosque," he said, settling on the most obvious.

"If it wasn't for you, it wouldn't be my mosque." Aariz smiled as he returned to the microphone. "Tate has proven his acceptance in the most difficult way possible..." He glanced around the room, looking at Tate last. "Change."

Tate was too overwhelmed to think straight, eyes darting around the room in search of a familiar face. Cameron's smile was impossibly larger than before, Max surprised but also proud as he gave Tate a supportive nod. "Tate's father was taken during 9/11," Aariz continued. "For a while, Tate didn't know what that meant. He was confused by our people, and perhaps a little wary. And if we're being honest..." Aariz looked around the room before turning to Tate, "...our people were a little wary of yours, too." The room nodded in collective agreement, and for the first time, Tate saw through their eyes. How hard it was for them to be blamed for something they didn't do. How scary it was to be hated as a whole for something done by a few. "But through music and friendship, Tate was able to change his views, to become a man that accepts everyone as his equal."

A man.

"Now you can use this scholarship however you choose." Aariz held up his hand, feigning a whisper. "But we all hope you use it to march in the parade."

The crowd applauded again, Aariz motioning Max and Cameron back to the stage as Tate stood rooted to the floor. "At the risk of overstepping," Aariz said. "I was hoping you boys would give us an encore."

"We don't have another song prepared," Tate whispered, his stomach lurching at the thought of disappointing a crowd who had given him so much. Aariz just winked and strode offstage as Max and Cameron took their places. Tate shouldered his guitar and waited for Max to count them into a song they already played. But he didn't.

When he turned to look, Max just smirked, jutting his chin to the side of the stage. Tate looked to the side, where the crowd was now parted around a rich blackness.

The piano.

Although she was hidden from the crowd, Tate's stomach lurched as Lyle smiled up at him, seated at the piano she swore to never play again. It felt like midnight, their eyes only on each other as the darkness of the night wove them together, Lyle's fingers gracing the keyboard as she began to play.

The familiar handful of notes rang through the lobby, and with a heart full enough to burst, Tate began to sing.

The boys held back, allowing them their moment as Tate sang along to the song only Lyle knew he needed. He looked out the window, the stars in the night sky an audience of the masses. He knew his father was one of those stars, watching him perform at this very moment, and all at once, Tate was singing to him.

His fingers found the guitar strings as the boys joined in, the song exploding at the jerk into a performance of the ages. The beat thumped in time with Tate's heart as he moved around the stage, the crowd bouncing and dancing along with him. He held nothing back, and one glance at Max and Cameron indicated they were doing the same.

Tate made his way to Cameron as the second verse began, whose grin was blinding as he rocked his little heart out. There wasn't one ounce of worry on his face as he sported his punk t-shirt and shredded that guitar. Tate spiked Cameron's blond spike a little higher before returning to center stage. Lyle remained at the piano, and Tate thrust his arms wide in her direction, as if showing her what it looked like to finally have everything they wanted.

The song shifted to the bridge, the lyrics registering in Tate's body as his eyes found Rawel in the back. His nod was subtle, but it was there, patting the scar beneath his shirt as Tate touched his own. After everything they went through, their scars bound them with a common past and bonded them for the future, and for that, Tate was thankful.

His voice was hoarse from the passion behind his singing, but Tate didn't care as his eyes found Aariz next to the case of money. They connected as he sang, a million apologies and thanks dancing on the melody between them. Without warning, Aariz pulled the drawstring, the velvet tumbling to reveal a wooden sign that knocked the air from Tate's lungs. It was beautifully stained, with a painstakingly carved font that read:

We remember and honor all whom we have lost.
May they live on through our music forever.

Tate managed to find his voice again as the song continued, but his body stilled as his eyes bore into the dedication in front of him. It faced the stage, a window through which their loved ones could watch him perform, and Tate felt their energy fill him from the inside as he broke into the final chorus. He regained feeling in his legs and joined Max at the drums, who was pounding them so hard he bounced on and off the stool. The bruise around his eye was fading, and the possibility of paving the way to a better future shone through every inch of Max's face in a smile Tate thought he lost when his mother left. Max stood as Tate put his arm around him, continuing to play as they took in how far they managed to come together.

The energy of everyone around and within him burst forth as Tate returned to center stage and held out the last note. As the music faded, Tate couldn't hide his crooked smile as he looked into Lyle's big blue eyes, and with a heart more full than it had ever been, tossed her his guitar pick.

EPILOGUE

Cameron stood amongst the other saxophonists, all of whom attended his spelling bee competition last night. The entire band had filled the audience, arriving in New York City a day early to watch Cameron's victory and advancement to the next stage. Wilson hadn't made the cut, but Cameron had been too focused on the cheers of Max and Tate to care. When it came down to it, he was where he wanted to be: part of the marching band, a rock band, and a group of real friends. The Shiners played at The Carry Out every Friday night, raising money for various community support initiatives. He wore his marching uniform with pride as he waited for his cue, and for the first time in his life, Cameron King felt accepted.

. . .

Drumbeats bounced off the skyscrapers from their place in the street, louder and more pronounced than ever. Max's body was all but healed, the bruises from his past replaced by possibilities for his future. Although his mother was not yet in the country, Aasimah was working her through the process, and Max was able to speak to her by phone almost every night. His father was anonymously reported for child abuse, launching Max and Tate headfirst into the foster care system. Luckily, their foster father was a great man who didn't hesitate to take them as a package deal, supporting Max's dream of college and Tate's passion for music. Max became his carpentry apprentice in the workshop below their apartment, and although he and Tate still shared a room, this one had walls. The drumsticks spun around his hands between beats as he waited for his cue, and for the first time in his life, Maxwell Moore felt like himself.

. . .

Rawel had insisted their firetruck be first in line, and Lyle could see the entire band from her vantage point. The crowd looked different since the last time she was up there, full of smiles, families, and hope. Although she had never lost hope, Lyle's shifted to hope of a better future, instead of a better past. She was slated to accompany the winter performance of the select chorus, and she already had a page-turner lined up. Although they lived in separate apartments, their bedrooms shared a wall, and every night she leaned against it as Tate serenaded her in the darkness. She fingered his guitar pick Aariz had fashioned into a necklace, and although there were hundreds of people in front of her, she couldn't take her eyes off the drum major. The sirens were silent as they waited for their cue, and for the first time in her life, Delilah Kaminski felt whole.

. . .

As he stood in front of the marching band, baton in hand, Tate couldn't shake the feeling this was all a dream. He wanted this for so long, but as he stood at the ready, it didn't feel anything like he had expected. He thought marching would fix him, heal him, but as he stared at his bandmates, Tate realized he was never broken, just lost. Great friends and an amazing girl was all it took for him to find his way again, and he could now say without a doubt he was exactly where he wanted to be. For too long, Tate had planned for this, and as he looked at Cameron, then Max, then Lyle smiling back at him, he was never more content to live in the moment. Tate raised his baton, his father's golden chain pressing against his bare chest beneath as he took his first step in the Macy's Thanksgiving Day Parade. He could feel his father in the sunshine, smiling down on him, and for the first time in his life, Tatem Rodriguez felt proud.

CPSIA information can be obtained
at www.ICGtesting.com
Printed in the USA
BVHW041038050721
611053BV00027B/1223